War Cry

About the Author

Ian Ross was born in England, and studied painting before turning to writing fiction. After a year in Italy teaching English and exploring the ruins of empire reawakened his early love for history, he returned to the UK with a fascination for the period known as late antiquity

His six-novel 'Twilight of Empire' series, set in the late Roman world, was published in the UK and worldwide between 2015 and 2019.

More recently, he has turned his attentions to the medieval period, and in particular the tumultuous era of mid 13th-century England.

Also by Ian Ross:

Battle Song

'Twilight of Empire' series:
War at the Edge of the World
Swords Around the Throne
Battle for Rome
The Mask of Command
Imperial Vengeance
Triumph in Dust

War Cry

Ian Ross

HODDER &
STOUGHTON

First published in Great Britain in 2023 by Hodder & Stoughton
An Hachette UK company

1

Copyright © Ian Ross 2023

The right of Ian Ross to be identified as the Author of the Work has been asserted by him
in accordance with the Copyright, Designs and Patents Act 1988.

All rights reserved. No part of this publication may be reproduced, stored in a retrieval
system, or transmitted, in any form or by any means without the prior written permission
of the publisher, nor be otherwise circulated in any form of binding or cover other
than that in which it is published and without a similar condition being imposed on the
subsequent purchaser.

All characters in this publication are fictitious and any resemblance to real persons, living
or dead, is purely coincidental.

A CIP catalogue record for this title is available from the British Library

Hardback ISBN 978 1 399 70888 3
eBook ISBN 978 1 399 70889 0

Typeset in Perpetua Std by Manipal Technologies Limited

Printed and bound in Great Britain by Clays Ltd, Elcograf S.p.A.

Hodder & Stoughton policy is to use papers that are natural, renewable and recyclable
products and made from wood grown in sustainable forests. The logging and
manufacturing processes are expected to conform to the environmental regulations of the
country of origin.

Hodder & Stoughton Ltd
Carmelite House
50 Victoria Embankment
London EC4Y 0DZ

www.hodder.co.uk

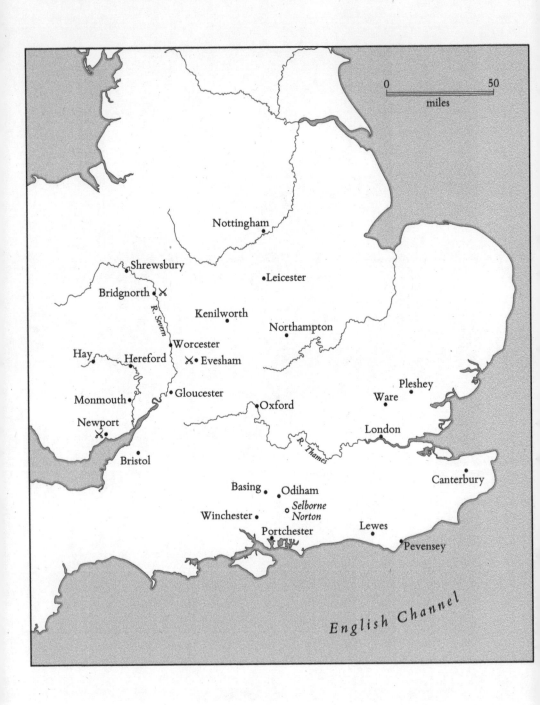

0   50
miles

Nottingham

Shrewsbury
Bridgnorth ✕

R. Severn

Kenilworth

Leicester

Northampton

Worcester
✕ Evesham

Hay
Hereford

Monmouth

Gloucester

Oxford

Pleshey
Ware

Newport ✕

London

Bristol

R. Thames

Canterbury

Basing

Odiham
Selborne
Norton

Winchester

Portchester

Lewes

Pevensey

English Channel

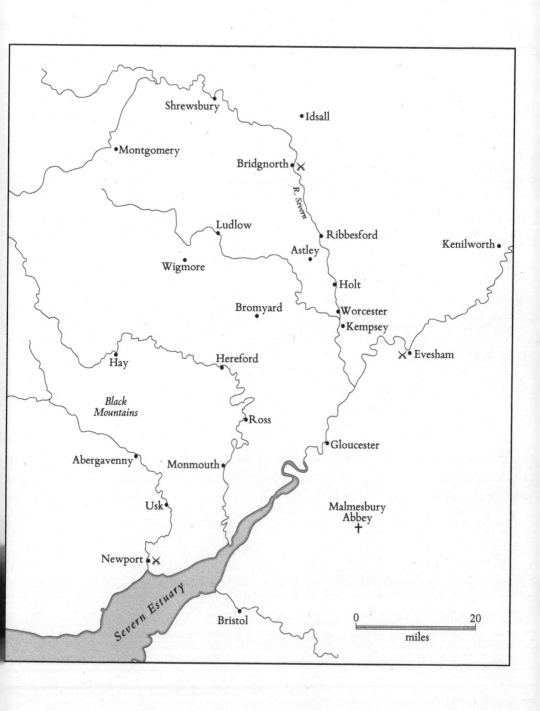

1264: at the Battle of Lewes, rebel barons led by Simon de Montfort, Earl of Leicester, win a crushing victory over the royal forces of King Henry III. The king and his son, Lord Edward, together with some of the greatest magnates in the land, are taken captive.

In the aftermath of battle, Simon de Montfort rules England in the king's name, promising to restore the rights and liberties enshrined in Magna Carta. But as he seizes ever more wealth, lands and honour for himself and his sons, even his own friends and allies grow wary of his power.

Meanwhile, the king's scattered and exiled supporters gather their strength, vowing to strike back against de Montfort and overthrow his new regime. England is troubled by grim portents and evil rumours, and many dread a far greater turmoil to come.

PART ONE

Chapter 1
September 1264

The Forty-Eighth Year of King Henry III

The riders emerged from the dappled shade of the woods onto the dirt track that led towards the manor. Pigeons rose from the shorn stubble of the fields, fluttering against the autumn sky. At the edge of the village, men were working at the threshing floor. The percussive thudding of their flails fell silent, and the women alongside them ceased winnowing the grain. Chaff drifted on the breeze. The riders passed on up the track, and the villagers gazed warily after them. Travellers seldom came this way, and these men were armed.

In the lead rode a man dressed in a dusty green tunic and mounted on a palfrey. His gilded spurs and the fine sword belted at his side marked him as a knight, no less than the powerful warhorse he led behind him. He was young, barely more than twenty, with dark curling hair, but his narrow features had a weathered look that belied his age. Four other riders followed him, with three loaded packhorses and a pair of Franciscan friars striding along beside them.

They rode onward, the hooves of their horses thudding, their bridle trappings clinking. In the far distance figures ran from the fields towards the village, little dark specks of movement. As the riders passed the boundary fence of the hall a dog began barking, then another, and then a frenzy of noise erupted from the kennels. The horses came to a halt, tails whisking. Nobody spoke.

Before them, across the yard, three men stood in the angled sunlight before the cob and timber hall, so alike they could only be brothers. The foremost of them laid one hand on the hilt of his sword. His spreading beard was dense and black, and his close-set eyes seemed to glare out across the top of it.

'Fulk Ticeburn?' the leading rider said.

The bearded man nodded. His two brothers remained standing, one of them carrying an axe and the other with a growling mastiff heaving at the end of a short leash. From the kennels the fury of the other dogs had dropped to a steady low growl.

'Then you'll know who I am,' the rider continued. 'And what I'm here to do.'

Fulk Ticeburn stared back at him for a long moment. His beard twitched. 'Not sure about that,' he said, in a voice like grinding millstones. 'All sorts of folk hereabout, in these troubled times. Robbers and disturbers of the peace, ravaging with horses and arms.' He paused, scuffing the toe of his shoe in the dirt. 'I even hear,' he said, 'that the King of England has been seized by a band of them, and made to do their bidding.'

'Goodman!' the younger of the two friars called, emerging from between the horsemen. 'Goodman, let us have no violence here, in the name of God! We have come to see justice done.'

'You think there is justice in England, friar?' one of the brothers said with a scoffing laugh. 'You're mistaken. Swords are the only law in this kingdom now.'

'Fulk Ticeburn,' the older friar declared, stepping forward to join his colleague, 'we swear upon our oath that Adam de Norton, son of James de Norton' – he gestured towards the young man in the dusty green tunic – 'has done homage for this manor before King Henry, and is the rightful holder of this land and all the estates and tenements attached to it, just as his father once was. Three times you have been ordered by the sheriff to vacate this place, and yet here you remain!'

'Here we *all* remain,' the third Ticeburn brother replied.

'I'm the appointed bailiff of my lord, Hugh de Brayboef,' Fulk said, raising his voice, 'and he has ordered me to hold this manor in his name until he returns—'

'Hugh de Brayboef is an enemy of England!' the friar broke in. 'He has abjured the realm, and his lands have been seized by the king—'

Adam de Norton held up a gloved hand, silencing him. 'Enough idle words,' he said. 'They know full well what we're about.'

He slipped his foot from the stirrup and dismounted. Keeping his eyes on Ticeburn, he walked across the yard to face him. Three more figures lingered in the shadowed doorway of the hall, perhaps another two just visible within. At the margin of his vision Adam could make out a slack-jawed man near the stables, holding a bow with an arrow nocked to the string. Fulk remained motionless as Adam halted before him. A fly circled in the still air between them.

Adam drew off his leather riding gloves and tucked them beneath his belt. 'My name is Adam de Norton,' he said, 'and I am the rightful possessor of this land. I gave you many chances to depart, and you ignored them. So now I must tell you in person, man to man.'

Fulk Ticeburn narrowed his eyes. He was a big man, bigger even than he had appeared from horseback, with a barrel chest and a wrestler's arms. 'I take orders only from my lord, Hugh de Brayboef, and from the Almighty,' he said, shrugging. 'Not from you, *boy*, and not from your master Simon de Montfort either. From my lord I've heard nothing. Perhaps I should wait for a sign from God?'

Adam felt the man's gaze pass over him, then saw the glint of a smile through the black beard. Yes, he thought, Fulk Ticeburn was a big man. But he had not fought at the Battle of Lewes, nor had he stormed the breach at Rochester Castle. He had not spent most of the past three years on the tournament fields of France and the Empire, learning how to fight, and to win. A spike of cold anger fixed Adam's nerves. He had not wanted this confrontation. No honour to be gained here, and only humiliation or bloodshed if he failed.

From behind him, he heard a dry click as one of the two mounted serjeants accompanying him cocked his crossbow. Adam's other companions, a plump man wearing a broad-brimmed hat, and a boy who carried a lance over his shoulder, were keeping well back from the confrontation. Fulk's brothers had moved slightly closer. Warin and Eudo were their names, although Adam could not tell them apart. But the figures lingering in the shadows of the hall showed no inclination of joining them, and the archer had not yet bent his bow. Adam smiled, exhaling slowly and letting his muscles ease. Then he took two long strides forward.

Ticeburn snatched for the hilt of his sword, but Adam was faster; with his right hand he drew his own sword up from its scabbard at an angle, slamming the heavy iron pommel into the bridge of Ticeburn's nose. As Ticeburn staggered and fell backwards, Adam reversed his blade. Standing over the fallen man, he levelled the tip of the sword to his neck.

'You have your sign,' he said.

Ticeburn sprawled in the dust, blood in the crease of his brow, his own weapon spilling loose from its scabbard. For a few gasping breaths he appeared too stunned to react, then he pushed himself up on his elbows, blinking. Clenched teeth showed through his beard.

'I give you until the sun drops below the trees,' Adam said, motioning with his head towards the wooded hillside to the west, already dark against the afternoon sky. He turned the sword again and slid it smoothly back into the scabbard.

A last glance at the other two brothers, both poised and glaring, and the men lingering in the shadowed openings of the house, then Adam turned his back and walked slowly, deliberately, towards the horses. Only now did he see the people gathering at the far side of the open ground. Men and women from the village; at least a score of them already, Adam estimated. He forced himself to walk with a nonchalant swagger, but his breath was tight in his chest, his heart punched at his ribs, and his shoulders were clenched. At any moment he expected to hear the sound of charging steps from behind him, or to feel the searing impact of an arrow. But he walked on, one hand lightly on the hilt of his sword, repressing the fierce urge to turn and look back. When he reached the horses, he took the reins from the boy and continued towards the great oak that spread its shade at the top of the village.

The manor oak, it was called. Adam knew it well. Even through the glaze of nervous tension came the flash and dazzle of memory, like the splintered sunlight through high leaves and branches. Ten years, was it, since last he had seen this place? He walked on, and the assembled villagers drew back as he approached.

By the time he reached the tree he felt breathless, and his body was running with sweat. But as he turned again to face the house, he maintained his composure.

'That was coolly done, by God,' the plump man said, taking off his hat and fanning himself. Hugh of Oystermouth was his name, and his voice carried the accent of his native Wales. 'The size of him! – a beast! But you put your foot upon his neck, right enough. Sir Robert himself could not have made a better show, I think.'

His companions were dismounting beside him, saddle leathers creaking. Adam fought down a quick shudder of anxiety. Yes, he thought, it had been a show – he had not been himself out there, facing down Fulk Ticeburn and his brothers; instead, he had imagined himself to be Robert de Dunstanville, once his master, then his mentor, now his friend. A man whom Adam had come to respect and to admire. A hard man to emulate, nonetheless.

'Then again,' said Hugh, who had been de Dunstanville's herald before he joined Adam's own retinue, 'perhaps Robert would simply have killed the fellow, and put an end to the problem?'

One of the friars, overhearing, cast a disapproving glance. Adam coughed a laugh, feeling the lock of dread shift in his body. But this was not over yet. The anger was still there, burning inside him. It flared suddenly, and he felt the killing urge. He could mount his horse and ride straight up to the house, cutting down anyone who dared to oppose him. Was that really what Robert de Dunstanville would have done? Should he do that now?

Adam felt the heavy scrutiny of those around him. Of those in the house as well; he knew the Ticeburns were watching him carefully. The knot of villagers had drawn closer. They peered at Adam's weapons, the dress of those who accompanied him, and the heavy leather bags slung across his packhorses. Several of the men had threshing flails over their shoulders, while the women still carried their broad winnowing baskets. They carried the rich smell of the earth with them too, of the fields and the beasts they raised, of the sweat of labour. Some were dragging benches into the shade, bringing bread and cheese and jugs of ale for the newcomers.

One of the older villagers pushed his way through the throng and dropped to kneel before Adam. He had a creased brown face and a ploughman's massive shoulders. 'The sheriff's men said you were coming, lord,' he said. 'Many days we've been expecting you. My name is John Ilberd, and I was reeve here in your father's day, as my father was before me. If you've come to drive out these Ticeburns, then all our people here are with you.'

'Their hounds kill and maim our animals, lord,' said a hefty young man, who so closely resembled Ilberd that he must be his son. 'They give us no justice!'

Adam nodded, scanning the faces gathered in the shade or further back in the bright sunlight. Not all, he thought, looked firmly decided in their allegiances, for all the old reeve's claims. Doubtless there were some who felt loyal to Fulk Ticeburn and his brothers, and to their master Hugh de Brayboef. Once or twice on the ride here from London, Adam had felt a pang of distaste for what he had to do: this place had been home to the Ticeburns for many years, and now he had to evict them. Having seen them with his own eyes, though, he felt no unease in his task. And from the mood of the majority of those gathered to watch the eviction, Adam could guess that the Ticeburns had not used this manor gently.

'Is it true, lord,' one of the villagers said, raising his voice above the murmuring of the throng, 'that you are Simon de Montfort's man, and you fought beside him at Lewes, against the king's evil advisors?'

Adam said nothing, but he heard one of the friars shushing angrily.

'Is King Henry truly a prisoner now, lord?' one of the younger men called, as the others around him began to speak out too. 'Does the Earl of Leicester really lead him about on a golden chain?'

'Don't be daft, boy,' a stout woman in a straw hat told him, 'that's not the king – it's Lord Edward that's led on a golden chain.'

'Will the foreigners still come to invade us, lord?' another man asked anxiously, and crossed himself. 'Or have they been repelled, by the blessing of Christ?'

'The danger's not departed yet!' an older woman rasped. 'Have you not seen the fiery star crossing the sky each night? God sends these signs as a warning, for those who have eyes to see and brains to understand!'

Adam remained silent, unmoving as the clamour of questions died down once more. For a moment he saw himself as the people of the village must: an emissary from another world. A world of finery, perhaps, and bold deeds. A world of blood too, and sudden inexplicable violence.

More than four months had passed since Simon de Montfort's great victory at Lewes, when the king and all his forces
were overthrown and England made new. Now Henry sat on his
throne once more, but Lord Simon directed the kingdom in his
name. That fight at Lewes had been a personal victory for Adam
too; he had been knighted on the field of battle, by de Montfort
himself. And he had captured the Earl of Hereford, one of the
greatest magnates in the kingdom, in whose household he had
once served as a squire. The earl's rebellious son, Sir Humphrey
de Bohun the Younger, had purchased his father's ransom from
Adam for five hundred marks; already he had paid a portion of
that sum in coin, and Adam had brought some of it with him in
the leather bags on his packhorses, a great weight of new-minted
silver pennies, each one stamped with the head of King Henry.
The rest he had stored safely at the treasury of the Templars in
London; Sir Humphrey would deposit the balance of the ransom
fee there too, once he had secured his lands in the Marches of
Wales.

But the money paid so far had allowed Adam to equip both
himself and his small retinue in proper style, and to pay the fee
for taking possession of his ancestral lands from the king. Three
months ago, Adam had knelt before Henry in the hall of the bishop's
palace at St Paul's and sworn his oath of homage. He would have
hastened back here to claim his lands as soon as the sealing wax
had dried on the parchment, but knighthood brought duties, and
England had dire need of warriors.

Queen Eleanor, so the heralds proclaimed, had fled to France
after her husband's defeat at Lewes, and had petitioned King
Louis to lend her troops and money to retake England. Together
with the Earls of Pembroke and Surrey, the queen had assembled mercenaries from Flanders and France, from Brabant and
the Empire, from Savoy and from Spain, and filled the Flemish
ports with the ships of her invasion fleet. And on the downs of
Kent the men of England had assembled to repel them, knights

and barons bringing their retinues, the militia of the countryside pouring in from every village and every shire within reach of the royal summons. Such a host, men said, had not been seen in England since the day when William the Bastard led his troops to Hastings.

For the past fifty days, Adam had served with that army on Barham Down, awaiting the invasion from across the sea. Through August and most of September they had waited, tense with nerves and fractious with the anticipation of battle. But the great winds that roared across the downs, creaking the sails of the windmills and whipping sparks from the campfires, roared also in the narrow straits of the Channel. Weatherbound, the ships of the invasion fleet had remained sheltering in their anchorages, and Queen Eleanor had remained in Bruges as her treasury drained away. Without food and fodder and ready coin, her army had drained away too, and by the middle of September it was clear that England would be saved from the storm. For this year, at least.

Adam had not been the first to leave the muster. Plenty had departed before him, militiamen slinking back to their villages, keen to throw off helmet and gambeson and pick up their sickles for the harvest. Some of the northern barons, too, had already gathered their men for the long march home. Adam had served ten days longer than the forty that was his duty as a vassal knight, but he needed to ensure that the claim to his lands was settled before Michaelmas, when the manorial accounts were drawn and the year reckoned up. No man could begrudge him that.

Hugh de Brayboef, who had married Adam's widowed mother and then claimed his father's estates when she died a year later, had also been with Queen Eleanor and her army of invaders across the sea. He had fought for the king at Lewes, and fled after the defeat. But a change of fortune's wind, Adam knew, and his enemies would return and seize everything from him. Men like

Hugh de Brayboef, and his follower Fulk Ticeburn, would rule the land once more.

After so many years longing for knighthood, his own manor to hold, and the chance to prove himself in the world, Adam felt uncomfortably exposed and vulnerable now.

Beneath the great oak the shadows moved, and he stood and stared across the open ground and the empty yard towards the house beyond. No sound came from within, and no figure showed at the doorways. The two serjeants that Adam had hired back in London were lounging at the base of the tree, drinking ale with great enthusiasm, but both kept their weapons close at hand. The grave-looking boy, Adam's groom and servant, remained with the horses, directing a forbidding gaze at anyone who approached the baggage. Hugh of Oystermouth, meanwhile, was sitting on a bench, eating and drinking and appearing entirely pleased with the world and everything in it.

'Lord,' one of the villagers asked Adam, sidling closer and nodding warily towards Hugh. Adam caught a warm gust of his oniony breath. 'Is this follower of yours truly a Welshman? My brother told me that the Welsh are a terrible savage people, with bare red legs, who eat nothing but raw meat. But this one sits there properly shod and eating bread and cheese like a Christian . . .'

'What marvels the world holds, eh?' Hugh of Oystermouth called from his bench, pausing as he chewed. 'I do believe your brother must have met my father!'

*

The sun was glinting through the treetops on the western heights when the first signs of movement came from the house. Adam drew a breath, his gaze sharpening instantly. A man ran from the hall door to the wagon-shed on the far side of the chapel. A moment later other figures appeared, running between the buildings. A slow ripple of sound passed among the watching people, an exhalation and then a suppressed cheer. A few of the assembled villagers called out mocking words, now that their persecutors were showing their heels at last.

From inside the house came the crash of wood and the snarl of raised voices. The dogs began their furious barking once more, the noise merging into a steady ragged pulse. As Adam watched, a pair of servants dragged the wagon from the shed and began flinging things into it: boxes and bales, furniture, sacks, quilts and straw mattresses. One of the friars gave an angry start, but the other restrained him. The Ticeburns were leaving, that was the important thing. Only at the last moment, with the barest gleam of sun showing above the hilltop, did Fulk Ticeburn and his two brothers emerge from the hall. They took the larger dogs from the kennels and secured them in the cart among their piled possessions, then mounted their horses. With a gang of servants on foot, more dogs running behind them and two women perched on the cart's tail, they rode out across the yard and turned onto the track that led northwards. Fulk Ticeburn reined in his horse and waited until all of them had passed. He stared at Adam, who stood in the last of the sunlight with his shadow stretched long across the ground.

'You'll see us again,' Ticeburn called. 'Before Saint Francis has come and gone, I promise, you'll see us. I swear upon the blood of Christ.'

Then he tugged angrily at the reins, kicked his heels, and rode on after his brothers, their servants and their wagonload of women, dogs and piled belongings.

'Doubtless they will return indeed,' the older and wiser of the two friars said, once the Ticeburns were gone. 'We must leave you on the morrow, but I suggest you maintain at least one of these goodmen to watch over your lands.' He gestured towards the two serjeants.

'I will,' Adam said. 'And I thank you, brother.'

Together they walked across the open ground and into the yard. The muck of dogs and horses lay caking in the dust, circled by flies, and the doors of the house hung open.

'I shall carry word of your possession of this manor back to Waverley Abbey, and the court in London,' the older friar said, and pursed his lips for a moment in thought. 'You also hold lands of William de St John of Basing, I believe? You should pay your homage to him as soon as you can. He is a powerful man in this district, and he may be able to keep the Ticeburns and their savage ilk from your throat.'

'I'll do that,' Adam said.

Leaving the friar in the yard, he stepped across the threshold into the gloom of the house. From the passage, he turned and entered the hall. It was smaller than he remembered, although it was open to the blackened rafters high overhead. Smaller and darker, and a lot dirtier too. The Ticeburns had broken what they could not carry away with them; shattered furnishings, ripped rags and broken pottery lay amid the wrack of churned straw underfoot. Adam sniffed, then winced.

'They've cleared out the buttery and the pantry,' Hugh said as he entered the hall, 'and even tried to rip out the painted altar screens in the chapel . . .' He paused, then coughed.

'Not so sweet, is it,' Adam said.

Beside the hearth, a spreading puddle of urine darkened the earthen floor.

*

Night had fallen before the work was done. Hall and hearth were swept and scrubbed, the mess of rubbish and filthy straw cleared into a heap in the yard for burning. John Ilberd the old reeve and his people had all given their assistance, and Adam had sent to the priory for a keg of good ale to refresh them. Even now, with the work done, the fire burned down and the villagers departed, the house felt grimy, ill-used and sour with resentment. It would be many days before the last traces of the Ticeburns were scoured from it, and Adam could feel that this was truly his home.

Hugh of Oystermouth was sleeping in the hall with young Matthew and one of the serjeants – poor lodgings, but they had known worse. Adam had offered to share the upper chamber with the two friars, as they would be leaving early the next morning. They lay on the floor now, wrapped in their cloaks beside the wreck of the bedframe, one of them letting out whistling snores with every few breaths.

Quietly, Adam opened the window shutters to the cool breeze. He listened for a moment: the other serjeant, and two village men and their dogs, were outside keeping the night watch, and he could just make out the quiet stir of their voices. Then he turned his head to the sky. For a few moments he stared into blackness. Then he angled his head again and his breath caught; there it was, directly above him and as clear as a line drawn in chalk upon a black wall.

The comet had appeared back in August, at first in the hours before dawn but then steadily earlier, until its trail was clear to see as night fell. Hugh of Oystermouth, who had studied the heavens, said that it was tracing a course towards Mars in the sign of Taurus, and that it was a harbinger of great violence and turmoil to come. Many agreed with him, and every night as the burning line in the sky grew starker and stronger their dread had increased. The men of the great army gathered on Barham Downs that summer had seen it, and spoke anxiously of what it foretold. The comet was a heavenly spark, they said, igniting all that lay beneath its course and spreading the flames of war and bloodshed.

Surely, Adam thought, with the threat of invasion from across the sea now fading, the comet should fade too? And yet there it was, as fierce and proud in the night sky now as ever. Perhaps, then, the true danger lay not across the sea, but closer to home? Perhaps it was from England that the threat came?

Abruptly Adam dropped his gaze from the skies and stared into the darkness. Something out there had caught his eye. Something moving – a man, perhaps, or a beast – out beyond the boundary fence and the ditch. Tensing, he stared and felt another presence staring back at him. Almost he could make out a shape in the darkness, and as his vision sharpened, he believed it was a human figure, a man, motionless and staring back at him. His right palm itched, and he closed his fist. His sword lay in its scabbard on the floor behind him, but he dared not move. The darkness seemed to pulse as he stared into it.

A long moment, then Adam exhaled. He blinked, and saw only the yard beyond the boundary fence, empty under the troubled stars. Somewhere outside a dog whined, and a watchman's gruff voice spoke a soothing word. In the darkened chamber, one of the sleeping friars let out a slow throaty snore. Adam stepped back from the window, then dragged the shutters closed and fastened them against the night, and all that it concealed.

Chapter 2

They came five days later, on the Feast of St Remigius. The church bell was ringing for evensong, and across the fields the plough teams were returning from their work breaking the fallow ground for the autumn sowing. Adam stood before the manor house, just as Fulk Ticeburn had done, and watched the riders approaching from the hazy calm of evening. Matthew passed him his sword belt, and he fastened it and settled the familiar weight on his hips. There was no time to put on armour. Five days. The Ticeburns had not even waited for St Francis.

Since the morning after his arrival Adam had toured his lands, from the main manor of Selborne Norton and the attached estates of Hawkley and Blackmoor to the smaller manors of Wyke and Neatham, meeting his tenants and assessing their holdings. At Michaelmas those same tenants, both freemen and villeins, had sworn their yearly fealty to them, kneeling before him as he clasped their hands between his palms. They had paid their taxes and given their gifts, the newly reappointed reeve John Ilberd had settled the accounts, and Adam had laid on a feast for all that had worked on his demesne lands over the harvest, feeding them on roast pork washed down with good ale while Hugh of Oystermouth sang in Latin and his native Welsh.

The following day, Adam had summoned his first manor court
to meet beneath the oak, and presided for several hours over the
deliberations and disputes of a year's worth of local grievances
– the Ticeburns having cared nothing for such matters. In truth
there had been little reason for his presence; he was a symbol,
that was all, a representation of good lordship and authority,
like the sword he had placed on the tabletop before him. But
he was trying to do right by those he sought to govern, and to
stitch himself more closely into the weave of life in this place.
And now, he told himself as he watched the file of mounted
figures crossing the field from the edge of the woodland, it was
all about to unravel.

Hugh of Oystermouth strolled from the door of the hall, then
made a choking sound as he spied the horsemen and stepped
back indoors again. William Tonge, the serjeant that Adam had
indentured to remain in his service, came from the stable with a
spanned and loaded crossbow.

'They're carrying weapons,' said Matthew. 'That's a destrier
one of them's leading too.' There was a question in his voice that
Adam took a moment to notice.

Now that the riders had crossed the field and were moving
up the track towards the house Adam could see that there were
only four of them, with a riderless warhorse, sure enough, and
several loaded pack animals behind them.

'Is it . . .?' Matthew asked, lifting his palm to shade his eyes.

Adam squinted, his chest tightening. The leading rider wore a
travelling cloak and a hood pulled over his face, only the tip of his
beard showing. But the destrier he led behind him was distinctive enough. Adam would know that iron-grey horse anywhere.
He grinned.

'Strange welcome in these parts,' the hooded rider said as he
drew to a halt. His beard twitched in the direction of the serjeant
with the loaded crossbow, then back at Adam standing with his
hand on the hilt of his sword.

'If you'd only sent word, I'd have hired some minstrels,' Adam replied. He signalled to William Tonge, who lowered his bow and loosened the cord.

Robert de Dunstanville swung his leg over his horse's rump and dismounted stiffly. He paused to flex his shoulders, wincing, then threw back his hood.

'Lord of the manor, then,' he said, studying Adam through narrowed eyes as he paced across the yard.

'As you see me.' Adam shrugged and spread his hands. Then Robert's face creased into a smile and he closed the distance between them, catching Adam in a rough embrace.

Robert de Dunstanville was more than a decade older than Adam, and did not wear the years lightly. But there was a sinewy vigour about him all the same, even after several days in the saddle. The slash across the cheek he had taken at Lewes had healed to a thin pale scar, and he looked all the more devilish for the disfigurement. De Dunstanville had not attended the great muster on the downs of Kent, instead leaving in July with Sir Humphrey de Bohun for the Welsh Marches and Shropshire. He was going to reclaim his old lands near Shrewsbury, he had said, and had given Adam no idea as to when he might return. Now here he was, appearing without warning from the ebb of the dying day.

That morning he had ridden from Winchester, he told Adam, and he would leave the next day to continue his journey to London. 'You're a little out of my road,' he said, 'but Wilecok here insisted that we should not neglect your hospitality.'

Wilecok, Robert's gnarled and grimy servant, sat on the second horse. He grimaced at Robert's words, but before he could make some carping reply, Hugh of Oystermouth strode from the house and dragged him from the saddle, embracing him in fellowship. Behind the servant rode his Gascon wife, heavily pregnant but enduring the discomfort of travel with her usual silent fortitude. The fourth rider Adam did not know but guessed his purpose. This was Robert's new squire; his own replacement.

Darkness was gathering by the time they sat down for a late supper in the hall. The hearth was piled with fresh logs and a fine blaze dispelled the early autumn chill. It was Wednesday, a fish day, but there were dishes of buttered eggs, spiced frumenty porridge with almonds and raisins, fresh bread and jugs of ale and wine. Hugh of Oystermouth sat at the lower table with Matthew, and Wilecok and his pregnant wife. They were joined by the new reeve John Ilberd, his son and the village hayward. Very soon their voices rose, and gusts of laughter came from the far end of the hall. Adam and Robert shared the high table with Robert's new squire, Giles de Wortham. He was two or three years younger than Adam, a square-jawed and sandy-haired youth who ate hungrily and remained entirely silent throughout the meal. *As I once would have done myself,* Adam thought.

This was, he realised, the first time he had hosted guests at his own table, in his own hall. The realisation brought a deep contentment and satisfaction, like a homecoming at last. Granted, the tables were crude boards on rough trestles, put together by the village carpenter to replace the ones stolen by the Ticeburns, and the bowls and spoons were carved wood instead of silver. The household was short-handed too, with only a half-dozen people from the village to work in hall, kitchen and yard. Two women served at the tables, bringing platters and jugs. The younger one, Edith, had a rounded figure and a soft receding chin; Adam noticed Hugh of Oystermouth turning from his bench to watch her as she passed him. The older woman noticed too, and shot Hugh a scowl.

'You've done well for yourself here,' Robert said as he wiped bread around the inside of his bowl. 'A good hall, and good land from what I've seen of it. Your tenants seem happy as well. They must prefer you to de Brayboef, or these Ticeburns you mentioned.'

Adam had already told Robert of what had happened when he arrived at the manor. He had made light of the confrontation, and of Fulk Ticeburn's threat to return.

'And this is surprisingly good wine,' Robert said, swirling his cup.

'It's Italian,' Adam told him. 'The prior of Selborne sent me over a cask of it. I think he is very keen to be friends with the friends of Lord Simon.'

Robert laughed, then raised his cup towards the far corner of the ceiling. '*Sanctificetur bonum vinum!*' he intoned, then drank deeply. 'You're using de Bohun's money well too, by the look of things,' he said as he refilled his cup. 'Has he paid you any more of it yet?'

'Not yet,' Adam said.

'I'll make sure he does,' Robert said gravely. 'Too easy for the wealthy to forget these trifling things. I travelled with him from Gloucester down to Winchester – you know he's been appointed constable of the castle there?'

Adam shook his head. Winchester was only an easy day's ride to the west.

'You should attend his court,' Robert said. He would not meet Adam's eye as he spoke, but his voice took on a rough edge. 'Lady Joane is with him too, of course.'

Adam's throat tightened. 'She's well?' he managed to ask.

'Oh, very well. Being mistress of a great household suits her nicely. And one day she'll be Countess of Hereford, which will suit her even better.' Robert drank again and set his cup down, rather too hard. 'As for her relations with Sir Humphrey,' he said, 'I cannot say. But she did not appear to me like a creature caught in a hunter's net.'

Adam turned his head away, unable to hide his expression. For months he had been trying to put Joane de Quincy – Joane de Bohun, as she was now called – from his mind altogether. He had last seen her in London, on the day of her wedding to Sir Humphrey. Adam had stood among the crowd outside the Church of the Austin Friars, watching as the vows and gifts were exchanged beneath the porch. With the rest of them he had filed into the church for the wedding mass. He alone had been unable to share the gladness of the day. Instead, he had felt only a plummeting black misery that brought him close to rage.

Joane de Quincy was the only woman he had ever loved. Once he had dared to hope that she felt similarly towards him. But now she was gone, sealed behind the gates of holy matrimony, with one of the wealthiest and most powerful men in the land, Adam's own benefactor: Sir Humphrey de Bohun, Baron of Kington, Lord of Brecon, Lord of Kimbolton, Keeper of Haverford Castle and now Constable of Winchester. One day soon to be Earl of Hereford and Essex too. How could a man like Adam, whose lands brought him less than thirty pounds a year, hope to compete with one whose property earned him at least twenty times as much?

At least the current Earl of Hereford, Humphrey's father, had not attended the wedding; it would have been too humiliating for Adam to have seen him again, so soon after capturing him on the battlefield of Lewes, and to have had to accord him once more the respect due to his rank. Caught in his black reflections, Adam had left the church as soon as he was able, forsaking the wedding banquet entirely, and had seen nothing more of Joane since that day.

And now here she was, back before his eyes as clearly as if she had walked into the hall. His heart pressed tightly in his chest, and he could say nothing. Robert's words, he knew, had been deliberately harsh, intended to stamp out any last embers of possibility Adam might still have nursed. But it was hard to feel grateful for them, however necessary they were to hear.

Robert, though, seemed oblivious to Adam's miserable state. He poured yet another cup of wine from the jug as he spoke expansively about the lands he had regained in Shropshire and elsewhere.

'Adderley was a barony once, you know,' he said, his voice a little slurred. 'It could be again! But a castle, now . . . a castle would be the best thing. I have my eyes on Whittington. Fitz-Warin used to hold it, but he died at Lewes – drowned in the river, so they say, while he was trying to escape! Hamo L'Estrange has most of the surrounding estates, even now, and he's no friend of mine, nor of Lord Simon. Were I granted Whittington, though, I might hold the balance of power in the northern marches—'

'You speak as if we're still at war,' Adam broke in, unable to escape his bleak mood.

'Are we not?' Robert said, widening his eyes. 'Ha! If this is peace, then it is ill-made.' He grinned at his squire, Giles, who appeared half asleep.

'But L'Estrange and the other Marcher lords promised to abide by their oaths, I thought,' Adam said, and scrubbed a knuckle across his brow. 'After Lewes, when Lord Simon gave them leave to return to their lands.'

'Oh yes, he gave them safe passage,' Robert replied, with bitter scorn in his voice, 'on the promise they would return and stand trial before Parliament. Mortimer and de Clifford, L'Estrange and the rest. And did they? Will they? Ha! *No.*' He slapped the tabletop loudly. 'And this is why you should never extract promises from men with swords at their necks. It was foolish of Lord Simon ever to believe things would be different.'

Adam sighed deeply. These months since Lewes should have been a time of celebration, a time of renewed peace. But, instead, there had been nothing but the threat of further conflicts to come. Robert's obvious relish for possessions, for lands and titles, sounded ugly in Adam's ears. But was he not the same? Ultimately, he thought, perhaps property was all that mattered, and was the root cause of all the evils of the kingdom too.

'It's a strange thing,' he said to Robert. 'The tenants here – some of them anyway – have a great admiration for Simon de Montfort.' He had dropped his voice so those on the far table would not overhear him, although they were speaking in French and the reeve and the others would be unlikely to understand. 'They've all heard tales about the deeds of Lord Simon,' Adam went on. 'How he drove out the foreigners and the king's wicked advisors, and freed the realm. The defender of England, they call him, and the guardian of liberty.'

Robert let out a scoffing laugh. 'What do they know of liberty?' he said. 'They're serfs! It's not good to raise the hopes of the common people.'

'You don't share their enthusiasm?'

Robert opened his palms and shrugged. 'Simon de Montfort has the king in his power, and the king's brother and son too. And he rules like a king, though he will never be one. He's granted one of his sons all the de Braose manors in Sussex, and another the Earl of Cornwall's lands, did you know that? He may as well make his third son Archbishop of Canterbury.'

'Can he do that?' Adam asked, perplexed.

'The king could, as a favour. King Henry will do anything for his great friend Simon nowadays, his most loyal subject, upholder of his dignity . . . and anyway, the current holder of the title is a fugitive in France!' Robert laughed again, but his voice was bitter now. 'So yes, Lord Simon is the great power in the land. But the guardian of liberty? I think not.'

He picked up the wine jug and upended it. A few last drops fell into his cup. The boisterous laughter from the far table had grown quieter now. The fire burned low and no longer held the darkness at bay. Giles de Wortham was already dozing on folded arms.

'Listen to me,' Robert said, speaking low as he seized Adam by the arm. 'Keep to your lands, and do not stir even if you are called. You've got the coin to pay *scutage* – shield money – instead of doing military service. Use it.'

'It would be my duty,' Adam replied, startled. 'How could I refuse?'

Robert choked back a curse. 'Easily. Plenty of men do. Look,' he went on, easing his grip on Adam's arm, 'if God provides, we'll have another rebellion in Gascony soon enough, or a new fight with the French, and we can wet our blades with honour. But there is bad war coming to this land, mark me well. The Marches are buzzing like an angry hive. All the lands north of Gloucester are filled with men with swords in their hands and little in their heads, and sooner or later they'll get to hacking. Don't be caught in that bloody mill, Adam de Norton.'

'So I sit idly while others fight?' Adam asked, leaning back in his chair.

'No, no,' Robert said, then smiled and hunched forward across the table. 'You mind your estates, keep your people fed, and see the Ticeburns don't come back here barking and snapping around your door. Find yourself a good plump wife, and forget Joane de Bohun, for the love of Christ!'

*

Night filled the hall. Only embers remained of the fire, and one of the servants lowered the cover across it as Hugh and the others blearily spread their mattresses on the floor. Adam stretched, and felt the fumes of the wine in his head. Leaving Robert at the table he went out into the yard.

The air was crisp and cold, the stars bright and the moon a waxing crescent above the black trees. Adam crossed to the midden behind the kitchens, then pulled up his tunic and unlaced his braies. He breathed deeply, letting the clean air fill his lungs, drive out the muddiness of the wine and still the churn of his thoughts. As his bladder emptied into the darkness, Adam stared into the sky and for a moment saw nothing. Then he picked out the pale streak of the comet's tail. *Still there.*

At one time, he considered as he gazed upwards, Robert had thought differently about the state of the realm. Adam remembered

very clearly the things he had said, when first they met, about the
fury of England, and how it would shake the throne and bring
justice once more. But now that justice had flickered so briefly
into life, returning to Robert the lands and the standing in society
that he craved, he seemed content to let things return to how they
had once been. Land and titles, it appeared, weighed heavier than
justice, or honour. For Adam himself it was different. All that he
possessed now was the gift of Simon de Montfort, more or less. If
de Montfort fell, Adam would lose it all.

He was just lacing his braies when he heard footsteps crossing
the yard, and another figure loomed at his side. Robert cursed
under his breath, then sighed deeply as he began to piss.

'That lad in there,' Robert said, nodding back over his shoulder towards the hall. 'Your new groom or servant, or whatever
he is. I know him, don't I? That's the boy from the Jewry, whose
family were slain in the massacre.'

'Matthew. He's called Matthew now,' Adam said, still resentful
of Robert's attitude. 'And he's baptised, or so he claims.'

Robert grunted. He stared down at the dark midden, jogged
on his toes, then relaced his braies. 'You don't worry?' he asked.
'His people died at the hands of Christians . . . you don't fear
he'll cut your throat one night, as vengeance?'

'No,' Adam replied curtly, not caring to hide his annoyance.
'I do not.' Matthew was the name the boy went by nowadays,
although until three months ago he had been called Mosse. He
was about thirteen years old, a sturdy and dependable lad despite
his wiry frame, and he learned fast. He was good with horses, and
had developed a fierce devotion to Adam as well. If he was never
seen at mass, said no Christian prayers and never ate pork or oysters, then neither Adam nor his retinue made any comment.

'No,' he said again. 'If I worried that anyone would cut my
throat in the night, it would not be Matthew.'

He turned to leave and go back inside, but then paused. 'Will
you see Elias in London?' he asked. 'And Belia?'

Robert paused momentarily before replying. 'Yes,' he said. 'Yes, I will.'

'And will you ask her to come with you? To your lands in Shropshire?'

Moonlight picked out the angles of Robert's face, and Adam saw him wince. 'Perhaps,' he said. 'I need to speak to her about that. And to Elias. I have not . . . I've not yet raised it with them. But I hope . . .'

His voice choked off. Adam stared back at him, suddenly ashamed of himself. Many years before, he had learned of Robert's love for the Jewish widow Belia, the sister of the moneylender Elias of Nottingham, and glimpsed for the first time the depth of raw emotion that the knight concealed with his caustic attitude. It was wrong of him to have raised the subject now, probing the wound just to see if Robert still flinched from that pain. Perhaps, if he was honest, intending to inflict a little pain of his own.

Abashed, he just made a slight sound of acknowledgement and turned away towards the house. He had only taken a few paces before Robert spoke again.

'I was thinking,' he said, 'that I might stay on here a little longer. It's only two days till the Feast of St Francis. I'd like to take a look at these Ticeburns, and see what they might do.'

'You would?' Adam said.

'What sort of friend would I be, eh,' Robert asked, 'if I ate a man's food and drank his wine, and did not stand by him in his hour of need?'

*

Rain fell the next day, streaming from the eaves of the hall and the stables and turning the yard outside to puddled mud. Adam had slept badly: he had shared quarters with Robert and Hugh countless times when they rode the tournament circuit, but already he had forgotten how Robert muttered and ground his teeth in his sleep, and how often Hugh farted. Down in the hall William Tonge was taking his crossbow to bits on the dining table, cleaning and greasing each part, while Hugh made persistent attempts to engage Edith the kitchen maid in conversation as she came and went about her chores. Weary of pacing the floor and circling the hearth waiting for something to happen, Adam threw on a cloak, pulled up the hood and went out into the rain.

He found Robert and his squire Giles in the empty wagon shed. Robert had exercised his grey destrier at dawn, and now his squire was rubbing the animal down and cleaning the hooves of mud and stones.

'So,' Robert said briskly as he sat near the open door, polishing his axe and sharpening the wicked curve of its blade, 'these Ticeburns – what do you know of them?'

'The elder one, Fulk, was once de Brayboef's chief huntsman, I believe, or kennel master,' Adam told him. 'But the sheriff came by on Michaelmas eve, and he knows them well enough. The Ticeburns, he says, are not men to shrink from evil deeds.'

Robert nodded, then ran his thumb along the edge of the axe. He stood up and hefted the weapon, flexing his right arm and cutting great sweeps of air. 'Do they have friends? How many could they muster?'

'There are two brothers named Pescod,' Adam said, 'related to the Ticeburns by marriage. And there's a gang living in the woods up near Alton, so the reeve tells me. Masterless men and outlaws, but the Ticeburns trade with them for game and supplies.'

Robert grunted, still swinging his axe. He tested the edge again, and appeared satisfied. 'So,' he said. 'They could come in force, if they so desired.'

Adam nodded. He had been thinking the same thing. The manor was not fortified or enclosed, beyond a sagging fence and a ditch on three sides intended to stop grazing cattle and horses from the rear paddock from straying into the yard. The reeve had sent men from the village to watch the tracks to north and south, and boys were perched up trees to scan the further approaches, but if the Ticeburns returned with a large band of men – armed and determined men, with horses – the fight could be brief, and bloody.

'What of William de St John, the lord of Basing,' Robert said, laying down his axe once more. 'Have you spoken with him?'

'Not yet.' That was, Adam realised, the second time he had been asked that question. William de St John's moated hall and court at Basing lay half a day's ride north; Adam had been there with his father several times, a decade or more ago, but knew little of Lord William now. 'He fought for the king at Lewes, didn't he?'

'As did many. But he's no zealot for the royal cause, like some. Go to him, give him your respect. He could help you, in times to come.'

When I'm gone, Robert meant; Adam understood that well enough. Already he was wondering whether Robert regretted his offer to stay a few more days. He had a distracted air about him, an eagerness to be elsewhere. In London, Adam guessed, with Belia; he wondered whether Robert would be able to convince her to return with him to Shropshire. Doubtless Robert himself was wondering the same thing.

By that evening there had been no sign of anyone approaching the manor, only a band of pilgrims on foot, trudging through the rain on their way to distant Canterbury. Adam and his household gathered once more for supper, all of them together at the same board this time, but the mood was altogether more sombre.

'Perhaps they won't come at all,' Hugh of Oystermouth said. 'Men make these bold threats, then after sleeping on it they come to appreciate the wisdom of tolerance.'

'Certainly it would have been convenient if they'd suggested a more exact date for a reunion,' said Robert. He leaned back in his seat, stretching his legs beneath the table, then cleared his throat. 'Either way, if they do not come tomorrow then we must leave the following day.'

'Of course,' Adam said. It was becoming an embarrassment, he thought, to have detained Robert at all. Silence fell, undisturbed by the sound of dripping water; the rain had stopped, at least.

That night they went quietly to their beds, but Adam lay sleeplessly once more. He heard the watchman pacing beneath the window of his chamber, the distant whine of a dog. Robert ground his teeth in the darkness, and Hugh rolled onto his side and let out a slow, whiffling fart. A day's ride to the west, Joane would be sleeping in her chamber in Winchester Castle. Not on a straw pallet unrolled upon the floor either, but doubtless in a great canopied bed with feather mattresses and quilts. Was Humphrey de Bohun sleeping beside her? Angrily, Adam drove the thought from his mind. For a long time he lay in restless agitation, until sleep finally took him.

Then suddenly a bell was ringing, and somebody was shouting. Adam opened his eyes to grey light, the barking of dogs, and cries of alarm.

'Up,' Robert shouted, flinging himself from his mattress. 'Rouse yourself, for Christ's sake!'

It was the Eve of Saint Francis, and the Ticeburns had kept their promise.

Chapter 3

Hoofbeats from the rear yard, and as Adam threw open the window shutter a rider passed directly below him. Smoke trailed from the bundle of straw and tow that the man carried on a stick. A burst of flame as the bundle ignited, searingly bright in the grey of dawn, then the rider tossed the burning straw onto the thatched roof of the kitchen.

Adam glanced to one side, drawn by a flicker of movement. An archer down by the boundary fence bent his bow, aimed directly at him, then released. Adam pulled his head back sharply and slammed the shutter closed just as the arrow struck. The barbed iron head punched through the boards.

'Stay here,' he told Hugh of Oystermouth, who was still scrabbling up from his mattress. Where was Robert? The knight had vanished. Adam pulled on his shoes, dragged a tunic over his head, then snatched his scabbarded sword from the floor and ran down the stairs to the hall.

William Tonge was aiming his crossbow out through the crack between the shutters and the wooden window bars. The serjeant was a stocky bow-legged man with a belly like a keg, but in London Adam had seen him put a bolt through the bull's-eye at a hundred paces. He shot, the string of the bow thwacking, then spat through his teeth. 'Clipped one of the buggers.'

A flurry of arrows banged into the window shutter, the thick oak of the door, and the cob of the front wall. Matthew came running from the kitchen, trailed by the young maid Edith. 'Get into the buttery and shelter there, both of you,' Adam called, fastening his belt. There was a smell in the air: burning thatch, the sharpness of smoke. Noise of horses from directly outside, the wild yells of men, snarls of command.

Wilecok was at the front door, peering through the slot in the oak boards.

'How many of them are there?' Adam asked.

'Fair dozen or so,' Wilecok replied, and sucked his teeth as he squinted into the slot. 'Half of them on horses.'

'Where's Robert?'

'Out there,' Wilecok replied, motioning with his head. 'I tried to stop him, but . . .' Adam was already pulling the locking bar from its socket and dragging the door open.

'Have a care, they've got—' Wilecok had time to say, before Adam was across the threshold, sword drawn.

Dogs. They had dogs – three big mastiffs, off the leash and running at the door with foam-flecked jaws. Fulk Ticeburn and his brothers were in the yard, with another man, all mounted. No sign of Robert. Adam took a step back, raising his sword. He had no shield, no armour. *God's blood.*

The first dog was almost on him already. Adam slashed his sword, roaring, and it reared back and snarled at bay. He could hold off one of the beasts, but if two or even three came at him he was in trouble. An arrow slammed into the doorframe behind his head. The archer was somewhere beyond the far fence, lofting his shafts high to avoid the riders. Swinging his blade in wide arcs to keep the first two dogs back, Adam searched for Robert. Instead, he glimpsed two other figures, running across the open ground from the village. The reeve, John Ilberd, and his son.

Fulk Ticeburn saw them too and circled his horse to cut them off, but Ilberd's son had already bent his bow, leaning into it as he ran and pumping an arrow straight through the throat of the third dog. The animal went down running, muzzle in the dirt.

'In here, quickly,' Adam shouted to the two village men, as Fulk Ticeburn spurred his horse into a charge towards the doorway, sword raised. Ilberd bolted past Adam, in through the door, while his son paused and stooped, shooting another arrow at the dogs. At that range he could barely miss. The first animal was fleeing as the second whined, shot through the hindquarters. Then Ilberd's son was over the threshold and Adam retreated after him, sword still levelled. Wilecok slammed the door closed behind them all, as they heard the hooves battering past outside.

'Who are they?' Adam gasped. 'I see the Ticeburns. Who else?'

'Pescods,' the reeve said. 'Walter and Richard. I don't know the others, lord. Men from Alton, I'd say.'

Another arrow whacked into the far side of the door.

'Typical Alton bastards, wouldn't dare aim at us when we could shoot back,' Ilberd's son said.

Adam threw open the slot in the door again and peered out. Ticeburn's brother Eudo went cantering past, hefting a boar spear and laughing like a maniac. It was still too dim to make out the ground beyond the boundary fence and ditch, the sun not yet risen and everything hazy in the grey-blue light. But Adam could see a faint glow in the sky to the left of the house, and embers of burning tow were drifting on the breeze.

'They've fired the kitchen roof,' one of the servants said, stumbling into the passageway. 'Thatch is still wet from the rain, but it's catching . . .'

'Douse it from the inside if you can,' Adam said. His thoughts were slow, his mind reeling from sleep. The stink of burning thatch was getting stronger, and smoke was hazing the passageway. *The stable*, Adam thought suddenly – that too had a thatched roof.

'Matthew,' he shouted, and the boy appeared instantly from the door of the buttery. 'Follow me,' Adam said, already moving down the passage towards the rear door. Leaning against the wall was a spare shield he had been using in his sparring practice, and he snatched it up as he passed. 'Get to the stable as quick as you can,' he told Matthew. 'Loose the horses – every one of them, and make sure they're safe. Understand?'

Matthew nodded. Ilberd's son was at Adam's heels, tucking three arrows through his belt. Adam threw aside the locking bar from the rear door, pulled it open and ran outside with the shield raised before him.

Two riders in the rear yard, and at least one archer in the paddock beyond the boundary fence; the same man that had shot at Adam when he appeared at the solar window. Ilberd's son leaned into his bow and pumped an arrow flat and true towards the fence. Adam saw the archer jerk upright as if he had been stung, then tumble backwards into the ditch behind him.

'God forgive me,' Ilberd's son said.

One of the riders carried a stick wrapped in burning tow, but at Adam's shout he turned his horse and spurred towards him, throwing down his flaming brand and drawing a falchion from his belt. Crossing the yard at a canter, he swung the weapon above his head, his horse's hooves kicking up the wet dirt. He seemed to expect Adam to run; instead, Adam charged back at him, shield raised, yelling. At the last moment he stepped to one side, caught the man's blade on his shield and then slashed back. His sword cut through the man's forearm, shearing off his right hand. Blood sprayed, and the man doubled over in the saddle, the horse rearing. Adam snatched for the bridle, but the animal was panicked. The rider was still in the saddle as Adam seized the reins, but a moment later he slumped sideways and slid from the horse's back. An arrow was jutting from his shoulder. When Adam glanced upwards, he saw Hugh of Oystermouth leaning from the chamber window, bow in hand.

The horse reared again, pulling the reins from Adam's grip, then charged for the far fence. The dying man was half out of the saddle, one foot still caught in the stirrup, and the horse dragged his body as it ran. Another arrow spat from the chamber window, and the second rider lowered the spear, tugged at his reins, and rode swiftly after the fleeing horse. Damp smoke billowing from the kitchen roof hid them both.

Matthew had darted across the rear yard to the stables, but the attackers had not yet managed to fire the thatch. As the boy threw open the stable door, Adam heard Hugh call from above him.

'Guard yourself!'

He spun on his heel, instinctively lifting his shield, as a bearded man in a gambeson ran at him from the corner of the house with a levelled spear. Adam swung his shield just in time, the spearhead ramming against it and then skating downwards. He felt the point jab into the flesh of his left hip, grating against the bone. Pain shot through his body as he shoved the spear aside and aimed a low cut with his sword. The spearman had dodged backwards, readying himself for a second strike.

Sword and shield up, Adam braced himself on his back foot. He was wounded, blood running down his thigh, but not too badly that he could not fight. He had trained for this, to deflect the next attack and then to flow forward into a reaping cut. The spearman, however, had not. Adam saw the wild panic in the man's eyes, his bristled jaw clenched and his throat working as he saw the yard beyond emptied of his brethren and a trained fighter confronting him. For a moment he hesitated between flight and fury. Fury took him, and he let out a strangled cry and aimed another stab with his spear. Adam smashed it aside, lunged forward, and cut the man's leg out from under him.

The spearman went down in the dirt. He dropped his weapon and Adam staggered slightly as he kicked it aside. A sudden crash came from the front of the house, a wail from within. Adam could hear Fulk Ticeburn's grinding voice as he yelled orders. Another crash: the attackers were ramming at the front door, perhaps the windows, trying to break their way inside. The fallen spearman was still writhing in the mud clutching his injured leg with bloodied hands, seething curses between his teeth.

'Stay there,' Adam called to Ilberd's son, who had remained at the back door with an arrow nocked to his bow. No time to bind his wound; the bleeding was not too bad, although the left side of his body felt numb. Instead, he ran to the corner below the chamber window, and the muddy path along the side of the building from which the spearman had attacked him. His heel slipped as he ran, and he stumbled and almost lost his grip on the battered shield. Then he was out at the front corner of the house, and the yard was before him.

One of the Ticeburn brothers — Eudo, Adam reckoned — and another man were still mounted, cantering circuits by the far fence and trying to stay out of the shooting arc of William Tonge's crossbow. A horse was down and kicking in the middle of the yard, the head of a quarrel jutting from its neck, the fallen rider sprawled beside it. But Fulk Ticeburn himself with two other men had dismounted, and their archers had flung aside their bows and taken up a heavy log. Together they swung it at the front door of the house, while Fulk and his accomplices stood with swords and axes ready, poised to storm inside as soon as their makeshift ram broke through.

Another shivering crash as the log swung. Adam was still at the corner of the house, gripped by indecision. His intention had been to seize one of the mounts from the riders in the rear yard; instead, he was on foot, wounded, without armour or helmet, and facing two armed horsemen and six or seven other foes.

A shout, and Adam turned to see Eudo Ticeburn wheeling his horse and spurring it towards him, a blade raised in his hand. He shrank back against the corner of the house, his shield up, hoping that he could hold the rider at bay long enough to make a retreat. But he was outnumbered, with only the wall at his back as a defence. Fear iced his blood.

Then a pale shape appeared from the morning greyness, gathering form as it approached. One of the gang by the door cried out a warning, and Eudo Ticeburn looked back over his shoulder and dragged at his reins. Now all could hear the beating of hooves as Robert de Dunstanville rode at the gallop from the direction of the wagon shed. His charging destrier was bridled but not saddled, and Robert rode bareback, bareheaded, wearing only a padded aketon over his linen shirt. His black hair streamed loose, and he swung his war axe above his head as he bore down on the other rider.

Eudo Ticeburn was trying to wrestle his horse around to face the oncoming threat. Too slow: the grey destrier was upon him in three heartbeats, as Robert brought his axe down in a powerful arc. The blade chopped into Eudo's skull and cleft it in two, biting as deep as his jaw, and as Robert ripped the weapon free, gore sprayed bright pink in the early light. Then the destrier crashed against the dead man's horse and blasted it aside, the grisly corpse swaying and toppling from the saddle, and Robert charged on towards the house and the men gathered before the doorway.

For a few long moments Fulk and his men appeared paralysed, gaping at the vision of sudden death bearing down on them. Then they fled, running for their own tethered horses as the men with the ram threw down their burden and scattered. Smoke billowed across the yard and Robert rode through it, shortening his reins to slow his charge and bring his horse around.

Adam ran from the corner of the house, managing to slip his sword back into his scabbard. His jaw tight with pain, he seized the bridle of Eudo Ticeburn's panicking horse, then got his foot in the stirrup and swung himself into the saddle. His left boot felt like it was full of blood. The horse circled beneath him, still jittery, and Adam clung tight with his thighs and kicked with his heels until it suddenly bolted forward.

The door of the house burst open, and Giles de Wortham came forth with William Tonge and the reeve, all of them armed. Two of the remaining attackers had already thrown themselves down on their knees, begging for quarter, while the others fled on foot. But Adam could see Fulk Ticeburn and his younger brother Warin riding at full stretch towards the distant woodland, revealed now in the gathering daylight.

Turning his horse, Adam urged it along the path beside the house and out into the rear yard. Ilberd's son flexed his bow as he turned from the doorway, and Adam waved a quick acknowledgement to him as he passed. Kicking at the horse's flank, he galloped through the lingering drift of smoke from the thatch. With one leap the horse cleared the boundary fence and ditch. A burst of pain from Adam's hip as the animal came down and he was jolted forward in the saddle. Then he was galloping again, across the stubbled wheatfield, closing in on an oblique course with Ticeburn and his brother as they made their escape.

Fulk snatched a backward glance as he rode, then his horse stumbled and slackened speed. Adam kicked his heels again, reaching for the hilt of his sword, but pain stabbed at him, punching into his chest. Robert was coming up in support, but it was just him and Fulk Ticeburn now. The bearded man twisted in the saddle, fumbling his sword from the sheath at his side. Adam closed at a full gallop, and at the last moment flung his shield at him. As Fulk swayed back in the saddle, startled, Adam stretched out his arm and seized him around the neck.

Ticeburn roared, fighting back against him. He had managed to draw his sword and was trying to angle the blade to stab across his body, but Adam dragged at his reins and the horse beneath him halted suddenly, rearing. Pain erupted through his body as his muscles tightened, but he dragged Ticeburn from the saddle as the other man's horse bolted forward. For a moment Fulk clung to him, his bearded jaw ramming into Adam's face, his teeth open as he screamed, then Adam released his grip and let him drop.

Pulling at the reins once more, Adam circled his horse. Fulk Ticeburn lay on his side in the trampled wheat stubble, one leg bent beneath him, his face white with terror above his black beard. Overcoming another sickening wave of pain, Adam dropped from the saddle and drew his sword. Ticeburn stared back at him. His own weapon had fallen from his hand, and his shoulder looked dislocated. Adam stood over him, gasping for breath, pain filling his mind with white fury.

'By the cross of Christ, spare me . . .' Ticeburn managed to say. 'Don't kill me, I beg you. I am wounded and unarmed! It would be an evil deed—'

'Evil I leave to the Devil,' Adam said. He turned the sword in his hand, gripped it with both fists, then dropped forward onto his knees as he plunged the blade downwards.

*

'Now *that* was a tournament move,' Robert said later. 'Wrestling him from the saddle – nicely done. Did I teach you to do it?'

'Probably,' Adam replied.

They were in the hall, pale morning sunlight streaming through the windows and the sound of cocks crowing from the village. Adam tightened his jaw, as Hugh knelt beside his chair and stitched the wound in his hip with silken thread.

'Still,' Robert said, 'you should have killed him.'

'That would have been the right thing to do?'

'No, it would have been the wrong thing to do. But you should have killed him anyway. Better to be sure, in these matters.'

Robert had arrived upon the scene moments later. He had found Adam kneeling beside the fallen man, his sword driven halfway to the hilt into the earth only inches from his head. Fulk Ticeburn had sworn upon his soul and the souls of his brothers, upon the lives of his remaining family, upon the holy sacrament, that he would not trouble Adam again, nor show his face within ten miles of the manor. Adam, in return, had promised to raise the hue and cry against him if he should break his promise, and make sure he was hanged as a disturber of the peace.

Still, Adam thought, perhaps he should have killed him anyway?

They had heard the wailing as they returned to the house. In the buttery, stretched on the beaten earth of the floor, they had found Edith the kitchen maid with an arrow in her chest, Wilecok's pregnant wife kneeling over her. One of the archers in the front yard had shot a stray arrow through the chink between the window shutters, killing Edith instantly without even seeing her.

Now her body lay in the pantry, decently covered and watched over by the older serving woman. In the yard outside, four other bodies lay stretched in the dirt. Eudo Ticeburn's ghastly head injury was covered by a cloth. Two of the archers lay beside him: one had been slain by an arrow from Ilberd's son, the other shot with one of William Tonge's crossbow bolts. Once the sun came up, the villagers had found him sitting in the boundary ditch in a lake of his own blood, and he was dead before they dragged him back to the house. They had found the mangled corpse of the rider that attacked Adam in the rear yard as well; his horse had dragged him almost to the edge of the woods before the stirrup leather broke. Hugh of Oystermouth had looked at the corpse, the stub of his own arrow still jutting from its back, and turned white and sickly. Adam had assured him that the man would probably not have survived having his hand severed and falling from the galloping horse, but Hugh was convinced that he had killed the man himself.

Outside, the house servants had dragged the smouldering thatch from the kitchen roof. They had doused the flames, but the house and rear yard still smelled of smoke and blood. The prisoners were secured in the old kennel at the back. Two of the men who had swung the ram at the door had been captured, with an archer Robert had ridden down as he tried to flee, and the spearman Adam had wounded during the fight in the rear yard.

'They said there would only be one man here, lord,' the spear-man told him, when Adam limped out to question the prisoners. 'A green youth, they said, who could not fight, and a few old servants. But they said there was silver, lord. Great bags of silver, and we could take as much of it as we could carry, if only we helped them.'

'Kill him now,' growled William Tonge. 'Or bag him and tie him until the sheriff gets here. Then we'll watch him and these other churls hanged for murder, sure enough.'

'Save us, lord, I beg you,' the archer cried. 'We were misled, that's all. We never meant no harm to you or yours!'

'You meant assault and robbery,' Adam told him, leaning on the gatepost, 'and breaking into my home. I cannot forgive you that.' But he was more troubled by the thought that somebody in the village had passed word to the Ticeburns about the silver coins he had brought with him from London.

Walter Pescod had ridden back to the house and surrendered himself too, on pledge for the life of his brother Richard, who was still unconscious after William Tonge had brought down his horse with a crossbow bolt. 'I swear to you on the holy body of Christ, we'll not trouble you again,' Pescod had promised. 'This was none of our devising – it was that fool Ticeburn who wanted this, and we owed him the favour. But we never laid a blow on any of yours, I confess it.'

'Will Fulk Ticeburn come back?' Adam asked him.

Pescod pondered a while, then shook his head. 'I'd say you learned him well enough,' he said. 'And his brother Warin's a spine-less coward – he won't quit his galloping till he's past Farnham.'

Adam took the Pescods' pledge and allowed Walter to leave in peace, his brother tied across the saddle behind him. He released the other captives too, and let them take one of the captured horses to carry their own injured away. The dead men they would bury in the churchyard, once the coroner had exam-ined them and the sheriff had pronounced their deaths justified.

Edith they would bury too, with far greater sadness. As for Fulk Ticeburn, Adam could only hope that he kept to his pledge, and never showed his face again. He was determined not to dread the man's vengeance.

*

Robert de Dunstanville and his retinue departed the next morning, after hearing Mass in the chapel. He would ride for London, and then back north and west to his lands in Shropshire. Wilecok was eager to get back there before his wife was due to give birth; Adam had offered to let them remain with him, to spare the woman the rigours of further travel, but both Wilecok and his silent wife had declined the offer.

'When my son is born,' Wilecok declared, 'he will be the finest horseman in all this kingdom!' His wife had just sat on her pony and shrugged. Adam had known them both for years, and knew their unshakable devotion to Robert; he was not surprised that neither wanted to leave his retinue now. He was more surprised when Hugh of Oystermouth appeared, booted and clad in his travelling clothes, leading his saddled rouncey and packhorse from the stable.

'I've decided I too will abide with Robert for a time,' Hugh said, not meeting Adam's eye. 'The death of that man sits heavy upon me, you see, for all his villainy. The death of that poor maid Edith, too.' He shook his head sadly, then frowned. 'Besides, I've a mind to revisit my homeland,' he said. 'In a dream last night, I saw my father lying in great distress and pain, begging I repent of my sins . . .'

'You'll go back to Wales?'

'For a spell, yes. But I shall return, I expect, in the spring when my soul is no longer oppressed. Will you give me your blessing?'

'Gladly,' said Adam, though he felt a deep pang of sadness. The Welsh clerk had been his companion for many years, and with his departure Adam would be sundered from all his old friends.

'I'll send word when I reach London,' Robert told him. 'And again once I'm back home. And if you should ever venture north of Worcester, be sure to come and find me. Though I cannot promise you as much sport as you've shown me here!'

'I shall,' Adam replied. Only now was he realising how much he would miss Robert too. He stood at the doorway as the knight and his party assembled their pack animals and rode once more towards the woods and the track that led north to the highway. Hugh rode at the rear, and as he passed through the fence, he turned in the saddle and pointed to the sky. 'Have you seen?' he called back. Adam shrugged, frowning.

'Look to the heavens tonight!' Hugh said. Then he grinned as he rode off after Robert and the others.

The last few days had been cloudy, and the night sky obscured. But once darkness fell, Adam limped out across the yard to the break of the fence, beyond the reach of the hearth glow from the open doorway, and saw that the clouds had passed. The moon was near full, the stars bright, but as he turned and scanned the black heavens Adam's heart skipped in his chest.

The comet was gone, and the sky was clear.

He drew a long breath, feeling the chill in the air, the first taste of coming winter. Yes, the comet was gone, carrying its dire portent with it.

And perhaps now, Adam thought, all the perils had truly passed, and England would know peace at last.

Chapter 4

The hunters assembled at daybreak. Frost lay blue on the ground, and the breath of the horses steamed. Beyond the palings at the bottom of the slope the woods were ashen grey and threaded with early mist. With the first light in the sky, the scent-hounds were already coursing through the nearer thickets and the shrill bleating of the horns was driving off the darkness of the winter night.

'We were robbed of our hunting season this year, my friends,' Lord William de St John said, as he sat in his saddle and drank from a cup of warmed and spiced wine. 'For now, all I can offer is a mere *battue*, a winter deer drive, but I promise you that once the summer comes again, we will chase the stag with strength of hounds!'

Lord William was a vigorous man in his late fifties, with a broad handsome face and a curling beard the colour of straw shot through with grey. Adam had been surprised how well he remembered the man from his childhood; his father had brought him several times to Basing to attend Lord William's court. Strange, he thought, how much he had forgotten of those years.

'I knew your father well,' the baron had told him, when Adam first presented himself at Basing to give homage for the land he held of the St Johns. 'A good man, and gone too soon, may

God grant him mercy. It's good to see you taking up his possessions once more.' And he had clapped Adam on the shoulder and
grinned in genuine pleasure.

Adam felt that same warmth from him now, radiating through
the morning chill. William de St John, he was discovering, was a
man of great heart and strong passions, and determined to show
the guests at his Christmas Court, whether friends or tenants,
the best of hospitality.

'Now,' William cried, straightening in the saddle. 'Let's away!'

A chorus of horns, and the hunting party moved forward.
There were a score or more mounted hunters, both men and
a smaller band of ladies accompanying them. Servants attended
them on foot, dressed in grey drab and winter brown, with the
greyhounds swarming around them.

Adam had attended hunts like this before, although he was
more familiar with boar hunting in winter, or the great summer
stag chases that the Earl of Hereford had conducted on his Welsh
estates. There would be nothing like that today; their prey would
be female deer only, the fallow does and the hinds. Once the hunters had taken their places among the trees and readied their bows,
the animals would be driven forth by dogs and beaters, to be shot
with arrows while the unleashed greyhounds brought down the
wounded deer and the stragglers alike. Not as honourable as the
stag chase, but there would be a far greater haul of venison.

'But is it not cruel to kill only the females?' a young woman
said as they rode, her voice carrying clear through the misty air.
'Especially when they have no way of escaping the park.'

Adam glanced back but saw only the shrouded figures of the
ladies who rode behind the main body of hunters. He heard one
or two of the men laughing.

'Not cruel at all, my dear,' an older woman replied. It was
William's wife, Lady Agnes. 'We must cull the females in winter,
you see, or there won't be sufficient forage to keep the whole
herd alive until summer.'

If the young woman made any further comment, Adam did not hear it. Instead, he was distracted by two of the riders ahead of him, whose voices rose as they approached the park palings. They were Sir John de Cormayles and Sir Martin des Roches, both guests of Lord William, and lords of nearby manors.

'It happened on St Lucy's Day, so my messenger tells me,' des Roches said. 'Lord Simon brought his army to Worcester, and the Welsh came down from the west and trapped the Marchers against the river. All of them agreed to the peace, every one of his adversaries from the greatest to the least – he gave them no choice. They swore to abjure the realm and go to Ireland with all their households and retinues for a year and a day.'

'Does anyone believe they will?' John de Cormayles said with a laugh.

Adam listened with interest; the summons to muster for military service against the rebels in Wales had gone out the month before, but he had paid the *scutage* fee as Robert had suggested, rather than attend.

'And what of Lord Edward?' de Cormayles went on. 'De Montfort may keep him chained, but the Leopard still has his claws, and his teeth are sharp!'

'Why do they call him that?' asked Lucy des Roches, who had ridden up to join her husband. 'I know that the beasts on the royal arms are called *leopards*, but why should the king's son be known by that name?'

'Because he is fierce as *leo* and cunning as a *pard*, my lady,' de Cormayles said, with a condescending smile. 'And Lord Simon should watch his back!'

Laughter from the other men, some of it scornful and some rueful. But Lord William's voice silenced them. 'Peace, friends, enough talk of conflict now,' he said. 'We are at peace here, and with God's blessing we are done with wars in England.'

Adam caught his eye. There were several among the gathering, he knew, who claimed to support Simon de Montfort and his governance of the kingdom, but Adam himself was the only man here who had fought on de Montfort's side at Lewes. William and two of the other knights present had been fighting on the opposing side that day. Since then, William had made his peace with the victors, and had spent two months serving under de Montfort's son at the fruitless siege of Pevensey Castle, where a band of royalist supporters still held out. But were they really all friends here now?

As he reached the park palings, Adam saw that another small group had arrived to join them and waited beside the gateway, two well-dressed men on horseback each with a foot servant and a bow-bearer. The older of the two horsemen was around Lord William's age, with a glowering pink complexion and a jutting brow, and the younger man appeared to be his son. Something about them sparked a memory in Adam's mind, but for several moments as he rode closer he could not place it. Only when he heard one of the men ahead of him greet the newcomers by name did recognition dawn on him. A heartbeat later, the man with the florid features noticed him too, and smiled at him, cold-eyed.

'I thought you were still overseas, Sir Hugh,' Adam said as he drew level with the mounted pair. Hugh de Brayboef, once and briefly Adam's stepfather and possessor of his estates these past ten years, inclined his head slightly, but his smile did not waver. 'A man must concede when the game is lost,' he said. 'After all, are we not all good Englishmen, and loyal to the king?'

Adam had never really known Hugh de Brayboef, having only seen him once or twice when he was still a child. The man's son was close to Adam's age, and he remembered him rather better, although he would not have recognised him without his father at his side. Geoffrey de Brayboef had inherited his father's heavy brow and pink complexion, but his stare was flinty and lacked even the semblance of good humour.

'Your servants, the Ticeburns, would not see things in so peaceable a light,' Adam said.

Hugh de Brayboef merely shrugged. 'Ah, yes,' he replied. 'I heard of their antics. A shameful thing, and none of my doing. I have expelled them both from my service and from my lands; and if I see them again, I shall hang them for their crimes.'

'Or I shall,' Lord William said, appearing at Hugh's side. 'Give no mind to them in future,' he told Adam, who felt considerably more reassured by his promises than by those of Hugh de Brayboef.

'Come, clasp hands in friendship,' William went on, taking Adam's hand and drawing his arm towards de Brayboef. A clumsy gesture; Adam could tell that this encounter had been intended, and William was uncertain of its outcome. But he extended his hand, and after a moment's pause his former stepfather clasped his palm in a tight grip. Their horses moved closer, and the two of them leaned from the saddle and embraced.

'Don't think I've forgotten,' Hugh breathed in Adam's ear. 'I may forgive, but I never forget.'

Adam drew back quickly, startled and then repulsed. But de Brayboef was smiling again, as if he had said nothing. Several of the other mounted men had moved up around them, and Hugh and his son pulled at their reins and joined the cavalcade as it passed through the gates and into the deer park.

'You did well,' Lord William said quietly to Adam, still riding at his side. 'I feared that if I told you they would be joining us, you wouldn't come out today. But we need to heal these old scars, if we are to live together in peace, do we not?'

'We do,' Adam replied. But his thoughts were in turmoil, and his body felt flushed with a strange emotion that he could not name. Anger mingled with trepidation. It was not just the prospect of the hunt that fired his blood.

They were following a track that ran through the lower wooded stretch of the deer park, and the bare trees and thorn bushes closed around them so that for a stretch the hunters had to ride in single file. The darkness lingered here, and the thickets were still hung with morning mist. Off to his left Adam could hear the sounds of the beaters forging their way through the denser scrub.

As the path widened he glanced to his right and saw that Hugh de Brayboef's son Geoffrey had dropped back to join him. 'You're comfortably settled on your estates, then, I suppose?' the man asked, his voice low and rough with scorn.

'I am,' Adam replied. He had no wish to speak with Geoffrey, but for the time being he could not get away from him.

'They should have gone to me, you know. If your Lord Simon had not seen fit to settle them on you, as a reward for your services to his cause . . .'

Adam's shoulders tightened, but he kept his voice calm. 'Those lands are my birthright,' he replied. 'My inheritance from my father.'

'They were your mother's inheritance, and you know it,' Geoffrey de Brayboef said, dropping his voice to a hiss. 'And when your mother married my father, they came to him as her dowry. God knows that truth, and one day I shall see justice done.'

So that was it, Adam realised: the de Brayboefs had no intention of giving up their claim to his lands. But before he could form a response a gap opened in the column of mounted hunters and Geoffrey de Brayboef spurred his horse forward.

Seething, Adam waited only until the other man was out of sight ahead of him, then he turned his horse onto a branching path that led to the left into the denser woodland. Already the hunting party was quickening its pace as they approached the open stretch of land where the deer would be driven to be shot, the feuterers drawing their greyhounds on ahead to take up their positions around the margins of the sward, ready to unleash the dogs once the prey appeared in view. Adam himself had made no great practice with the bow and did not care to risk embarrassing himself with his poor shooting; instead, he had volunteered to aid the beaters in driving the deer out into the open.

As he plunged off alone into the thickets, his mood soured and the excitement of the hunt was lost on him. Lord William's attempts to make peace between him and the de Brayboefs seemed unendurable now. Quickly the noise of the hunting party fell away behind him, the thud of hooves and the pant and whine of dogs muffled by the misty thickets all around him. From ahead came the bleat of the hunting horns, the *touroo-roo-roo* of the lymerers and the crash of the undergrowth as the dogs surged through the morning gloom. Now and again a dog let out a swift bark, although they were trained to keep quiet on the scent.

Adam shortened his reins and rode off the path a little, letting his palfrey pick a route through the deep muffling leaf-litter. Shafts of light filtered down between the trees, and when he looked up, Adam saw that the sky was brilliant blue above him, the bare branches that rose from the misty gloom trapping the sun in a glowing tracery of orange and gold. Birds wheeled and soared in the brightness of the morning.

Abruptly his sour mood was gone. Adam breathed deeply and inhaled the scents of the dawn woodland, the dampness of the mist in the air, the mould and the leaves, the good warm sweat of the horse beneath him. A nudge with his spurs, and the palfrey neatly leapt a fallen tree overgrown with brambles. Four more cantering strides and Adam rode out into a clearing between tall elms and birch trees, where the angled sunlight illuminated a carpet of dense golden-brown bracken. He drew in the reins and the palfrey slowed to a halt.

Something moved from the far side of the clearing, but in the dimness Adam sensed it rather than saw it. The shape formed from misty shadow, and Adam's breath caught. It was a great fallow buck, almost the size of a stag in its coat of dark shaggy winter fur. The animal emerged into the clearing and stepped gracefully onto a mossy log among the bracken, then halted and lifted its head. Lit by the shafting sun, its antlers spread like the palms of open hands, tipped with stiff spiked fingers. For a long moment there was silence, the distant sounds of the hunting horns and the dog pack falling away.

Adam knew the old hunter's lore; a deer will flee from a man on foot, but will often ignore a man on horseback, taking him for a fellow four-legged creature. He trusted to that adage now, as he held himself motionless in the saddle. The buck twitched its ears, moved its head slightly, scenting the damp air.

Then Adam saw that he was not the only person in the clearing. On the far side, almost concealed by a stand of birches, was a woman mounted on a small jennet pony. She was wrapped in a woollen cloak, but Adam could see that she was watching the fallow buck, transfixed just as he had been. Then, as if drawn by his gaze, she looked at him.

He had seen her the day before, at the Nativity feast in Lord William's hall, but he had not been introduced to her. Somehow, he was sure that she was the young woman who had spoken earlier, during the ride down to the park.

Adam's palfrey snorted and shook its mane. A moment later the blare of a hunting horn sounded between the trees, and the cries of the men urging on their scent-hounds: 'Ho moy! Ho moy!'

A flash of movement, and the fallow buck was gone, leaping from the log and bounding across the clearing and into the sheltering shadow of the trees and thickets. Adam heard the woman on the jennet stifle a cry of surprise, or perhaps of disappointment. Before either of them could move, three does came dashing through the clearing, bounding in high leaps as they cleared the log and vanished into the thickets on the far side. Almost at their backs streamed the running dogs, grey and speckled hounds rushing quick and silent through the golden bracken, with the huntsmen coming after them with their horns.

Adam held his palfrey back to let the men and dogs pass, then when the clearing was empty once more he rode out into the heart of it. The young woman joined him.

'You saw the fallow buck?' Adam asked.

'Yes,' the woman replied. 'He was beautiful.' She appeared troubled, gazing after the huntsmen and their running pack. 'Will the dogs take him, do you think?'

'We must hope not. This area should have been cleared of male beasts. But if he runs with the does then the greyhounds may catch him . . .'

He broke off, noticing the woman's quick shudder, and recalled what she had said during the ride to the park. 'You do not care for the hunt, my lady?'

'I do not. I only came out for the exercise, and because everyone else would be here. But I would gladly let the beasts live freely if I could.'

Adam smiled, remembering for a moment Joane de Quincy and her relish in sending her hawk against wildfowl, her love of nature's savagery. This young woman seemed to share none of that. They set off together after the hunters, their horses side by side.

'You don't remember me, do you?' she asked Adam, with a glance that mingled challenge and amusement.

'From the feast yesterday?' he asked, but then saw at once that she meant something different. She was familiar indeed, he had known that at once. A bird burst from the tangle of a bush directly ahead of them, and the woman's jennet flinched and shied. Adam caught the bridle, and as he did so he noticed the little shield-shaped pendant on the pony's harness, enamelled with the arms of the St Johns: bright white with a bar of red at the top, bearing two golden stars.

'You're Lord William's daughter,' he said, once she had calmed her horse. 'I must have met you when I came to Basing as a child. Agnes, is it . . .?'

'Agnes was my older sister,' the woman said. 'She died four years ago.'

'I'm sorry,' Adam said quickly, 'I did not—'

The woman raised her palm in demurral. 'I'm not surprised you remember her better,' she said with a smile. 'I was only six or seven years old when we last met.'

'Isabel,' Adam said, smiling as the name rose from distant memory. The woman smiled too and inclined her head, as if in congratulation.

They were walking their horses once more as they spoke, the barking of dogs and the bleating of the horns a distant noise that came and went around them. Yes, she had changed a lot, Adam thought. He remembered her as a thin pale child, slinking in the shadows of the hall while her boisterous brothers held forth and her older sister preened. He had been a very minor visitor to Basing then, the son of a country knight and tenant, of little regard. But now Isabel de St John was fully a woman, her face pink with life and her blue eyes gleaming.

The rough path they had followed from the clearing appeared to be leading them into ever denser thickets, thorny bushes closing in on either side. 'I'm not entirely sure where we are,' Isabel said, turning in the saddle and peering around her. 'These woods grow so tangled in winter. I'm afraid I broke away from the others soon after we arrived.'

'I'll take you back to join them,' Adam said. In truth, he doubted that she needed a guide, but he wanted an excuse to spend longer in her company.

They rode together for a short way further, their knees brushing as they passed through an enclosing thicket; a loop of bramble caught at Isabel's cloak, and Adam helped her tug it free. The sounds of the hunt had faded, and for a while Adam could almost imagine that they had passed into some secret and enchanted woodland, like the ones in the songs and stories.

Then they emerged abruptly onto the bank of a stream, and saw to their left a bowl-shaped sward, the frosted turf washed in pale wintry sunlight. Now, as if a door had been flung open, they heard once more the *touroo-touroo* of the horns, the shouts of the dogboys as they uncoupled and unleashed the animals, and the rapid excited barking of the greyhounds. Around the sward they could see the standings where the archers waited with bows strung and readied, and already the first few deer had been brought down.

'Look!' Isabel cried, catching Adam by the arm and pointing. In the middle distance, towards the far side of the sward, Adam picked out the raised antlers of the fallow buck they had seen in the clearing. As yet neither the dogs not the other hunters appeared to have noticed it.

A pair of does raced from the cover of the thickets, driven forth by the shouts of the beaters. Adam saw Martin des Roches lift his bow, draw and hold for a moment's aim, then release. The arrow went wide, the deer skittering towards the far trees. At the next standing, Lucy des Roches and Amicia de Cormayles aimed and shot; one of them cried out in triumph as her shaft struck the flank of a running doe. At once the sleek greyhounds went racing across the grass, bounding and seizing the wounded animal as it staggered to its knees.

Adam heard Isabel's warning, and looked across the sward towards the fallow buck. But Isabel called out again, more urgently; this time he understood her, and turned quickly in his saddle.

Geoffrey de Brayboef stood beside a tree, half hidden in the shadow, his bow bent. Adam saw the barbed steel arrowhead moving, tracking him. Then de Brayboef shot, and Adam only had time to throw himself forward in the saddle as the arrow skimmed across his bent back.

'Did he hit you, are you hurt?' Isabel called, turning her pony swiftly. She had put herself, Adam noticed, between him and de Brayboef's archery position.

'He aimed for me!' Adam said under his breath. He straightened, half expecting to feel the pain lancing up his back.
Amazingly, the arrow had cut a rip through the wool of his cloak
but had not even nicked him. 'You saw him?'

Isabel nodded. But Geoffrey de Brayboef was already striding forth from his tree, arms spread, holding his bow in an
outstretched hand. 'Forgive me!' he called. 'There was a deer
directly behind you, and you moved forward just as I released!'

Adam glared at him, fighting the urge to strike the man. But
he would not fight here, not in front of Isabel. Had that been
what de Brayboef wanted to provoke?

'I appear to have survived, thanks to God,' he said, his voice
catching.

A chorus of shouts came from across the sward, and all turned
to see the fallow buck galloping out from the cover of the trees.
The greyhounds, already loosed after the fleeing does, went for
it at once.

'Ware, ware!' Lord William shouted from among the trees.
'Feuterers, call off the hounds!'

'Let them run, William,' Hugh de Brayboef called to him.
'The buck's one of mine – he escaped from my deer park at
Hackwood not a month ago. I make of him a Christmastide gift
to you, my lord!'

It was too late, Adam could see, to save the buck. Some of the
more eager archers had already loosed arrows at it, and bright
fletchings jutted from its dark fur. The greyhounds whirled as the
big animal tried to turn back and seek shelter. Instead, the stream
lay before it, and the buck plunged into the icy water, tossing its
head to try and strike the pursuing dogs with its antlers.

But even the dogs could not bring down the wounded
beast. In the end, when the buck had staggered and thrashed
two bowshots or more along the stream, Lord William's chief
huntsman rode in close and slashed at its hamstrings, crippling it. Hugh de Brayboef himself dealt the killing blow,

stabbing it between the antlers with the long spike of his
hunting knife.

*

'There's many a man been struck by a chance arrow while hunting,' William de St John said. 'Kings of England among them, so
they say . . . No harm was done, I understand?'

'None,' Adam said, and forced himself to smile. 'Except to
my cloak. And it's true I should not have been there – my place
was back with the beaters. I'd only come forward to escort your
daughter.'

Lord William's relief was palpable. He appeared caught
between anger and embarrassment at what had happened. But
as the host, he could not allow a dispute to grow between his
guests. He had already spoken terse words to Hugh de Brayboef,
who in turn had spoken sharply to his son.

But now all were distracted by the ritual of the unmaking. The
grass of the sward, pocked by the hooves of the fleeing deer, was
dyed and dappled with their blood and viscera. The slain does –
nine of them, at the final tally, all fat with winter grease – had
been swiftly undone, fleaned and brittled. The noble hunters had
watched from horseback while the huntsmen and their servants,
all of them red to the elbows and spattered with gore, had done
the cutting and skinning. Steam rose from the carcasses, and the
cold morning air was charged with the coppery reek of blood
and flesh.

The slain fallow buck, however, demanded greater ceremony
in its unmaking. While the greyhounds were kept back in a baying, milling throng by the staves of the dogboys, the servants
hauled up the animal's legs and secured them to poles. Then the
work of the knives began. The chief huntsman flayed the hide,
opened the chest and then the belly, and his two assistants carefully tied the bowels and sliced free the viscera. The clamour of

the dogs had settled to a constant yapping and whining as they circled with weaving tails, waiting for their reward. Above them all the sky was noisy with birds, the crows and ravens circling too, and settling along the bare branches of the trees.

'Always there at the death, our sable friends,' John de Cormayles said, gazing upward with a grimace. 'We must be sure to throw them their fee.'

Geoffrey de Brayboef had joined the huntsmen in the dismemberment of the carcass. Adam watched him as he worked with his hunting knife, and remembered the man's look of cold calculation before he released his arrow. He had aimed to kill, no doubt about it. Adam's gaze drifted to Isabel de St John, who had remained in the saddle, keeping her distance from the blood and gore. She was trying to appear unmoved by the scene of slaughter, but Adam noticed that her distaste was not solely for the butchering of the animals.

A horseman sidled up beside Adam's mount, Hugh de Brayboef leaning towards him from the saddle as he followed the direction of Adam's gaze. 'I see you've become friendly with Lord William's daughter,' the older man said, barely above a whisper. 'Quite a peach, isn't she?'

Adam turned abruptly to stare back at him, his jaw tightening with affront. De Brayboef's ruddy features creased into a smile, almost a wink.

'She's been betrothed to my son Geoffrey these last five years,' he said softly. He gave a last nod, then shook his reins and jabbed with his spurs, moving away to join the other hunters as they laughed and shared cups of heated wine.

By now the slaughtered buck was fully unmade, the head with its fine spread of antlers cut off and mounted on a pole, the organs and genitals displayed on a forked stick, the meat expertly divided to be carried back to the hall. Upon the flayed hide the huntsmen spread the chopped offal, and the hounds rushed in a baying tumult upon their bloody reward. The huntsmen blew

their horns in wild cacophony, and the dogs reddened their muz-
zles as they fed.

Geoffrey de Brayboef came from the scene of the unmaking,
holding outstretched in one hand the severed forefoot of the
buck. Walking up to Isabel de St John, who remained on her
pony at the margin of the mounted group, he presented her with
the trophy.

Lord William gestured impatiently, and Isabel took the severed foot between finger and thumb. It looked obscene, a baton
of stripped bone and sinew, tipped with the animal's delicately
slotted foot. 'For the fairest,' Geoffrey said, grinning. Blood was
smeared on his cheek.

Adam turned away, unwilling to see more, as the other ladies
and some of the men cried out their congratulation, and the
frenzy of the feeding dogs went on.

*

The hunting party returned to Basing Court in time for dinner,
the huntsmen bearing the buck's head on its pole before them,
the organs slung on their fork just behind, and the long line
of carts carrying the carcasses of the does as the hornblowers
sounded the mort.

'Plentiful venison, once it's hung,' Lord William said to Adam
as he rode at the head of the column of mounted hunters. 'I'd say
some of it should be good to eat by the Feast of Epiphany.'

Adam nodded, although he was not intending to remain
at Basing anything like that long. In fact, he wanted to return
home as soon as he could without giving offence. But he needed
to speak with Lord William's daughter once more before he
departed; to let their subtle play of attraction end so soon would
be unendurable. It was late that day before he had a chance; the
light was already fading, the feasting was done and the servants
were lighting the big nests of candles at the corners of the hall,

and he met her by chance in the dimness of the passageway as he returned from the stables.

'He should not have done that,' Isabel said at once, dropping her voice. 'Given me that grisly foot, I mean. And after so open an attack on you too. He had no right!'

'What did you do with it?' Adam asked.

'I gave it to the cooks. They can use it in broth if they like, I don't care.'

Adam twitched a smile, but his heart was beating faster. They were standing very close in the shadows of the passageway, the candlelight through the open hall door barely reaching them. 'Hugh de Brayboef told me you are betrothed to his son . . .' Adam began.

Isabel cut him off with disdain. 'I am not!' she said. 'I was, I mean, but as soon as I was old enough to understand what sort of a man he is, what sort of men both of them are . . . I spoke with Father and he agreed to break off the engagement. He claimed there was some issue of family affinity, but Geoffrey and his father both act as if nothing has changed.'

Adam, speechless, found to his surprise that she had taken his hand as she spoke. Apparently, she was just as surprised herself, and released him again.

'I saw him shoot that arrow at you as well,' Isabel said, almost whispering. 'I doubt he meant to kill you – even he would not be so bold. It was intended as a warning, you understand. That unless . . .'

'Unless?' Adam asked, as she fell silent. He was sure that he could hear her heart beating, even above the steady thump of his own. Then Lord William's voice rose from the hall, calling everyone to join him before the hearth, now the candles were lit and Christmastide cheer was restored. Hippocras and wafers would be served, a troupe of minstrels would play for them, and the hall would be cleared for dancing.

*

Epiphany had come and gone by the time Adam made his way home from Basing. A light dusting of snow iced the fields and the bare trees, and as he rode, Adam recalled that morning years before when he had first set out from Pleshey with Robert de Dunstanville. How much had changed in that short space of time.

But very soon his mind turned once more to the events of the past two weeks. Adam had known the festivities of a great household when he had been a squire of the Earl of Hereford, but at Basing he had not been an onlooker but an honoured guest and participant. Hugh and Geoffrey de Brayboef had made their silent departure the day after the hunt, and from then on Adam had spent his days in feasting, and riding out to exercise the horses with William's sons and household knights. During the short winter evenings there had been music, and firelit recitations of chivalric romance. Adam had even told the story of his own experiences at the Battle of Lewes and the Siege of Rochester, being careful to accord equal honour to both sides in the conflict.

But through all of it there had been Isabel. The pleasure of her memory warmed him as he rode. The pleasure too of thinking – he was sure that it was not his imagination alone fooling him – that she had enjoyed his company just as much. And for the first time in nearly a year, he realised, he had thought nothing of Joane de Bohun. For the first time he had allowed himself to think of a different fate, a different future that spread before him like a golden sunrise.

He caught himself and shuddered. The image came to him of Geoffrey de Brayboef's eyes narrowing as he took aim. The flash of barbed steel through the cold air. How quickly everything he had gained, everything he wished for, could be taken away from him. He must not grow complacent.

The horse tossed its mane, breath pluming as it stamped the frozen mud of the road. With a touch of the spurs, Adam urged the animal onward, before the barren desolation of the winter landscape seeped into his soul.

Chapter 5

It was a grey day in late March, just before Holy Week, when Hugh of Oystermouth returned to the manor. His arrival was unannounced, and sooner than expected.

'Not that I relish creeping back here like a dog with his tail between his legs,' he said as he sat in the hall by the fire, eating a lenten meal of bread and herrings and washing it down with ale. 'But sad to say my return to the Gower was not what I'd hoped.'

'Your father was not sick and begging your repentance, then?' Adam asked.

'Not a bit. He was in rude health, and my family were not inclined to treat me like the prodigal son either. In fact, they beat me savagely, and demanded that I return the money they'd spent on sending me to university in Paris.'

Adam gave him a wry smile. 'You seem to have escaped,' he said.

'Aye, but my purse is cruelly deflated.'

In fact, Adam noticed, Hugh looked quite deflated himself. He had lost his plumpness and ruddy complexion, and appeared almost gaunt and grey. For all his usual jovial spirits, it was clear that he had not been well treated by fortune.

'To be quite honest,' the Welshman went on, taking another deep swig of ale, 'I'm completely penniless. I was hoping you might be able to offer me a position in your household.'

Adam frowned and rubbed his jaw, feeling the prickle of fresh stubble. Over the past six months he had restored the manor and its adjoining estates as best he could. The hall was laid with fresh rushes, the walls whitewashed and painted with a tracery foliage pattern in red and green, and the tables and sideboards had covers of embroidered linen and were set with polished silver. Above the dais hung a large wooden shield with Adam's heraldic arms, a golden lion rampant on a green field.

He had restored his household as well, which now comprised twenty manorial officers and servants, from the steward and bailiff who managed his estates to the household clerk who compiled his accounts, the cofferer and chaplain, the cooks and grooms and stableboys, and the laundress and her maids.

'I've got all the followers I need,' Adam said with a rueful shrug.

Hugh's face fell, although he tried to hide it. 'Ach well,' he said. 'Perhaps I could just trouble you to put me up for a few days—'

'Stay as long as you like,' Adam said, cutting him off. He was far more comfortable in his role as lord of the manor now, and less inclined to observe distinctions of birth and status. Besides, he was only now realising how much he had missed Hugh over the past half a year, and all his old friends. 'Call yourself my herald, if you like, or a valet,' he offered, unable to hold back his smile. 'I'll pay you a valet's fee, anyway, and we can decide what that might involve later.'

'Thank you, my friend!' Hugh said, seizing Adam's hand. For the first time he seemed once more to resemble his old carefree self. In celebration, he poured himself another brimming cup of ale. 'And as your herald,' he said, raising a finger, 'I bring you news from the outside world!'

In truth, Adam had been too concerned with the tasks of the manor over the months since Christmastide to inform himself of events in the wider kingdom. He had picked up scraps from the occasional passing traveller who sought hospitality under his roof, and from the sheriff and the prior of the abbey, and from William de St John. But all of them knew that Adam was Simon de Montfort's ally and they should not speak too freely. Hugh, he guessed, would be a surer informant.

'I've just come from Odiham,' Hugh said. 'I left there this morning. Lord Simon's living at the castle with Lady Eleanor and their sons, and they've got the king and Lord Edward with them too. Not that I got a look at any of them! Nearly two hundred knights and squires arrived with Simon, and it's no big place. They must be packed tight as cordwood in the hall and solar, and sleeping like dogs in kennels.'

'Lord Edward's been freed then?' Adam asked, frowning. He had heard that the king and magnates were negotiating to that end.

'Oh yes!' Hugh said, and drank again. 'By order of the parliament at Westminster. Lord Simon never lets him out of his sight, even so – both the king and his son are his *honoured guests* nowadays, whether they like it or not. Edward's agreed to hand over all the lands of the Honour of Chester and the Peak to de Montfort too, which didn't please the Earl of Derby, who'd seized them from Edward's men last year during the war. Now Lord Simon's summoned the Earl of Derby to London, and had him seized and locked up!'

'Earl Robert de Ferrers?' Adam asked. He had heard plenty about de Ferrers, supposed to be the greatest magnate in the north of England, and a man of fierce pride and furious anger.

'The very same. *The Devil of Derby*, as some call him. Nowadays the devil of a small cell in the Tower of London!'

Adam snorted a laugh. 'And this did not please the other earls and barons, I assume?'

'Not at all. In particular it displeased the Earl of Gloucester, who's been nursing a great swelling of grievances against de Montfort ever since Lewes, it turns out . . .'

Adam frowned. Several times he had encountered the hot-
headed, red-haired Gilbert de Clare, and had reason to distrust
him. De Clare was a powerful magnate too, Earl of Gloucester
and Hertford, and Lord of Glamorgan. He was even younger
than Adam himself, but despite his youth he had commanded
the largest retinue in de Montfort's army at the Battle of Lewes.
A phrase came to Adam's mind; something that the Countess
Eleanor had once said of Lord Gilbert: '*he wants more than any
man can give him, and he wants it immediately.*' If he was growing restless and dissatisfied, and his alliance with Lord Simon
was unstable, the continuing peace of the kingdom could not
be assured.

'But it's not just Gilbert the Red who tugs at the bit,' Hugh
went on, dropping his voice to a confidential hushed tone. 'Quite
a few men are pointing out that Lord Simon talks of justice and
liberties, and has the king reissue Magna Carta, while behaving
like a tyrant himself.'

'Which men? Who says this?' Adam asked urgently. But Hugh
merely shrugged and took another deep swig of ale.

'Robert de Dunstanville says this – is that what you mean?'
Adam had heard nothing from Robert since his departure nearly
six months before, but he remembered the knight's caustic
words about de Montfort.

'Ach, no, not exactly,' Hugh replied. 'Sir Robert is . . . bound
up with his own concerns, we could say. He's constable of
Bridgnorth Castle now – Lord Simon gave him the post, in the
king's name, back in January. A great honour! As a royal castle,
you see, it's usually held by the Sheriff of Shropshire, but he's got
enough to do keeping hold of Shrewsbury, with those Marcher
lords snapping at him—'

'So you've been there? To Bridgnorth?' Adam broke in. 'How
is Robert?'

'Oh, very well,' Hugh said, and leaned forward over the table
as he lowered his voice even more. 'He has the Jewess Belia living

with him, as his wife. Not that anyone knows of her true identity, of course.'

Good, Adam thought. He had often wondered how fortune was treating Belia, and her brother Elias. Often he had wanted to pray for them – but would Christ and his saints accept prayers for Jews? He did not know.

All the same, he realised, Hugh would not have left Bridgnorth and returned to Hampshire if all was well there. Again he considered what Robert de Dunstanville's reactions to the state of the kingdom might be. Where did his loyalties lie now? Hugh seemed suddenly unwilling to say more.

'But what of you?' Hugh asked abruptly, thwacking Adam's shoulder with his fingers. 'How have you kept yourself these six months past?'

Still troubled by his reflections about Robert, Adam began to answer as he had intended, keeping only to practical matters. But as soon as he began to speak his words became freer, and soon he was telling Hugh about the Christmas Court at Basing, and his meeting with Isabel de St John. Several times since then he had returned there, and at every meeting their bond had grown stronger. As he spoke, he found himself grinning, glowing, illuminated by the mere thought of her.

'Well then,' Hugh said with a sly laugh, and spread his palms. 'This would be a propitious time for a union, you know, with the sun in Aries and Venus entering the tenth house. Besides, taking a wife would be good for you,' he went on, glancing around the hall. 'I mean, this is a fine place, but it has all the womanly charm of a Templar Preceptory. And a marriage connection with the St Johns of Basing would be most beneficial too. Though I'm sure that's not crossed your mind.'

Adam laughed wryly. In truth, the thought that people might believe he was seeking marriage with Lord William's daughter for material gain and influence was one of the things that stood in his way. He felt inexpert in courting too; his youth in the household of the Earl of Hereford had involved no lessons in it, and the stories of chivalry offered few hints. In Isabel's presence he felt the surety of their mutual attraction, but otherwise he felt as if he walked in a field of tangled briars.

'I don't suppose that you still have thoughts for the other one?' Hugh asked, in an angling tone. 'For the de Quincy woman?'

Adam shook his head in curt denial. But Hugh had found him out. His lingering passion for Joane de Quincy stirred in his heart, for all that he tried to deny it. On a thong around his neck he still wore the medallion of St Christopher that Joane had given him years before. And in his chamber, in the chest beside his bed, he kept the creased page of parchment she had cut from her Psalter, the protecting psalm that had kept him safe in the battle at Lewes. Why he still held on to these tokens he could not rightly say.

Perhaps, he thought that evening as he lay sleepless in bed listening to Hugh's familiar grunt and mumble from the pallet on the floor, if he could commit himself to marriage then he might finally banish the shade of his desire for Joane. She belonged to the darkness now, to past lives and regrets. Isabel de St John, by contrast, was a figure standing in the sunlight. With her at his side, his sense of belonging in the world would finally be complete.

Or so he told himself, as he lay with one hand on the medallion at his throat.

*

At the far end of the paddock, Adam wheeled his horse. Lance upright, he set his feet more firmly in the stirrups, then kicked with the spurs. The stallion surged into motion at once, mane and tail flying in the damp air, hooves kicking up clods of wet earth. At the last moment Adam lowered his lance, dropping the steel tip in a smooth arc to bring it cracking into the centre of the shield-shaped wooden target. The horse did not slow its charge, and Adam heard the big swinging counterweight whip the air behind his back as he galloped on up the course. He drew the reins in, slowing the charge, then wheeled again and cantered back.

'You see?' he called to the waiting rider as he drew to a halt. 'Drop the lance smoothly, like a plunging hawk, to strike the target. That way the shaft doesn't bounce in your grip as you ride, and your aim remains true. Here,' he said, and tossed the lance to the other man.

It was the Eve of St Anselm, a damp day two weeks after Easter, and the sky was knuckled with dark clouds that threatened further rain. Those few villagers who were not at work in the fields were lining the fence at the side of the paddock, watching Adam training his new squire in riding at the quintain. Hugh of Oystermouth sat on the upper rung of the fence beside Ilberd's son, the two of them passing a flask of ale.

Benedict Mackerell was a spotty gangling youth of seventeen, and sat his horse as if he had been draped over the saddle. He was the son of one of William de St John's vassal knights, but so far Adam had not detected in him any great aptitude for horsemanship, martial skill, or anything else. Then again, Adam suspected that he may have appeared that way himself, at that age. Benedict's attempts to both strike the quintain's target and avoid the weighted sack swinging on the tail of its pivot had so far been completely unsuccessful, to the raucous amusement of the onlookers. At least, Adam hoped, he might manage one or the other before the light faded or the rain set in once more.

Hunched in the saddle, the squire urged his horse around at the far end of the paddock. His lance wavered, then the horse bolted suddenly forward. Jolting in the saddle, Benedict brought his lance down too early and fought to control it as he rode, the tip veering wildly. Adam caught his breath as the youth approached the quintain, then let out a cry of satisfaction as the lance clipped the target. His cry turned to a groan as he saw the weighted sack swing around in its arc and whack Benedict between the shoulders. The squire clung to the saddle for three more galloping strides, hauled at the reins, then plunged forward over the horse's mane and toppled into the mud.

A woman's voice came from behind him, and Adam turned in the saddle.

'Is he hurt?' In the greyish light, it took Adam a moment to recognise Isabel de St John as she stood at the paddock gate.

'Well?' Adam called back across the field.

Benedict Mackerell scrambled quickly to his feet, blushing heavily, mud smeared over his chest. Too quickly — his legs buckled beneath him and he fell again. Hugh ran to assist him, as Matthew went after the squire's capering mount.

Turning his horse, Adam cantered over to the gate and drew to a halt, swinging himself from the saddle as he did so. Isabel stood beside her grey pony, dressed in a blue mantle and white headcloth. Two grooms and a maid, her travelling escort, waited behind her with their own horses.

'I'm sorry to arrive without sending word,' Isabel said. 'I've been on the road since daybreak, but I think my jennet has worked a shoe loose. I'm afraid she'll go lame if it isn't fixed.'

Adam called to one of his own grooms, ordering the boy to take the pony to the farrier in the village. 'You arrived at a good time,' he said. 'I believe my squire has taken enough falls for today.'

'I was admiring your charger,' Isabel said, stepping closer and rubbing the bay stallion under the chin. 'He's quite magnificent.'

'He's called Fauviel,' Adam said. 'Trained as a racer, I think, but I'm hoping to work a bit more agility into him.' The animal had cost him more than an entire year's income from his estates; often he remembered the tournament fields of France, where men would ransom captured horses and armour, and felt dizzy as he contemplated the fortunes won or lost in a sword's stroke or the clash of a lance.

As he walked with Isabel back towards the hall, her attendants trailing behind them, she noticed the freshly dug ditch and chest-high palisade of green timber that surrounded the compound of the manor buildings. 'Do you fear an attack?' she asked, frowning.

'Not any more,' Adam said. In fact, he had seen and heard nothing of the Ticeburns or their gang over the months of winter, and they seemed to have vanished entirely. Hugh de Brayboef and his son had made no appearance either, and he was glad of that.

Inside the hall they pulled up benches and sat beside the glowing embers in the hearth. Isabel took off her damp mantle and spread it over a stool to dry, then unwrapped her headcloth. Beneath it, her curling blonde hair was secured only by a linen fillet. She was on her way home from her father's estates at Halnaker in Sussex, she explained as the servants brought them cups of spiced wine; she had left Petersfield that morning, but it was still a good half-day's ride back to Basing. Her maid and grooms sat on the far bench, stooped over the wan glow of the fire and clearly not relishing the thought of once more setting out on muddy roads under a lowering sky, but Isabel herself appeared undeterred by the prospect.

'I was at Odiham with my mother just before Hocktide, visiting the Countess of Leicester,' she said. 'She's very grand these days, isn't she? And she remembers you well too.'

Adam caught her glance, her quick smile, and looked away. Odiham Castle was only five miles from Basing, but nearly a year had passed since his last brief visit there, and that had been in the febrile days leading up to the Battle of Lewes. Countess Eleanor, Simon de Montfort's wife, had trusted him with a letter then, but they had not communicated since. Perhaps, like her husband, she seldom forgot a face or a name.

'Lord Simon is no longer at Odiham, then?' he asked.

'No, he left before Easter with the king and Lord Edward, and all that vast retinue of theirs, and rode to Northampton. There's another tournament planned there, supposedly, but Earl Gilbert de Clare won't be attending – he refuses to speak with Lord Simon or recognise his authority, and he's gone off to the Marches of Wales instead.'

Adam grimaced. 'These magnates are petulant as children.'

Isabel drew in her shoulders, trapping a shudder. 'My father's been summoned to join Simon's son at the siege of Pevensey again,' she said, and her voice took on a low confidential tone. 'But he won't attend – he said the castle can hold out until the crack of doom for all he cares.' She looked at Adam, her brow creased, and her blue eyes caught the pale light from the windows. 'What about you?' she asked. 'If you're summoned to join Lord Simon, or the king, would you go?'

Adam thought for a moment. 'If I were summoned in person,' he said, 'I would have to.' Geoffrey de Brayboef, he thought, had been correct in one thing at least: the lands that Adam held were the gift of Simon de Montfort, given as payment for service, and in expectation of further service to come. So far, Adam had taken Robert's advice and deferred that service. But he could neither defer nor delay for ever. Isabel nodded, but he noticed that she appeared dismayed for a moment. Had she come here to sound out his true allegiances? He shook off the thought, and soon they spoke of other things.

The clouds had parted by the time the grooms returned with Isabel's horse, and they walked from the hall into springtime brightness. The new-turned soil steamed in the sun, and the sky was filled with birdsong. For a few moments they stood in the yard and looked out over the lands of the estate. Only now was he beginning to feel that this place was truly his home, no longer just a memory of childhood, or his father, but something he could truly appreciate and love. And with Isabel standing beside him that sense of belonging only deepened.

'It must make you proud to hold all this,' she said, shading her eyes.

He looked at her, and she held his gaze and smiled. Compared to her father's estates this manor was insignificant, but Adam could see that she understood what it meant to him. The realisation of that understanding, that shared awareness, warmed his heart. But then her maid and her grooms appeared once more, horses stamping around them, and the moment of departure had arrived. She could not stay longer, Isabel said, as her mother was expecting her at Basing before evening.

As Adam watched her ride off along the track beside the woods, Hugh sidled up beside him.

'Frankly,' he said in a low tone, 'I don't see why you delay.'

Adam frowned a question at him.

'Come now,' Hugh said, then widened his eyes and spread his palms. 'The sun comes out when she gazes upon you! Marry her. Or, if her father is unwilling, elope with her and marry her in the greenwood.'

Adam laughed wryly. 'You think she desires that?'

'Put it like this,' Hugh said, 'there was nothing wrong with her horse. Matthew had a look when they took it down to the farrier. I believe she is a woman who knows her own desires, and tends to get them too.'

*

The messenger arrived on a Friday in the middle of May. Adam had returned from riding to find the man already in the buttery, sucking down ale to wash the dust from his throat. Now he sat in the hall as his steward stood before him, both of them staring at the letter on the table between them. It bore the royal seal.

Adam drummed his fingers on the white linen tablecloth. 'Open it,' he said.

The steward, a bald grey-bearded man with an air of great solemnity, picked up the scroll with due reverence and broke the seal. '*Given at Hereford, on the day of the Translation of Saint Andrew, the forty-eighth year of King Henry,*' he read, turning the parchment to the stripe of daylight falling through the open window. He cleared his throat and read on: '*As it is necessary to make powerful provision for the defence of the realm, the king commands Adam de Norton, under pain of losing what he holds of him, to come with horses and arms manfully and with all speed to join us at Hereford, before the Feast of Pentecost, and to proceed with us forthwith against the enemies of our peace.*'

Adam steepled his fingers and pressed them to his lips. Without knowing it, he had been expecting this moment for some time. He calculated quickly: nine days until Pentecost. The last news he had of the king and Lord Simon had been shortly after Easter, and placed them at Northampton, far away from Hereford. Why had they travelled there? And who were the *enemies of our peace*?

Abruptly he stood up and paced to the open window. Outside, swifts and swallows circled the eaves above, darting against the cloudless blue. The Feast of Ascension had just passed, and the land was verdant in the spring sunshine. The fields of winter wheat were ripening from green to gold, the barley sown in March already sprouting, and the meadows and the woodland beyond were lush under the noon sky. But behind the tranquil calm Adam sensed the rolling thunder of coming events, the drumming of massed hooves and the distant screech of battle trumpets far across the horizon of tomorrow.

He sensed, too, a gathering obligation, a debt he had still to pay. This time he must answer the summons. And even as he made that decision, he knew that the time had come to set aside his doubts.

'Send word to Lord William de St John at Basing,' he told the steward, turning from the window. 'Ask that I might join him for the Feast of St Dunstan, next Tuesday.'

As the steward bowed and departed, Hugh of Oystermouth came in from the yard. 'We must prepare ourselves,' Adam said, handing him the letter. 'We depart three days from now, on Dunstan's Eve, fully provisioned, with horses and arms.'

'We travel by way of Basing, then?' Hugh asked, raising an eyebrow as he looked up from the parchment.

Adam nodded, and noticed Hugh's sly smile.

*

'No, I received no summons myself,' William de St John said. 'I'm not sure if I'd have answered it, if I had. I've done quite enough for the de Montforts this last year, and whatever their quarrel with the Earl of Gloucester might be, it's no concern of mine. Or of the realm, I might add. But you must act as you see fit.'

They were in his upper chamber at Basing Court, shortly after vespers. Lord William sat on a stool, flanked by his two favourite greyhounds, while Adam stood by the window gazing out into the evening sun as it lowered over the river and the distant hunting park beyond. He was not surprised that the baron had not been called to join the king; the summons had been a personal one, sent only to those men that Lord Simon believed he could reply upon. Those men who owed him everything they possessed.

'But loyalty is important now, I suppose,' William went on, and sighed. 'Loyalty and friendship. Earl Gilbert of Gloucester, they say, has gone over to the Marchers with his whole affinity and retinue. He grows stronger in his opposition to de Montfort with every day that passes.'

'Does he have good cause for that, would you say?' Adam asked. Always before he had guarded his words when he talked to William of the affairs of the kingdom, and the baron had done the same. But now there was no time for evasion.

William sighed again, more heavily, and cupped the sleek head of the nearest greyhound in his palm, rubbing the animal beneath its jaw. Adam had a sharp memory of those same jaws ripping into the flesh of a deer the previous winter. 'Perhaps,' William said. 'My wife's brother Thomas – the Lord Chancellor, I should call him – tells me that only Simon de Montfort can hold the realm together, and without him there would be anarchy. But these great men would plunge England into bloodshed just to soothe their scalded pride. And as for Gilbert de Clare himself, I care little for him – he's the arrogant whelp of a vain and devious father. To be honest, I can almost admire Simon de Montfort for trying to hold that red dog by the ears!'

He tugged at the ear of the greyhound, and it let out a low affectionate growl as it gazed up at him. 'Now,' William said, 'we can only pray for peace and justice once more to prevail in England.'

Adam muttered his agreement, and crossed himself. He had asked to speak to Lord William alone, but had not expected the baron to share his concerns for the state of the kingdom.

'I have something to ask you,' Adam said. Now that the moment was upon him he felt very nervous. The possibility of acting foolishly, clumsily, of disgracing himself and offending both Isabel and her father, pressed upon him.

'Ah,' Lord William replied, still playing with his dog's ears. He seemed unwilling to return Adam's gaze.

'I wish to marry your daughter,' Adam told him abruptly, almost choking on the words. 'I wish to marry Isabel.'

'Ah,' William said again, then drew a breath. 'And what does she have to say about this?'

'I haven't . . .' Adam began, hesitant, 'had a chance to ask her yet.'

William made a low sound in his throat, then shouted, loud and abrupt. When the steward appeared at the chamber door, he told him to summon Isabel. She returned very soon afterwards, flushed and slightly breathless, as if she had run up the stairs.

'I'll leave you to talk then,' William said gruffly as he got to his feet and paced towards the door. 'Come, Blondeau, Roquart . . .' The two greyhounds uncoiled themselves and rushed after him, claws scratching the floorboards.

Isabel stood in the middle of the chamber, her hair unbound and her simple tunic of sky-blue wool lit by a beam of low sun from the window. She was beautiful, more so than ever before, and for a long moment Adam could not find the words to speak. He cleared his throat, and his fingers darted to the medallion at his neck. With an effort he let his hand drop.

'Isabel,' he said, his voice hoarse. 'Will you take me for your husband?'

At first she made no reply. Adam saw a frown crease her brow. 'You're about to ride off to war,' she said. 'Would you make me a widow before I've even been a wife?'

'I'll return, I promise,' Adam said. 'I'm pledged to serve for forty days, six weeks at most. I'm sorry I have no ring, no gold to seal the pledge, but I give you my word. I want you to be the woman to whom I return.'

She dropped her head, pressing her hand to her mouth. Adam saw the trembling of her shoulders, and for a pained heartbeat he thought she was weeping. Then he heard her muffled laughter. She dropped her hand. 'So grave,' she said.

She raised her head once more, squaring her shoulders. 'Yes,' she declared, and grinned. 'Yes, of course I will. I wanted that from the first moment I saw you, back in the woods just after Christmas.' She threw her arms around Adam and kissed him, and in the perfection of that moment all his fears, all his misgivings, were gone.

*

The following day there was feasting in the great hall of Basing
Court. A banquet for St Dunstan, and to celebrate the betrothal.
Lord William, when he learned of his daughter's decision, had
accepted it immediately and become boisterous in his approval.
Now all was agreed and arranged: the wedding would take place
on the Feast of St Oswald, in less than three months' time; long
enough for Adam to discharge his service to the king, to return
home and to prepare himself to be wed. Adam and Isabel were
seated on the dais, between William and Lady Agnes, and in the
warmth of the fire and the food, the laughter and the song and
the pleasure of Isabel's presence, he felt sure of his decision. He
placed his palm over hers, and as she tightened her grip their
fingers entwined.

But the next morning, in the darkness before dawn as he mustered his retinue to depart, Adam felt once more the weight
of his uncertainty. He had slept badly, and for the first time in
months he had dreamed of Joane de Quincy. A tender and terrible dream: he had seen her kneeling beside him, bathing blood
from his face with a cloth, and had known from the sorrow on
her face that he was dying. In the depths of the night he had
woken, strangling a shout in his throat, and lain awake until the
hour came to depart.

Now the horses stamped and blew in the cobbled court outside the hall, dogs prowling between them. Metal clinked and
leather creaked, and the figures silhouetted in the open doorway
threw shadows into the twilight gloom. Hugh had a guilty and
evasive look as he sat slumped on his pony. Nearby, Benedict
Mackerell looked pale and ghastly, his eyes red rimmed.

'Hugh,' Adam said. 'You seem to have led my squire into
debauchery.'

'Ach, a few extra ales last night. A bad brew, I suspect. But
how was I to know the lad would take it so poorly?'

Matthew was already mounted, with Adam's bay stallion on
a leading rein. Two other figures stood beside their horses, both

wrapped in cloaks and resembling father and son. Adam held his lands of the king for the service of two knights in wartime. His main manor sufficed to support him, but none of his other estates and manors were large enough to support a second knight, so he had to make up the deficit by providing two serjeants instead. William Tonge had been in his retinue since the previous summer; he was harsh-tempered and hard to like, but doughty and dependable. Adam was less sure of his second serjeant. Thomas of Hawkley was the son of one of Adam's free tenants. He claimed to have fought in Wales, though he scarcely appeared old enough, but seemed capable in his horsemanship and skill at arms.

Isabel stood wrapped in a woollen shawl as Adam swung himself into the saddle. She took his hand, and pressed it to her chest, and he leaned from the saddle to kiss her. As they parted, she slipped a small silk bag into his palm. Inside was a string of prayer beads, a paternoster in ebony and silver.

'You are in my prayers,' she told him. 'Return soon.'

His throat clenched, and Adam could only nod. He straightened in the saddle, raised a hand to Lord William's bulky form in the doorway, then pulled at the reins and turned his horse towards the gateway and the long road beyond.

As the sun rose, the long shadows of the riders stretched ahead of them. Adam tried not to think of his dream, tried not to believe that it had been a premonition. He turned only once to gaze behind him, into the glare of the dawn.

A flutter of black wings crossed the sun, and Adam shuddered and rode onward.

Chapter 6

They left Gloucester to the ringing of the matins bell, riding out of the town and crossing the Severn on the bridges and long causeway. No fellow travellers shared this stage of their journey; the bands of pilgrims and merchants that had accompanied them for the past four days from Basing through Newbury, Marlborough and Malmesbury went no further west. With rumours of war and conflict thick in the air, few dared to risk the roads that led towards the Welsh frontier. Adam's retinue seemed all the smaller now, and they pressed on swiftly through the morning, keeping close together on the narrow track as it wound between the upland slopes and dales. Adam himself had put on his mail hauberk that morning, and kept his shield slung over his shoulder. The two serjeants wore gambesons and kept their crossbows ready, while Matthew and Benedict carried lances, all of them keeping a close watch on the steep wooded hills to either side. Only Hugh of Oystermouth gave no sign of vigilance. He jolted along on his pony, swigging frequently from a flask of ale he had brought from Gloucester.

'He's more scared than any of us!' said the younger serjeant, Thomas of Hawkley, with a laugh. 'The closer we get to Wales, the more he fears he'll meet some of his family out on the road hunting for him with their red fists!'

'It's more the thought of your own countrymen that concerns me, boy,' Hugh replied grimly. 'And a certain *red dog* in particular.'

Adam could only agree. They were passing through the fringes of Gilbert de Clare's territory now, and the lands of de Clare's vassal John Giffard. Both men had fought for Simon de Montfort at Lewes. Now they were perhaps his enemies, while other men that had fought for the king on that same battlefield now backed Lord Simon's rule. The strange turns of fortune and allegiance were baffling. More baffling still the inconstancy of great men, who turned against their oath, it seemed, without a moment's hesitation.

Two nights before, in the guest hall of Malmesbury Abbey, Adam had heard a story that William de Valence the Earl of Pembroke, and his comrade John de Warenne the Earl of Surrey, had landed at the western tip of Wales with a force of mercenaries, determined to raise the standard of revolt against Lord Simon. But how likely was it that two of the greatest magnates in England, the queen's most vigorous supporters, should have sailed all the way from France without being detected or halted? He was inclined to discount the rumour. He was likewise doubtful of the story he had had been told the night before at Gloucester, that Gilbert de Clare and Lord Simon had mended their quarrel and agreed to an alliance once more. The fate of the kingdom, it seemed, could change on a momentary decision, a lapse of judgement, a bold move or a failure of nerve. Adam tried to give little thought to such things. Only when he reached Hereford, he told himself, would he and the men of his little retinue know for certain what was happening.

Before noon they descended from the hills and crossed the Wye on a stone bridge at the town of Ross. For the next few hours they traced the valley north-west, the sinuous river looping away and then slinking towards them again as they rode, and the dark mountains of Wales looming on the western horizon. This was sheep-farming country, open slopes covered in tufted pasture, little stone villages studding the valleys between, and several times they passed pack animals carrying heaped bundles

of fleeces towards Hereford or back towards Ross. The herd-
ers pulled their animals off the road as the armed men passed,
watching them with wary eyes.

It was early afternoon, and they were descending a ridge of
pastureland into a wooded vale when Adam heard a warning
shout from behind him. William Tonge was bringing up the rear,
and he was pointing away to his left. Following his gesture, Adam
saw the line of horsemen appearing along the ridgeline. Six of
them at least, maybe more, all with shields and spears.

A quick glance forward: too far to the shelter of the trees, even
at a downhill gallop. Adam circled his hand, and the riders of
his retinue turned to face uphill with the pack animals between
them. He pulled up his mail coif to cover his head, slid his forearm
through the shield straps and took the lance from Matthew. The
two serjeants hauled back the cords of their crossbows. Adam felt
the breath tight in his chest, the blood beating in his neck, all the
fatigue of the long journey dispelled at once by the sharpening
possibility of combat. They were outnumbered by two to one in
fighting men – Adam was not sure if he could yet trust Benedict
in a fight – and their opponents commanded the high ground. But
still there was a chance they could win.

The six riders had fanned out as they descended from the
ridge, one of them advancing ahead of the others and approaching
Adam. They were rough-hewn men, long haired and hard faced,
a couple wearing gambesons. All were keeping their weapons
ready, but they made no immediate move to attack. Adam kept
his eyes on the leader. There was something immediately familiar
about him. Something very strange about his features as well. It
was only as he got closer that Adam realised who he was, and
what he was looking at.

'You have writing on your face,' he said.

'Ah yes, I do!' the man replied, and showed broken teeth as he
grinned. 'A vow I took at Easter . . . I must bear the Holy Name
of the Saviour upon my brow until Pentecost, as proof against

the Devil, and in certain expectation of the Apocalypse, when He shall come again to sit in judgement upon all the sinners!'

Squinting, Adam could make out the smudged black letters scribed across the man's forehead, in either ink or paint: *IHESU NAZAR*. He wondered if the man's brow was not wide enough for the full name.

'What happened to your holy string?' he asked.

'I still wear the string of St Thomas!' the man proclaimed, clapping a palm to his midriff. 'Tighter than ever it was, and as sure a defence against evil!'

Although he had recognised him, Adam could not recall his name until he made out the streak of white through his lank black hair: *Le Brock*. He remembered the last time he had seen the man too, when he had tried to rob Adam of a letter he was carrying from Simon de Montfort, on the orders of his master.

'You still serve Gilbert de Clare?' Adam asked.

Le Brock merely smiled again. The riders behind him had not relaxed their vigilance, and at the margins of his vision Adam could see William Tonge and Thomas of Hawkley had their cross-bows cocked. Clouds crossed the sun, throwing moving shadows over the hillside.

'But look at you, your own man now!' Le Brock said, his smile widening to a ghastly smirk. 'Gilded spurs, belted sword . . . A real knight, may God bless you, lord!'

'I'm travelling to Hereford to join the king,' Adam said brusquely. Watching Le Brock's mouth moving was turning his stomach. 'Do you and these men you're leading intend to stop me?'

Le Brock pouted, covering his terrible teeth. 'Us? Why, no! We have no dispute with you, nor does our master with the king. He has nothing but love for your master Lord Simon — all their strife is ended, did you not hear?'

Adam frowned, unwilling to accept the man's word alone. He recalled the rumour he had heard back at Gloucester that the two great magnates had been reconciled, but still thought it dubious.

'Then why do you waylay us on the road, armed and in strength?' Adam asked.

'Merely to bid you good day, and see who you might be . . .' Le Brock said. He opened his mouth to say more, but suddenly there was the snap of a crossbow, and one of his men let out a shout as his horse skipped sideways and almost threw him from the saddle. At once all the other riders had lifted their spears, and Le Brock had plucked an axe with a cruelly hooked blade from behind his saddle.

Thomas of Hawkley had one open hand raised. 'Sorry, I'm sorry!' he cried. The crossbow dangled from his other hand. 'It just went off – my finger slipped on the trigger!'

'Never span an arbalest unless you know how to use it, youngster!' Le Brock snarled. 'And you, lordling,' he told Adam, gesturing at the serjeant, then at Matthew and Benedict, 'don't put deadly weapons in the hands of such children as these!'

'Is your man unharmed?'

Le Brock looked back at the rider, who was twitching and breathless but otherwise intact. The crossbow quarrel had missed him by a hand's span, but had startled his horse.

'Yes, thanks be to the Saviour!' Le Brock said, and slapped the blade of his axe into his open palm. 'Maybe life would have turned bad for you, if it were otherwise.'

Adam just inclined his head. 'Then we shall delay no longer,' he said. 'I aim to be in Hereford by vespers.'

Le Brock and his men sat on their horses and watched as Adam gathered his followers into column once more and set off down the slope towards the trees. All the way they rode in silence, and Adam could sense that each member of his retinue was as tense in the saddle as he was himself, expecting at any moment the shout of command from behind them, and the wild thunder of the downhill charge.

'Do that again, lad, and I'll murder you myself!' William Tonge snarled, once they were through the woods. Thomas of Hawkley cowered in the saddle, his face dark with shame. As they climbed the far slope Adam turned and looked back, but the mounted men had already retreated over the ridge behind them.

'What did they really want, do you think?' Benedict asked.

'They're just watching the road for Gilbert de Clare, I would guess,' Adam said. 'Seeing who's going to Hereford to join Lord Simon, and what sort of strength they have. They'll send a rider to report back to their master.'

Soon afterwards they came up with another band of travellers on the road, a dozen militiamen of the Gloucestershire levy, striding along with bows and spears and staves. Their commander, a grey-bearded serjeant, was only too glad to fall in with Adam's retinue. They too, he reported, had encountered Le Brock and his road patrol earlier that day after setting out from Ross. Even slowing their pace to the speed of the marching men, Adam and his party made good time, and before the sun was low in the west they crested the last ridge and saw in the wide bowl of the valley ahead of them the glimmer of the Wye once more, and on the far bank the red sandstone walls of Hereford, the cathedral and the castle keep on its tall mound, and the blue haze of a hundred cooking fires rising into the clear sky.

*

'God's mercy,' Benedict said, wide-eyed and gazing, 'are there so many people in all the world?' They were forging their way up the lane from the bridge, into the tight web of streets around the cathedral, and all around them were mobs of men and jostling horses.

Adam had been to Hereford before, many years ago when he was a young squire in the household of Lord Humphrey de Bohun, but it was transformed now. The town was heaving with newcomers, from the men of the royal household and the huge retinues of Simon de Montfort and his principal baronial followers to independent knights like Adam, riding in with only a handful of followers. The levies of three shires and half a dozen towns were here as well, sturdy bowmen and spearmen propping the walls and lining the benches outside the alehouses in every street and alley. The band of militia that had accompanied Adam on the road had already thrown themselves down outside the first hostelry they found after crossing the bridge. Every stable yard was packed, and the narrow streets were heaped with dung and flowing with horse piss, trampled into a rich-stinking mire.

'Takes me back to the old days of the tournaments!' Hugh said. 'Do you remember those towns along the Rhine? All of them like this, and scarcely a bed to be had! We'd best look sharp for lodgings, or we'll be camping outside the walls.'

Sure enough, Adam thought as he surveyed the scene around him, accommodation in Hereford would be hard to find. Above the seething throng hung bright banners and shields, displayed outside the houses and hostelries where the various retinues had already billeted themselves. Adam spotted several that he recognised from the field of Lewes; Lord Simon's summons had drawn knights from as far away as Lincolnshire and Yorkshire, Suffolk and distant Kent. Peering into the crowd, he hoped he might see a face he recognised, somebody who might offer to share their billet, but everyone he saw was a stranger.

Adam ordered his men to dismount, as the crowd in the street had grown too dense. Leaving William Tonge to mind the horses, he sent Benedict, Thomas of Hawkley and Hugh of Oystermouth to scour the rest of the town for lodgings, while he continued with Matthew towards the castle.

As the street widened, he saw above the heads of the crowd the west façade of the cathedral, with its soaring windows and turrets glowing pinkish in the afternoon sun. The castle lay on the far side of the cathedral precinct, beside the river, and Adam led Matthew around to the left of the building, into the open area outside the north porch. Bells rang overhead, clear and

bright in the late afternoon air; it was vespers on the Eve of
Pentecost, and hordes of men from the knightly retinues were
streaming into the cathedral for evensong. So many spears, pen-
noned lances, axes and bowstaves were stacked in the porch that
it resembled an armoury. Here and there priests and their servants stood aside, ashen faced and trembling at the sight of the
rude mob filling the portals of their church.

Now he was in the open Adam could make out the more
prominent figures among the crowd. He saw Nicholas de Segrave, grave and long-faced in his black surcoat. Beside him was
the stocky, muscular Henry de Hastings. Then, a short distance
away, Adam spotted John FitzJohn. His shoulders tensed as a cold
sensation rose through him. The scowling young baron had been
at the forefront of the violence against the Jews in London the
previous summer; Adam had seen FitzJohn murder a prominent
moneylender with his own hands.

Matthew had noticed the man too. He was poised and alert as
a scent-hound, but it was not fear or nerves that had caught the
boy – Matthew was transfixed by hatred. He recognised FitzJohn,
sure enough, and knew what sort of man he was, what sort of men
so many of those gathered here must be. Adam clapped a palm on
the boy's shoulder, and felt his muscles drawn tight as bowcord.

'Softly now,' he said quietly, and felt he was trying to calm a
restive horse. 'Say nothing and do nothing. We must pass them,
and not see them.'

Keeping his head turned from the group of noblemen, he
strode onward, leading Matthew across the open area towards
the street on the far side that would take them to the castle gates.
The king and his court would be lodged in the castle, and Adam
would have to present himself there before doing anything else.

But even as he ignored the nobles, their presence clouded
his mind. For the last year, Adam had pretended to himself that
Simon de Montfort and his cause were principally supported by
men like himself, or the sort of man he wanted to be. Men like

Robert de Dunstanville, at least. But now he was forced once more to accept that Lord Simon's main strength lay in men like John FitzJohn and Henry de Hastings, ruthless men of proud ambition and limitless greed. Men of violence and bloodshed.

Maybe, he thought, William de St John had been right in his misgivings? Maybe Robert had been correct as well, and Adam should have refused the summons. He had been scanning the banners and shields around him since he entered Hereford, alert for any glimpse of Robert's familiar red lattice on white, *argent fretty gules*, with the red quadrant and the golden lion *passant*, but among all that riot of heraldry the de Dunstanville arms were nowhere to be seen. Was Robert still holding Bridgnorth Castle? Had he retired to his own lands in Shropshire, to play no part in the struggles of the kingdom?

A sudden shout of laughter from behind him broke into his thoughts. Matthew had already paused and turned to look back. Adam took a moment longer to compose himself. Even after a year, he knew the sound of that scornful mirth too well.

'By the holy name,' the familiar voice said, 'what impoverished knights we are making in England now! This one presents himself here with only a single boy as his retinue!'

Richard de Malmaines came to a halt four paces away, a gang of his own squires and serjeants at his back. He was unchanged, tall and handsome as a knight from a chivalric tale but still with the thin smirk that Adam remembered from their first meeting, still the strange mad gleam in his protuberant eyes. He wore a blazing red tunic and surcoat and had his thumbs hooked in his belt, his sword proudly displayed.

'The last time I saw Adam de Norton here,' de Malmaines said, speaking over his shoulder to his retainers, 'he was still a squire.'

'And the last time I saw you,' Adam replied, turning to face him, 'I was dragging you from the battlefield at Lewes, after saving your life. And you gave me your word that the feud between us was over.'

'Oh!' de Malmaines said. 'A promise given under duress, of course. But I'm quite willing to honour it all the same. I have no quarrel with you.' He shrugged as he spoke, then shot a grin over his shoulder once more. 'All the same,' he said to Adam, his smile souring, 'a man who wears the belt and spurs of knighthood should never retreat from a challenge. And one of these days you may receive one from me, so step carefully.'

Adam forced himself merely to nod and to make no reply. That de Malmaines was refusing to honour his promise came as no surprise. Ever since their first encounter many years ago at a tournament in France the man had insisted on this senseless competition. Adam had managed to avoid him the previous summer, during the muster in Kent; de Malmaines' estates lay very close to Barham Down, and he had remained at his own manor for most of the time. In fact, Adam realised, he had almost managed to forget about the man entirely.

'What's the matter with your boy, your shield-carrier there?' de Malmaines asked, flinging a gesture at Matthew. 'He looks like he's about to throw up!'

Matthew took a step forward, and Adam seized him by the shoulder and steadied him with a firm grip. De Malmaines was already walking away, laughing once more with his retainers.

'You've seen that man before?' Adam asked the boy in a low voice.

Matthew nodded tightly. 'I remember him now,' he said. 'He was one of them. He was the worst.'

And at his words Adam saw once again the scenes of horror in London the summer before, the firelight reflected in the blood that pooled between the cobbles of the Jewry. He saw Richard de Malmaines appearing from the smoke and darkness, a reddened sword in his hand, on the night that Matthew's family had been murdered.

'Stay away from him, you understand?' Adam said firmly, still clasping Matthew by the shoulder. 'Stay away from all of them . . .'

The boy nodded, sullen and silent, but in his eyes Adam saw a new focus and determination. Foreboding clouded his mind, and a disturbing suspicion. Had Matthew intended Adam to lead him here, on some mission of vengeance?

'You are my groom, my servant, remember that,' he said in a hiss. 'Attend to your duties, and do not so much as glance in the direction of that man.'

Matthew shrugged, and seemed to nod. But before they could exchange another word, the brassy note of a horn carried across the cathedral green, and the crowd parted.

Adam took several paces in the opposite direction to de Malmaines and his retinue, drawing Matthew with him. Crossing the green from the far street was a group of mounted men, and the crowd fell away at the heavy thudding of the hooves and the clinking of bridles.

A squire rode at their head carrying a blue banner with six golden lions rampant and a bold white diagonal emblazoned with fleurs-de-lis. Adam knew the arms all too well. He had hoped that Sir Humphrey de Bohun might remain in Winchester. But here he was, riding behind his banner bearer. De Bohun sat heavily in the saddle, his deep blue tunic and green cloak of the finest wool, and his belts and brooch of gold set with gemstones. He had grown a short bristling beard on his chin, which only accentuated the coarseness of his features, but otherwise he appeared unchanged by a year of peace. Around him trotted a column of mounted squires and serjeants, all in his blue and white livery.

But among them was a very different figure, a young lady riding slim and tall in the saddle of a sleek jennet, carrying a hooded bird of prey on one gloved hand. Her copper-coloured hair was secured in a jewelled net, a white silk neckcloth and fillet encircled her face, and her pale green gown was edged in gold.

She glanced in Adam's direction as she passed, and for a moment he felt his heart still in his chest. Joane de Bohun's grey eyes widened briefly as she saw him in the crowd.

Then the mounted cortege rode onward, and she was gone.

Chapter 7

'Is it true that you're living in a brothel?' Sir John de Kington asked, the following day. They were in the great hall of
Hereford Castle, the tables around them thronging with over
fifty guests assembled for the Pentecost feast. The noise was
voluminous.

'Not exactly,' Adam replied, raising his voice. 'But lodgings
were hard to find . . . my herald found a place eventually, but it's
not in the noblest of locations . . .'

'*Gropecunt Lane!*' a knight on the next table guffawed.

Adam mimed a smile in his direction, and tried to hide his
blush as he bent over his trencher-bread and the slices of roast
venison. Hugh of Oystermouth had indeed found accommodation the previous evening in Hereford's least salubrious quarter,
east of the market. Adam and his retinue now occupied one
long wooden room above a cattle byre they used as a stable.
The byre opened onto a yard behind another building owned by
two sisters, Dulcia and Idonea Makepays. The queues of men in
the street outside left the trade of the Makepays sisters and the
girls they employed as no secret. And with the town full of men,
trade was brisk: the wooden room had not been cheap.

'No matter, we'll be gone from here soon enough,' John de
Kington went on. He and Adam had met the year before when

they were both squires. 'With Haverford fallen, there's nothing to stop de Valence and de Warenne from marching against us. We'll surely be taking the field to oppose them.'

Haverford Castle was one of de Bohun's strongholds in west Wales, and news of its capture after a week-long siege by the earls of Pembroke and Surrey and their mercenaries had reached Hereford only that morning. The two great magnates had raised their Welsh tenantry, the messengers had reported, and were now marching east, taking further castles as they came.

'I wouldn't start making plans to leave just yet,' said William de Boyton, a young knight from Suffolk who sat at the next table. 'Haverford's at least ten days march away——'

A blast of trumpets cut him off, as the next course was carried into the hall. While some servants removed the remains of the venison, others bore wooden pallets holding whole roast swans, decked in their own white plumage. Others still passed along the tables bearing jugs of wine, and ewers and basins for the diners to wash their hands between courses.

Adam and his mess companions were packed together on benches at the lower end of the hall. Above them the linen-covered tables stretched along either side, right up to the raised dais at the far end where the king, his son and Simon de Montfort were seated. In the cleared area before the dais a troupe of dancers were capering, all of them dressed in the shaggy green costumes of woodwoses, while musicians raised a skirling music on bagpipes, nakers and vielles. Certainly, Adam thought, few people here seemed unduly concerned about the activities of de Valence and de Warenne far away in the west of Wales.

As the carvers removed the plumage of the swans and sliced the meat, he let his gaze drift along the table opposite. He saw Richard de Malmaines, but avoided his eye. John FitzJohn and Henry de Hastings were seated towards the upper end of the hall, both bellowing with laughter and hurling scraps of food at the dancers. Lord Simon's younger son Guy was roaring along with them, his face hot with glee beneath the lick of black hair that cascaded over his brow.

King Henry and Lord Edward sat on canopied chairs at the centre of the high table, with Simon de Montfort seated by the king's right hand. From the corner of his eye, Adam watched the three of them carefully. He had seen the king the evening before, when he had presented himself at the castle and knelt before his throne. Henry, third of that name, by God's Grace King of England, Lord of Ireland, and Duke of Aquitaine had not appeared to recognise Adam at all, or to remember why he was there. Even now, presiding over the feast in the cavernous hall of the castle, the king appeared distracted and barely aware of his surroundings, as if he were entranced. And some did say, Adam knew, that Lord Simon had used sorcery to bend the king to his will.

Simon himself, by contrast, was fully in command of the situation. Grey-haired, firm-jawed, he sat with his elbows on the table, eating and talking and laughing with easy confidence, his eyes constantly roving over the scene before him. Astonishing to consider, Adam thought, that de Montfort and King Henry were almost the same age; beside the hardy, vigorous-looking Earl of Leicester the king appeared a feeble old man.

And on the king's other side, Lord Edward, too, looked fully in control of himself. But where Lord Simon was secure and confident, Edward's tensed discomfort showed clearly in his posture and expression. The Leopard, men called him — yes, Adam thought, he could see it now. The king's eldest son was only four years older than Adam himself, but even sitting down he was tall, sinuous and imposing; his short beard and curling hair, once golden, were darkening with age, but his eyes were fierce and proud, the slightly drooping eyelid he had inherited from his father giving him a contemptuous glare. For a moment, from the far end of the hall, Adam felt that glare fall upon him, and quickly turned away.

Instead, as the woodwoses gave a last caper and a shout, he found himself looking across to the far corner, below the dais.

He saw Joane glance back at him, and this time he held her gaze. She was one of only a handful of women in the hall, most of the knights and magnates having left their wives at home. Adam had noticed her the moment he entered, and had been trying not to look in her direction throughout the meal. Trying, and failing.

She had been listening to the lady sitting next to her, Baron Marshall's wife, who was holding forth to the company, but Adam saw her gaze shift to meet his own once again. Joane raised her cup to drink, but held it for a moment, as if in a toast. Adam raised his own cup likewise, and was rewarded by Joane's brief smile. For a moment his breath caught, and then he drank to hide his discomfort. When he raised his eyes once more she had turned back to speak to her friend; she raised her hand, and the rings on her slender fingers caught the light. Adam let his gaze linger on her for a few heartbeats more, then compelled himself to look away.

Already the servants were bringing the next course: capons with pomegranates, and a blancmanger of veal minced with cream and almonds. At the far end of the hall the prancing wood-woses had now been replaced by a pair of tumbling girls in flimsy gowns. FitzJohn, de Hastings and Guy de Montfort watched them avidly, calling out lewd suggestions.

'But Sir Humphrey will not sit idly by while de Valence and de Warenne plunder his Welsh lands with impunity,' John de Kington was saying, his voice emphatic. 'We have to march out against them sooner or later—'

'But don't forget, we have Gilbert de Clare to the south of us,' de Boyton broke in from the next table, 'and Mortimer and the Marcher barons to the north, ready to fall on us the moment we stir!'

'De Clare is no threat to us now,' de Kington declared. 'He and Lord Simon are allies once more, and as for the Marchers—'

'I hear Bridgnorth Castle's already surrendered to Hamo L'Estrange,' a man further along the table commented.

'What did you say?' Adam demanded, as a spike of sobriety rose through him. 'Surrendered by whom?'

His brow prickled with cold sweat. Robert de Dunstanville was still constable of Bridgnorth, and since he was not here in Hereford, he should still be at the castle. But he could not believe that Robert would have surrendered so easily while he still had life in his body, and especially not to the Shropshire baron Hamo L'Estrange; the pair of them hated each other.

But before anyone could speak another word there came another blast of trumpets from the upper end of the hall, and all stood up. King Henry was on his feet, and Lord Edward too; the king raised his hands, palms spread, in blessing to the gathering, then turned and made his way with shuffling steps from the dais, his son and Simon de Montfort following. Immediately upon their departure, the servants rushed to the dais and began snatching the uneaten food from the platters and draining the wine from the goblets, as the two dancing girls wrapped themselves quickly in woollen mantles and dashed from the hall.

*

The banquet was finished, and the men who had crowded the benches were now pressing through the doorway of the hall and the passage beyond, and spilling out into the bailey of the castle. Adam followed the horde, and found his squire Benedict waiting in the passageway. He could see no sign of the man who had made the comment about Bridgnorth. Surely it was untrue, a mistake or a mere rumour. But he could not shrug off his mood of disquiet. As they made their way towards the outer door, Adam felt a heavy palm fall on his shoulder, and Humphrey de Bohun appeared at his side.

'Walk with me a moment, if you please,' the baron said. 'We have things to discuss.'

Adam had known Humphrey de Bohun, eldest son of the Earl of Hereford, nearly half his life but had never liked the man. Once de Bohun took Joane as his wife, Adam's dislike had turned to loathing. But the link between them seemed impossible to sever: Adam had saved his life at Rochester the year before, and Sir Humphrey had threatened him with death over Joane, but now it seemed that all was forgotten and forgiven. The baron himself appeared to regard Adam as a member of his affinity, and sometimes even as a distant sort of friend. It was hard to believe that Sir Humphrey and Robert de Dunstanville were half-brothers, although Robert was illegitimate and the connection was never made publicly.

'Find some food, and then make your own way back,' Adam told Benedict. 'I'll meet you at . . . at our *lodgings*.'

Once the squire had made his exit, de Bohun conducted Adam from the passage through a low arched doorway and up a flight of stone steps built into the thickness of the wall. 'It's a shame we haven't yet had a chance to speak,' de Bohun said over his shoulder, breathing heavily as they climbed. He appeared to have indulged fully in both food and wine at the feast. 'I trust you understand why I've been unable to provide any more of my father's ransom payment as yet? The demands of war, of course, must take precedence.'

'Of course,' Adam replied, and was glad that de Bohun could not see his twitch of annoyance. Even with his lordship of Brecon in the hands of the Welsh prince Llywelyn ap Gruffud, and the Marcher barons threatening his holdings in the border country, Humphrey de Bohun was more than wealthy enough to have paid the full promised sum by now. But Adam's mind was still on other matters.

'Has there been any word from Bridgnorth?' he asked. 'I just heard a rumour that the castle had surrendered to Hamo L'Estrange—'

'Then you should give no credence to such things,' Sir Humphrey answered curtly, cutting him off. 'Bridgnorth holds, and Robert de Dunstanville remains constable.'

'You have this on good authority?' Adam asked in quick relief.

'I heard it from Lord Simon, earlier today,' de Bohun said, reaching the top of the stairs. He motioned towards an arched doorway ahead of him. 'But I'm sure he can tell you of it himself.'

A pair of men at arms stood sentry before the arch, and stepped aside to let them pass. De Bohun opened the door and gestured for Adam to precede him into the chamber beyond. Five men were seated there, a low table between them with cups of wine and a dish of sweetmeats, but none were eating or drinking. The rowdy festivity of the feast seemed to have deserted them altogether.

'Adam de Norton, welcome.'

Simon de Montfort, Adam knew, never forgot a face or a name. He and his companions appeared to have been speaking together in hushed voices moments before the door opened, but Lord Simon stood up at once and gestured for Adam to approach. His sons Henry and Guy were with him, along with the square-headed justiciar Hugh Despenser, Joane's cousin. All of them had fought at Lewes, and Adam knew them by sight. The fifth man, however, he did not know, although he had seen him at the feast. He was young, barely more than a youth, but already wore the belt of knighthood. His sandy hair and sharply pointed features appeared familiar, but Adam could not place the resemblance.

'I'm happy to see you here,' Lord Simon said. 'We need men around us that we can trust. Men who have served us well in the past.'

His words were warm and friendly, but Adam caught the chilled hostility of the other men in the room. Guy de Montfort and the sharp-featured youth seemed particularly unhappy.

'Tell them what happened yesterday, on the road,' Humphrey de Bohun said as he followed Adam into the room. He stooped and seized one of the cups of wine from the table, draining it in one swallow. Briefly Adam recounted the meeting with Le Brock and his riders a few miles to the south of Hereford.

'And he told you he was a retainer of Gilbert de Clare, you're sure of this?' Henry de Montfort demanded, almost before Adam had finished speaking.

'He . . . did not confirm it,' Adam said, thinking back to the meeting. 'But I'd seen the man before, at the siege of Rochester, and I know he is one of the Earl of Gloucester's serjeants. Earl Gilbert sent him to waylay me when I carried the letter to your wife, my lord.'

'Yes,' de Montfort said, sitting forward with a smile and raising one finger. 'I remember the occasion. You served me well that day – and this was the same man, you're sure?'

'He is very recognisable, lord.'

'But he did not confirm that he was still my brother's serjeant?' the sharp-faced youth asked. At once Adam realised the resemblance. He was younger, and lacked the flaming red hair that distinguished his brother Gilbert, but otherwise they appeared very similar.

'This is Thomas de Clare,' Humphrey de Bohun confirmed, gesturing to the young knight.

'The man you speak of could have left my brother's service at any time in the last year,' Thomas de Clare went on, addressing Simon and the others in the room. 'He could be a mere renegade, trying to rob travellers on the road.'

'He told me that his master's strife with Lord Simon is ended,' Adam said. 'Who else might he have meant?'

'I agree,' Humphrey de Bohun said. 'It can mean nothing else. Lord Gilbert has not retreated to his lands in Glamorgan, as he promised, but remains close to Hereford, watching our movements.'

Lord Simon pursed his lips and nodded. Then he glanced towards young Thomas de Clare, a question in his eyes.

'My brother is tempestuous and proud, but he is true to his oath,' Thomas said. He spread his hands, shrugging. 'I cannot speak for him, but if he promised to go to Glamorgan then I must assume that he is there. And any stray dogs left wandering the roads,' he said, shooting a barbed look at Adam, 'are master-less whelps.'

Lord Simon nodded once more but said nothing. For the first time Adam could see the tension in his features, the clench of muscle around his jaw and the creases graven into his brow. His eyes held a hard and sorrowing pain. The man carried the weight of a kingdom on his shoulders now, but the rancorous dispute with his former ally Gilbert de Clare had cut notches into him.

'You were once squire to Robert de Dunstanville, is that not so?' he asked abruptly.

'Yes, lord,' Adam replied, his senses sharpening. 'And his friend still, although I haven't seen him since last autumn.'

'He was known for his devious ruses and stratagems on the tournament field, as I recall. A man of twists and turns,' Simon went on. 'And yet I made him constable of Bridgnorth, one of the most powerful strongholds in the borderlands and the key to the northern Severn. Now he fails to respond to my messages, although our spies report he still holds the castle. Sir Humphrey here tells me I am right to maintain my trust in him. Would you agree?'

'Entirely, lord,' Adam said, and caught young Thomas de Clare's twitch of disdain. He knew now why Sir Humphrey had been so quick to deny the rumours of Bridgnorth's fall. 'Robert de Dunstanville is his own man, but he is true to his word. I would stake my life on that,' he said, and hoped that his misgivings remained concealed.

'Good,' de Montfort said. 'Then I shall accept your judgement of him. As for you yourself,' he went on, 'I think perhaps we may put you to good use. Your current lodgings are not what might be desired, I think?'

Adam coughed and nodded. *Had everyone heard?*

'Then we must find you a better alternative. Lord Edward, as you know, is my guest here. I've appointed an escort of young knights and nobles to keep him in honourable company . . .' He

seemed momentarily unsure of something and looked to his son
Henry, who nodded in confirmation.

'Very well,' Simon acknowledged, and looked to Adam once
more. 'I believe you might be suited to the role. Robert de Ros is
Lord Edward's chief custodian – speak to him and he will find you
quarters in the castle bailey and show you to your new duties.'

'My lord,' Adam said, bowing.

Humphrey de Bohun appeared satisfied; no doubt he had
put Adam's name forward. 'Just be grateful for what fortune
bestows,' he said, as he and Adam returned down the stairs and
along the passageway. 'And remember from whose hands that
fortune comes.'

Adam frowned, unsure whether he meant Lord Simon, or
himself. But now they had reached the outer door of the hall. As
they stepped over the threshold, a squire came from the passage
behind them and summoned de Bohun back. 'You must excuse
me a moment,' Humphrey said to Adam. 'Wait for me, and I'll
join you shortly.'

He returned to the hall, leaving Adam on his own. It was still
broad daylight and hours yet until vespers; Benedict had long
departed, and Adam had left Matthew with the horses to keep
him out of trouble. He had no desire to spend any more time
in Sir Humphrey's company, and would not wait for him. But
as he walked from the hall in the direction of the stables, Adam
saw Joane waiting with a group of her ladies outside the castle
chapel. Too late to retreat; she noticed him too, and smiled.

'You act like a stranger to me these days,' Joane said to him as
he joined her. 'You try not to see me, whenever we meet. I could
easily take offence.'

'I did not expect you to be here at all.'

'Neither did I,' Joane said brightly, in a light and conversa-
tional tone that barely masked the tension in her voice. 'But my
husband thought that having the granddaughter of Llywelyn the
Great at his side might aid him in overawing the Welsh.' She

affected a frown. 'Now I find myself in the midst of an armed camp – although I believe Humphrey intends to find a castle with a tall tower to keep me in.'

Adam had not seen her in more than ten months, but despite her more sumptuous style of dress, Joane appeared outwardly little changed by marriage. Her manner, though, was different. The crisp sarcasm in her voice, the deliberate languor of her attitude, felt like something she had adopted from the other ladies around her. Joane's Flemish maid Petronilla was shooting Adam dark stares from beneath lowered brows, which he attempted to ignore.

'I think you know why I act as I do,' he told Joane, dropping his voice. 'But I'm sorry if it seemed obvious.'

'I don't think I've seen you since my wedding, in fact,' Joane went on, as if he had not spoken. 'All those months I was in Winchester and you did not come to visit me. This is not the behaviour of a friend, I would say.'

'Are we friends, my lady?'

She paused a moment, as if startled by the direction their conversation had led them. They were standing close together now, apart from the group around the chapel.

'I do not know what else we are,' she told him. 'Would you have us be enemies?'

'You know well what I would have.'

She blushed quickly, and he saw her throat tighten. 'And you know well you cannot,' she said. Then she was smiling once more. 'I hear you are betrothed to William de St John's daughter.'

'News flies in these lands.'

'It does. And your new squire likes to talk. And my similarly garrulous cousin Elizabeth has large ears and fondness for family tittle-tattle. I wish you God's blessing on the match. She's beautiful, I hear.'

'Not a relation of yours?' Adam asked. He had often been amazed and bemused by the complicated family connections of the aristocracy; Joane's de Quincy lineage stretched far and wide.

'No. But I believe her mother is one of the de Cantilupes,' Joane said with a playful air, 'so you'll be related by marriage to the Lord Chancellor, and the Bishop of Worcester too. And I believe one of her cousins is the wife of Henry de Hastings. You've done very well for yourself!'

Adam had seen the elderly Bishop Walter de Cantilupe at the feast; he remembered him blessing the assembled troops on the dawn of battle at Lewes too. Strange to imagine that Isabel was related to such a man. A connection with the bullish Henry de Hastings was less appealing.

'And what of you?' he asked Joane. 'Marriage suits you, it appears.'

'Oh, does it appear that way?' she said, and her smile became suddenly bleak. 'Appearances can deceive.'

And just at that moment Humphrey de Bohun came booming from the hall, calling orders to his squires and grooms. He swept past Joane and seized Adam by the arm. 'Come with us,' he said. 'We're lodged next to the Bishop's Palace, and we'll be hearing vespers in the cathedral this evening. We can take supper beforehand.'

'Thank you, but no,' Adam said, detaching himself. The food he had already eaten sat heavily in his gut, and the effects of the wine no longer felt pleasing. 'I need to speak to the custodian Robert de Ros and find new quarters. May God give you a good night, my lord.'

He bowed to Sir Humphrey, and then to Joane, trying not to meet her eyes again. The thought of the two of them lying together in their big bed, in their chamber adjoining the Bishop's Palace, brought a flush of cold nausea. But Joane's closing comment lingered in his mind as he turned away and stalked across the bailey. *Appearances can deceive.*

It meant nothing, he told himself. Nothing at all.

Chapter 8

The keep of Hereford Castle was a round tower, set within a tight ring of walls at the top of a steep-sided riverbank motte. It was the Monday after Whitsun when Adam first scaled the creaking wooden stairway to the tower's iron-studded oak door. Behind him came two servants, the first carrying a platter of food and the second a jug of wine.

Through the door, in the narrow stone entrance passage, the servants set down their burdens while a guard checked them for hidden messages or concealed weapons. Only then did Adam lead the way up a twisting spiral stair built into the thickness of the wall. Three turns brought him to the door of the upper chamber. The guard on duty there unlocked it, then took a few steps further up the stairway to let Adam and the servants pass.

The chamber beyond was circular, narrow windows in deep embrasures letting in the daylight. The floor was covered with fresh rush matting, the walls with deep tapestry drapes. Beasts cavorted in gold embroidery on the red silk hangings of the canopied bed, and on a table of dark polished wood a chess-board was laid with pieces in amber and jet. Lord Edward was known to enjoy the game, and often played long into the night with Thomas de Clare or Henry de Montfort.

'Set it down there,' the Leopard told the servants as they entered, gesturing to a low side table. With averted eyes they placed the platter and jug on the table, bowing all the while, then shuffled backwards from the room. Adam watched them carefully, waiting until they had departed before making his own bow.

'Remain,' Edward ordered. He was standing by the window embrasure, gazing out into the light. Adam gestured for the guard outside to close the door. As they heard the locking bar drop Edward turned from the window.

'Do I know you?' he asked.

'We've met before, lord,' Adam told him. He had remained standing beside the door, one hand on the hilt of his sword. 'The tournament at Senlis, three years ago.'

Edward frowned a moment, then raised an eyebrow. 'Oh, perhaps I do remember you,' he said, and stabbed a finger towards Adam. 'You were a squire then, I think?'

And I saved you from capture in the melee, Adam thought. He remembered all too well kneeling before the injured Edward in his tent afterwards, begging him to pay Robert de Dunstanville's ransom. He remembered Edward's callous refusal.

'Your name?' Edward asked, prowling across the floor to take a cup of wine.

'Adam de Norton, lord.'

'I like to know the names of all my jailors, you know.'

'I'm no jailor, lord.'

'I see,' Edward said, and a smile flashed quickly across his face and was gone. 'So if I hammered on that door and overpowered the guard, you'd make no move to stop me leaving this place?'

'Lord,' Adam said, 'there are four more guards in the chamber above us, another on the stairs and three in the chamber below, besides the sentinels on the rampart. Unless you can transform yourself into a bird and fly from that window, you won't be leaving here today.'

Edward laughed coldly. 'You know, I often imagine that. What's the story where the knight turns into a falcon and flies to the lady's tower prison?' He glanced again towards the window and sighed. 'No matter,' he said.

At close quarters, Lord Edward was a formidable presence. Over six feet tall, he moved with a supple energy. The slight cast in his left eye only served to sharpen the intensity of his gaze, and the trace of a lisp gave his words a keen hissing edge. As he spoke he ran his fingertips through the soft curls of his beard.

'Come,' he said, and gestured for Adam to follow him to the embrasure. Together they gazed out into the daylight, over the roofs of the town and the cathedral towers, and Edward pointed to the dark line of hills just visible on the horizon.

'Those hills are filled with men who love me, and my father,' he said quietly. 'No friends of Lord Simon there. No, he will find few supporters beyond the walls of this town, I think.'

Adam had been told that he should be on his guard against any attempt to turn his allegiances, or to recruit him to carry messages. Even communications between Edward and his father the king, who was lodged in the royal chambers in the castle's outer bailey, were forbidden. Father and son could meet only in the presence of Simon de Montfort himself, and by his permission. Adam said nothing now, merely nodding in acknowledgement of Edward's words. He did not doubt the truth of them.

'So what do you think, Adam de Norton,' Edward went on. 'Is my situation just? Is this an honourable way to treat the son and heir of the king? Denied the company of my father and my friends, even the company of my wife – is that justice? You're a knight now, and you bear your own arms, I see. You hold land too, I expect, yes? So you've performed homage to my father for those lands. You've sworn your oath of fealty to him. To the king. Or does your Lord Simon compel his knights to a different oath nowadays?'

'I have taken only the single oath, lord. To your father.'

'Oh? So we will not be seeing *King Simon* in England soon? No?' Edward let out a dry laugh, prowling once more on a circuit of the room. 'Then how is it, do you think,' he said, gesturing rhetorically, 'that this unkingly man, this royal subject the Earl of Leicester, can issue orders to the king? How can he subjugate my father, while you, for example – the king's loyal subject – do nothing to uphold the dignity of the crown? Hmm?'

'Earl Simon wishes only the best for the realm, lord,' Adam said with great care. The words tasted bitter on his tongue, and sounded ugly. 'He wishes only the best for you, and for your father the king—'

Edward let out a sudden roar. With one kick he upended the low table, sending the platter of food flying and the jug of wine toppling to the floor, then took a long stride towards Adam. He towered over him, his face flushed, spittle flying from between his clenched teeth.

'I am trapped in the throat of that cursed dragon!' he snarled. 'But some day soon I shall spring forth, and then I shall rend the bodies of all those who oppose me! Oh yes, I shall rend them with great wrath!'

Wine was spreading over the floor from the fallen jug, soaking into the rush matting. Adam had taken a step back, shocked by Edward's eruption of fury, but compelled himself to retreat no further. His back rigid, his left hand tight on his sword's grip, he stared up at Lord Edward and held his savage gaze.

A long slow growl crept between the man's teeth, then abruptly he smiled and stepped back. 'You hold your ground well,' he said lightly. 'Perhaps one day I'll test you properly, eh?'

'I shall be ready for it, lord,' Adam said.

Edward had paced back to the window once more, spreading his long arms to brace himself in the opening of the bay. He stood like that for a few moments, silhouetted against the glare of daylight.

'You are dismissed, Adam de Norton,' he said.

*

The visitors arrived at the castle on the afternoon of the following day, an hour before vespers. They rode in across the drawbridge and beneath the stone arches of the gatehouse, white pennons raised above them and a crowd of curious onlookers gathered at the far side of the moat to watch them pass.

'This is a mistake,' John de Kington said, as the newcomers emerged from the gatehouse and dismounted in the outer bailey. He too had been appointed to what they called, with only slight irony, Lord Edward's *honour guard*; he and Adam had been sparring with wooden clubs and shields in the bailey when the new arrivals were announced.

'Either a mistake, or a brilliant ruse,' Adam replied quietly. 'We'll find out soon enough.'

He knew one of the visitors by sight. The Kentish baron Roger de Leyburne had been one of the leading defenders of Rochester Castle the previous summer, and had personally slain Robert's serjeant, John Chyld. But Adam had met de Leyburne long before that, on the tournament grounds of France. He knew him as a skilled and redoubtable warrior, and a sworn enemy of Simon de Montfort.

De Leyburne's companion, Roger de Clifford, was a powerful Marcher baron, and similarly a foe of Lord Simon. They had three knights and four squires with them, of their combined households, but they left their attendants with the horses as they strode across the bailey, between the tents and the storage sheds. The two Rogers wished to present themselves to the king, of course. But to do that, they had first to present themselves to their hated adversary.

'Look at them,' John de Kington said quietly, smiling. 'Doing their best not to gag and puke!'

Simon de Montfort met them in the yard before the great hall, and they exchanged embraces and the kiss of peace. Both de Leyburne and de Clifford had been granted safe conduct to come to Hereford and meet with Lord Edward, simply – so they claimed – to assure themselves that he was alive and being treated with dignity. Few in Simon's camp believed that, but fewer knew why he had granted them the terms they asked.

Now Edward himself came striding from the inner gatehouse, accompanied by his custodian Robert de Ros, a brisk northerner of around thirty who appeared to regard most younger men as fools. Henry de Montfort and Thomas de Clare were with them, and Richard de Malmaines too – to Adam's disgust, he had also joined Lord Edward's guard. The two groups met in the yard, with further embracing, and then filed into the royal chambers to present themselves to King Henry. Adam, John and the other knights of the escort waited outside.

'No doubt Simon will be keeping close to the two Rogers,' John said. 'Making sure they speak no subtle words to Edward, and pass no written messages.'

Sure enough, Lord Simon was walking between the king's son and his visitors when they emerged once more. They all stood together in polite conclave, with Thomas de Clare and Henry de Montfort standing off to one side, and then Edward was once more escorted back to the keep while the two Rogers returned to their horses.

'Do you think they got all they wanted?' John de Kington asked.

Adam just frowned. Simon and his sons may have been able to prevent the visitors speaking in private with Edward, but there had been plenty of time for them to speak to other people. And if there was one among them who could not be trusted, Adam thought, then all their precautions had just been rendered useless.

That evening, as the eastern sky darkened into night, he stared from the window of the tower he had been allotted as his lodgings, across the bailey towards the keep on its high motte. A light was glowing from the slit window of the upper chamber, where Edward was taking a late supper. More than anything, Adam longed to gather his retinue and leave this place. To ride back to his manor, to the lands he had made his own. To Basing, and to Isabel.

Flicking his fingers over the string of ebony and silver beads, her parting gift, he muttered his way through the Paternoster and the Ave, and prayed that his days of military service would pass quickly. Thirty-six more, he thought, and then he would be gone. And Simon de Montfort could go to the Devil if he chose.

*

Early in the morning, two days later, Adam and the rest of the escort took their horses out to exercise on the broad meadows to the north of the town. It was not the first time that Edward had been permitted to accompany them; there had been some talk of arranging a tournament, or at least a jousting match, and with so many knights billeted in the town with horses and arms and little to do, the prospect lifted the spirits of many.

The church bells had not yet rung prime, the air was still fresh, and the streets of the town near empty as the iron-shod hooves clattered over the castle drawbridge. Adam was riding his destrier, the bay stallion Fauviel, and he could feel the animal twitching with anticipation beneath him as he rode. Several days in a cramped stable with only an evening walk around the bailey was insufficient exercise for a trained warhorse. All of the destriers were high spirited and mettlesome, eager to stretch out and gallop freely in open country.

Lord Edward rode near the front of the group, between Robert de Ros and Thomas de Clare. Adam and John de Kington followed, with Richard de Malmaines and William de Boyton at the rear. Each of them had their own mounted squires accompanying them, and de Ros had brought half a dozen grooms leading remounts and a troop of serjeants and foot soldiers too. The horses raised a fine thunder in the narrow streets of the town. Cockerels were crowing and dogs barking wildly as they passed, and a few early risers crept back into the doorways and alleyways and watched the cavalcade ride by.

'By God, what a fine morning!' Edward cried as they rode through the Widmarsh Gate towards the fields beyond. 'Glorious, isn't it, to see far horizons once more, unconstrained by walls? A shame that Henry and Guy could not have come with us,' he went on, turning to Robert de Ros. 'I know they have some fine horses between them!'

'We have horses enough, my lord,' de Ros replied curtly.

But not riders enough, Adam thought. 'We should have brought greater strength,' he said to John de Kington, as the three leading men cantered on ahead of them.

John just laughed. 'Robert de Ros is no fool,' he replied with a grin. 'He's brought a small army!' He gestured back with his thumb at the column of men following them.

'Perhaps de Norton grows scared of his own shadow?' Richard de Malmaines asked, riding up alongside. He barked a laugh, then spurred his horse on after Lord Edward.

Half a mile from the town, Edward and de Ros turned off the northward road into the broad meadows. This was marshland in winter, but in the warmth of late May the ground was firm and dry beneath the horses' hooves. Stretching in the saddle, Adam gazed up at the clouds moving across the vault of blue sky above him. Then he dropped his gaze, scanning the horizon in a half circle to the north and west. There were no other riders in sight, no figures at all. Just a few placid red cows grazing in the further meadows, sheep nibbling the gentle green slopes to the north. So why did he still have such a sense of imminent threat?

Edward's mood had seemed overly boisterous, even joyful, since the evening before. Was it only the thought of the morning ride, or the promise of a jousting match some time soon, that had raised his mood so dramatically? Adam doubted it. The young prince's high spirits were more the product of nervous tension than genuine happiness. He was trying to cover his anticipation with a display of levity.

'Are you always so dull on a summer's morning?' Thomas de Clare said, walking his horse closer. 'I'm sure your friend Robert de Dunstanville would not shirk the opportunity of a bit of sport. I've heard he's a good man for a wager too. Here, drink!' Grinning, the young knight tossed Adam a leather skin of ale.

Adam drew out the bung and took a swig. Most of the other riders had dismounted, and were breakfasting on bread sopped in ale, with a little cheese and dried sausage, while their horses cropped the grass. The serjeants and soldiers accompanying them had spread out in a wide cordon around the meadow.

'Now, friends, let's see which of these horses shall win the mastery,' Edward declared. 'The owner of the most excellent charger shall have a purse of silver from my hand before vespers this evening!'

The promise of silver added a hard edge of competition to the morning's exercise. The blood of the horses was up, their eyes bright and their chests proud, as the knights mounted for the first race. A yell from Lord Edward, and the animals leaped into motion, stretching out quickly from a canter to a fine gallop over the level meadowland. None of the riders wore mail, and they were using light saddles rather than heavy padded war-seats; without the added encumbrance the horses could run freely. Adam felt the air rushing around him as he stooped over his stallion's flying mane. The drumming of the hooves on the turf merged to a steady rapid pulse, and Adam saw first one rider and then another fall behind him. Soon only Edward still outpaced his rushing steed.

Whooping as he rode, lashing at his horse's flank, the king's son appeared to be enjoying himself immensely. His long brown-gold hair whirled in the breeze, and his surcoat of brilliant scarlet lined with sky-blue silk flickered as he drew his horse around in a sharp turn at the far end of the meadow and began to ride back.

The horses were lathered with sweat by the time they reached the starting position once more, but there was only time for a swift drink of water before Edward once again called for a ride. This time only he and two or three others raced, Edward on a borrowed horse. The clouds had cleared and the day was growing hot. Adam was rubbing down his horse with a handful of dry grass by the time Edward returned.

'De Norton,' the king's son called as he vaulted from the saddle of his sweating charger, 'that's a fine animal you have. Spanish blood, if I'm not mistaken – what's he called?'

'Fauviel, lord,' Adam replied, who had bought the stallion from a London dealer the previous summer, and knew that its ancestry was far from exotic.

'And is he as wild as his name suggests, would you say?' Edward asked.

'Not quite, lord,' Adam said with a smile.

'I do remember you, you know,' Edward told Adam, rubbing the bay horse's muzzle. 'The melee at Senlis, as you said. You aided me then, and I never repaid you as I should have done.'

Adam found no words to reply. He had not expected this. What was it Lord Simon had said of Edward on that day? *He has not yet learned what a debt is worth.*

'I shall make amends, I promise you that,' Edward said, with an air of sincerity only slightly belied by his lisp and drooping eyelid. 'But first, let me try your Fauviel. You can take my grey remount there – I find him too mettlesome, but perhaps you'll have better luck.'

Adam gave Fauviel's neck a last rub and then handed the bridle to Edward. The grey horse was standing nearby, in the care of one of Thomas de Clare's squires. It was a powerful looking destrier with a proud chest and muscular haunches, but almost shied as Adam tried to mount. The squire fought it under control, and Adam swung up into the saddle. Stamping the turf, the grey pulled at the bridle. Was the bit too tight, Adam wondered, or poorly fitted?

Already Edward had set off once more across the field, flogging at Fauviel with his goad, just as he had done with the previous horses he had ridden that morning. Adam bared his teeth in a grimace. The king's son might treat high-quality horseflesh as he pleased, but to lesser men it was painful to watch. And when he shook the reins of the grey the horse took only two steps sideways and blew angrily.

'It's no use, sir,' the squire said as Adam dismounted. 'The beast must be gassy, or have a touch of colic.'

'Then you should have been more careful with the feed,' Adam said, his teeth still clenched. He stared at the distant scarlet and blue flash of Edwards' surcoat as he turned again at the far end of the field. Then he bent to examine the hooves of the grey.

Sure enough, he found what he sought when he checked the rear left hoof. As the squire held the horse steady, Adam raised the foot and drew a knife from his belt. A quick hard jab and a levering twist freed the stone pressed beneath the edge of the horseshoe.

'An old tournament trick,' Adam told the squire. 'Intended to make a horse look lame, or skittish. Did you do it?'

'No sir!' the squire exclaimed, wide eyed and blushing. Adam could not tell whether he was genuinely surprised, or just trying to hide his guilt.

Edward came riding back, Fauviel lathered and blowing beneath him.

'Wonderful charger, de Norton!' he cried as he leaped from the saddle. 'I'll buy him from you – how does a hundred marks of silver sound?'

'Lavish, lord,' Adam said. That was almost half of what Humphrey de Bohun had so far paid of his father's ransom. 'But I could not afford a better horse for twice that sum.'

Edward laughed, tossing Adam the reins, then snatched a flask of ale from one of the grooms and drank deeply. Both horses and men were sweating now. Adam let Fauviel drink, the horse sucking up water from the trough, and rubbed the animal down once more.

'I see you've cured the grey,' Thomas de Clare said, leading his own charger towards the field. 'Are you a horse-doctor too?'

'Just a stone in the shoe,' Adam said. 'Anyone might have seen it.'

De Clare narrowed his eyes, then mounted his horse and cantered off across the meadow once more. Richard de Malmaines fell in with him as he rode.

Robert de Ros and some of the other knights and squires had thrown themselves down on the grassy bank to drink and rest in the sun while their horses recovered from the morning's exertions. Off in the far distance, most of the men guarding the perimeter appeared to be resting too. Some had retreated to the shade of a stand of trees. Lord Edward swung himself into the saddle of the grey and walked the horse forward, leaning from the saddle to pat the animal's shoulder.

'Lordlings!' he cried, standing in the stirrups and turning to address Robert de Ros and the others on the bank. 'Lordlings, I've remained with you too long. Greet my father the king when you see him, and tell him I'll meet with him again soon – in freedom!'

Startled, the men on the bank just stared in confusion as Edward let out a wild whooping cry, pulled at the reins, and turned the grey towards the meadow. Then he dug fiercely with the spurs and the horse erupted instantly into motion.

'My lord!' Robert de Ros yelled, scrambling to his feet. 'My lord, no, you cannot do this . . .!'

'De Clare will stop him,' one of the other knights said, pointing towards the middle of the field. 'De Clare and de Malmaines, look . . .'

Already they could see the figures of the two horsemen riding to intercept Lord Edward's flight. But rather than opposing him, they turned and galloped alongside him. And three of the men that had been attending them now rode with them as well; one, Adam noticed, was the squire who had been holding the grey horse.

'Ride, all of you!' shouted Robert de Ros. 'Chase them down, for honour's sake! For our lives' sake!'

Adam was already mounted. His own horse was both the fastest and still the least wearied; he spurred the stallion forward in pursuit not caring if any others followed. The fugitives had the advantage: Thomas de Clare had ridden only once or twice that morning, de Malmaines barely at all. Both of them, and the men that attended them, had been preserving the strength of their mounts for this very moment, just as Edward had kept the grey horse back and deliberately exhausted the others. Now they were easily outrunning their pursuers, while Lord Edward's grey shot across the field like the fletchings of an arrow.

At the far edge of the meadow, where no guards remained to oppose them, the fugitives turned towards the north and easily vaulted the boundary ditch. Adam was beginning to gain on them at last, but his stallion was heaving beneath him, sweat spattering from its flanks. Ahead he could see Edward lashing at his grey, his spurs scoring bloody gashes into the animal's hide.

They had soon covered nearly a mile, up a rough track that rose from the meadows onto the higher ground. Above them Adam saw another mounted figure silhouetted against the sky, close to a copse of trees on the hilltop. The figure was standing in the stirrups and waving something above his head. Lord Edward let out another triumphant yell, and lashed at his horse with greater fury.

Richard de Malmaines veered ahead of Adam, turning in the saddle as he drew his sword. Spitting a curse between his teeth, Adam snatched his own blade from the scabbard. He let out the reins, hoping he might charge past de Malmaines or even ride him down, but the other knight had veered his horse even closer to cut him off from his pursuit.

'Oathbreaker!' Adam snarled, aiming a blow from the saddle as de Malmaines flinched away from him. The other man made a backhand cut, and Adam parried it aside. They were still riding, their horses jostling flank against flank; Fauviel arched his neck and bit at the other animal's head. Both horses were wild, as fierce as their riders. Adam swung again, and the tip of his blade cut at de Malmaines's shoulder. One of de Clare's squires had doubled back; Adam saw him coming and disengaged at once. As de Malmaines rode onward, stooped over the saddle bow and clutching his wound, Adam spurred his horse directly at the squire, sword raised.

The squire, his face blanched with fear, had already screwed at his reins and turned, his horse rearing. Adam was closing fast, but the other fugitives were far ahead of him now. He heard John de Kington call his name, and when he raised his head and stared up the track his heart clenched in his chest.

The hilltop was lined with men. Men armed and mounted for war, wearing mail and carrying banners. Scores of them that Adam could see, and plenty more in support. He could only watch as the armed riders opened a lane between them for the fleeing Edward and his companions.

De Kington grabbed the bridle of Adam's horse. 'There are too many of them, we need to be gone from here!' he cried.

Adam sawed at the reins, turned his sweating horse, and rode after John de Kington. When he looked back a few moments later he saw the mass of riders still waiting at the crest of the hill, their banners silhouetted against the sky.

'God damn your souls!' Adam yelled, choking back tears of fury and frustration.

Because the Leopard had slipped free of his cage, and now his wrath would be unleashed.

*

'*The deceiver!*' Simon de Montfort roared. He stabbed his finger at his chest. 'That viper Thomas de Clare has wounded me in my heart!' But his rage was not unbridled; he appeared to blame himself as much as anyone else.

They were gathered in the chamber adjoining the hall of the Bishop's Palace, where de Montfort had his lodgings. It was crowded with men, all of them pressing close around Lord Simon.

'We trusted him,' said Guy, the earl's younger son. 'We trusted him and he tricked us.' He was weeping openly – Thomas de Clare had been his own age, and the two of them had appeared to be close friends. But Guy's older brother Henry did not weep for the escape of his own friend Edward. His face was pale with fury.

Yes, Adam thought, the ruse was clear to all now. When Roger de Leyburne had come to Hereford, it had not been to Edward that he passed his secret messages. There was no need; the visitors had been allowed to speak freely with Thomas de Clare, and with de Malmaines too, and they had arranged the plan between them without a word passing to the king's son before that very morning. The de Clares held lands in Kent, Adam remembered; had Richard de Malmaines been their man all along?

'And what of those set to guard our friend?' Henry de Hastings snarled. His face was reddened, glowering. 'What of you, de Ros? Were you dozing when Edward made his gallop for freedom, eh?'

Other men shouted in angry agreement. The chamber was packed, the air dense with fury and fear. 'Or did his other custodians conspire in this as well?' de Hastings said. He swung to confront Adam. 'What do you say, boy? Are you a traitor too?'

'If I was, I'd be halfway to Wigmore by now, and not here looking at you,' Adam replied calmly.

Simon de Montfort ignored the comments, rubbing his jaw. 'So – Lord Edward, Mortimer, the Earls of Pembroke and Surrey, de Leyburne and the Marchers . . .' he said, as if to himself. 'And now the Earl of Gloucester and his brother too. All our foes are boiling together in one pot.'

'We still have the king,' Robert de Ros said.

'Oh, do we really?' Henry de Hastings replied scornfully. 'Perhaps one of us should go and check, and make sure he hasn't flown off as well, while nobody was looking?'

'Peace, friends, *peace*,' Lord Simon declared, raising his hands to quell the angry stir of voices. 'We must be united, or we are lost. Our enemies may be inspired by the Devil, but the king is indeed with us, and we still have a great strength of men and horses.'

'So we must take the field then,' Henry de Hastings said, 'to a chorus of agreement. 'Strike them now, before they can combine their forces!'

'Not so soon,' Simon replied. He closed his eyes, pressing his knuckles to his brow, and for a moment he appeared so pained, so lost, that every man in the room felt his heart quail inside him. 'Our enemies have outpaced us this once,' Lord Simon said, 'but we can still outwit them. For now let us guard ourselves, and pray to God.'

Adam heard Henry de Hastings's sigh of dismay. He felt it too. Surely they must take some action in response to what had happened? Inertia would cripple them. For all their faith in Simon's strategic abilities, his luck and his piety, they needed more now than he could give them.

'I shall send messengers to my wife, the Countess Eleanor, at Odiham, and to my son Simon,' de Montfort declared. 'They will raise troops in the south and in London and march to reinforce us here. Until then, we must ensure that we keep what we hold, and avoid any further disasters.'

Adam lowered his gaze. The shame of this day, the failure, was partly his; he bore that weight, and he could not blame Lord Simon for being unable to ease it. When he looked up he realised that de Montfort was staring directly at him.

'Adam de Norton,' the earl said, 'you are to go to Bridgnorth and reinforce Robert de Dunstanville there. Discover his loyalties, and ensure that he is upholding his duties to the full. And if he is not, you will replace him. Do you understand?'

Adam nodded. It was hard not to see this as banishment.

'When should I set out, lord?' he asked.

'At once,' Lord Simon said forcefully.

Part Two

Part Two

Chapter 9

Morning. Sounds of voices, distant birdsong, shuffling steps on a stone-flagged floor, then the ringing of a bell. Adam opened his eyes to the faint grey light. He was still clutching Isabel's string of beads in his hand.

Bromyard, he thought. He was in the guest hall of the old bishop's palace at Bromyard, a half day's march from Hereford. William Tonge was stamping about in the adjoining chamber, rousting the men from their pallet beds.

'Up!' the serjeant barked. 'Up, you beggars, and show your-selves to God, lest the Devil sees you first!'

Matthew was already awake and dressed; he brought Adam a bowl of water from the well in the yard to wash, and a cup of ale. Adam splashed his face, swallowed down a few gulps, then swung himself up from the mattress and pulled on his tunic and hose. On the far side of the room, Benedict Mackerell was crawling from his blankets, bleary and grumbling.

'All up and about, lord, and ready to move,' the serjeant said, appearing in the doorway. Adam nodded. Along with his own retinue, he was escorting a band of soldiers, sent to strengthen the garrison at Bridgnorth. Eight crossbowmen and twelve spearmen had tramped along the dusty road from Hereford behind his mounted retinue; Adam had put William Tonge in charge of them, and the barrel-bellied serjeant had taken to the duty with grim relish.

The cockerels were crowing and the first sunlight glinting above the church tower as Adam went out into the yard. He stretched and yawned, waiting for Matthew and Benedict to bring his horses from the stable. He would wear armour today, he decided; their road would take them close to the fringes of Marcher territory.

But it was liberating to be away from Hereford. They had set off the previous afternoon, slipping out by St Owen's Gate as quietly as five horsemen, twenty soldiers, a string of packhorses and remounts and a light baggage cart ever could. A pall of suspicion and dread had seemed to hang over the town. News of Lord Edward's escape could not be kept secret, and already the rumours had been flying. Some people were angry and fearful, others were secretly exultant, but many more were just quietly apprehensive of what might follow. Few could believe that the shining young prince they had cheered through their streets could be returning soon at the head of an army of ferocious Marchers, who would besiege their town, plunder it, and lay waste to it all.

Yes, Adam thought, it was good to be free of that mood of impending doom. But so swift had his departure been that he had not had any chance to bid farewell to Joane. Perhaps, he thought, it was better he had not. Perhaps it would be better if he never encountered her again.

Hugh of Oystermouth had not accompanied him from Hereford. 'What with Mars in Cancer and on the cusp of entering the twelfth house,' the herald had told Adam, 'I would consider this to be far too volatile a moment for travelling, unless strictly necessary.'

'What if I made it strictly necessary?' Adam replied.

Hugh had pulled a pained expression. 'To be quite honest,' he said, 'when I last parted with Sir Robert it was not on the best of terms. He would not, I think, be happy to see me again so soon.'

Adam had been unable to extract anything further about what had happened, and there was no time to try and convince Hugh

to overcome his misgivings. The herald would remain in Hereford, they had decided, and take up his lodgings once more with
the Makepays sisters.

'Keep your ears open,' Adam had told him, strangely dismayed
to be parting from Hugh so soon, but unwilling to show it. 'I'll
want to know of all that's happened, and all that's been said, as
soon as I return.'

'You will,' Hugh replied. Although the look in his eye told
Adam that he doubted that moment would come soon.

Adam's irritation with the Welshman had lingered over all the
thirteen miles to Bromyard. Only later, lying in the gloom listening to the snores and grunts of twenty soldiers sprawled on
their mattresses on the floor of the next chamber, did Adam find
himself missing Hugh of Oystermouth. The shame of his failure
to prevent Edward's escape gnawed at him, and the prospect of
what he might find at Bridgnorth was no solace. In the darkness
he had flicked through his beads, silently shaping a prayer that
might ease his soul, and found himself thinking once more of
Isabel. It was the thought of her that had finally stilled his mind,
and allowed him sleep.

By the time the sun was above the line of hills to the east they
were several miles on along the road. A guide had accompanied
them from Hereford, who claimed to know the best route to the
Severn above Worcester. Adam kept his horse to a steady walk,
the pace of the soldiers straggling along the road behind him
with their two-wheeled baggage cart. All through the day they
rode and marched, and the guide took them over the long hills to
the north of the Malverns, across meadows of long grass await-
ing the haymaking scythe and uplands wooded with beech and
oak, before leading them down into the valley of the Severn.

They made camp on an open heath, a mile or two beyond the
village of Astley. This was the southern fringe of Wyre Chase,
a hunting reserve that belonged to the Marcher baron Roger
Mortimer, and Adam set men to keep watch through the hours

of darkness. After attending to his horses, he sat near the fire cleaning and oiling his sword and belts and listening to the low voices in the dusk as the soldiers lingered over their supper of bread and ale. All knew they had another hard day's marching ahead of them, and before the light was gone from the sky most were rolled in their blankets and raising their snores to the stars.

Only Matthew remained awake, rubbing down the horses and checking their tack and bridles. Adam joined him in the twilight. The boy had been more than usually taciturn all that day, turning away from Adam's glance, clearly disturbed.

'You missed your chance with him, didn't you?' Adam asked. 'De Malmaines, I mean. He escaped you, just as Edward escaped us.'

Matthew paused in his work, and Adam saw the muscle tensed in the boy's neck. He nodded.

'And that was the sole reason you joined my service, wasn't it?' Adam asked quietly. 'To find the man who killed your family, and take revenge.' He felt the regret in his words as he spoke. He had not truly wanted to believe this. But he saw Matthew nod once more.

'So what do you want now?' Adam asked. 'You need not remain with me.'

'Train me at arms,' Matthew said, blurting the words. 'I'll be fourteen next month. Train me to be a knight.'

'You can't be a knight! You're a . . .' Adam caught himself. 'You're an apothecary's son.'

'A serjeant then, like him,' Matthew said, motioning towards the sleeping form of William Tonge. The barrel-bellied crossbowman had never treated Matthew with anything but scoffing condescension, and had never allowed him to as much as handle his weapons. Hard to see the serjeant as a man to emulate.

Adam exhaled. 'We'll see about that,' he said wearily. 'You're a good enough groom, for now. Sleep, and we'll talk more of this another time.'

*

Morning sun woke them, the dew on the grass and the views across the Severn in the dawn light refreshed them, and after a breakfast of sops they were soon on the road again. They needed no guide to follow the course of the river northward, and the rough tracks led them up onto the high ground to the west of the valley, through the fringes of the Wyre woodlands. They passed through villages, low dark places of wood and straw, and encampments of charcoal burners, but saw no other armed men, and by the time the shadow of the trees had covered the road, Bridgnorth was in sight before them.

The castle stood at the southern extremity of a ridge above the deep valley of the river, and the low sun lit the ramparts and the towering keep a reddish gold against the darkening woods below. No banner flew from the top of the keep, and Adam could see no men on the walls as he rode slowly down the track that descended to the river valley. The slope of the ridge was dense with scrub and outcrops of rock, the wall and rampart at the top black against the sky. The line of men behind Adam were silent now, their footsteps and the sound of the horses drowned by the noise of the river to their right as it swirled beneath the wooden palings of the bridge. Then they were climbing again, the track scaling the side of the valley and looping back to the town that spanned the top of the ridge. Here and there a figure appeared at the low doorway of a house or workshop, blank faced and silent as the horsemen and the footsore infantry went by. There were a few chickens scratching in the dirt of the wide central street, and a large pig gazed placidly back at Adam from a fenced sty. But most of the remaining inhabitants were keeping out of sight.

At the top of the street Adam saw the mighty outer gateway, the barbican that guarded the approach to the castle bailey. The drawbridge was down, the cables cut and hanging slack, and the top of the arch was blackened by fire. No sentries stood in the gateway. None watched from the battlements above. Only crows perched along the wall top, watching the approaching riders with black and glittering eyes.

'Is it abandoned?' Benedict Mackerell asked in a hushed and anxious voice. 'Are they all dead, do you think?'

Adam made no reply. The gates were open, one of them hanging off its hinges, but he had the strong sense that he was being watched. Nerves bunched his shoulders as he nudged his horse forward and rode across the charred planks of the drawbridge and into the gateway.

The outer bailey lay before him, a rectangle of walls and ramparts enclosing houses, workshops, stables and barns. One glance told Adam that there had been fighting here too; around half the buildings showed marks of fire, and several of the doors had been scarred by axes. But the violence had not been recent. Weeds grew in the blackened shell of a house near the gate, and grass sprouted from the wrecked thatch of a stable. On through the bailey they rode, every man peering to left and right, the two mounted serjeants with loaded crossbows. The infantrymen had slung the shields from their backs, and the few who had helmets pulled them on.

At the far end of the bailey was the inner gate, not as massive as the outer barbican but defended by a deep moat cut down into the bedrock. And this time the drawbridge was raised, and there were men on the ramparts above it. The area before the gate had been cleared of buildings for half a bowshot's distance. Adam rode slowly up to the moat, into the shadow of the gateway, and craned his neck to gaze upwards. He saw no banner, no pennons, and the men on the wall shouted no challenge.

'My name is Adam de Norton,' he called. 'I come in the name of the king, and of Lord Simon de Montfort. Open the gates!'

A distant voice from somewhere within the walls. Heads bobbed along the parapet, men peering down at him and then vanishing again.

'Open up, for the love of Christ!' one of the soldiers behind Adam called. 'We're thirsty, and we're out of ale!'

A boom from within the gatehouse, then the creaking of cables and timbers. With a rumble of counterweights, the drawbridge began to descend. The portcullis within rattled upwards, and the gates swung open. And there, striding out of the darkness of the gate passage into the light of the evening sun, was Robert de Dunstanville.

'Thanks be to God,' Adam breathed.

*

'When we saw you coming up the valley, I told myself there's only one man in this kingdom who carries a green pennon on his lance,' Robert said with a grin. 'But then I reasoned that this could not be Adam de Norton, who is safe on his estates in Hampshire, far from these lands of warfare and turmoil, and enjoying the fruits of the earth and the blessings of nature.'

'He asked me,' Belia added, '"*who has stolen Adam de Norton, and replaced him with this valiant leader of men?*"'

Benedict Mackerell sat with his mouth hanging open, clearly unsure whether he should find the exchange amusing or not. Matthew, sitting on a stool beside the hearth, listened in silence. They were in the lower chamber of the castle keep; usually the constables of Bridgnorth lived in the great barbican of the outer bailey, but with that gatehouse burned and the bailey itself largely abandoned, Robert had moved his small household here instead. A fire burned in a wall hearth, the smoke curling out through a vent in the massive stonework above it, but the chamber was dark, and growing darker as evening deepened into night. Robert's squire Giles had joined them at the table, and Robert had ordered a late supper for the new arrivals. Now the servants were carrying the platters up the external stairway from the kitchens in the ward outside: herring and a little salt cod, bread and cheese, and pickled eggs.

'We've been short of supplies for weeks now,' Robert said, as Adam chewed on the bland food. 'I'm glad of the extra men you brought with you, but a cartload of grain might have served us better.'

'It looks like there's been fighting here,' Adam said.

Robert made a dismissive gesture. 'Most of the damage you see happened over the winter. We had to drive Hamo L'Estrange out of the castle, and out of Shrewsbury too. That was a tough little campaign, at the end of December. Freezing weather.'

Adam recalled the season well. He had been at Basing then, hunting with William de St John, and meeting Isabel. It was strange to think that men had been fighting and dying in this place at that same moment.

'They haven't returned since then?' he asked.

'Not in person. But their people are all around us.'

Adam noticed that Robert had dropped his voice as he spoke, and cast an apprehensive look towards the open door. 'The towns-people mainly support the Marcher lords,' Robert went on. 'They've been all the law and power in Shropshire for genera-tions. You won't find that many folk praising Simon de Montfort in Bridgnorth, or talking about the rights and liberties of Englishmen.'

'They threw two royal messengers in the river last week,' Belia said. 'Somebody claimed they were de Montfort's men, and the mob seized them. We watched them do it from the ram-parts.' She shuddered quickly, and pulled her mantle around her shoulders.

'They survived,' Robert said lightly. 'But the greater problem is that half my garrison used to serve under L'Estrange. And the half that didn't are assaulted in the marketplace whenever they leave the castle walls . . . Or they used to be, before most of the townsfolk packed up and fled. Often I'm tempted to go back home myself.'

Robert caught Adam's eye for a moment. A furtive look crossed his features, and he looked away.

'So tell me,' he said abruptly, 'why did you decide to give up the blessings of peace and come all the way here? Did life on that manor of yours grow too comfortable? I told you, did I not, that you should pay *scutage* and keep clear of de Montfort and his campaigns?'

'I did exactly that, the first time, back in the winter,' Adam told him. 'But when I was summoned again, I felt I had no choice.'

'You always have a choice,' Robert broke in, 'despite what lords and kings may tell you.'

'But you're here, aren't you?' Adam replied, with an accusatory edge.

'True enough!' Robert grinned wryly. 'But I'm an older campaigner than you are, and I take to peace less easily.'

Adam noticed Belia's look of discomfort as Robert spoke. She appeared to have aged by more than the year that had passed since last he saw her; her face was graven by weariness, but when she had met him in the bailey outside he had been struck by how well she played the role of Robert's wife, and how happy she appeared to be in his company. She still wore the neat white head-covering of a married woman, carried over from her widowhood, although she now wore a Christian medallion on a slim chain around her neck. Adam wondered if her claims of conversion went any further than that. He detected a subtler and more profound change in her as well, but he said nothing.

'So, tell us what you've been doing over all these months, Adam,' Belia said, changing the subject quite deliberately. 'Other than growing broader in the shoulders, it seems, and collecting squires.'

She smiled at Benedict Mackerell, who bobbed his head and blushed.

Adam shrugged, composing in his mind some innocuous answer. But suddenly he could not resist the urge to speak more freely. 'I'm betrothed,' he said, and a smile broke over his face as he blushed as deeply as Benedict. 'To the daughter of William de St John of Basing. Isabel. Her name is Isabel.'

Robert leaped up, roaring his congratulations and seizing Adam in an embrace. Belia embraced him too, kissing him. 'You deserve this,' she said. 'You deserve true happiness, at last. What do you think, Robert, is his heart true?'

'I believe so,' Robert said, sitting down again. 'Sincerity is painted all over his face, I'd say!'

He called for a jug of good wine, and they drank to Adam's impending marriage and the bliss that would surely follow, Matthew and the two squires joining them in the toast, and for a few long moments the dread and foreboding that had gathered throughout the day was dispelled.

'There, you see,' Robert said, 'all the more reason to return home as soon as you can. Let us pray that nothing happens to detain you.'

'Well, things should be quiet enough as long as your Simon de Montfort holds on to power,' Belia said, 'and keeps the king and Lord Edward under his control.'

Benedict Mackerell made a choking sound and swallowed thickly. Adam just blinked slowly, and found he could not speak. He set his cup down.

'What?' Robert said sharply.

And so Adam told them, hesitantly at first but then withholding nothing.

Belia drew a quick breath as he spoke, her hand going to her throat and then her belly. Robert just stared, his jaw set.

'When did this happen?' Robert demanded, when Adam was done.

'The day before yesterday, around terce.'

'Christ's blood,' Robert said, and sat back heavily in his chair. 'Edward's supporters could be at Shrewsbury by now. Or here . . .' He gripped the bridge of his nose, his brow creasing, then shook his head. 'No, they'll more likely gather at Wigmore Castle, or Ludlow . . . But this will have been planned well in advance – L'Estrange and the other Marchers must have known of it long ago.'

'And you saw all this? The escape, everything?' Belia asked.

Adam nodded. 'I could do nothing to stop it,' he said bleakly, his head hanging. 'I was fooled just like the others. But I should have known, I could have——'

'No,' Belia said, cutting him off. She reached across the table and took his hand. 'You are not to blame. The responsibility for this — it's not yours.'

Adam tried to thank her but the words caught in his throat. He had not wanted forgiveness. But to hear it now was a blessing, and a balm to his soul.

Later, once Belia had retired to the upper chamber and Matthew and Benedict had stretched out on their bedrolls in the corners, Adam and Robert pulled their benches over beside the last glow of the hearth and sat together as they finished the wine. Adam could hear Benedict's rasping breath as he slept; the day had been long, and he too felt the weariness in his muscles and bones. But he was unwilling to surrender the last hour of evening just yet.

'Belia is expecting a child?' he asked quietly.

Robert turned his head, and his eye caught the firelight. 'I did not think you would notice,' he said, with an approving tone. 'She's nearly four months gone. It's . . .' He seemed speechless for a moment. 'It's a blessing from God. She did not believe, you see, that she could bear children. That was why she never remarried, after her first husband died. But now, it seems, things are quite different . . .'

'And . . . difficult?' Adam asked.

'No,' Robert said quickly. 'Not at all. It's quite astounding how much simpler everything seems now, in fact.'

'But you're not married, not by law at least,' Adam said, whispering now. 'Unless she truly becomes a Christian, you never can be.'

Robert hissed between his teeth. 'We're as married as I've ever been,' he said. 'And I see no reason why anyone should know different. If the law or the Church takes issue with that, then to hell with them.'

For a while they sat gazing into the embers of the fire, the last pulse and flare of heat and colour among the ashes. Robert drained his cup and set it down.

'Simon de Montfort sent you here to spy on me, did he not?' he said. 'To discover my allegiances, I suppose.'

'That was what he told me, yes,' Adam replied. 'But that was not why I came.'

'No?' Robert asked sharply, turning to face Adam. The glow of the fire etched his face in shadows.

'I came because I wanted to,' Adam said. 'And because I find I need to trust somebody.'

Robert grunted. He stared into the fire, then grinned. 'Now that's a dangerous thing to admit,' he said.

*

The next day was Trinity Sunday, and Adam attended mass with Robert in the little chapel in the bailey. Belia was with them too, although Matthew found something to do in the stables instead. As they left the church after the service, Robert called Adam to join him, and led him up the worn stone steps to the rampart walkway. From that vantage, Adam could get a much clearer impression of the castle's size and arrangement than he had the previous evening.

The inner bailey was shaped like a shield, with the apex to the south at the tip of the ridge. On one side stood the keep, a rectangular block of masonry rising sixty feet to its battlements. A dividing wall to either side of the keep enclosed an innermost ward, where the royal hall and chambers, the kitchens and the kennels stood. Outside in the bailey were the stables, armoury and smithy, the chapel and a wooden barracks for the castle garrison.

'If you look towards the middle of the bridge down there,' Robert said, pointing out between the stone merlons of the wall-top ramparts, 'you'll see where the two royal messengers were thrown in the river last week.'

Adam gazed downwards. The river shone in the morning sun, and birds circled above the deep valley. From up here the castle seemed impregnable, set upon its rocky eminence with sheer slopes on three sides and powerful defences on the fourth. But when he looked along the rampart walk, Adam saw only a handful of men standing watch. A few more lurked glumly around the inner gatehouse. Robert had abandoned the outer bailey entirely and used what men he had to turn the inner bailey and keep into a redoubt.

'Since January I've been petitioning de Montfort and the king to send building materials and skilled men to repair the damage to the outer gates and the bailey,' Robert continued, as he led Adam along the rampart. 'But I've heard nothing. I had barely sixty in the garrison before you arrived, and only one in ten mounted. Half of those that remain are Welsh.' He paused, squinting into the morning sun. 'But I have just about enough strength to hold the inner wall circuit and gate,' he said, 'when the attack comes.'

'*When*, you say,' Adam replied. 'You're sure L'Estrange will try and take the castle back?'

'He'll try.' Robert shrugged. 'The townsfolk knew about it days ago, which is why most of them packed up and fled. If anyone else were constable here, L'Estrange might just blockade the place, but as it's me – yes, he'll try.'

Adam remembered meeting L'Estrange years before, at the first tournament he ever attended. 'So his grudge against you is personal?' he said.

'He used to be my brother by marriage.'

Adam looked at him, startled. 'Why have I never known of this before?' he asked.

Robert shrugged again and smiled. 'It's true, I chose not to speak of it,' he said. 'But my late wife was Hamo's younger sister, the daughter of John L'Estrange. She was a widow herself when we married, and brought a considerable dowry. But she died barely a year later, and I lost it all. Hamo always blamed me for her death.'

Adam nodded, a frown knotting his brow. Robert had told him once, and once only, about his marriage to a wealthy widow. It had sounded all too much like Hugh de Brayboef's marriage to Adam's mother; Robert too had tried to strip the woman's sons of their inheritance. But Adam had long been resigned to his friend's imperfections.

'So you'll hold the castle against him?' he asked, following Robert as he paced on along the rampart.

'Yes,' Robert said over his shoulder. 'To the extent that I'm able, with what strength I have. And you can tell Simon de Montfort that, when you see him next.'

They reached the southern point of the rampart walkway, and Robert paused again, leaning against one of the merlons and staring out into the gulf of sunlit air, towards the distant blue hills.

'You know, I used to hunger for castles and land,' he said. 'To be a powerful baron, a Marcher lord in my own right, seemed a glorious thing. Now I'm not so sure. Honour and fame drive us forward, but seldom to an honourable end.'

He turned from the rampart. 'Maybe I'm just getting old, eh?' he said, then began to descend the steps to the bailey once more.

Adam followed him back towards the keep and the gate of the innermost ward. A band of soldiers were returning from a foraging expedition in the town – Robert had ordered that anything abandoned by the inhabitants could be requisitioned for use by the castle garrison. Two of them, Adam noticed, were dragging the large pig he had seen the day before. Another band of soldiers were sitting around a cooking fire outside the barracks; among them were men who had marched from Hereford with Adam. He saw them gazing at Robert as he stalked by, their eyes cold and hostile.

'When the child is born,' Adam asked, lowering his voice as they neared the keep, 'will you raise it as Christian or Jew?'

'Christian, of course,' Robert snapped back immediately. 'Although, maybe . . .' He paused again, grimacing and scratching at his beard. 'It's not an easy thing to discuss.'

The priest came from the chapel, and Robert raised his hand in greeting.

'Hugh of Oystermouth, you know, became quite insufferable on the subject,' Robert went on as he led Adam towards the keep once more. 'He thought it madness that I live here with Belia as my wife. People would suspect her, he said, and drive us out, and any child born to us would be pulled between worlds, as he put it.'

He let out an abrupt laugh, and turned to Adam. 'I told him that he of all people should know all about that! Our discussion grew heated, and I ordered him from my presence.'

'I understand,' Adam said. He knew now why Hugh had been so unwilling to return here. Robert could be ferocious when he was angry, and slow to forgive.

'I am a proud man, though I can be humble if necessary,' Robert said, gazing up at the keep looming above them, and the arched windows of the solar chamber on the upper floor. 'For her, though, I will admit no humility. For Belia, and for the child she carries, I will fight to the last, and God damn any man who goes against me.'

*

No alarms were raised that day, no riders came with news of an advancing foe, but the sense of threat remained. In the evening, an hour after vespers, Adam walked along the ramparts once more. The moon was rising full in the blue sky, hanging over the wooded hills. No smoke drifted up from the houses of the town, and only the sounds of the river flowing through the bridge piers and the birdsong from across the valley carried to the men standing watch on the castle walls. Adam looked down at the tranquil scene, the peace gathering in the early twilight, and knew how deceptive it was.

Earlier that afternoon he had spoken to Wilecok, whom he found working in the kitchen behind the keep. The servant's Gascon wife had a baby girl now; they had named the child Edith, in memory of the maid killed in the attack on Adam's manor.

'I've seldom known the master so ill tempered,' Wilecok had told Adam. 'He's divided in his mind – it's been the same since Mistress Belia joined us here. Not that I would speak a word against her, of course . . .' Wilecok's dislike of Jews, Adam had noticed, seemed a thing of the past.

But the servant went on in a low tone, rubbing at the side of his nose with a grimy forefinger. 'He's just not the same, young sir. Robert, I mean. He doesn't trust himself like he used to do. And there's plenty around here who don't trust him much either.' He rolled his eyes meaningfully, encompassing the full extent of the castle with his implication.

'It's different for me now, suffice to say, being a family man and a father,' Wilecok said, and with a proud sniff he motioned towards his wife, who sat on the hearthstone breastfeeding her infant with a look of stolid forbearance. 'All this confusion, everyone at cross-purposes. It's not good! Not a harmonious state at all!'

Robert de Dunstanville went early to bed that evening, climbing to the solar chamber of the keep with Belia. For another hour Adam sat awake in the hall, drinking wine and listening to the mournful singing of the soldiers on watch outside. But the night grew dark and still, and he knew he needed to rest. He lay down on his mattress near the hearth, his scabbarded sword placed beside him, and ran through the beads of the Paternoster while he waited for sleep to take him. An image rose in his mind, of Isabel riding in the dawn woodland near Basing. But then, eclipsing it, came an image of Joane instead. He did not notice when he slipped into dreams.

Solid darkness when he woke again, hearing muffled sounds and harsh words. He sat up, grasping his sword. Cries came from outside, and the clatter of footsteps on the outer stairway. Moments later the door creaked open and a faint grey light spilled across the chamber.

'What is it?' Adam called. 'What's happening?'

'Word from the sentries, my lord,' the guard's anxious voice replied from the doorway. 'The valley's filled with horses and men, they say – an army arrayed with banners!'

Chapter 10

An hour after daybreak and the men on the ramparts stood ready, the crossbowmen with their weapons spanned and loaded, every archer with an arrow nocked to his bow. Beside them on the walkways lay sheaves of fresh arrows and bundles of quarrels; Robert might be short of both men and food, but Bridgnorth was a royal arsenal and did not lack for ammunition.

'Wait for them to get close,' William Tonge called, crouching beside the rampart wall. 'Don't waste your shot. Take your time to aim. Then stick every son of a bitch.'

The barrel-bellied serjeant had an ugly temper, but fighting was his business, the only thing he appeared to enjoy, and he was very good at it. For all that he had endured of the man's company, Adam was glad to have him here now. The other men on the wall seemed bolstered by his confidence too. Either that, or they were just scared of him. Between the bowmen stood others with slings and spears, and piles of rocks to drop on the attackers. From the ramparts flanking the gateway, the men of the garrison looked out over the ravaged expanse of the outer bailey. On the far side, among the ruined buildings and fences, the enemy were massing for the first assault. Already bands of them were advancing into the cleared ground between the last of the buildings and the castle ditch.

Most were militiamen in tunics and linen coifs, some bare-legged and even barefoot. They carried spears and short bows, and many were lugging big crude shields made of planks and wicker. But Adam could see better-equipped men among them, serjeants in gambesons and iron helmets, some in mail.

'Look at them!' William Tonge cried with incredulous scorn. 'A gang of cut-throats! Welsh reavers! Come on then, bastards!' he yelled, craning his head up above the parapet. 'Come here and die!'

Beside Adam, a crossbowman nervously smoothed his palm along the stock of his weapon, muttering a prayer through clenched teeth. An archer to his other side flexed his bowstave, the muscles of his arm bunching and relaxing.

Still none of the defenders loosed a shot. A wail went up from the enemy ranks, the high screeching battle cry of the Welsh, and the sound of it seemed to echo back off the wall before them. Adam's throat tightened at the sound, and he felt a chill up his spine. A few of the Welshmen among the defenders let out answering screams of defiance. Here, as in the rest of England, men would be battling against their own kin.

In the shelter of the inner bailey, behind the gatehouse, Robert was waiting with his reserve of mounted serjeants. Adam glanced down from the wall and saw Robert summoning him with a gesture. Shuffling along the narrow walkway to the steps, Adam descended quickly, then jogged across the open ground to join Robert. The knight sat calmly in the saddle chewing on bread and cheese as if nothing unusual were happening.

'What is it? Are they about to attack?' Adam asked breathlessly.

Robert shook his head. He smoothed his moustache with his thumb. 'They're just testing our resolve. A demonstration of force. But it appears your crossbowman up there has everything well under control.' He nodded towards William Tonge.

Adam frowned, perplexed. But only a moment later he heard the horns bleating from the outer bailey, and the cries of the enemy serjeants calling their men back from the open ground before the castle wall. The men on the rampart hooted and jeered, and a few stepped up onto the parapets, backs turned and tunics raised, to slap their naked buttocks at the retreating foe.

'Now,' said Robert as he swung down from the saddle, 'we get to the talking. You'll want to see this, so follow close.'

They crossed to the gatehouse, and Adam followed Robert up the narrow spiral stairway. A tough climb in full armour, and he was breathing hard by the time they emerged onto the rampart of one of the round towers flanking the gate. It was still early, but already the day was getting hot, and the low sun glared from the eastern sky. Shading his eyes, Adam saw with a shock that their enemies appeared to have doubled in number. They filled the far side of the outer bailey, some of them busily ripping apart the houses and buildings to construct new ladders and mantlets to screen their archers. As Adam watched, the ranks of the waiting army opened and a mounted group rode forth.

In the lead was a man bearing a white pennon, the sign for parlay. The rider behind him carried a red banner with two prowling white lions, paws raised in defiance. 'Hamo L'Estrange?' Adam asked.

'It is,' Robert replied. 'That's him in the leading group.'

'If Hugh were here he might be able to identify the others,' Adam said, squinting to pick out the heraldic devices on the shields, surcoats and saddles of the riders.

'Well, I grant that chatty Welshman does have his uses,' de Dunstanville said. 'But in this case he wouldn't be needed. I know them well enough. The white lion rampant on blue is Roger de Mohaut. White with two red chevrons is de Grendon, and the white eagle on blue is de Ridware. This is good.'

'It is?' Adam said, frowning.

'Certainly. All of them come from the surrounding region. It means that Lord Edward and Gilbert de Clare haven't sent anyone to reinforce them yet.'

'And they don't have any siege engines either!' Adam said, his frown lifting.

Robert gave him a tight smile. 'God may yet be on our side.'

By now the group of riders had come to a halt ten paces from the ditch and gateway. Hamo L'Estrange rode to the front of the party and gazed up at Robert, one fist on his hip, his mail coif thrown back. He was around Robert's age, strongly featured, with a beak-shaped nose and thick black hair.

'Why do you keep to your walls, de Dunstanville?' L'Estrange called. 'Do we frighten you? Why not come down and speak like men, face to face?'

'Your rabble smell too bad,' Robert called back, leaning from the parapet. 'The air's fresher up here. Besides, I can hear you well enough.'

'Then tell us,' L'Estrange called, raising his voice, 'by what authority you hold this castle against us?'

'By the authority of the king,' Robert replied. 'Whose constable I am.'

'By the authority of that traitorous excommunicate Simon de Montfort, you mean,' the other banneret, de Mohaut, shouted, rising in the stirrups, 'who forces the king to do his bidding!'

L'Estrange calmed his companion with a raised hand. 'Your master de Montfort is a traitor, sure enough,' he called to Robert. 'And he will die a traitor's death before long. But surrender the castle to us now and there need be no more strife between us. You can leave this place with your arms and honour intact. Refuse, and every man of your garrison will be hanged from the walls.'

'You can't have the castle, L'Estrange,' Robert replied. 'It doesn't matter how nicely you ask.'

Adam heard L'Estrange's contemptuous snort. 'So be it,' the knight said, then signalled to his companions, tugged at his reins and rode back to join the rest of his force.

'Now we wait for the real fighting to begin,' Robert said quietly. He was stroking his moustaches with finger and thumb, and appeared to be enjoying the situation. Or perhaps, Adam thought, he had just enjoyed the opportunity to bid defiance to his former brother-in-law Hamo L'Estrange.

*

Hours passed, the sun climbing in the eastern sky, and the men on the ramparts sweated in their padded gambesons and mail as they waited for the assault. From the ruined buildings of the outer bailey came the noise of axes, hammers and adzes, and by mid-morning the enemy had begun to edge forward a line of mantlets, heavy sloping screens of wicker and hide, even sections of thatch torn from the houses. The archers on the walls sent arrows arcing over towards their foes, but the shafts vanished into the blue, and after a while the serjeants called for them to save their ammunition.

Benedict Mackerell sat below the rampart, in the scant shade of one of the merlons. He looked spottier than usual, and even less resolute, and Adam realised that the youth had never seen real combat before. He realised too that he himself had been failing in his duty towards his squire. Stooping, he made his way along the rampart walk and sank to a crouch beside Benedict, laying a hand on his shoulder.

'You're troubled by what lies ahead?' he asked.

Benedict nodded, his chin bobbing. 'Yes, but . . . it's not just that.'

Adam frowned a question, and the squire glanced to left and right and dropped his voice. 'Some of the men . . . I've heard them talking. They say that Sir Robert has become Jewish! That he's been ensorcelled by a Jewish witch, and he's leading us all to hell!'

'Christ's wounds!' Adam swore. 'Which of them said this?'

'I don't know . . . several of them,' Benedict said, evasive. 'But Thomas of Hawkley was among them . . .'

Adam drew a breath between his teeth, casting around for a glimpse of his second serjeant. But Thomas of Hawkley was not to be seen. He might have expected such things from the irascible William Tonge, perhaps, but Thomas had seemed less prone to vicious rumours.

'Idiots!' Adam said, with a scoffing laugh. But the news twisted in his gut. Once he might have believed such things himself. 'Robert de Dunstanville has shed his blood for Christ in the Holy Land!' he said. 'And the Lady Belia is . . . Have they not seen her attending mass?'

'I know, master, but they're scared . . . They heard what the baron out there said, about hanging them from the walls. They fear for their souls.'

Adam's roving gaze fell upon Matthew, standing with the horses in the open ground inside the gateway. The boy had found a sword from somewhere and belted it on; he was almost tall enough now to wear it properly. Matthew noticed him, and looked away quickly.

'If you hear anyone saying these things,' Adam told Benedict, stressing the words as his grip tightened on the squire's shoulder, 'then you must quell the rumours, understand? We must not let them eat away at our resolve.'

Benedict nodded glumly, but Adam was left wondering whether the squire believed the stories himself.

And still the line of mantlets crawled forward across the outer bailey, edging closer to the castle ditch. Smoke rose from among the wreckage of the buildings beyond them, where L'Estrange's men had set up field armouries and cooking fires. The noise of construction work was unabating, chipping away at the stillness of the day, chipping away at the nerves of the defenders as they waited for the attack to commence.

*

It was just past noon, the hottest time of the day, when the horns wailed from beyond the wall and the enemy raised a shout that started the birds from the trees across the valley. Adam scrambled to his feet and stared across the battlements. Finally they were coming. Beyond the wall of mantlets the attackers were assembling in their companies, hundreds of them massing darkly in the sunlight. Speartips and blades glinted as the enemy passed crudely constructed ladders and rough shields forward to those who would lead the assault. Then the horns cried again, the shouts of command rang out, and the tide of armed men began flowing forward through the gaps in the mantlets and streaming across the open ground towards the castle defences.

They were coming in a rush, hoping to overwhelm the defenders in one swift wave. And there were far more of them than Adam had feared. Boiling forward with shouts and guttural cries, they swarmed towards the ditch with the ladder-carriers running in the lead. William Tonge called his order, and the bowmen on the wall stood to the embrasures, aimed, and loosed.

The first flurrying volley cropped down a score or more of the attackers. Staring from the gap between the merlons Adam watched them fall, amazed that the survivors still pressed the assault after taking such losses. One man, an arrow through his throat, staggered right to the lip of the ditch and then toppled forward. Others, shot through their limbs, writhed in agony on the dusty ground. But their comrades just leaped over them, and kept on coming. The bowmen on the wall managed another shot, leaning from the embrasures, and then the enemy were scrambling down into the ditch and piling towards the base of the wall, struggling to haul their ladders across and swing them into position.

Screams from along the walkway; Adam saw a flickering in the air, and heard the brittle clink of steel against stone. With a start he realised that the enemy archers and slingers were shooting back at them from behind the line of mantlets. Arrows were striking the merlons or arcing between them. Slingshot cracked against the masonry; one struck a man standing a few feet to Adam's left, bursting a red wound in his forehead and knocking him back off the parapet to plunge twelve feet into the bailey behind him. A crossbowman lay twisted in agony beneath one of the merlons, an arrow jutting from his chest.

'Keep shooting, you dogs!' William Tonge bellowed, as several men went to help the wounded. 'Drive them back. We're all dead men if they get in here!'

But the storm of arrows and slingshot from the outer bailey was taking effect. The attackers had ten men for every one of the defenders, and for all their appearance of wild indiscipline the archers and slingers among them were keeping up steady volleys, directing their aim at particular areas of the wall. Two of the men on the rampart heaved a slab of sandstone up between them and toppled it over the edge; Adam heard it crash into the ditch, and then the screams of the men it had struck as it fell.

Already the first of the ladders was clattering against the wall, the men below raising a cheer. Even without leaning out from the battlements, Adam could tell that it was too short – with its foot in the ditch, the ladder would never reach the crest of the wall. A few men were scrambling up even so, shields held above them, yelling taunts at the defenders as the archers in the outer bailey kept up their stinging volleys.

To his right, Adam could see another group attacking the gates. These had longer ladders, and ropes with iron hooks as well, and they were trying to haul down the drawbridge. Smoke rose between the gatehouse towers, a thin smudge against the blazing noon sky. Robert de Dunstanville was up on the ramparts between the towers once more, leading the defence; he gave an order, and three of his men lifted a steaming cauldron and edged it to the parapet. With a grunt and a heave they tipped their load, pouring a torrent of boiling water down over the gates and drawbridge below them. Scalded attackers howled and tumbled from their ladders. But another band were scrambling down into the ditch below the gatehouse, ready to take their place.

Adam was in a fury of impatience, all his nervous anxiety turned to aggressive energy. But his desire for combat was frustrated; trapped on a narrow walkway with men to either side of him he could do little but watch what was happening in other places. The pressure of remaining crouched below the parapet while arrows and slingshot cracked off the stones and whipped overhead was telling upon him too. He was sweating heavily, his stomach cramping and the blood flaming in his head. The grip of his sword felt slimy in his fist.

A cry from behind him, and he turned to see Matthew running from the direction of the keep, holding his scabbard away from his legs so it did not trip him. 'They're climbing up the western slope to the postern,' the boy reported, breath heaving. 'They've got ladders, and ropes . . .'

Adam cast one look back towards the gatehouse, where Robert was still yelling orders as the enemy mustered for a renewed attack. Further along the rampart walkway he could see William Tonge, bending to span his crossbow before taking aim once more. But down in the bailey the reserves, four men at arms and six spearmen intended to reinforce the defenders wherever they might be needed, were leaderless. They stood waiting beside their horses, gazing up at the ramparts. Adam saw at once what he needed to do.

Calling for Benedict to follow him he ran down the steps to join Matthew. Thomas of Hawkley was among the reserves and had already seen him. No time to worry about the man's attitudes now.

'With me, all of you!' Adam yelled, and pointed with his sword towards the arched gateway of the inner ward. A couple of the men at arms leaped into the saddle and rode ahead of him, the rest followed Adam on foot. Through the open gateway beside the keep he entered the ward at a run, his body flowing with sweat beneath his heavy armour. Belia was at the top of the wooden steps of the keep, and she pointed towards the wall beyond. Already Adam could hear the shouts from the parapet, and from the attackers on the far side.

A square tower jutted from the wall above the western slope, guarding a small postern gate that led to a snaking path down the steep hillside beneath it. Robert had known it was a potential weak point, and had stationed a dozen men in the tower and on the walls flanking it. Now the enemy had identified the weakness too, and sent a force to assault the postern while their main force distracted the castle defenders with an attack on the northern ramparts.

As Adam ordered his men to follow him he could hear the gnashing thud and rip of an axe against the postern gate. He found six men waiting before the gate arch, nervous as the hacking blows fell on the far side. But the gate was heavy ironbound oak, double barred and bolted, and six defenders were more than enough to hold the narrow entranceway even if the attackers chopped a way through it. Adam ordered two of his own men to reinforce them, then led the rest up the cramped spiral stair inside the tower towards the battlements above the gate.

Swinging his shield from his shoulder, he lifted it before him as he scaled the stairway, his mailed left shoulder grating against the curve of the wall. The noise of the men climbing below him thundered in the darkness. As he neared the wash of daylight at the top a tumbling figure blocked the upper doorway, and Adam barely had time to tighten his grip on his shield before the falling man crashed against him. Shoving the body to one side, he clambered over it and continued upwards. He could hear fighting on the rampart walkway now. The attackers had brought ladders with them, he realised, and had already got up onto the ramparts while their comrades below them battered at the gate. Stumbling up the narrow wedge-shaped steps, his chest heaving and his breath loud in his ears, Adam pushed himself to climb faster.

Another turn of the stairway and he was at the landing. To the left, an arch opened onto the walkway. Two defenders cowering on the stairs above him, three more in the tower chamber to his right. As Adam emerged into the daylight he saw another man in a gambeson and helmet, an axe in his hand, clambering over the parapet. On the walkway below him a band of his comrades were locked in combat with the last few defenders.

Shield up, sword levelled over the top edge, Adam paused just long enough to draw breath before charging from the tower archway onto the rampart walk. Benedict was right behind him, Thomas of Hawkley and three more men at his heels. The first attacker he took by surprise. The man turned, startled, and Adam rammed his shield straight into him with all the force and momentum of his charge, toppling him off the wall. But the next two and the axeman were ready for him, snarling as they raised their weapons. The walkway was only two paces wide; enough for a single man to fight another, but no more. Adam blasted aside a swinging mace, then crouched and cut low beneath his shield, hacking at his opponent's legs. The man with the mace went down, and Benedict stabbed with his sword over Adam's back at the man beside him. A crossbow smacked, the quarrel striking sparks from the stone parapet and veering away.

Two steps, another shove from behind his shield, and Adam drove the next attacker backwards. The man stumbled over the body of his wounded comrade, and with a cry of triumph Adam wheeled his sword and slashed the man across the face, opening his cheek to the bone. Blood spattered as the man collapsed, hands scrabbling at the wall, and his comrade with the axe pushed past him. To the left of the narrow walkway was a drop of twelve feet; a chasm, it appeared now. Adam dodged closer to the parapet just as the defenders on the tower battlements loosed their crossbows. The axeman spun as one of the bolts struck, staggered once, and toppled from the walkway.

Hard breaths, blood beating. Dead and wounded at Adam's feet, and only his own men standing now. They were yelling over the wall in defiance as Adam heaved the ladder away from the battlements. Benedict rushed to help him. Beneath them, the noise of the axes hacking at the gate had doubled in volume.

'Guard yourselves!' a voice yelled from above, and Adam glanced up quickly to see two men on the tower top, dark against the sky as they hefted a broad iron basin onto the ledge. He crouched quickly, lifting his shield to cover himself and gesturing for Benedict to get his head down. There was a hissing rush, a wave of dry heat flowing through the air, then they heard the screams from below them. Adam's gut clenched. He had seen the effects of burning sand once before, during the attack on Rochester. When he straightened up, squinting, he could still feel the whirling particles in the air, stinging his face.

Below them the men attacking the door had received the full blast of the sand. Adam leaned over the parapet: two still lay writhing on the threshold, clawing at their padded garments as the fiery grains worked their way deeper, burning their skin. Three other men were sprawled at the base of the wall, dead or dying, beside the fallen ladder and the scattering of rocks flung from above, while the rest were scrambling away in flight down the slope below the postern.

Adam drew rapid breaths through his teeth, the sweat flowing in runnels from his brow. He still expected another attack, another rush of armed men from along the walkway. Had they got a ladder up on the far side of the tower as well? Braced between the merlons, he recited the Paternoster through parched lips.

Yells came from deep inside the postern tower, echoing up the funnel of the stairs. Thomas of Hawkley, standing beside the doorway with streaming eyes, blinked and rubbed his face and then hefted his sword. Benedict had time to give a warning before a man appeared from the darkness of the stair, a grimy reeking figure with a knife in his hand. Teeth snarled from a blackened face as the man lunged at Thomas of Hawkley and drove the knife into him. Then somebody below on the stairs grabbed the man's ankles and pulled him down. Benedict stepped forward, and with one swift blow rammed the point of his sword between the man's shoulders.

'He came up through the latrine chute!' the man on the stairs cried. 'He killed Hywell too!'

'He's dead now,' Adam said, as one of the serjeants rolled the intruder off the rampart walkway.

'Master,' Benedict said, turning to Adam. 'You're hurt.'

Adam frowned – surely he was mistaken? – but when he looked at his right arm he saw blood streaming red through the links of his mail. He snatched a breath, calmly handed his sword to Benedict, and shucked his hand from the mail glove at the end of his sleeve. Blood webbed his fingers and slicked his palm. Peering at his shoulder, he saw the gash where a crossbow bolt had punched through the mail and into the flesh of his arm. He had not even felt it. A sudden wave of nausea flowed through him; a handspan to the left, and the bolt would have pierced him through the neck. Now that he had seen the wound he felt it for the first time too, branding his whole right side with its fire.

Swallowing back the pain, his right arm hanging and his fingers dripping red spatters onto the rampart walkway, Adam shuffled towards the stairs. It was only then that he noticed Thomas of Hawkley slumped by the door to the tower, teeth clenched as he pressed his hands onto the knife wound in his side. The blood flowing between his fingers looked unnaturally bright in the dusty air.

Chapter 11

'Hold it here,' Belia said. Adam gripped one end of the linen strip while she bound it around his upper arm and tied it. Her maid had already washed the wound, sewn it closed with stitches of silken thread, and anointed it with honey. Adam, stripped to his braies and hose, sat bare-chested between the two women.

'You're very good at this,' he said.

'Not as good as Wilecok's wife,' Belia replied as she finished tying the bandage. 'She's down below, attending to your serjeant and the other wounded. But do not imagine,' she went on as she got up and went to pour another cup of wine, 'that every woman you meet is a leech, or a physician. I, for example, am a money-lender, and a very astute one – or I was, until recently. Now I am . . . who can say?' She turned to Adam with a smile. 'Apparently some people here consider me a witch.'

They were in the upper chamber of the keep, the solar that Robert and Belia used as their private lodgings. Belia had led him up here to attend to his wound in person. Rush matting covered the floors, but the room was still dim, the narrow windows in their deep embrasures giving little light. Austere as well, with its white-washed walls and dark wood screens. Here and there Belia's own possessions brightened the chamber. The bed was large and old, with thick hangings; Adam instinctively averted his eyes from it.

'That should keep the wound clean at least, and allow it to heal,' Belia said, studying the bandage again. She passed him the cup of wine. 'You'll have trouble using your arm for a while. Do not exert yourself, or the stitches could open.'

Adam gave a dry laugh. The first attack on the northern rampart had been driven off, but the enemy were once more massing outside and preparing for a fresh assault. Exertion was a near certainty. But he felt better now, and the spiced wine that Belia had poured from her own private supply had raised his spirits and dulled the flare of pain to an itching throb.

'I hear more men have deserted,' Belia said, pouring herself a cup of wine and taking a sip. 'They were supposed to be guarding the eastern wall, but during the attack they let down a rope from the battlements and ran away. Luckily somebody noticed the rope and drew it up before the enemy discovered it. Why do they do it?' she asked, with a rhetorical air. 'Is it due to my presence here?'

'No!' Adam said. 'Cowards have their own reasons, but you are not to blame for this.'

'Cowards, yes,' Belia said, not meeting Adam's eye. 'Oh, but I should never have come here!' she went on with sudden force. 'I should have stayed in London with my brother Elias, or gone to Nottingham to be with the rest of my family, I see that now!'

Adam said nothing, He understood that this was a debate Belia had been conducting with herself – and perhaps with Robert too – for some time.

'And what about you?' she asked abruptly. 'Why did you come here, Adam de Norton? Oh, I know you say that Simon de Montfort ordered you, but he is not the king, or your lord and master. Why did you really come to Bridgnorth?'

Adam took a moment to compose his reply. He had not thought clearly about the question himself. He realised now that he had been avoiding it. 'I still felt guilty, about Lord Edward's escape,' he said. 'I felt I had something to prove. A debt of loyalty to pay . . .'

Belia gave a dismissive snort of laughter. 'Loyalty? After all this time? Surely all your debts are paid.'

'I did not mean a debt to Lord Simon,' Adam went on quickly. 'If Robert were not constable here, I would not have come.'

'You would have ridden home to your manor,' Belia said, 'and the woman who is to be your wife?'

Adam had the sudden and distinct sense that she was testing him. 'Yes,' he said. He hoped his answer sounded sincere.

Belia crossed the chamber and sat on the stool beside him. Her maid was busy at the far side of the chamber, scrubbing Adam's bloodied tunic in a basin of warm water and giving no impression of listening to the conversation.

'So if Robert declared that your debt to him is paid, that you owe him no further service or loyalty, then you would leave here with an open heart and return to your home, your marriage, and your life?' Belia asked.

'Not while the enemy are at the gates,' Adam said with a bemused frown. 'Robert stood with me when I was in danger, and so I will stand with him.'

Belia reached over and traced Adam's jaw with her fingers. 'Yes,' she said. 'We both must stand with him. But we must listen to reason too, when it speaks.'

*

The sun was gone, the summer twilight deepened towards night, and still the enemy did not stir from their encampments surrounding the castle. From the walls, the defenders of Bridgnorth could see the cooking fires of L'Estrange's men, and even hear their songs, crude verses that mocked Simon de Montfort and his sons. Nerves strained, they waited for an attack which may not come until dawn, or may never come at all. Perhaps the enemy, thrown back from the walls, had decided merely to blockade the castle and starve out the defenders? The deserters would certainly have reported that the garrison was short of supplies.

Throughout the afternoon the line of big mantlets had edged further forward; now they made an unbroken wall of hides and wood and thatch protecting the enemy archers. Anyone who showed their head above the parapet instantly became a target for the bowmen concealed behind their screens. During the earlier assault the attackers had dragged down the drawbridge, hacked through the cables and wedged it open, but the gates and portcullis had held them back. Now the timbers of the gateway were pitted and scarred, bristling with arrows.

Just after evensong the castle chaplain had made a tour of the defences, offering to hear the confessions of any who desired absolution, in fear for their mortal soul. But he had been drinking since noon; he stank of ale and wine dregs, his voice was slurred, and William Tonge had barked at him to get back to his chapel lest he cause even greater dismay among the men. It had not seemed a good sign. But it was a warm evening, the breeze soft after the scorching sun of the day, and the weary soldiers manning the walls and camped in the open bailey were content to enjoy a few hours of relative peace as the moon rose over the valley and smoke drifted from the camps of their enemies.

Adam stood on the northern rampart, at his accustomed place, and Matthew brought him a bowl of potage and a crust of bread as a late supper. Earlier, Benedict had returned from the armoury with Adam's hauberk. The smith had managed a crude repair of the broken mail: four new links riveted into place to close the rent in the upper arm. With Benedict's help Adam had dragged the mail coat back on, gasping through clenched teeth as the metal tightened over his wound. But it felt better to be back in armour. Even if he could not use his right arm effectively, either to swing a sword or to climb a ladder, he could at least feel like he was aiding in the defence.

'You think they'll come again tonight?' Benedict asked him, as they crouched on the rampart looking out over the parapet.

Adam nodded. 'They're making too much noise,' he said. 'Their serjeants are keeping them lively. I would guess they'll start their assault as soon as it's fully dark.'

Sure enough, by the time it had grown too dim to make out the shapes of the ruined buildings at the far end of the bailey, the noise of horns rose once more from the enemy encampments. Torches flared, baffling the vision of the men on the walls, but those who squinted tightly enough could make out a massive, bluntly angled shape rolling slowly forward out of the dusk, men crowding behind it as it came. They heard a distinct heavy rumbling too, the steady low chant of voices and the shriek of wood turning against metal.

'It's a wagon,' said Matthew, who had joined Adam on the rampart. He stared, eyes narrowed. 'A wagon stacked with logs.'

As the shape approached the walls, Adam could distinguish it more clearly. It was a big two-wheeled farm cart, with a gang of men between the shafts pushing it towards the gates. The bed of the cart was piled with heavy beams, built up around it as a bulwark. Archers advanced alongside, unleashing a withering hail of arrows that drove the defending bowmen down into the cover of the merlons.

'They're going to use it as a ram,' Adam said, under his breath. He could see it now: the attackers would heave the cart forward across the fallen drawbridge and smash it into the portcullis and the gates behind it. Others had realised the same thing, and a wave of panicked cries flowed along the rampart, until William Tonge ordered everyone to be silent.

Smoke was rising from between the gatehouse towers, and Adam caught the acrid reek of hot pitch on the breeze. Still the cart rolled closer. The men between the shafts kept up their hoarse chanting as the ironbound wheels turned and the lumbering vehicle rolled towards the gates. Most of the advancing enemy were screened by the wooden bulwarks, and the few archers and crossbowmen on the walls who dared emerge from cover could only snipe at the men who dashed forward to clear the wreckage from their path.

The stink of pitch grew stronger as the wheels of the cart rolled onto the battered timbers of the drawbridge. A shout of command, and the men above the gate hefted a great steaming cauldron up onto the parapet. Another shout and the cauldron tipped, sending an ink-black torrent spattering down onto the drawbridge and over the heavy wooden cladding of the cart. Too soon, Adam realised. Most of the ram had remained untouched, and the men pushing it had been shielded from the hot pitch.

Then a spark fell, a flaming torch dropped from the gatehouse rampart. Another, and the pitch flared and smoked. Flames licked upwards, curling beneath the arch of the gateway even as the attackers heaved the cart forward through the blaze. Craning from the wall battlements, Adam saw the light of the pitch-fires illuminating the figures below him.

A shuddering crash as the cart rammed into the portcullis. Undeterred by the flames, the attackers dragged the vehicle back. With a harsh collective yell they rolled it forward again and drove it a second time into the opening of the gate. Sparks billowed into the night, and the whole gatehouse was lit by the flames. The cart itself was burning now. A cheer and a shout, heavy wheels rumbling on the drawbridge. Another crash, and the rending of timbers.

'The portcullis is broken!' a voice shouted. 'They're up to the gates!'

William Tonge was yelling orders, calling men from the ramparts to help him reinforce the guards holding the gate passage. Adam signalled to Benedict to follow him, and made his way along the walkway. Other men were already running down the steps ahead of them, and as he approached the stairhead Adam found the serjeant in front of him. William Tonge had left his crossbow on the rampart and armed himself with a short-bladed falchion.

'Best stay up here, master,' he said, with a grimace that the flickering firelight turned into a sneer. 'Maybe some rough work ahead.'

Adam shrugged off the affront. His right arm might be injured, but he could still hold a shield. Shoving his way forward, he followed the serjeant down the steps into the gulf of darkness behind the wall.

From the foot of the steps, the gatehouse was a black silhouette against a fiery sky. With six men behind him William Tonge jogged forward into the vaulted passage beneath it. Flames raced beneath the arch of the gateway. But the heavy bar that locked the gates shut was holding, even as the burning ram slammed against it once again.

'Put your shoulders to it!' Tonge yelled, his voice echoing beneath the stone vaults. 'Put your shoulders to it, and by Christ's blood and bones *shove!*'

The men around him did as he ordered, all of them pressing hard against the planks of the gate and the locking bar even as the wood creaked and shuddered under the blows of the ram and the dark passage filled with smoke. Adam stumbled forward into the smoke, intending to join them, but Benedict took him by the arm.

'No, master, stay back,' the squire said urgently. 'Remember you're wounded . . .'

Adam turned with a curse on his lips, but he knew that Benedict was right; even running down the steps had brought a pulse of hot pain to his upper arm. Instead, he fell back with the squire and band of others who formed a rough cordon around the mouth of the gate passage, and slipped his left arm into the straps of a shield. Robert de Dunstanville strode out of the darkness to join them, his own squire Giles and four other men in armour accompanying him. Robert's face was streaming with sweat inside the glittering oval of his mail coif. In his hand he held his axe, the blade burnished.

'Hold them here,' Robert said to the men around him, his voice low and hard. 'If the gate goes down they'll rush the passage. We're the last line of the defence.'

A thunder of straining timbers, shrieking iron. A line of men were passing buckets from the well, and hurling water onto the back of the gates. The wood steamed, the locking bar cracking under the pressure from the far side even as William Tonge and his men heaved against it.

'They're breaking through!' a voice yelled, and a bellowing cheer came from the men outside. They dragged back the cart, taking the pressure off the gates for a few heartbeats, then rammed it forward once again to slam against the battered wood. Fire licked between the gates as they strained apart.

Adam heard William Tonge's furious yells, and then his voice cut off. A pair of men appeared out of the smoky darkness, dragging the body of the serjeant between them.

'Is he dead?' Robert demanded.

The men shook their heads; William Tonge was alive, burned and bloody but still spitting furious orders even as they carried him to safety. Waves of heat rolled from the vaulted passage, and smoke streamed from its mouth. Another cheer from outside, and the next blow of the ram brought a sudden shattering crack as the locking bar broke and the gates burst open.

Adam felt himself shouting, but could not hear his own words. Beside him Robert stood with feet planted in the dust, axe raised. Sergeants flanked with him levelled spears.

A tumult of voices echoed from the gate passage, but for a moment in the fire and the dense smoke it was impossible to see what was happening. Men were pushing forward through the broken gates, Adam realised with a clenching chill. He saw them as they clambered over the smouldering wreckage of the cart: hard determined-looking men with axes and spears. Their yells were triumphant, but edged with terror as they stormed through the funnel of the gate passage to fling themselves at the last cordon of defenders.

'Hold them back!' Robert cried, and the cordon of blades and shields tightened around on either side of him. Adam had his shield raised, his left shoulder forward and Benedict protecting his right.

Then the wave of attackers swarmed forward out of the smoke of the gate mouth, and Robert struck. Three long strides, and he whirled his shield up and swung a blow with his axe below the rim. Blood sprayed black in the darkness, and the first man went down, dead before he could even see his killer. Already a second attacker was lunging at Robert with a spear; the backswing of the axe drove the weapon aside, then Robert's shield punched into the man and knocked him down. The sergeant at his side despatched the man with a swift stab of his spear.

There were too many of them, Adam thought; the enemy were massing in the passage now, seeing the determined ring of steel that confronted them, but soon their numbers would be overwhelming.

One of their serjeants yelled a command, and with a roar they surged forward again, out of the shelter of the passage with spears levelled and axes raised. Blades rasped and clashed in the darkness. Adam saw one of Robert's sergeants hacked down. Swiftly he leaped to cover the man, swinging up his shield to block the next blow. An axe blade struck the shield, and he felt the shock of it through his whole torso. Benedict was yelling in his ear. The squire jabbed his sword over Adam's right shoulder, and the attacker reeled back and vanished into the darkness.

'Close up!' a voice shouted hoarsely. 'Close up or they'll break us!'

Before Adam could move to defend himself, another man had darted in from his left, lunging forward with a spear. Swinging his shield down with a grunt of effort, Adam managed to deflect the blow. But now his whole body was exposed, and he had no weapon.

The spearman was drawing back his arm for another strike at Adam when a figure darted between them; Matthew, with a long knife in his hand. With one swift movement, the boy darted inside the spearman's thrust and slammed the knife into his chest, just below the throat. The man went down at once, the knife still jutting from the wound.

'Thank you,' Adam gasped, the breath gone from his body. But Matthew appeared oblivious. The spearman lay dead at his feet, but his face was blank of any expression as he fell back behind the cordon of defenders once more.

Another rush of men came from the gateway, and Adam moved up to close the gap in the line with his shield. The attackers came on more cautiously now, picking their way over the bodies of their fallen comrades.

'Drive them back!' Robert commanded. 'Don't give a foot of ground!'

Advancing to the gate's mouth he launched himself against the attacking horde, the blade of his axe weaving in the glow of the flames. A man cut at him with a sword and Robert feinted, backstepping, before swinging the axe in a horizontal arc. The blade bit, and another body fell. Adam moved up to protect Robert's left, but his friend needed no help. Invulnerable in his full mail, he advanced steadily and left bodies in his wake. The attackers were retreating into the gate passage again now, abandoning their wounded and slain as they fell back before Robert's killing fury. Archers and crossbowmen had come down off the walls and were shooting over the heads of the defenders, directly into the mass of enemy troops packed in the gateway. Few of them had shields, and at a range of only a few paces every arrow and bolt found its mark.

Then, just as the men in the passage pressed tighter and their sergeants began ordering them forward once more, there came a sudden hissing and spitting from above them. Boiling water gushed down through the vents in the passage vault, falling in a scalding torrent upon the men trapped below. Adam was grateful that he could see little of it. The screams alone chilled his blood.

A few men staggered forth from the passage, shrieking and terrified, only to be cut down by the merciless defenders. Steam wreathed from the gate passage, bringing the stink of burned flesh and charred timber. The horns were blowing in the outer bailey, the enemy commanders urging their men forward. But the survivors of the attack were retreating in panic now, scrambling back over the wreckage of the gate and across the burned ruin of the drawbridge. Up on the gatehouse the defenders jeered and yelled abuse as they saw their foes scattering into the darkness. Robert just stood where he had fought, wiping the blood from the blade of his axe. His face was grim with fury.

'What a waste,' he snarled. 'What a damned waste of lives.'

*

In the candlelit chapel, Adam knelt beside the body of William Tonge. The serjeant was still alive, barely conscious, propped on his side on a straw palette. One side of his body and face was horribly burned, the flesh blackened and splitting to raw red flesh. His remaining eye glared out from swollen lids, and he breathed slow pained sobs through clenched teeth.

'Will he live?' Adam asked quietly as he straightened up. It was uncomfortable even looking at such injuries. Too much to imagine the pain the man must feel.

The chaplain sucked a breath. He was sober now, but still stank of sour sweat. 'Hard to say,' he told Adam. 'If God is merciful . . . But he won't use a crossbow again. There's nothing I can do for him now, and little enough for these others but pray. And dig their graves, come the morrow.'

Adam stared into the deep shadows of the little chapel, and saw figures laid out on palettes all across the floor and around the altar. The dying and the dead. The air stank of blood, filth and burned flesh. Only a dozen men had been slain in the attacks on the walls that afternoon, and six more in the fighting around the gateway. But as many again were seriously wounded and at least nine had fled over the walls and deserted. Now Robert had fewer than fifty able soldiers remaining to defend the castle against an assault that seemed certain to come in the hours around dawn.

At the chapel door Adam paused, turning to cross himself and dip his head towards the altar. Easy to forget this was a holy place, and not merely a charnel house. He took a flask of water from Benedict, who waited in the porch, and splashed his face, then swigged the warm liquid down.

A figure formed from the darkness of the bailey; Giles, Robert's squire.

'My master wants to speak with you, sir,' he said, and gestured towards the gateway of the innermost ward, where the keep rose in a block of shadow against the night sky. Adam signalled for Benedict to come with him, and then followed Giles. As he crossed the open space of the bailey he looked towards the northern wall and the gatehouse. No fires burned now, but he could make out the shapes of men on the rampart walks and the gate towers. Robert had ordered the gate itself blocked with timbers and rubble, but it was a desperate expedient. How much longer could they hold out now? Could they still hope to repel the morning's assault, with so few men? Slowing his steps a moment, Adam muttered a prayer. *Good Lord protect us in the hours of darkness, and in the dawn* . . . Then he hurried on after Giles.

Robert was waiting in the great chamber of the keep, standing with his fists braced on the table before him and the same grim look on his face that Adam had seen earlier. Belia and her maid were with him, and Adam was surprised to see that Wilecok and his wife had joined them, and a couple of the serjeants of Robert's retinue. The chamber was hot, lit by clustered candles on tall sconces, and Adam could feel the tension that charged the air as he entered.

Matthew was sitting in the corner behind Belia. Hunched on a stool in the shadows, he appeared almost a child again, with no trace of the cold-eyed killer he had so recently become. Belia stood before him almost protectively.

'We will not stand another day of this,' Robert declared, before Adam had crossed the room. 'Our numbers are low, too many have deserted, and those that remain are losing heart.'

Adam glanced at Belia, and saw the colour rise to her face.
Wilecok could not meet his eye. 'So,' he said, hesitant. 'So . . .
we must fight our way out of here.'

'And abandon our wounded to be butchered by the enemy?'
Robert asked, lifting his gaze for the first time. Adam saw the
grim intensity in his eyes, lit by the candles. But he knew what
Robert really wanted to say; once again he looked at Belia. She
would not fare well if they had to make a fighting escape. Nor
would the child she carried in her womb.

'I think not,' Robert said, straightening up and addressing
everyone in the room. 'In fact, I think there is only one option
remaining. Tomorrow at dawn I shall send an offer of surrender
to Hamo L'Estrange.'

'No!' Adam cried, unable to bite back the word.

'I shall not offer to surrender the castle *to him*,' Robert went
on, ignoring Adam, 'but only to Lord Edward, in person. I shall
demand that everyone in the garrison be permitted to leave hon-
ourably, with our arms and our wounded, and make our peace
with Edward. We will not be treated as prisoners, or as captives,
and there will be no ransoms . . .'

'Would L'Estrange agree to that?' Belia asked.

Robert nodded. 'I believe he will. He knows he will lose many
more men taking the castle, and this way he gets to present it to
Edward as a gift.'

'And then . . . what?' Adam managed to say. He could feel his
face burning, his throat growing tight. Still the words pressed
into his mouth. 'You said you would fight to defend this place,
fight to the last—'

'I said I would fight to defend *what is mine*!' Robert said, raising his voice to a shout. He turned for the first time to look at
Belia. 'I will not allow myself to be taken as a prisoner or held
for a ransom that I cannot afford. I will not allow those I love
and support to be cast out as homeless beggars . . .' His voice
choked off.

'Then you'll give your oath to Lord Edward?' Adam asked quietly, into the silence.

Robert nodded briskly, tightening his jaw. 'If that's what is required of me. An oath not to take arms against him. Or . . . or to bear arms in his cause, if he so demands.'

'Against Lord Simon? You'd fight *against* Simon de Montfort?' Adam heard his own voice as he asked the questions, and it seemed to come from far away.

'I ask you now, Adam de Norton,' Robert said, with cold gravity. 'Will you do as I do?'

Adam drew a slow breath. He could sense the pressure gathering, the gazes of everyone in the room locked upon him. 'I cannot,' he said, his mouth dry.

'I do not want to meet you on the battlefield, you know that.'

'Such things,' Adam said, feeling the itch in his right hand, 'are determined by God, not by men.'

Robert nodded once more, and his face appeared suddenly weary and greatly aged. 'So be it then,' he said. He made the slightest gesture with his hand.

Adam snatched for his sword hilt, turning towards the door. Too late. One of the serjeants behind him grabbed him around the waist, while Giles de Wortham snatched at his arm. The wound in his shoulder screamed as Adam drove his elbow back into the serjeant's face, but he felt the man's nose break. Then two other men rushed from the doorway and grappled him, and he was pinned between them as Giles de Wortham unfastened his sword belt and slipped it from his waist.

To his left, Adam saw Benedict shrinking back against the wall, Wilecok's dagger at his throat. The fight died from him, and only the agony remained. From the far side of the room, Belia watched with her hands pressed to her face. Matthew sat beside her, impassive.

'I'm sorry it turned out this way,' Robert said. 'But from this moment on, Adam de Norton, you must consider yourself my prisoner.'

Chapter 12

For hours he lay awake in darkness. At first his mind churned sickeningly between fury and despair, but soon enough shame consumed him utterly. Benedict must have felt the same; for a long time, Adam listened to the young squire sniffing back tears as he lay on his straw mattress, and was glad when the sounds shifted to the slow rasp of exhausted sleep.

Their prison was an old storage shed or tack room, adjacent to the stables and backing onto the castle wall. The straw they lay upon was the only furnishing, and once the guards who had led them from the keep closed the heavy wooden door and dropped the bar in place, there was no light at all. After some time – hours, Adam guessed – a faint wash of moonlight began creeping in through a ventilation slot above the door, and as his eyes adjusted he could make out the shape of the room, and Benedict's sleeping form in the opposite corner. As his thoughts stilled, he cast about desperately for any possibility of escape. Three walls were heavy timber, with the rough masonry of the castle wall forming the fourth. Beams and slats formed the sloping ceiling, and packed dirt the floor. The vent above the doorway would be too narrow to wriggle through, even if he could dislodge the bars that closed it. Adam tried to imagine himself scratching a hole between the rough stones of the outer wall, or scrabbling a tunnel in the floor.

Hopeless, he knew. It would take days, and he had no weapon or tool to dig or to scrape. The guards had taken his waistbelt and purse, and his eating knife too.

With Benedict's help he had shrugged himself out of his mail hauberk and chausses at least; without his belt to take the weight at his hips the armour had pressed upon his shoulders, and the wound in his arm had burned. Now the mail lay in a heap of steel links beside him, with his stained linen aketon laid beside it. Otherwise he had nothing. The room was hot and close, and the straw of the mattress made his back itch, and Adam concentrated his mind upon the discomfort and tried to block out all other thoughts.

Pointless to ask why Robert had betrayed him. Pointless to wonder how lightly his old friend had taken that decision, and the decision to throw aside his duty as constable of the castle. Perhaps, in Robert's position, he would have done the same. And yet he asked himself those questions again and again, drawn back helplessly to his torment. Robert had told him that he did not want them to meet on the battlefield – he did not want to find himself fighting against Adam, perhaps having to kill him. But that was the scene that Adam's anger and despair conjured for him now. He pictured himself cutting Robert down, hacking his blade into his friend's flesh, stabbing him and watching the blood flow from his wounds. Then his mind rebelled and pulled him back with a sickening lurch. He had known Robert for so many years, loved him like a brother, respected him like a father. He knew that he had no choice in his decision. So why did Adam conjure scenes of his death so avidly?

Somewhere in the depths of the night, closing his eyes against the faint moonlight, he dropped into a shallow turbulent sleep. He dreamed he was at Basing, and William de Saint John had imprisoned him in a tower to prevent him marrying Isabel. But he could hear her, somewhere down below in the yard. Calling up to his window. Calling his name . . .

'Adam! Adam, are you awake?'

Tensing, drawing a sharp breath, he lay with his eyes open trying to discern the shapes in the darkness. Benedict had not risen.
The voice came from outside the door, and a spill of candlelight
showed through the barred vent above it. Sitting up, dazed and
unsteady, he rolled to his knees and crawled to the door.

'I'm here,' he said, pressing himself against the rough oak boards.

A scrape as the locking bar was lifted, then a heavy tap as it
was set aside. The hinges creaked, loud as trumpets in the silence
of deep night, and then the candle's glow filled the room.

Belia stood in the covered passageway outside. Matthew was
beside her holding the candle. The boy had a bag slung over
his shoulder, and Belia carried Adam's belted sword. For a few
moments Adam just knelt, staring at them. He heard Benedict
stirring behind him as he dragged himself to his feet. The wound
in his arm was flaring and pulsing, but the sense of awakening
possibility drowned out the pain.

'We must move quickly,' Belia said in a low voice. 'It's still an
hour until dawn.'

'Why?' Adam managed to ask. 'Why are you doing this?'

'Robert fears you'll rejoin de Montfort if he lets you go free,'
Belia said quickly. 'He fears you'll meet as enemies in battle . . .
and what might happen when you do.'

'You don't fear that?' Adam asked.

'I prefer to trust in your judgement,' she said, with a thin
smile. 'You told me yesterday of your debt to Robert. Now that
debt is discharged, nothing is stopping you from returning to
your home, and your betrothed. You'll do that, yes?'

It was not entirely a question, Adam knew. But he nodded anyway.

'I do not make you promise, you notice,' Belia said. She spread
her fingers and pressed her palm to his chest, and for three
heartbeats they stood motionless. 'I'm just trying to save you
both from actions you may regret,' she said, breathing the words.
'May God forgive me. And may Robert forgive me too.'

Matthew had already moved along the passageway, taking the candle with him, and darkness was eclipsing them once more. Benedict was already on his feet; he reached for the bundled mail and aketon, but Adam halted him with a gesture; it grieved him to abandon it, but whatever the coming hours might hold, stealth and silence would be of more worth than heavy armour. But as he belted his sword around his waist, he felt instantly restored to life and purpose.

Along the passageway, following the wavering star of Matthew's candle, they emerged into the night air close to the postern gate and tower. The black shadow of the wall above them blocked the faint glow from the sky, and for several steps they groped along blindly until Matthew uncovered his light once more.

'There are no sentries on the wall above us, or in the tower,' Belia said, holding Adam's shoulder as she whispered into his ear. 'There's a rope there – two more men deserted before midnight, and they left it tied to the merlon.'

'The postern gate would be easier,' Adam said, sudden fear gripping him.

Belia shook her head quickly. 'It's heavily barred and the arch is sealed with rubble,' she said. 'The rope is the only way out of here now. Quickly, up the steps and over the wall, before daylight comes.'

Directly above him, Adam was shocked to see that the night sky was already gathering the first faintness of dawn, all but the brightest stars snuffed out.

'Thank you,' he said, taking Belia by the arm. 'From my heart.'

'Remember,' she told him. 'No promises. But listen to the voice of reason, and let it be your guide.' And she embraced him quickly, kissing him. 'Let us hope we can meet again in better times.'

When Adam turned to the low archway that led to the tower stairs, he saw that Matthew had passed the bag he was carrying to Benedict. He was expecting the boy to follow him, but instead he hung back.

'Mosse stays with me,' Belia said from the darkness.

It took Adam a moment to remember the boy's real name. Yes, he thought, *of course*. It was better this way. Belia knew who the boy had been, and had seen what he was becoming. She was determined to save him if she could. A last nod of gratitude, and he ducked his head through the arch and followed Benedict up the narrow spiral stairway to the battlements.

The moon was gone, but even the last stars shone unnervingly bright as Adam emerged from the stairs and stepped out onto the rampart walk. Below him to his right was the darkened gulf of the castle's inner yard; he could just make out the pale smudge of Belia's headcloth. The western sky, behind the keep and the opposite wall of the castle, glowed with the approaching dawn. To Adam's left, beyond the rampart, the ground dropped away steeply into a valley consumed by shadow as still and deep as midnight. The rope was clear to see, coiled on the walkway with one end tied around a merlon, just as Belia had reported.

Hardly daring to think about what he was doing, Adam peered over the parapet at the ground below, then tossed the coil of rope over the side. A moment to secure it around the stone of the merlon, then he swung himself up into the gap in the crenellations.

'Let me go first,' Benedict whispered. 'Your arm—'

'I'll be fine,' Adam replied tersely. He did not want to think about his wound, which was already smarting more painfully. How much weight could he put on it, before the stitches tore open? The night air was warm, the slight breeze gentle, but Adam was sweating cold and sour. He wished he had waited to get clear of the walls before fastening his sword belt, but there was no time to alter that now.

Metal scabbard fittings scraped as he edged clumsily over the parapet, achingly loud in the stillness. The drop below him seemed immense, although he knew it could only be about twenty feet to the rough slope at the base of the wall. He grasped the rope in his good hand, looping it around his forearm, then edged himself backward until he hung suspended with his feet braced against the outside of the wall. Breath tight, teeth clenched against trapped breath, Adam seized the rope with his right hand as well and let it take his weight.

Almost at once his feet slipped from beneath him, and he swung heavily against the stones of the wall. Choking a cry in his throat, he felt the pain of his wounded arm ripping through the right side of his body. Desperate, Adam clung to the rope, muscles bunched as he tried to hold himself with one arm, suspended over the gulf of emptiness. Benedict was above him, leaning out from the parapet, but there was nothing the squire could do for him now. The rope burned Adam's palm as he eased himself downwards, kicking at the wall to try and gain some foothold upon it. The toe of his boot caught and he managed to take some weight from his arms, then he was easing himself down again, grunting with the effort. His palms were filled with liquid fire, but he held his grip as he descended in juddering drops, catching himself each time.

At last he could cling on no more. Kicking himself away from the wall he released his grip on the rope and let himself fall. The ground raced up beneath him and he fell sideways, collapsing into the dirt and the dry thorny scrub. A long breath, then Adam grinned. He was down; he had only dropped the last few feet, and he was uninjured.

Quickly, as silently as he could, he scrambled back upright and tugged on the dangling rope. He saw Benedict above him, already climbing out over the parapet with the bag slung over his shoulder. From here, the sky appeared already pale, the shape of the climbing man perilously exposed.

Adam moved away from the wall with crablike steps, feeling his way down the slope a short way. There was a path somewhere here, leading from the postern gate, but in the greyish half-light it would be near impossible to find. Adam lifted his gaze, and with a shock like a punch to the chest he realised that he could clearly make out the shapes of an encampment in the valley below him, the low humps of tents, the forms of horses, even of men. Distantly a gleam of firelight flared, and then was gone.

A sharp yell from behind him, then a scrape and a heavy thud. Adam turned, crouching instinctively, and saw the rope swinging against the wall. Benedict was sprawled on the slope below it, one leg twisted beneath him. He had let himself drop too soon, and fallen badly.

'Can you stand?' Adam asked in a rasping whisper as he joined the squire.

Benedict nodded quickly, but then gasped in pain as he tried to move, baring his teeth. 'My ankle,' he said.

Adam sat back on the ground. In less than an hour the sun would rise behind the castle wall, and they would be exposed to the eyes of the sentries in the encampment in the valley. He could take Benedict with him, he thought; perhaps the two of them could struggle through the lines of the besiegers unseen?

It would not work. And from the look of woe on Benedict's face it was clear that he too was aware of the impossibility. 'I think it's only sprained,' he said, scrabbling to sit upright. But the sweat was standing out on his forehead in drops, visible even in the twilight.

'Here, give me what you're carrying,' Adam said, easing the strap of the bag from Benedict's shoulder. 'There's water here,' he said, feeling inside the bag and pulling out a flask. He drew out the bung and gave it to Benedict, who drank gladly. 'Keep it with you,' he said.

'You can't leave me . . .' the squire began, clasping at Adam's tunic.

'The men on the walls should see you when the sun comes up,' Adam told him. 'Tell them who you are and call for Robert. They'll get you back inside the castle, and you'll be well enough looked after. Once I'm gone, Robert will have no reason to treat you as a prisoner.'

Benedict said nothing for a moment, still clasping the water flask. 'I'm sorry,' he said, his voice breaking.

'Don't be,' Adam told him.

Then he turned and began picking his way down the slope into the deep shade of the valley.

*

Hamo L'Estrange's troops may have been resolute enough at assaulting the walls, but they were far less capable when it came to guarding their own perimeter. There were camps scattered up and down the slopes to the west of the castle, but few had sentries posted or patrols moving between them. Dropping slowly down the hillside through the rustling thickets of scrub bushes, Adam could easily see the open areas between the camps, and made his way towards them. Only once did he halt and crouch in shelter, as two men strolled from the darkness along a pathway, spears across their shoulders. Neither looked in his direction, and after a few moments they were gone and he moved on once more. The laxity of the besiegers was almost maddening; a determined sally from the postern gate, Adam thought, could have scattered them like chaff. But it would take a truly daring man to risk such a thing.

Only now he was clear of the castle walls did Adam begin to consider what he was doing. His liberation had been so swift, so unexpected, that he had not paused to consider what he would do after his escape, or where he would go. He had nothing with him but his sword, and the sack that Belia had given him. His armour, shield and helmet, his horses and saddles and all his other possessions were lost to him now. Several times as he made his halting progress through the darkness he glanced back at the castle, silhouetted now against the lit western sky, and thought of his destrier Fauviel, still in the stables of the inner ward. How much he would give for a good mount now . . . With an ironic smile he remembered Lord Edward offering to buy the horse from him for one hundred silver marks. Only a few days had passed since then, but so much had changed in his fortunes it was almost dizzying to contemplate.

By the time the first sun was picking out the ramparts of the castle behind him, Adam had crept past the camps of the besiegers. He kept moving westwards, up the slope from the valley and across rough ground, hoping he would not meet any of L'Estrange's foraging parties. The sky was bright blue and filled with birds, but the land still slumbered in twilit darkness. Only when he had covered a mile or more from the camps did he pause, crouching in the lee of a hawthorn hedge to gaze back at the castle. How long would Robert wait before he sent out his offer of surrender? Would he already have discovered Adam's escape? And when he did so, Adam wondered with a frown, would Robert be furious, or relieved?

Weariness was stealing through him now. He had slept only briefly during the night, and he felt his mind becoming glazed and his limbs aching. The wound in his upper arm was a steady itching throb, but the wound seemed to have remained closed; the bandages were still tight and no fresh bloodstains showed through the wool of his sleeve. Still, he was not safe here. Willing himself to activity, to alertness, Adam pushed himself to his feet and turned his back on the castle, setting off westwards once more.

He crossed the hilltop, pushing through tangled bushes and over strip fields and open meadowland. On the far side the ground dropped once more, and he found himself beside a stream. Falling to his knees, Adam cupped water in his hands and splashed his face, then drank. It was cold, and instantly refreshing. When he raised his head once more a heron stood in the reed-grown shallows on the far bank, its spiked beak twitching as it returned his stare.

Back on his feet, he stumbled further along the marshy water-side, following its course downstream. Sooner or later, he knew, it must reach the Severn, and from there he would follow the river south towards Worcester. Morning sunlight angled down between the trees, but the streambed was still in shadow, and Adam's feet were sinking into the wet ground. His scabbarded sword kept catching at his legs, and he took off his sword belt and slung it over his shoulder, carrying the weapon across his back. He pushed himself onward for another mile, his mind fogged with weariness, and finally reached a pool of open water fringed by willows and alder, and a dry grassy sward at the bank where he could throw himself down and rest.

He was not aware of sleeping, but when he opened his eyes again the sun was high and beaming through the trees, and he knew that several hours must have passed. Raising his head from the grass he saw a kingfisher dive and swoop across the surface of the water, flashing brilliantly through the sunbeams. A moment of alarm tensed his body and he sat upright, gazing around the margins of the placid pool, the trees still threaded with morning mist, but there was nobody in sight. Adam was alone, miles from Bridgnorth, and he was safe.

The banks of the pool were muddy, but a short distance away he found a rill of clear water flowing over stones. He washed his face and drank deeply, then returned to the grass where he had been sleeping and opened the bag that Belia had given him. As he had hoped, he found bread and cheese, wrapped tightly in clean linen. His eating knife too, and his belt pouch containing flint and steel, a purse weighty with silver pennies, and his string of pater-noster beads, Isabel's gift. At the bottom of the bag, wrapped in rags, were his gilded spurs. Grinning, Adam turned his face to the glory of the morning and gave thanks for the mercy of God, and for the charity of friends.

Once he had eaten and washed once more, he gathered his possessions and set off, following the bank of the stream that flowed from the pool. Trees grew close along the waterside, and the ground between them grew marshy once more. Adam found himself having to climb further from the bank as he traced the course of the stream. He was still intending to find the Severn and follow it south, but after an hour of picking his way through the trees the twists and turns of valley had confused his sense of direction. Instead, he hiked up the slope, through the thorny bushes and the ferns until he reached the summit of a hill and could make out the position of the sun clearly enough to use it as a guide. Keeping it to his left, he turned southward and set off across country.

This was the Wyre Chase, the hunting reserve of Roger Mortimer that he and his men had skirted on the journey to Bridgnorth, and Adam kept a keen watch in all directions as he walked. He found a path which led him in the right direction, a narrow dirt track snaking through sunshot glades and patches of grassland grown wild. He moved southward, keeping clear of the few small abandoned-looking houses he passed along the way. At one point a pair of mounted men appeared in the distance, and Adam stepped back off the path and remained concealed in the trees until they had passed.

He still had no clear idea of what he would do once he reached the districts he recognised once more. The thought of returning to Hereford, of having to report to Lord Simon the surrender of Bridgnorth and Robert's treachery, was not appealing. But to do as Belia had asked and simply return home after losing everything and abandoning his oath and his honour, seemed worse. He imagined himself appearing at Basing and presenting himself to William de St John in his current guise, a wanderer without horse or shield or armour, his sword slung over his shoulder and his spurs hooked to his belt. The disgrace of that would be unbearable. If he thought too closely about his options, he felt the shame and despair welling up in his heart, threatening to overwhelm him. The future branched ahead of him, like the branching paths in the wood through which he walked, and every path led to disgrace. So he kept walking, and tried to block such thoughts from his mind.

By late afternoon the path he was following had led him almost to the southern margin of the Wyre, and he walked through cultivated lands of strip fields and open pastures. Descending from the ridge he entered a wooded valley, oaks and beech growing densely along the banks of a brook, and he paused once more to rest and eat what remained of his bread and cheese. The brook flowed in pools and rills through the shadows beneath the trees, and as he sat on the bank Adam saw plump fish moving in the limpid depths, dark against the pale stony bed. Weariness stole over him once more; he was unaccustomed to covering long distances on foot, and the wound in his arm was sapping his strength. Just as he lay back against the roots of a tree, he heard the slow beat of a horse's hooves, and a moment later saw the animal and its rider appear between the trees a little way upstream.

Lying motionless, Adam watched as the man dismounted and tethered his horse to a branch. He could make out no livery, no painted shield or coloured surcoat, but the man was wearing a gambeson and appeared to be a serjeant or squire. As Adam watched, unseen, the man shed the padded garment, stripped off his shoes, his hose and tunic, and waded into one of the larger pools wearing only his braies and linen coif.

Eyes narrowed, Adam slid himself upright. The horseman was thigh-deep in the pool now, stooped and peering into the water with his hands stirring just below the surface, obviously waiting for one of the plump fish to swim closer so that he could seize it. His tethered horse stood placidly by the bank, stretching its neck to lap from the brook. The man had not even troubled to remove the saddle or bridle from his mount, and in the filtered sunlight small insects whirled around the animal's hot hide. Bending, Adam fastened the spurs to his ankles and tightened the buckles. Then, moving slowly and quietly, lifting his feet through the undergrowth, he edged through the trees towards the horse.

He had almost reached the tree where the animal was tethered when the man in the pool straightened, flicked the water from his hands and glanced in his direction. For a moment the man was too startled to make a sound; by the time he drew breath to shout, Adam had already slipped the tether from the branch and set his foot in the stirrup.

The man yelled, inarticulate, and surged towards the bank. He tripped at once on the stony bed and subsided face-first into the pool. 'Thief!' he gasped, hauling himself up again. 'Stop him! He's got my——' Again he fell, and his words were drowned in the noise of the splashing water.

Adam swung into the saddle, the horse startled and frisking beneath him. Drawing the reins tight he pulled the animal's head around, bringing it under control as he jabbed with the spurs. By the time the other man had waded from the pool, crashing and blustering through the shallows, Adam was riding fast back up the path between the trees, heading for higher ground.

But the rider had not been alone. As Adam broke from the trees and gained the open pasture, he saw two other horsemen further along the slope to his right. Already alerted by their friend down in the brook, they were spurring their horses in pursuit. One had a spear, and the other a sword at his side, and they came after Adam at a brisk uphill canter.

Head down, stooping over the animal's mane, Adam spurred his horse to greater speed. The land ahead was unknown to him, but it appeared rough and tangled with patches of woodland and bushes. He braced himself in the saddle as the horse rode at an overgrown ditch, then swayed upright as the animal vaulted across and came down on the far side. Another tug at the reins, and the horse turned neatly into the deep shelter of curving hawthorns, a tunnel or a sunken lane. Bright flashes of light overhead, plunging gloom all around, then Adam was out into daylight once more. He could hear the two pursuing riders behind him somewhere, shouting to each other, and he let out a cry of laughter as he realised they had lost the chase.

Over an open slope of tussock grass, sheep bounding away in fright, Adam rode on down into another patch of woodland. Only when he reached the shelter of the trees did he slow his pace, drawing the sweating horse to a walk. For a few long moments he hoped he had thrown off his pursuers altogether. Then he heard their distant cries, and caught the shape of a horse and rider between the trees to his left. Once more he kicked with the spurs, and the stolen horse bolted forward.

Through the last fringe of trees, Adam rode out from the woodland's dappled shadow into a wide grassy area with a dirt track running across it. He caught a gust of woodsmoke, and to his right he saw figures gathered around a fire. Tethered horses too, and men putting up tents. He pulled at the reins, trying to turn his horse and ride back the way he had come before he was seen, but the animal jinked and stumbled, and already it was too late.

Kicking with the spurs, he drove the horse forward instead. But at once he realised his error; the group he had seen around the campfire was only the edge of a much larger encampment which spread away along the open ground fringing the track. In the middle distance were banners raised above pavilions, horse lines and carts, and the smoke of many fires. And he was riding right into the heart of it.

'Take him, he's a spy!' somebody yelled. Men swarmed around Adam's horse, rushing from all sides with hands outstretched to seize at the bridle and reins, others brandishing spears or spanning crossbows. Panicking, the horse tried to rear, but the men clung on tight and got its head down. Adam had reached for the hilt of his sword, still slung clumsily over his shoulder, but one man grabbed his arm and another shoved his foot from the stirrup. A spearhead jabbed at his back, and then Adam was toppling from the saddle into the arms of his captors.

He tried to fight them, but he was beaten to his knees, his arms wrenched down behind his back and tied at the wrists. Dragged between them, he managed to get his feet under him and stumbled along, head down. One of his captors managed to unfasten his belt and take his sword, pouch and knife. A few struck at him with their fists or the shafts of their spears, but Adam barely felt it.

'He stole one of our horses!' another man was calling from somewhere behind him.

Abruptly Adam was dragged to a halt, men pressing in on all sides. He heard the snarl of their voices, the excited frenzy. A fist gripped his hair and pulled his head up, and as he blinked the sweat from his eyes he saw the face of the man before him. His heart clenched in his chest.

'What do we do with him?' one of the other men said.

Fulk Ticeburn grinned through his beard. 'He's a spy, or a horse thief,' he said. 'Either way – *hang him!*'

Chapter 13

His captors shoved Adam along between them, his wrists bound and arms pinned, a knife jabbing him between the shoulder blades with every step. Fulk Ticeburn walked on one side of him, and his brother Warin on the other, and the rest of the mob thronged around them.

'Kept my pledge, didn't I,' Fulk was saying, whispering, his face so close that Adam could feel the man's beard prickling his ear. 'Kept my oath, yes – didn't come near your place, did I? Didn't raise a hand against you. Now, though – now *you've come to me*! And that makes things different. Now you won't escape me with any clever ruses.'

'You're going to die,' his brother Warin was saying, over and over, his eyes shining with passionate hatred. 'You're going to *die!*'

On the far side of the open ground was a grassy knoll, crowned with an isolated stand of trees, and the mob of soldiers were bearing him towards it. Seemingly they were all content to follow the Ticeburns' lead; Fulk appeared to have gained a bullying mastery over them. One of the trees had a low horizontal branch jutting from the trunk, and two men were slinging a hempen rope over it. Adam saw them knotting the dangling end of the rope into a noose, and only then did the horror burst through him. His capture had stunned him, but now the full awareness of what was about to happen crashed over him.

'I'm not a spy!' he managed to shout. 'I'm a knight . . . I'm a messenger, from . . . from Roger de Mohaut and Hamo L'Estrange!'

Fulk Ticeburn's fist smashed into his jaw, and Adam tasted blood filling his mouth. He gasped and spat, sucked air, tried to shout again. But Warin Ticeburn seized his chin and stuffed a filthy rag into his mouth, choking off his cries.

Now they were herding up the side of the knoll towards the tree and the dangling noose, a dozen or more of them gripping him between them. They were common soldiers, militia spearmen and archers, a few crossbowmen and serjeants among them. But Adam could see nobody leading them, nobody directing what was happening. In vain he stared into the crowd of coarse reddened faces and vicious grins for anyone he recognised, anyone to whom he might ask for quarter or mercy. But Fulk Ticeburn and his brother seemed to have taken charge of them all.

Beneath the tree they held him upright, hands grappling him on all sides. Many of them were laughing now, hooting and jeering at the prospect of his death. Adam pressed his chin down, trying to spit out the wad of rag, but Warin grabbed a fistful of his hair and pulled his head up again. The rough noose slipped over his neck and pulled up tight against his throat.

'Look at him, wriggling like a fish on a line!' one of the men laughed.

'He'll be jerking all the harder when we stretch him!' another cried.

Kicking and twisting, Adam tried to free himself from the grip of his captors. But the rope was already pulling taut and he could feel the rasp of the noose at his neck. Another moment and he would be lifted off his feet, hoisted above the heads of the mob to die writhing in agony. Desperately he tried to shape the words of a prayer, something pious at the moment of death, but red rage and blind terror filled his mind and the only words he could summon were curses.

'This is your payment for the death of Eudo,' Fulk Ticeburn hissed in his ear, one hand gripping the rope above Adam's head. 'For my brother's death, and for robbing us of our lands. To the Devil with you, de Norton!'

He stepped back, with a last tug on the rope. 'Haul him!' he cried.

Adam inhaled sharply and tightened the muscles in his neck as the noose drew taut and he was pulled up onto his toes. For three heartbeats he danced like that, feeling his every muscle stretched and screaming.

His neck burned, and as his face swelled he bit down hard on the wadded rag. This could not be his end. One toe was still on the ground but the rope was dragging him upwards. This could not be his end, he told himself, even as he felt death enfolding him.

Then another voice was shouting, a gruff yell through the baying of the mob. Adam's eyes were tight shut, the blood beating in his temples. Abruptly the rope that suspended him went slack and he collapsed onto the springy turf and spat the rag from his mouth. One heaving breath, and he rolled to his knees. He expected at any moment the noose to haul him up again. Men were jostling around him, the voice he had heard before still rising above the clamour. He knew the voice but could not place it.

'Look at his ankles, messires! See those gilded spurs? He's a knight sure enough – so why would he want to steal one of your wormy old nags, eh?'

'A spy then!' Ticeburn snarled. 'He's our prisoner – we took him, we dispose of him!'

'A spy, you say?' the other man said, drawing nearer now as the crowd parted. 'Yet he claims to be a messenger . . . Either way, won't Lord Edward and Lord Gilbert want to know who sent him? Won't they be wrathful that you've done him to death,

a belted knight of unknown origin, without so much as questioning him first?'

Throat burning, pain beating in his neck, Adam managed to
raise his head. The Ticeburns still flanked him closely, but the
newcomer was drawing the mob onto his side. They shrank away
from the tree and the noose now, as if they wanted nothing more
to do with it.

Adam squinted, then coughed a laugh. He recognised the
newcomer's voice now; he had heard it first on the river near
Rochester, on the night they attacked the castle, and again on the
road to Hereford only a month before. His saviour wore a grimy
aketon, and greasy black hair marked with a white streak spilled
from his linen coif. Beneath it, his creased face was still mottled
with dark lines and patches, the remains of the lettering that he
had not managed entirely to scrub from his skin.

'Besides,' Le Brock said as he looked down at Adam, 'I believe
I know this one.'

*

Lord Edward's army had pitched their tents on the crest of a rise,
looking east over the valley of the Severn. They had marched
from Ludlow the day before yesterday, so Le Brock told Adam,
and further contingents had joined them along their route. Now,
Adam estimated as he passed through the encampment, they
must number in their thousands. Many were rough-looking militia infantry of the sort that had captured him earlier, but there
were crossbowmen and men at arms among them, and many of
the tents flew the banners and pennons of knightly retinues.

'I've freed you of your bonds, but I'm trusting you to stay quiet
and douce-like,' Le Brock said from the corner of his mouth as
they walked. 'Your friends back there would no doubt be joyous
to catch you again and kill you quick, if you give them a chance.
Let's call it a matter of *parole* then, shall we?'

'I won't run,' Adam told him, and probed with his tongue at the wound in his mouth where Fulk had struck him. 'I give you my word.' *Not yet, at any rate.*

'Good fellow! What a perfect knight you are, if I may say so. And you must think me very *gentil* too, rescuing you like that. Especially as you once tried to get me hanged as a thief, as I recall.'

'A good thing you have such divine protection.'

Le Brock whipped a glance at Adam, his habitual leering smile shifting to a sour grimace. 'Oh yes,' he said, mirthless. 'Oh yes, don't you doubt it, boy. God and all his saints watch over me, and the saving power of the Cross that is our only redemption!'

They arrived at the perimeter of Lord Edward's own encampment, where mailed soldiers stood in a cordon. Adam was still a prisoner, even if he was no longer bound; Le Brock had retrieved his sword and belt, and a groom carried his possessions. Still he felt the hot choking rasp of the hemp at his throat, and his heart had not yet slowed its panicked beating.

Edward's tents were the largest and grandest of all, and the best sited. Over them stirred the red banner that Adam had first seen many years before, at the tournament town of Lagny: three prowling golden lions of England, with the blue bar of the eldest son and heir across the top. Outside the tent enclosure one of the sentries took his sword, while another went with Le Brock to report the capture. Adam sat on the dry grass, his head hanging, taking low slow breaths. He asked for water, and a servant rather grudgingly tossed him a flask. The liquid inside was warm and tasted of oily leather, and his throat still hurt when he swallowed, but he drank deeply.

'You,' a voice said from inside the enclosure. 'Come, now.'

In the cool and carpeted shade of the largest pavilion, Lord Edward was sitting over the remains of an early supper. On the table before him were cold meats and fine breads on polished trays, and silver cups of wine. The king's son glanced up with his lazy eye as Adam was escorted in. He looked smooth and relaxed, his face shaved clean of the light beard he had worn during his captivity. He smiled in recognition as Adam knelt before his couch.

'Ah,' he said. 'Now you have learned to approach me with due courtesy, I find.'

'By the arm of St James,' one of Edward's guests said, feigning amazement. 'We've seen this man only recently!'

It was Thomas de Clare, of course, the sharp featured younger brother of the Earl of Gloucester. And beside him sat his brother, Gilbert de Clare himself. Adam saw the resemblance between them clearly now. Both were slight of build and freckled, Gilbert's hair a fiercer red, their expressions alike in scornful amusement.

'We have indeed,' Edward replied. 'At Hereford, not a week ago. I was your prisoner then, Adam de Norton. But see – our positions are reversed!'

Adam hid his sour smile. A man like Lord Edward would never hold a position anywhere approaching his own, or even understand what it meant.

'But I wonder,' Edward said to his guests, 'how this Adam de Norton comes to be here now? And from the north, if our scouts are not mistaken . . . Up, man,' he ordered with a brusque gesture. 'Explain.'

Adam rose to his feet once more, trying to compose his expression and calm the maddened whirl of his thoughts. He had come up with a ruse while he was sitting outside. Less a ruse, perhaps, than a desperate gambit, but it was all he had.

'I've come from Bridgnorth, my lord,' he said.

'Oh!' Lord Edward replied, with a dry smirk at Gilbert de Clare.

'His old friend Robert de Dunstanville holds the castle,' Thomas de Clare explained.

'I have a message from Sir Robert,' Adam went on. He was trying not to touch his neck, which still smarted from the noose.

'He wishes . . . He wishes to surrender, but only to you, Lord Edward.'

'Ah!' Edward said. His expression remained closed and guarded. 'Strange. We had word only this morning that Hamo L'Estrange has Bridgnorth under siege.'

'Yes, the siege continues . . . But Sir Robert refuses to open the gates to L'Estrange. He sent me to find you, and to offer his terms to you directly.'

'A likely tale,' Thomas de Clare said with an easy smile, sitting forward on the facing couch. 'I'd say this fellow just slipped out of the castle to save his own skin, looking very much a vagabond.'

'Hmm,' Edward said, steepling his fingers and gazing at Adam across their peak.

'The traitor de Montfort has used this man to carry messages before,' Lord Gilbert said, circling his cup upon the linen table-cloth. 'Perhaps he carries a message from de Dunstanville now? Maybe he was on his way to Hereford, requesting reinforcements?'

'No, my lord, I carry only the message to Lord Edward,' Adam said quickly. 'Upon my oath.'

'Well, we shall find out soon enough, I suppose,' Edward said, and stood up abruptly. His height appeared exaggerated in the low tent, and Adam instinctively took a step back. 'We await word from Bridgnorth. If this offer of surrender is genuine then we shall hear of it. If not . . .' He turned his hand in the air, a strangely dismissive gesture that brought a cold chill to Adam's brow.

*

Between Lord Edward's tents and the wagons that carried his baggage, trestle tables had been set up near the cooking fire. A pair of serjeants escorted Adam to a table and stood over him while a servant slammed a cup of ale and trencher sopped with leek potage in front of him. Adam's throat was badly bruised, and he swallowed the food down with difficulty, trying to appear unconcerned while fear billowed inside him. If Robert had decided not to surrender the castle, or if Hamo L'Estrange had rejected the terms and stormed the place that very morning, or if no messenger came from Bridgnorth at all, then Adam's life was forfeit. Whenever he closed his eyes his saw the ugly noose dangling before him, and felt the bite of the rope at his neck.

From his vantage point he had a good view of all those who came and went from Edward's pavilion. Several were still dressed in mail, and a few carried helmets. The king's son was holding a council of war, it appeared. Roger de Leyburne went stalking past, with his friend de Clifford. William de Valence as well, the Earl of Pembroke; Adam had not seen the man before, but he overheard his guards talking about him. He and John de Warenne had joined Edward at Ludlow after marching with their troops all the way from the west of Wales. Roger Mortimer arrived last, accompanied by the largest band of retainers. He was a dark, aggressive-looking man in his early thirties, with a hard jaw and purposeful stride.

Only when all the magnates had entered the pavilion, leaving their household knights and squires thronging outside, did Adam fix his gaze beyond the cordon of guards. Fulk Ticeburn stood there with his brother Warin, both of them glaring back at him. Fulk pointed to his eye, and then at Adam, baring his teeth in a savage smile. His fingers went to his throat in a throttling gesture, then he mimed a rope tugged above his head.

Now his reeling confusion was beginning to ease, Adam knew that he should not have been surprised to see the Ticeburns here. Once he had driven them off his land, and the de Brayboefs had disowned them, they would have sought out any who might offer them work. Any who might stand against Simon de Montfort as well, and challenge his rule. If de Montfort were overthrown, they must have reasoned, then Adam too would be outlawed and their hold on the manor restored. Whether they gave their allegiance now to Gilbert de Clare, or John de Warenne, or one of the Marcher lords, was of no concern. They were here, that was all that Adam cared about. They were here, and they wanted him dead.

He looked away from the Ticeburns, determined to ignore their grimaces, and as he did so a knight in a red surcoat detached himself from the crowd of lesser men outside the pavilion and approached him.

'It really is you!' the knight said. 'I heard they'd caught a spy prowling about the camp, but I could scarcely believe it was my old friend Adam de Norton!'

Richard de Malmaines looked as lean, handsome, and deranged as ever. He was grinning as he sauntered up to Adam's table and propped his boot on one end of the bench. His eyes bulged, and his teeth gleamed unnaturally bright. 'Who would have thought we would meet again so soon,' he said, glowing with false cheer. 'The last time I saw you, I believe you were damning my soul to hell. Do you regret those words now?'

'I spoke in anger,' Adam said flatly. He remembered a remark of Lord Simon's, back in Hereford: *All our foes are boiling together in one pot.* Now all he needed was for Geoffrey de Brayboef to appear, he thought, and the array of his enemies would be complete. But no: John FitzJohn was still with Simon, and many other evil men as well.

'Well, you appear to have made plenty of friends already,' de Malmaines said, nodding towards the Ticeburns, who were still grimacing and hissing abuse from outside the cordon of guards.

'Yes, you really do have all the finest people here,' Adam replied.

Richard de Malmaines snorted a laugh. 'I shall have to keep a close eye on you myself then,' he said, leaning a little closer. 'And ensure nothing unpleasant befalls you.'

The guards had returned Adam's belt and knife, although they kept his sword. They returned his belt pouch too; the purse of silver that Belia had given him had vanished, but Adam was glad to see that his paternoster beads remained. Once de Malmaines was gone, he sat alone on the tail of one of the baggage carts, his guards standing idly nearby, and flicked through the beads to try and still his mind.

Pater noster, qui es in caelis, sanctificetur nomen tuum . . . A slow summer evening was falling, soft washes of light over the river valley, and the noises of the camp – the stamp and snort of horses, clatter of weapons, the *ting ting* of an armourer's hammer, the rough voices of men – faded into a hush. Adam thought of Isabel, who had given him the beads, and wondered what she might be doing now. Was she thinking of him too? She seemed at that moment unimaginably distant, almost the figment of a dream. Concentrating on running the beads between finger and thumb, Adam tried to summon the memory of his betrothed more strongly, as if he might draw her closer to him in spirit. As if her presence, even in his mind, might be a protection.

Et ne nos inducas in tentationem, sed libera nos a malo . . .

The drumming of hooves carried clearly, and Adam's thoughts vanished as he raised his head to track the galloping rider's approach.

A messenger, dusty from the road on a sweating horse. Impossible to say from which direction he had come. Adam remained motionless, feigning nonchalance, as he saw the messenger conducted to Lord Edward's tent. Steadily the light ebbed from the sky, the last sun gone behind the western hills. Flights of birds wheeled above the camp, streaming away along the valley. Adam heard laughter, and the sound of men cheering. He waited, counting off the beads once more.

Ave Maria, gratia plena, Dominus tectum . . .

'You there,' one of the guards said, and jerked his thumb.

Adam stepped down off the cart, placing the beads back in his belt pouch with deliberate care, then followed the serjeant back between the larger tents and around the far side of the central pavilion to a grassy area on the crest of the hillside.

Lord Edward was sitting on a folding stool, admiring the twilight over the valley. Several of the men from his war council remained: they stood around him, bulky in their mail, the colours of their surcoats glowing richly in the evening light. Now the council was over they held cups of wine.

'The messenger was from Bridgnorth,' Edward said promptly as Adam was announced. 'It seems you were correct. Hamo L'Estrange reports that de Dunstanville has offered to open his gates on terms, although to me alone.'

The wave of relief was almost dizzying. Adam's head reeled, and he exhaled slowly.

'So,' Edward said, standing up to his full height and turning to face Adam. 'Tell us, how much do you love Lord Simon now?'

Instantly, Adam's relief turned to a cold greasy fear that twisted in his guts. He had known this moment was approaching. Had been preparing himself for it, in fact, even while he desperately tried to turn his mind from it. Only one path remained before him, and he had no choice but to take it. But to perjure himself before God and men was no easy thing.

'I do not, my lord,' Adam said, not even knowing if it was a lie. He took another breath, willing himself to speak slowly, to appear resolute. 'I repudiate Simon de Montfort, and cast aside any allegiance to him.'

He saw Gilbert de Clare smirking, nodding slowly. He too, Adam remembered, had made this journey. 'He repudiates the traitor!' de Clare said. 'He casts aside the seducer!'

Roger Mortimer sipped wine, barely interested in what was happening. 'Why should the loyalties of such a person concern us?' he said with a dismissive shrug.

'Because, my lord Roger,' Edward said, with a strange intensity in his voice, 'where one comes, others may follow. And yet greater men too.' He gestured to Adam, just a flick of his wrist but eloquently compelling.

Adam knelt before him. 'I pledge my allegiance to you, my lord,' he heard himself saying. 'Upon my honour, I will bear faith to you of life and limb, and become your man, so help me God, and do you homage and bear faith to you of all folk.'

'In my father's name, I accept your pledge,' Edward said lightly. He raised Adam to his feet and kissed him. Summoning one of his men at arms, he took Adam's sword – the same sword that Simon de Montfort had presented to him on the battlefield of Lewes – and returned it to him. Then he dismissed him with a wave of his hand.

And Adam reversed his steps, head bowed, and only when he turned away did he feel the dread and shame burning through him.

*

'I don't believe you, of course,' Richard de Malmaines said lightly, the following day. 'I heard they put your head in a noose – such a thing can loosen the bonds of even the most loyal, I would imagine. The tongue serves where the heart will not.'

'Justice is all I care to serve,' Adam said quietly.

De Malmaines gave a hollow laugh.

They were both on horseback, up on the red sandstone bluffs above the Severn at Ribbesford. A line of men stripped to their braies and linen coifs stood waist deep in the flood, gouging and scraping at the submerged riverbed. The spray sparkled in the sunlight, and the water flowed clear upstream from the ford, and filthy brown below it.

Lord Edward and his retinue had set off upriver for Bridgnorth at first light, and would rejoin the army the following day if all went well. In the meantime, Gilbert de Clare and Roger Mortimer had set their troops to destroying the ford, digging out the bed to make it impassable to men and horses. Others scoured the riverbanks, destroying any boat or punt large enough to act

as a ferry. They were sealing the line of the Severn, Adam realised; with Bridgnorth in Edward's hands and Shrewsbury now
threatened by L'Estrange, de Montfort's supporters would soon
be unable to cross the river anywhere above Worcester. And
Worcester, as everyone knew, was the next target.

'It was all that talk of justice that turned me from Simon de
Montfort, you know,' Richard de Malmaines said. His lip curled,
and he spat the words. 'All his prating of *peace* and *righteousness*,
and the liberties of men . . .'

'You don't respect such things?' Adam asked him.

De Malmaines laughed again, his voice full of scorn. 'They are
words for women, and for priests,' he said, with an expression
that told Adam of his disdain for both. 'Weak words. And I despise
all weakness. Perhaps there is peace and justice in heaven, if such
a place exists. But here on earth there is only power and force.'

Sitting in the saddle, they watched the work of destruction
in the river for a while. A ragged man was roaming among the
soldiers and the attending knights, begging that somebody com-
pensate him for the wrecking of his punt, with which he had
supported himself and his family. Men laughed at him, shoving
him away.

'I'm surprised,' de Malmaines said, 'that after so long with
that devil Robert de Dunstanville you still manage to preserve
these pious delusions about the world. One might have thought
he would have beaten them out of you. I would have done.'

'Did you ever truly believe in de Montfort or his cause?' Adam
asked him, turning in the saddle.

Richard de Malmaines shrugged. 'He seemed attractive once.
Powerful men can have that effect. But Lord Simon is old, and
believes too many of his own lies. And his sons are fools. Lord
Edward is young, and strong, and he will win this war. Who
would not want to follow a winner?'

Adam could make no reply to that. He had repudiated Lord
Simon and sworn allegiance to Edward to save his own neck, and

to win sufficient freedom to act in his best interests. Even now, he was not convinced of what those interests might be. The lure of simply following Edward, in truth and not only in pretence, was compelling.

De Malmaines turned his horse. 'Remember,' he called to Adam over his shoulder, 'if you try to escape, I shall be the one to stop you. And you can be sure I will kill you this time!'

As he rode off along the riverbank he tossed a single penny onto the ground near the boatman, who picked it up and gazed at it in the palm of his hand, tears making runnels through the dirt on his face.

That night they camped by the mutilated ford, and the next day the army rolled on southward down the Severn towards Worcester in a torrent of men and horses, destroying crossing places as they went. At the vanguard the banners flew and the pennons and mail flashed in the sun. At the rear, the rabble of foot soldiers and camp followers dragged a dark tail of carts and dogs and sumpter beasts. Plunderers and ravagers spread out across the land ahead, seizing all that the army required and torching whatever remained, and the country emptied as they advanced. At Holt that evening Lord Edward rejoined them; Adam was glad to see that Robert de Dunstanville had not accompanied him from Bridgnorth. L'Estrange and de Mohaut were besieging Shrewsbury, the scouts reported, but would bring their forces down to Worcester as soon as the town capitulated.

The troops lit fires on the riverbank, and as night fell they roared their obscene songs about Lord Simon and his sons as the sparks whirled upwards towards the stars. Adam sat at the margin of the firelight. Two men at arms still accompanied him everywhere, and Le Brock came and went, checking on him. None of them trusted him, and nor would they until he had proved his new allegiance to Edward by some deed of arms or great daring. Somewhere out there in the gathering darkness Fulk Ticeburn and his brother were shaping their plans to kill him. They would not dare strike at him openly, Adam knew. But they were cunning men, and desperate for his murder.

No, he told himself, he could not remain in Edward's camp while such men were around him, or remain in the company of Richard de Malmaines either. His only option was to slip away, at the first opportunity. But what then? However he turned the question in his mind, no firm answer appeared to him.

The evening darkened, and Adam rolled himself in a tatty blanket and crawled beneath the bed of a cart to sleep. His two guards stretched themselves on either side of him, and other men with their dogs slept all around. Slowly the noises of the camp subsided, until only the calls of the sentries and the occasional muffled stamp and snort from the horse lines disturbed the quiet. Adam lay unsleeping, staring up at the blackness of the cart above him. The dog at his feet stirred and whined. He rolled onto his side, peering towards the nearest fire, where a group of men kept the night watch.

A figure passed before the light, stalking slim and silent through the darkened camp. For a moment the stalker paused, glancing towards where Adam lay. Then he moved on and was lost to the darkness.

Adam lay still, a name trapped in his throat. He had seen only a glimpse of the boy's features, but he was sure he had not been mistaken.

Matthew.

Chapter 14

Worcester surrendered to Lord Edward on the Morrow of St Boniface. The following day was a Sunday, the Translation of St Wulfstan, patron saint of the city, and the bells rang out from every church as Edward crossed the bridge on horseback and rode in through the river gate and along the main street. Only ten days had passed since his escape from Hereford, and now he would hear mass as a free man, a triumphant leader, in the great cathedral.

He had promised the city burgesses that there would be no sack. His troops would not rampage through the streets, ravaging and despoiling. Instead, the army of Edward and his allies remained in camp on the other side of the bridge. They would only cross the Severn, the commanders decreed, when they were ready to commence their southward march once more, towards Tewkesbury and Gloucester. Then they would destroy the bridge behind them, to deny the crossing to de Montfort.

Adam remained in the camp all through that day, staring over the river at Worcester. He had seen nothing more of Matthew, and had almost come to believe that he had imagined the boy's appearance that night at Holt, or dreamed it. His request to enter the city was refused – he had wondered whether, once in the narrow streets, he might be able to evade his guardians somehow.

Instead, he was confined to the familiar circuit of wagon camp, tent groups and cooking fires, with the constant prowling attentions of Le Brock and the Ticeburns. It had been more than ten days since he had changed his clothes, or bathed, and he felt filthy and ragged, unshaven and unkempt as the lowest beggar. Only the finely mounted sword at his side and the spurs at his ankles marked him as anything more than a common churl.

After evensong, once the liturgical day was considered over, the knights and younger barons laid out a course on a meadow near the river and rode practice jousts and mock fights. They tied a figure of straw to a stake and dressed it in a linen surcoat daubed with Simon de Montfort's red and white arms, then took turns riding at it with lance, sword and axe until it was slashed and battered out of human shape. Adam watched them, envying them their freedom and the exercise it allowed them. Richard de Malmaines, of course, had sneeringly suggested that Adam ride a joust against him, knowing full well that Adam had no lance, shield or armour, and had been given only a sway-backed old cob to ride.

'Those who come last to the table must be last to taste the meat,' de Malmaines said, sitting in the high war saddle of his glossy chestnut stallion. 'But if you pay attention, you may at least learn something of valour and skill at arms.'

Then he pulled on his helmet and rode out onto the course, where he broke three lances against his first opponent, and then drove another knight from the saddle on his second pass.

Night fell slowly over the camp, and until the curfew bell rang from the cathedral the lights of the city shone their reflections across the slow steady waters of the Severn. Adam sat against the wheel of a cart. He was thumbing through the paternoster beads once more, but his mind would not settle. Soon enough, news of the fall of Bridgnorth and Worcester would be carried back to Hereford, and would reach the ears of Lord Simon. News of his own and Robert's defections too. If Adam remained with

Edward's army when they marched south towards Gloucester, his chance to slip away from them would surely close.

But every time he anticipated some avenue of escape it would close before him at once, sealed by his own dread. His own cowardice, as he came to suspect. His drowsy mind tantalised him with memories of his manor, the days of autumn through into spring. Memories of Isabel, and all that he stood to lose.

'I'm not here for you,' a hushed voice said. 'I'm here for him.'

Adam's breath stilled, the beads motionless in his hand. He moved his thumb again, keeping his expression unaltered. The boy was behind him, beneath the cart and concealed by the spokes of the wheel.

'He's too strong for you,' Adam said, barely moving his lips.

'He's not. I've seen him sleeping. I almost held the blade to his throat. Tonight, I'll do it.'

'Why tell me then?'

For a long moment Matthew said nothing. Adam heard the rustle of straw. A dog nuzzled beneath the cart, tail thwacking.

'You can help me.' The boy said. The dog was licking at his palm.

Adam might once have relished the thought of Richard de Malmaines's death, but the idea of outright murder repelled him. Often in these recent nights he had feared the knife in the darkness, the keen touch of steel waking him from sleep, then the flash of pain as the blade severed his jugular. He was not even sure the boy had the strength or resolve to do it properly.

'It's madness,' he said, dropping his head and muttering the words into his shoulder. 'Even if you manage it, you'll die. Help me get clear of the camp instead, and I can ensure you get your revenge another time.'

'*This* is the time,' the boy hissed, and for a moment his voice cracked and dropped into a fully adult tone. 'Justice falls on him tonight, or never.'

A grunt from one of the men at arms sitting nearby, who turned and peered at Adam. His face bunched, then he shrugged and looked away again. Adam knew without turning his head that the boy was gone.

*

Midnight had passed, and the noises of the camp had grown stilled. Adam lay awake, turning his head from time to time in the direction of Gilbert de Clare's tents, where he knew Richard de Malmaines was camped. He could not allow Matthew to make his attempt at murder – it was sinful, even if de Malmaines deserved it. More importantly, the boy would surely die. How Matthew came to be in the camp at all, rather than back in Bridgnorth or wherever Robert and Belia had gone after surrendering the castle, was a mystery that Adam could not begin to unravel. The boy's burning hatred and desire for vengeance, his fixation on the one single figure of de Malmaines as a bloody recompense for the sufferings and deaths of his family and his people, was easier to comprehend, if no less terrible.

Rolling over, Adam dragged aside the blanket and clambered out from under the cart, trying not to disturb the other sleepers or the dogs that accompanied them. He failed: the whine of a hound, and the rough grumble of a man wakened from sleep. 'Where are you off?' one of the serjeants attending him said through a yawn.

Adam just motioned in the direction of the ditch they were using as a latrine. The serjeant growled in annoyance; he was supposed to accompany Adam everywhere, even on such journeys as these.

But before the man could crawl to his feet a spark of light caught Adam's eye. A flame, somewhere in the darkness of the camp. Somebody screamed, and a horse whinnied loudly. Fire danced in the blackness.

'What is it?' the serjeant demanded, getting to his feet. The other men were waking now, the dogs raising their heads, ears cocked. Adam could make out the shapes of running figures, the cries of alarm.

'It's an attack!' Adam said, the seed of an idea forced into bloom at once. 'De Montfort's men are attacking the camp!'

'Eh?' the serjeant replied, still dulled by sleep, scrubbing at his head.

Adam seized him by the arm. 'Rouse the others!' he said urgently. 'Rouse the whole camp – Go, man, before the enemy are upon us!'

He snatched up his sword as he spoke, and began striding towards the source of the disturbance. Already panic was beginning to spread. The serjeant had run to summon help from the nearest tent encampment, and a moment later the cries of alarm sounded, the bleating of horns and the wild barking of dogs. Fastening his sword belt and drawing his blade, Adam broke into a jog as he neared the flames that billowed from among the tents of de Clare's men. He had already guessed what was happening: Matthew had kindled a fire among the heaped straw gathered as feed for the horses. The flames had taken hold quickly, and were now spreading along the horse lines.

Grooms dashed from their tents, some still naked or dressed only in shirts, and tried to seize the panicking animals and lead them to safety. The squires and knights had stumbled from their beds too, all of them crowding in confusion, some armed and others empty handed, peering around into the reeling smoke and the chaos of rearing, plunging horses and desperate grasping hands.

'What's happening?' said one man, dressed only in his braies and holding a sword.

'The enemy's got inside the perimeter!' Adam told him as he jogged past, and gestured with his own weapon. 'They're over towards the river.'

'Merciful Christ,' the man said, and leaped back inside his tent bellowing for his squire to ready his armour.

Into the smoke and the fire's heat now. The flames cast mad weaving shadows between the tents. Adam tripped over a guy rope and jabbed the tip of his sword into the turf, then stumbled back upright. Easy enough to stab somebody by mistake . . . All around him were blades gleaming in the firelight, faces stretched taut with confusion or dread. A few voices were already call-ing for calm: there was no attack, it was an accidental fire, the enemy were not upon them . . .

Adam was peering into the smoky darkness for any sign of Matthew, or of Richard de Malmaines. But he could recognise nobody at all. A horse came towards him, the groom clinging to the bridle and fighting to control it. As Adam approached, the groom swung himself up onto the animal's bare back and shortened the reins, tugging its head down until it ceased to fight against him. It was a powerful charger, Adam noticed, a destrier or a fine-bred palfrey.

Striding up to the horse's withers, he grabbed the groom by the knee. The man slashed at him with the reins, but Adam was stronger and quicker. He shoved, and the groom toppled from the horse's back. Adam vaulted up in his place; the groom still had the reins, but one swing of Adam's sword and the man yelled and released them. The horse was wild again, bucking and fight-ing against the unfamiliar rider, and Adam struggled to regain control and to stay on the animal's smooth muscular back.

Pressing with his knees, jabbing with his heels as he shortened the reins, Adam got the horse under control. He had ridden bare-back many times, but with an unfamiliar mount it was always difficult. In smoky darkness filled with jostling armed men, it was near impossible. His spurs were hanging from his belt, but there was no time to fasten them in place now.

From his vantage point on the horse's back, Adam could see much more clearly what was happening around him. The

animal's panicked canter had taken him a short way from the
tents; behind him, the grooms and the servants had managed
to douse most of the fire in the straw. Smoke blew across the
camp ground, and as it parted Adam saw with smarting eyes a
bare-chested man in hose and braies, with a sword in his hand.
He recognised Richard de Malmaines at once. Then, even as he
watched, Adam saw the smaller figure detach itself from the
darkness and run at the knight from behind. He heard the cry
of fury, and saw the blade catch the weaving gleam of the fires.

Adam kicked with his heels, but the horse was responding
only sluggishly. De Malmaines turned, still dazed, and only
heartbeats before Matthew struck he saw his attacker and let
out a yell, dropping back into a fighting stance. Adam saw the
sword flash up. He saw Matthew pause, realising too late the
odds against him.

With a lurch that almost sent Adam tumbling from its back,
the horse bolted forward. Adam pulled at the reins, his knees
clasped tight around the barrel of the animal's chest. He shouted,
raising his own sword. Either the shout or the noise of galloping
hooves caught de Malmaines's attention and he turned on his
heel. The charger blasted past him as he dived out of the way,
Adam's blade cutting the air in a horizontal stroke.

Screwing the reins, Adam brought the horse back around. He
was scanning the darkness ahead of him, but saw only a chaos
of reeling forms. Through the smoke he made out the cathedral
tower to his left, black against the stars. To his right the loom
of hills. Then a shape lurched up ahead of him. For a moment
Adam thought that de Malmaines had somehow writhed across
the earth and was springing up to attack, then he caught the
shape of the boy's tousled hair.

His sword gripped beneath his left arm, Adam slowed the
charger's canter, then leaned from the saddle and seized Matthew
by the neck of his tunic. The boy cried out, and the cloth of his
tunic ripped. Muscles burning, the wound in his shoulder flashing

agony through his body, Adam heaved the boy across the withers
of his horse. The animal staggered as it took the extra weight,
then began to run again, wildly now towards the darkness and
the open ground.

*

They were a mile from the camp and riding freely by the time
the first pursuers appeared. Adam had fastened his spurs and
mounted Matthew behind him, the boy clinging to his waist.
They were following a wide track, a drover's road that took them
towards the hills, but at the first cries of pursuit Adam leaped the
horse over the roadside ditch and set off across open country.

'How many?' he said as he rode.

He felt Matthew twist to look backwards. 'I count four or
five,' he said. 'Ticeburn is leading them.'

Adam was about to commend him on his sharp eyesight when
he noticed that the scrim of cloud had shifted and the half-moon
was illuminating the land all around them. He needed to find
obstacles and broken ground, woods that might hide them from
their pursuers; the horse was powerful, but carrying a double
load it would tire quickly. Across broad strip fields of standing
wheat, they crashed through a fringe of trees and over a brook.
The horse barely broke its steady cantering gait, but Adam could
feel the animal's lungs working as it heaved breath, its sweat
gleaming.

Now the moonlight was broken, the landscape a shifting maze
of ashen grey and plunging black. Slowing the horse's pace,
Adam let it pick its own way across the broken ground and
through the wooded patches. He could still hear the pursuing
riders calling to each other, but they were growing more distant now. Then, as he rode on through another belt of trees, he
found a river before him. The horse came to an abrupt halt, head
down, and Adam was almost pitched forward over the mane.

The watercourse was much narrower than the Severn, but in the dark it was impossible to determine its depth, and the far bank was heavily overgrown and appeared impassable.

'I can't swim!' Matthew said.

'Then hang on tight,' Adam told him, and spurred the horse forward. The animal leaped from the bank into the water and forged its way into midstream. At first it was swimming, the two riders clinging to its back with locked thighs, but then the water ran shallower and the horse got its legs beneath it. Adam pulled at the reins, stopping it from bolting directly for the far bank and turning its head downstream instead. The water surged around him in the darkness, and Matthew's grip around his waist was fierce. Around a bend in the river, the horse swimming in the deeper stretches and wading through the shallows, Adam saw a break in the dense foliage of the opposite bank and nudged the animal towards it. Hopefully, he thought, they had moved far enough downstream to throw their pursuers off the scent.

Back on dry ground, he slipped from the horse's back and led it on foot through the rasping scrub and across an area of strip fields to the next copse. Shouts still came from far off to his right, but they sounded very distant now. When he reached a thick stand of hawthorns and brambles he motioned for Matthew to dismount, and drew the horse into the deep cover.

For around half an hour they waited, listening for the sounds of pursuit. Adam became aware that the boy was sniffing back tears. Back in the camp he had been bold and resolute, filled with steely purpose, but out here in the dark country he was trembling.

'I wish I'd killed him,' Matthew said in a whisper. 'I was close enough. I could have done it.'

'You could not,' Adam replied. 'You might have wounded him, but then he would simply have killed you. What purpose would that serve?'

The boy was silent, resentful. He sniffed again. They were both soaked from shoes to shoulders, their limbs daubed with mud from the riverbank, their hands and faces scratched by briars.

'Anyway,' Adam said, 'I believe we've stolen his horse.'

He flicked at one of the little enamel pendants dangling from the harness. The shape of a white hand, de Malmaines's heraldic blazon, gleamed from the shadows. Matthew sniffed again, but this time it was laughter he was suppressing.

Adam hissed for quiet, and both of them crouched. The horse remained standing, twitching slightly. Out in the moonlit field beyond the copse a horseman cantered into view. Adam watched as the man reined in his mount, standing in the stirrups to peer into the darkness. He was a long bowshot distant, but Adam could make out his black beard. He heard Matthew's rapid breathing beside him. The horse twitched again, stirred, and Adam willed it to remain motionless. His hand slid to the hilt of his sword.

Fulk Ticeburn turned in one direction then the other, his head bobbing as if he was sniffing the breeze. He leaned from the saddle, staring at the ground. Then Adam saw his shoulders bunch in a frustrated shrug. One of the other riders was calling from away beyond the next woodland, and Ticeburn pulled his reins and trotted his heavy cob in that direction.

Adam exhaled, a shudder running through his body. Slowly he eased himself up from his crouch. To his left he could still see the black shapes of the hills, higher here and more imposing than they had appeared when he crossed them on his way to Bridgnorth. He must be some distance south, he guessed. But he would need to ride further still to evade Ticeburn and the other searchers. He motioned to Matthew, took the horse by the reins and led it from the thicket. A long night lay ahead of them.

For several miles they tracked south, both Adam and Matthew walking and leading the horse to conserve its strength in case they needed to flee once more. At first they walked in silence, but after a while they began to speak of the events at Bridgnorth Castle.

'De Dunstanville shouldn't have surrendered like that,' Matthew said. 'It was cowardly. I would have fought to the last.'

'You know he surrendered to protect Belia, and to save the lives of his men?' Adam told him. 'You understand that, yes?' Only now did he feel he was coming to understand it himself. But Matthew merely shrugged and refused an answer. Looking at him now in the half light, Adam remembered how swiftly the boy had deserted him back at Bridgnorth and gone over to Robert.

'So what happened after I escaped?' he asked.

'William Tonge died before morning,' Matthew said, with no trace of compassion in his voice. 'Thomas of Hawkley was sick with a fever from his wound. He'll be dead too by now, for sure. But when Lord Edward arrived Robert opened the gates, and rode out with the rest of his men.'

'Where did they go?'

Matthew shrugged. 'Some place called Idsall. One of his manors, half a day to the north. I didn't go with them.' He fell silent for a while. Both of them were tiring, their strength flagging.

'I was supposed to keep Mistress Belia company,' Matthew went on. 'She wanted me to. She said I'd been . . . corrupted.'

'By whom?'

'By you. By him – Robert. By all the Christians. She wanted me to stay with her and return to the life I used to know. I told her I could not. That life is gone now.'

'So you slipped away and followed Lord Edward?' Adam asked.

He saw Matthew's nod in the darkness. 'It was easy enough. He had plenty of men with him, and they always need grooms and horse-handlers. I didn't have any trouble finding somebody who'd take me with them.'

'And all because you wanted to find de Malmaines again?'

Another nod. 'Find him, and kill him if I could.'

His tone was so coldly deliberate that Adam felt a momentary chill of unease. 'And die in the process?' he asked.

'How could you understand?' Matthew said, and there was a rough scorn in his voice that was suddenly fully adult. 'It's different for you – you're a knight, with your *honour* and your *prowess*. Fighting's just play for you. But I'm the son of a Jewish apothecary . . .' Matthew's voice caught, then he swallowed and spoke again. 'And my family are dead,' he said, spitting the words, 'murdered by that man and others like him. All I have in this world, my only purpose and desire, is to take vengeance upon him!'

For several long moments Adam was too startled by the outburst even to feel affronted by it. The sense of unease he had felt grew stronger, and he was glad that the boy was walking ahead of him and he could not make out his expression. For those few unnerving moments he felt that Matthew was no longer a boy, no longer fully human at all, but rather some devilish thing taken human form. Then he shook himself and the notion was gone.

'I understand more than you think,' he said quietly.

But Matthew just shrugged, and spoke no more.

Navigating by the stars, Adam led them on a wide loop to the west, towards the steep hills that marched in a solid line across the horizon. Before the first light was in the sky they were climbing on rough paths that scaled back and forth up the hillsides, through dense thickets of scrub and across sloping sheep pastures. They were far now from any possible searchers from the camp, but still Adam paused every few hundred paces and looked backwards over the great sweep of land behind them. Far to the north-east he could make out the tower of Worcester Cathedral and the line of the Severn. But no riders dogged their steps, and the country was silent and wrapped in early twilight.

They reached the summit of the hills before daybreak, an exposed ridge of sheep-nibbled turf that seemed in the faint light to undulate like the ridges of a toothless mouth. Stumbling with weariness, Adam secured the horse, then threw himself down to rest on the bank of a bramble-grown ditch. Matthew was already asleep.

Only an hour or two later, they woke to splendour. The sky all around them was filled with summer sunlight, and their hilltop stood like an illuminated island in a sea of milky mist that spread away to east and west. Crawling up to the lip of the ditch, Adam rubbed his eyes and checked that the horse was still where he had left it. Then he gazed around himself, over the dew-shining grass.

'What is this place?' Matthew asked. He was already awake, standing above the ditch with his hand raised against the bright sun.

'A fortress,' Adam replied. He scrambled upright, his legs aching from the long night's journeying. His clothes were still wet and clung to his limbs, and he was desperately thirsty. The horse stood nearby, head down and cropping the longer grass.

'Who made it?' the boy asked. He was staring away over the ditches and grassy embankments. They were overgrown in places by scrub bushes and banks of nettles, and the round summit of the hill rose between them like a bald green head crowned with rings of turf.

'Nobody knows,' Adam replied. He dragged off his damp shoes and hose, his mud-spattered tunics, and spread them in the sunlight to dry as best they might. 'The ancient pagans, maybe? Or King Arthur and his men?'

'Are there devils here?' Matthew asked, his gaze twitching.

'None worse than those we escaped last night.' Adam sat down again, and thought wryly of his delusion in the twilight that Matthew had become a devil himself. In the clear freshness of morning he was prey to no such fears. He peeled the bandage from his arm and was relieved to see that the stitches closing his wound had held. He took out his sword and wiped the blade, polishing it as best he could with a handful of damp grass.

'Rub down the horse,' he told the boy. 'We'll need to leave soon. There's no food or water up here.'

'You could use your sword to kill a sheep?'

Adam gazed at the boy, wincing. 'Do you know how to butcher a sheep?'

'No.'

'Neither do I. Rub down the horse.'

Already his stomach was growling, but the need for water was greater. Adam wished he had brought a flask with him from the camp. As it was, they would have to find a spring or stream and drink from cupped hands. He laughed suddenly. Only a few days had passed since his escape from Bridgnorth, but his fortunes had become steadily worse. Now at least he had a stolen horse, but not a penny or a change of clothes, or a mouthful of bread, and not even a cup from which to drink. He scrubbed his fingers through the stubble on his cheeks and grinned. At least he was alive, and free for the time being. He reached quickly for his belt pouch, terrified for a moment that his paternoster beads had been lost, then relieved to find them still there. He kissed the St Christopher's medallion at his neck, then knelt in prayer on the sunlit grass, hands clasped before him, giving thanks to God for his preservation.

He still had not considered clearly what road he might take. Hereford lay somewhere to the west, across that broad rolling country now emerging as the morning mist began to thin. As far as he knew, Lord Simon was still there. Humphrey de Bohun too, and Joane. Southwards, down the valley of the Severn, lay Gloucester and the route that would lead him back to his own manor, to William de St John's court at Basing, and to Isabel.

Even as he weighed his options, Adam knew he had little choice. The war had begun, and he could not stand aside from it now. He had betrayed Lord Simon once, in word if not yet in deed. With Edward now his enemy, he could not afford to do so again.

Briefly he allowed himself to imagine his return home, freed from the obligations of war. He pictured Isabel as he remembered her, as he had seen her once before, a figure standing in the sunlight. The phantasm danced above him in the morning brightness, but would not hold. No easy road would take him back to the life he had once believed he might enjoy. Whichever path he took from this place, it would lead him into the darkness, into the places where oaths are broken and honour is tarnished. It would lead him through bloodshed and peril. He could only hope and pray that the home he had forsaken, and the promise of his marriage to Isabel, still endured when he found his way back once again to the light.

'What shall we call this horse?' Matthew asked as Adam dressed himself.

'You decide.'

The boy tipped his head, studying the animal. In the sun its brushed hide glowed a rich chestnut. '*Red*, maybe? Like Lord Gilbert de Clare's head.'

'*Rous*,' said Adam. 'That's a proper name for a horse.' He looked at the animal and nodded, but it gave no sign of caring what name they gave it. Then he fastened his belt, slid the sword back into his scabbard and took the leading rein from Matthew.

Together they started off down the track that descended the hill, towards Hereford.

Chapter 15

'Swear upon the Holy Gospels,' the bishop ordered, 'that all you tell us is true.'

Adam laid his palm upon the book held before him. 'Upon my oath, all is as I have told you.'

'Not that your oath's worth anything, on your own confession!' Henry de Hastings snarled. He took a step towards Adam, bullish and livid, his hands balled into fists.

'Peace, sir!' the bishop demanded. 'Respect this holy place!'

'Sir Henry,' Simon de Montfort commanded, raising his voice only slightly. 'As Bishop Walter says, let us have peace here.'

Lord Simon had summoned his principal magnates to meet with him in the chapel of St Katherine adjoining the Bishop's Palace, so all could hear the news that Adam had brought. They gathered now before the apse, a shaft of light descending upon them from between the tall-pillared arches. Walter de Cantilupe, the elderly bishop of Worcester, had been particularly saddened to hear that the people of his own episcopal see had surrendered their city to Edward and the Marchers without a fight. The loss of Bridgnorth and the Severn crossings was a mild thing by comparison.

'We should have known that Robert de Dunstanville would prove to be rotten,' de Hastings said, with a shrug of contempt. 'He always cared more for himself than for honour, or loyalty.'

'From what I hear,' said John FitzJohn, through a leering half-smile, 'his courage was stolen by a Jewish fornicatrix!'

'Sir Robert only surrendered,' Adam said, 'when he saw the odds against him were too great.'

'Oh yes? And this was after an epic defence of . . . *a single day!*' de Hastings crowed. 'But it's only fitting that you defend him, de Norton, when you failed so grievously yourself!'

Adam knew that he must endure their taunts. This was his penance: to soak up the humiliation, to absorb the accusation and the abuse of his betters, and by so doing allay their own fears, and absolve them of their own guilt. Barely an hour had passed since his arrival at Hereford, and the joy of his return had evaporated. He was still unwashed, unshaven, clad in his muddy, sweat-stained tunic and hose. At least, he thought, he appeared properly penitent. Compared to the great men that surrounded him, in their fur-trimmed robes of silk and samite, their jewelled brooches and rings, their hair curled with heated tongs, he resembled the roughest of villeins.

Only Earl Simon de Montfort himself was dressed plainly, in a simple tunic and cloak of dark russet. His sons flanked him, both Henry and Guy looking casually elegant and deeply unimpressed with Adam and the news he had brought them. Adam had been careful to omit almost nothing; if de Montfort's scouts and informers had already reported on his apparent change of allegiance, it would be better not to attempt any concealment. All he had withheld was Belia's involvement in his escape from Bridgnorth.

'And so we must believe,' the justiciar Hugh Despenser said, pondering as he stroked his chin, 'that this young man slipped away not only from confinement in the castle, but also from the heart of Lord Edward's camp? That he was threatened with the noose at one moment and then clasped to Edward's bosom the next? An extraordinary tale. I am not sure I can fully swallow it.'

'Nor I,' said Guy de Montfort. 'How do we know that he hasn't come here on Edward's bidding? He's given a false pledge once, after all.'

'Yes, and he defends the treacherous de Dunstanville too,' Henry de Hastings added, stabbing his finger at Adam. 'What do you say, is Sir Robert still your friend and master? Did he send you here to spy for Lord Edward?'

'No!' Adam cried, and felt the heat rise to his face. No choice now, he realised as he saw the hostility, the accusation in the eyes of those around him. 'Robert de Dunstanville has betrayed his trust, I do not deny it,' he said with emphasis. 'He is no friend of mine. He is . . . he is a traitor and a faithless coward, without doubt.' Nausea surged hotly inside him, and he fought it down. John Fitz-John was nodding along with his words, a vicious smile on his face.

'Friends, this is no time for recrimination, or for suspicion,' Humphrey de Bohun declared as he stepped forward into the spill of light. 'Adam de Norton has brought us valuable intelligence of the enemy, though it pains us to hear it. We should be grateful to him.'

Adam heard Henry de Hastings's choked laugh, and saw the glance he exchanged with FitzJohn. *What did they know?*

'Quite so,' Simon de Montfort said. He took three steps and stood beside Adam, placing a hand on his shoulder. 'I thank you for returning here,' he said, with quiet sincerity. 'It cannot have been an easy journey.' Adam met his eye, and tried to detect any spark of anger or condemnation there, but saw only the cool flame of his indifference.

'At least now,' the earl said, raising his voice as he stepped away from Adam, 'we know that Edward has fully engaged with the enemies of our peace! I shall speak to his majesty the king this afternoon, and draft a proclamation condemning Edward and his actions, together with those of the faithless traitors Gilbert de Clare and Roger Mortimer, and all their adherents. May the Devil take them!'

The assembly broke up, the magnates strutting away towards their lodgings without another word, as if all were eager to be gone. Adam was just following them when he felt a touch on his arm.

'Walk with me a moment,' said Humphrey de Bohun. He led Adam a short distance along a covered passageway, between the chapel and the southern precinct of the cathedral.

'Thank you for speaking in my favour, my lord,' Adam said.

De Bohun just made a dismissive gesture. 'Only our enemies stand to gain from sowing dissent between us,' he said. 'I cannot fault you for what you said about Robert either, although any man would have done the same in his position.'

'Would you?'

Humphrey de Bohun's gaze was flat and empty. 'If Lord Simon had any sense he would have sent a greater reinforcement to Bridgnorth, and a garrison to Worcester too. He cannot expect the mere glory of his name to win wars for him everywhere. Fortunately, he's already despatched Robert de Ros and Geoffrey de Lucy with three hundred men to hold Gloucester. But some here are so impressed with his genius that they will fault nothing he does, and find others to blame instead.'

Adam was surprised to hear the anger in his voice. Never before had he heard de Bohun make any criticism of the earl.

'Listen,' Sir Humphrey said, turning to Adam and halting him as they reached a turning in the passageway. 'Simon's intending to make a pact with Llywelyn ap Gruffudd, who calls himself Prince of Wales.'

'Is Llywelyn not occupying your lands in Brecon?'

De Bohun nodded curtly, his expression sour. To their left, an archway opened into a herb garden, and the scents were heady in the summer air. 'Lord Simon wants military help against Edward and the Marchers,' Humphrey said. 'He's prepared to recognise Llywelyn's title in return, and grant him lands and castles – he's already in possession of many of them, but this would make his lordship permanent.'

Adam nodded. Now he understood why Humphrey had grown less enamoured of Simon's strategies. The loss of Brecon and his other lands in Wales would reduce his patrimony considerably. 'Is it worth it?' he asked.

The older man's face flushed with anger. 'No!' he said. 'But I must accept it, for now. I'd hoped, you know, that my wife's Welsh ancestry might win over some of my former tenants and bring them back to my control. But it appears I shan't be given that chance . . .' Just for a moment fury choked him, and he gazed unseeing into the sunlit garden with the muscle twitching in his jaw. For the first time, Adam saw in his features an odd resemblance to his half-brother Robert. An older, coarser version of his friend, perhaps, flushed and hefty with frustration.

'I may need your help,' de Bohun went on, and struck Adam's left shoulder lightly with his clenched fist. 'I intend to play along with this scheme to flatter Llywelyn, but only for as long as we need him. After that I shall use all the strength I can muster to oppose him and regain every last acre of what is mine.'

'I understand,' Adam said. Apprehension clouded his mind, and he seemed to hear the echo of de Bohun's own words from moments before. *Only our enemies stand to gain from sowing dissent between us.*

'I know I've been remiss in not paying you the remainder of my father's ransom,' Humphrey said, in a warmer tone. 'I can only apologise to you, man to man. These matters of war and land, and the difficulties with Llywelyn ap Gruffudd, well . . .' He smiled awkwardly, showing his teeth. 'But I wanted to make you an offer, which in time will yield great benefit. My father holds the manor of Crofton in Wiltshire – do you know it? Just on the southern edge of the Savernake forest. It's none too large, but it has estates attached at Wilton and Marten, and together the land's worth twenty-five pounds per annum. I want you to take the lordship of Crofton, as my tenant.'

'You father holds it, you say, and not you?'

De Bohun made an impatient gesture. 'I've taken on all my father's responsibilities, since you, uh . . . since *his capture* at Lewes. I'm Earl of Hereford and Essex in all but name now. So I can dispose of my father's lands as I see fit, and I wish you to have Crofton. Tell me you'll accept,' he said, dropping a heavy palm once more onto Adam's shoulder.

Adam considered for a moment. The lands de Bohun had described would nearly double his wealth, and spread his holdings over two shires. But if he took the lands, Sir Humphrey would become his overlord, alongside the king and William de St John. Was this merely a ploy to draw Adam into his affinity, and tie him more firmly to de Bohun's service?

'It's a generous offer, my lord,' Adam said. 'I must take some time to reflect on it, before I give you an answer.'

Humphrey de Bohun looked crestfallen, as if he had expected Adam to kneel before him at once and pledge his homage. But he managed to smile again, and tightened his grip on Adam's shoulder. 'Of course,' he said heavily. 'Of course. In these uncertain times, we should take no hasty steps. Just be certain,' he went on, his smile slipping as his gaze chilled, 'that you do not delay too long. We must be sure we know who our friends are, and who they are not.'

*

Warm sudsy water lapped at his chest as he sat back in the tub. Reclining against the linen-covered rim, Adam exposed his throat to the barber's swift and careful blade. The steel rasped, stroking up and under his jaw, and the man dipped the razor in the bath water and then wiped the blade on a rag.

'So you're a pimp these days then?' Adam said, his eyes closed. Late afternoon sunlight angled down into the yard around him.

'I wouldn't use a word like that, no, certainly not,' Hugh of Oystermouth said. He was sitting beside the bathing tub, holding Adam's towel and clean clothes. 'But I had to pay for my accommodation somehow, you see, while you were away. It's only accounts and suchlike that I do for Mistress Makepays and her sister, certainly nothing immoral!'

'He tried to argue that we should give him a wage,' Dulcia Makepays said. Adam opened one eye; the woman was leaning over the railing of the wooden balcony at the back of her building, which overlooked the yard where he was taking his bath. 'I told him, we're working women here – men pay us, not the other way around!'

Her sister Idonea, leaning over the railing beside her, gave a cracked laugh. Both women were in their early thirties, and while Dulcia was abundantly fleshed her sister was slim and stalklike.

'And how are *you* going to pay us, fine sir knight?' Idonea said. 'I don't see a purse of coin at your belt, and that great chomping beast you've put in our stable isn't going to buy his own oats!'

Adam smiled, enjoying the ebbing warmth of the bathwater. He recalled the occasion, the previous summer, when he and Robert had bathed in the courtyard of Elias's house in London, before riding out to war. How long ago that day seemed now, and how much had changed. The barber gave a last few smoothing strokes with his razor and then stood away from the tub, satisfied. Adam sat up while Matthew poured fresh water over his head and chest.

A short distance away, in the shade of the balcony, two of the sisters' girls sat watching him. One of them nursed a baby at her breast. Abashed by the frankness of their gaze, Adam turned his back as he stood up, until Matthew wrapped the towel around his torso. He was suddenly very aware of the bruises on his body, the cuts and abrasions, the rope-burn on his neck and the wound on his upper arm still raw and reddened after the surgeon had removed the stitches. These girls, he knew, had seen plenty of battered male flesh. Even so, he felt obscurely ashamed.

He had known women like them back on the tournament circuit, in France and Flanders and all across the Empire. Known them and loved them, however briefly. But nearly two years had passed since he had last lain with a woman; he endured the abstinence, but often a sweet ache of desire ran through him. Then again, he remembered that Robert had kept himself chaste for three years or more while he was away from Belia. Hugh of Oystermouth often maintained that doing without sex was harmful to a man's constitution, and caused the blood to clot in the loins and the seed to flow up into the brain, but Adam had learned to take many of the Welshman's pronouncements lightly.

'Ah, here are the Jews,' Dulcia Makepays called from the balcony, showing gappy teeth as she grinned. 'God's blessings upon you, Master Aaron!'

'Thank the saints somebody's still got money in this town!' her sister added.

Adam turned as he stepped from the bath, and saw the group of men entering the yard through the covered passageway from the street. Aaron of London was one of the most prominent moneylenders in Hereford; Humphrey de Bohun himself had recommended him. He was a lean man, neatly dressed in a long surcoat and pelisse of the finest blue, and his urbane smile did not shift as he paced across the yard. The two young clerks that followed him showed no such composure; their eyes darted everywhere. Behind them came four thick-necked men carrying an ironbound coffer.

'Sir Adam de Norton, may God keep you,' Aaron said, as Adam pulled on a clean tunic and buckled his waistbelt. The two of them met in the centre of the yard and exchanged a kiss of greeting. 'You know, you would have been welcome to visit me at my house,' the moneylender said, raising an eyebrow. 'A friend of Elias of Nottingham is no stranger to me. But this . . .' He gestured to the yard around him, the brothel and the lounging women, then nodded briskly. 'This is . . . certainly fine!'

Adam bowed his head. Matthew brought folding stools – Adam noticed Aaron glance at the boy, and a brief wordless communication pass between them. The moneylender and his two clerks both wore pale linen panels sewn to their mantles, the prescribed mark of the Jewish faith, but had thrown back the hems to conceal them.

'I'm happy to agree the loan you requested,' Aaron said as he waved the stool away. 'Twenty pounds, borrowed against the value of your fine warhorse, and repayable with the usual interest. My clerk here has prepared the *chirograph*.'

'I thank you,' Adam said as the clerk showed the loan document to Hugh. Twenty pounds was as much as he dared borrow. Even so, once he had bought a saddle and tack for his new horse, a replacement mail hauberk, shield and linen aketon, a riding palfrey and packhorse and a mount for Matthew, and also paid his retainers' wages and the Makepays sisters for their accommodation, almost the full sum would be exhausted. Bleakly he thought of his bags of coin still held in the Templars' treasury in London, inaccessible now on the far side of the guarded Severn. Annoyance rose once more within him; if Humphrey de Bohun had paid only a fraction of what he still owed, Adam could have afforded everything without the need for costly loans.

'A moment, perhaps, while our friends look over the documents,' Aaron said, gesturing for Adam to follow him. They crossed to the far side of the yard, both pacing slowly with hands clasped at their backs, as if they were discussing the loan. 'As you are a friend of Elias,' the moneylender said, 'I will assume you do not share the hostility of so many of your people for ours.'

Adam merely inclined his head in acknowledgement.

'Then perhaps you can tell me something of what might happen now?' Aaron asked, dropping his voice. 'Already Lord Simon makes exactions upon us. Only two days ago he confiscated, in the king's name, Jewish property in the town to recompense some householders for buildings destroyed during repairs to the walls. If he and his army stay here much longer, my friend, we could be ruined!'

'I'm sorry, I know no more of Simon's plans than you,' Adam said.

'And what of Edward then? A proclamation is being drafted, one hears, again in the king's name, calling him – what was it? – *credulous and easy to deceive*. Is that a fair assessment?'

Adam snorted and shook his head.

'I suspected it was not,' Aaron mused. 'And yet I suppose the king must be seen to make some comment on the activities of his eldest son. Perhaps Edward is proving rather more cunning than Lord Simon had assumed?'

'Perhaps,' Adam said, suddenly uncomfortable and unwilling to say more. It occurred to him that Edward and his allies doubtless had agents in the city as well.

They turned and made their way back to join the others. Aaron's clerk was cutting the loan document into two pieces along a jagged line. One half was for Adam, the other for Aaron of London. The two men shook hands, sealing their agreement, and the second clerk handed over a leather bag of coin from the ironbound coffer, a small amount in advance of the full sum.

As Adam accompanied Aaron towards the passage that led to the street, the moneylender halted him with a hand on his arm. 'That boy,' he said in an undertone. He was not looking directly at Matthew. 'I know well what he is,' he said.

'He is my groom and servant,' Adam replied.

Aaron looked at him, his smile gone. 'Whatever you've made of him, and whatever evils he has seen, I beg you to return him to wherever you found him. There is something in his eyes that does not speak of childhood.'

'Many younger than him have that same look,' Adam replied. 'As for Matthew, he knows his own mind.'

'Does he really? Ah well,' Aaron said, as he turned to leave. 'Then his fate shall be upon your conscience, in that case.'

*

It was a warm evening just before the solstice, the twelfth day after Adam's return to Hereford, and the light was fading as he made his way back from a visit to an armourer's workshop near the Eigne Gate. In the close heat of midsummer the town seethed with restless anxiety, the lid of low cloud sealing in the tensions of an army of men billeted here for more than six weeks now.

News had reached them only yesterday of the fall of Gloucester to Lord Edward's forces; Robert de Ros and his men had withdrawn to the castle, and were now under siege. Would Hereford be the next target for the Leopard's wrath? Would they be forced merely to wait while the noose closed around them, or would Simon de Montfort finally give the order to march out and confront the enemy directly? Lord Simon was delaying, some said, while he agreed his treaty with Llywelyn ap Gruffudd, or while his son Simon the Younger mustered a new army in London. But perhaps it was already too late? Perhaps their long inactivity had sapped their strength and turned them soft. If so, they would be easy meat for the swords of Lord Edward's followers.

The streets held a strange turbulent mood that evening, almost festive, but edged with lazy aggression. At one end of the marketplace a cluster of buildings in St Peter's Street had set up as alehouses, with bushy alestakes mounted over the doors and benches outside. Adam walked in the centre of the road, stepping around the mounds of horse and cattle dung, and kept clear of the boisterous crowd that thronged the benches to either side. Most of the drinkers were militiamen from the neighbouring shires, but there were a good few squires and grooms from the knightly retinues among them, and some who could be household knights as well. Tomorrow was a Sunday, but no piety restrained them now.

Benedict had remained back at the armoury with Matthew to oversee the last bits of work, and Hugh had vanished into the stews of the town. Adam was alone, his cloak thrown back to expose the sword belted at his side, but he expected no trouble here. Music reeled from the open doorways, and in places men and women were already lurching into drunken dance. Towards the far end of the street a cheering mob formed a ring around two men – one English, the other Welsh – who were laying into each other with their fists.

'Let Lord Edward fall on us now!' somebody shouted. 'Let the Marcher barons come – they can have the king and his crown too, for a song!'

As Adam reached the corner of the narrower way leading to the Makepays sisters' yard – was it really called *Gropecunt Lane?* – a figure appeared some distance ahead of him, darting between shadowed doorways. Another step, and Adam froze abruptly, tensed. The noise of the music and revelry from the street behind him faded. The lane was empty, but Adam could sense a presence there. The figure that he had seen moments before had been trying to keep out of sight.

His hand went to his sword hilt, fingers curling around the familiar worn leather of the grip. Above him, between the eaves of the houses, swifts flittered across the narrow gap of blue evening sky. Music wafted from the marketplace behind him, crass in its jollity. Breath tight, sword eased partway from the scabbard, Adam began to walk forward into the gullet of the lane.

A cat arched suddenly in a shadowed doorway, hissing, then raced across into the building opposite. Adam exhaled and eased his shoulders from their hunch. Three more steps and the entrance to the yard came into view.

'Somebody was just asking after you, lord,' a girl said, leaning from an upper windowsill. She was one of the Makepays sisters' workers.

'Did he give his name?' Adam asked.

'Oh no, lord – it was no man.' The girl grinned, and gestured towards the covered passageway.

Adam found his visitor waiting in the far corner of the yard near the stables, in the deepest well of evening shadow. She was wearing a travelling mantle, too thick for the season, with the hood pulled over her head, but even from behind he recognised her at once.

'Either you've posted a watcher in the lane, or you were followed here,' he said.

'No doubt one of my husband's loyal hounds,' she replied, drawing aside her hood to look at him. 'I thought I'd thrown them off.'

'Perhaps he sets them to protect your welfare, my lady,' Adam said. 'The streets can be perilous for a woman alone.'

'Then let's hope I need no protection from you, Adam de Norton.'

Adam had not spoken to Joane since his return to Hereford, although he had seen her from a distance in the company of her husband. He had been avoiding her, trying not to indulge temptation. Now, it seemed, he had no choice.

Unwilling to give the spy in the lane anything to report, Adam led her into the deeper darkness of the stable. They passed along the stalls, and Joane paused to rub the nose of the chestnut stallion, Rous, who stood patiently whisking his tail in the gloom.

'Do you recall the first time we spoke,' she said, 'back in my stable at Ware?'

'How could I forget?' Adam replied. That was the bitter winter when he had first become squire to Robert de Dunstanville, and had left the Earl of Hereford's household at Pleshey. Joane had been only sixteen years old then. She was not yet twenty now, but it seemed that whole decades had passed since, and they had become quite different people.

'You made me promise to guard Sir Robert from danger,' he said, smiling.

She laughed. 'As if he would ever have needed guarding! . . . Is it true what they say about him now? Did he betray Lord Simon and surrender Bridgnorth?'

'He did it for Belia's sake,' Adam said. 'If he'd allowed himself to fall into the power of Hamo L'Estrange, he would have lost everything. By surrendering to Lord Edward alone, he was able to safeguard his lands and leave in peace.'

'A pragmatic decision, I suppose,' Joane said. She ran her palm over the horse's neck once more, then paced a little further and turned to face Adam. 'It cannot have been easy for you to accept,' she said.

'It was not.'

'I won't ask why you've been avoiding me,' Joane said. She had thrown back her hood, and the braids of her hair shone a deep copper red in the faint light. 'I understand you have your reasons . . . But I came because I've heard some news that I thought you should know. News that might affect how you act.'

'Tell me,' Adam said with a frown.

'Firstly, Lord Simon intends to march out with his whole army in five days' time,' Joane said, 'on the Morrow of St John. His treaty with Llywelyn is all but agreed, and he hopes to draw Edward's forces away from their siege of Gloucester by attacking Gilbert de Clare's garrison at Monmouth.'

She had heard this from her husband, Adam guessed, or more likely overheard Sir Humphrey discussing it with his men. He would have learned of it himself soon enough. 'What else?' he asked, feeling apprehension stirring within him.

'A messenger came this morning, from Winchester,' Joane said, dropping her voice. 'It seems that William de St John has declared for Edward and raised his banner in Hampshire.'

Adam drew a breath, surprise blanking his mind for a moment.

'He has others supporting him,' Joane went on. 'Martin des Roches and John de Cormayles, Hugh de Brayboef . . . They've seized Odiham Castle. Winchester's opened its gates to them as well. Now they're supposed to be mustering an army to march against Portchester. Lady Eleanor was with her son at Pevensey when last we heard from her, and making for Dover.'

Adam remained stunned, the news sinking in slowly. William de St John, the father of his betrothed, was now his enemy. And if the de Brayboefs were on his side too . . . There could be no way back to the life he had once anticipated, and the future he had desired. No safe return home to his untroubled lands. No marriage to Isabel. Not unless he once again betrayed his oath and his trust and changed sides in this conflict. The great edifice of his future happiness had collapsed suddenly into rubble, and he felt the plummeting dizziness of its fall.

'I'm sorry,' Joane said. 'You deserved to know this.'

'Why?' he said, still caught in the furious churning of despair.

'So you can decide. You've done all you can for de Montfort. If you wanted to go, this is the time. Now, before the army musters once more.'

'You think I could simply give up and leave?' Adam asked, unable to keep the bitterness of accusation from his voice.

He saw Joane's jaw tighten, the blood rise in her cheeks. 'That's what Robert did, isn't it?' she said.

True enough, Adam thought. *To protect those he loved.* 'And what about you?' he asked.

Joane exhaled. They were standing very close together now. 'I have no choice,' she said. 'My husband suspects my every move, and believes every wicked rumour about me.' She gave an exasperated laugh that turned into a sigh. Adam's heart was beating fast, and a new and unnerving desire was rising through his despair.

'Humphrey's determined to keep me with him at all times,' Joane went on. 'But you – you can choose a different fate, if you wish it.'

Abruptly, as if she feared any greater intimacy, she pulled up her hood, then turned and left the stable without another word.

Adam stood in the doorway and watched her go. As she crossed the yard, the first raindrops fell from the lowering sky.

*

Five days later, Simon de Montfort's army mustered on the road outside Hereford. There were no orations, no prayers. Every man among them had spent the previous night in vigil, as the fires of St John's Eve smouldered in the drizzle. A single blast on a trumpet, and the column began to move, stretching out along the rain-drenched road south towards Monmouth.

Lord Simon and his retinue formed the vanguard, and behind them came the barons, bannerets and lesser knights, the mounted serjeants and the Welsh and English levy infantry. In the midst of the army, King Henry sat in the saddle with his back straight, his beard pearled with raindrops, acting as if he were in command here and not a virtual prisoner.

Adam rode at the centre of the column, clad in his new mail and mounted on his palfrey, with his warhorse Rous on a leading rein. Matthew and Hugh were riding behind him, drawing his solitary packhorse. He turned as he rode and looked back towards the retinue of Humphrey de Bohun, directly behind him; Joane rode alongside her husband, draped in a mantle to keep out the rain. She caught Adam's eye, and just for a moment a smile lit her face.

Under lowering skies they marched forth from Hereford, the hooves of the horses and the oxen pulling the baggage carts and artillery wagons mashing the dirt of the road to liquid mud. At the rear, the long train of camp followers tramped after them through the dung-spattered mire, leaving only the slinking scavenger dogs in their wake.

PART THREE

Chapter 16

They were blockading Monmouth when the enemy caught up with them.

Four days of siege, of drenching rain and bursting sun, and the castle still stood defiant against Lord Simon's army. It was neither a large fortification nor a strong one, just a ring of walls on a hilltop with a single round tower, but Gilbert de Clare's banner still flew above it, the red chevrons on yellow as bright as an enamelled pendant in the rain-washed air.

De Montfort's men occupied the town that spread below the castle to the bank of the Wye. They had dug trenches and erected mantlets to protect their archers, and set up the trebuchets and perrier catapults they had dragged from Hereford to batter the walls. But so far there had been no full-scale assault; Lord Simon did not wish to waste his limited manpower on taking such a minor place by storm. And so far the defenders of Monmouth had proved frustratingly tenacious.

The alarm sounded on a Sunday afternoon, the first trumpet blast answered by horns and cries rousing the camp into turmoil. Adam looked from his patched and leaking tent to see men running in confusion, stumbling between the guy ropes as grooms loosed their horses. The camp stood in the flat fields to the south of Monmouth; wooded hills rose on all sides, with the town clasped between them in a curl of the Wye. There was no enemy that Adam could see, and the castle garrison had not made a sally. He called for Matthew to saddle his horse, his new squire to bring his armour, and Hugh to find out what was happening.

By the time the herald returned, Adam was already dressed in mail and surcoat, Matthew standing with Rous saddled and ready as the squire fastened his belts. Eustace de Brumlegh was the son of one of Humphrey de Bohun's tenants; a truculent youth with a doughy face and a small feathery moustache, he gave the impression that he thought he was fated for better things. By comparison, Benedict Mackerell had been an Arthurian hero.

'Enemy horsemen to the north of the town,' Hugh reported, sucking breath.

'How many?' Adam demanded. He swatted away the squire's fumbling hands and fastened the sword belt himself, then took the reins from Matthew and swung up into the saddle.

'Couldn't say,' Hugh told him. 'Not a great number – but they could be an advance guard.'

John de Kington came riding past, wearing the blue and white of de Bohun's household. He waved for Adam to join him, and together they kicked their horses into a trot between the tent lines. Other knights joined them, with squires and mounted serjeants, all of them alight with the taut excitement of impending combat.

'Have a care, sirs! Have a care!' a man cried as they neared the edge of the camp. He was a tonsured clerk, waving his arms at the riders. 'His majesty is passing!'

At once the riders shortened their reins, drawing their snorting chargers to a halt. Before them a procession was approaching between the tents, moving at a stately pace towards the town on the far side of the meadow. King Henry walked at its centre, bareheaded and carrying a book clasped in his hands; many of the knights and serjeants dropped at once from the saddle and knelt on the damp turf, while the others just bowed their heads, teeth clenched in angry impatience as they curbed the vigour of their horses.

The clerks of the royal chapel accompanied the king, together with a band of monks that Henry had brought from Hereford to join his choir in singing psalms and the holy hours. Together they walked in slow procession across the meadow; the king had already heard mass twice that day, and now he would hear evensong in the priory church of St Mary in the town.

'Christ's nails,' said John de Kington under his breath, 'I swear he does this on purpose!'

The king's presence was a source of continual hindrance at the best of times. Henry's pavilions occupied nearly half the camp, and the constant sound of psalm-singing and biblical recitation wore at the nerves of men more accustomed to crude campfire songs than piety on campaign. True enough, the king's intense piety had a determined quality at times, as if he were mocking the martial efforts of Lord Simon and his followers with his displays of Christian virtue. Now, as he walked slowly, calmly, unmoved by the plunging horses and the armoured riders, anxious only to reach the church before the service commenced, King Henry appeared to be enjoying himself greatly.

By the time the king had passed, the noise of trumpets from the far side of the town was a constant clamour. Barely waiting for the last of the monks and clerks to pass, the knights let out their reins and dug in with their spurs, sending the clerics at the rear of the procession dashing for safety as they thundered past. Adam could see other bands of riders converging on the meadow to the north of the town. On the far side of the meadow, an army was drawn up to oppose them.

'They must have crossed the river at Flanesford,' Hugh Despenser was saying, as Adam and his companions joined the main force. 'They'll have left Gloucester yesterday, most likely.'

'Has Gloucester Castle fallen already?' somebody asked.

'No, surely not,' Despenser replied, musing, 'or we'd see Lord Edward and de Clare himself here. This will be a smaller force they've sent to oppose our siege.'

'Only two score pennons between them,' Henry de Hastings said, with a boastful laugh. 'We outnumber them thrice over!'

'Two score or fewer, and maybe five hundred infantry,' Despenser added, narrowing his eyes into the glare of afternoon sun. 'But they seek to challenge us all the same.'

'Is that Hamo L'Estrange?' Adam asked, peering at a red banner among the opposing horsemen.

John de Kington shook his head. 'John Giffard,' he said. 'Gilbert de Clare's chief man in these parts. Although his blazon looks similar. Three lions to L'Estrange's two.'

Adam nodded. He had spotted another blazon, on the lance pennon of a knight with Giffard's retinue. Three severed white hands on a red field. His chest tightened, and he settled himself more firmly in the saddle.

'Richard de Malmaines,' he said quietly. This time, de Kington agreed.

The enemy had taken a position a little more than a long bowshot from the town, between the riverbank and the Hereford road. Behind a screen of mounted knights and men at arms, their servants and footmen were already erecting tents on the pastures further upstream. It looked, Adam thought, rather like the scene before a great tournament. The meadow between the two armies was flat and level, grass cropped by the haymaker's scythe, ideal for mounted combat. John Giffard's force may be outnumbered by three to one, but clearly he intended to stand his ground, and expected de Montfort's men to fight.

Lord Simon came riding up from the town with his retinue of knights and squires around him and his red and white banners raised. The clouds had parted and the afternoon sun poured down hot upon them all.

'My lord!' Henry de Hastings shouted, 'give the order and we charge as one – we'll sweep them from the field!'

But de Montfort held up his gloved hand, commanding his men to keep their horses on a tight rein. Unlike most of those around

him, he was not wearing mail. Across the stubbled field the leading knights of the opposing force were riding out to challenge
them. Shields flashed, armour glimmered and the caparisons of
the horses moved in waves of flowing colour.

'John Giffard leads them, I see,' de Montfort said, in a carrying voice. 'William Maltravers is with him, look, under the sable
banner latticed with gold. And Richard de Malmaines is there
too. All three fought beside us at Lewes! All three have turned
traitor now, and rebels against their oath.'

'May the Devil burn out their eyes!' de Hastings growled.

Adam turned to his left, along the line of knights that were
forming up around Lord Simon. John FitzJohn had joined them
now, with Nicholas de Segrave, both speaking vigorously with de
Hastings. Humphrey de Bohun came riding up too, with the rest
of his mounted retainers under their blue and white pennons.
He was bringing a large number of infantry with him, Welsh
levy archers and spearmen, and English militia. Now the numbers on de Montfort's side were sufficient to overwhelm their
opponents. The dazzle of their heraldry alone was impressive;
but Adam would have given anything to see the familiar red and
white pennon of Robert de Dunstanville flying among them.

Guy de Balliol, the Scottish knight who served as Simon's
standard-bearer, rode out from the line and circled his horse. At
once riders came forth from the opposing army, calling out challenges. 'In the king's name, declare yourselves,' de Balliol cried,
'or lay down your arms!'

'Perjurer!' one of the opposing knights yelled back at him.
'You don't speak for the king, but for the treasonous old serpent
de Montfort!'

De Balliol just made a dismissive gesture, and rode back to
join Lord Simon.

'Traitors!' the opponents cried after him. 'Perjurers and dogs!'

'You are the traitors, not us,' John FitzJohn shouted across at
them.

'Come forth then,' one of the riders replied. It was their leader, John Giffard, brandishing a sword. 'Come forth, and bring your fork-tongued seducer Lord Simon! I'll cut off his tongue myself!'

'Where are Edward, and de Clare?' Adam heard Lord Simon say to Hugh Despenser. 'Until they take the field, this is nothing more than play.'

Adam's new squire rode up with his shield and lance. In the opposing encampment, several of the servants and soldiers had left off their work of erecting tents, turned their backs and bared their buttocks, slapping them derisively at de Montfort's men. Jeers and mocking laughter carried across the meadow.

'Give the word, my lord!' Henry de Hastings yelled. 'Give the word and we'll slay every one of them! By the teeth of God, we'll paste this field with gore!'

'No! Hold back,' de Montfort replied. 'They goad us, but we must not be provoked.' He sat impassively in the saddle gazing across at the opposing army.

'But lord,' de Hastings cried, exasperated. 'The enemy is before us! We should *attack*!' Already he was urging his horse forward, the rest of his retinue crowding after him, their fury barely held in check.

'I say again *no*!' de Montfort replied, standing in the saddle. Adam noticed that his face was shining with sweat. 'Do you remember, de Hastings – and you, de Segrave,' Simon shouted in sudden anger, 'how your recklessness almost cost us the battle at Lewes? Hold back, or may God damn you!'

Startled, de Hastings instantly pulled his horse around. His features were still glowing with fury, but a dangerous look of affront darkened them further now. All along the line the horses were milling, riders gripping the reins tight. On the far side of the meadow the enemy rode out and back, calling their taunts and challenges.

'De Montfort refuses battle!' John Giffard's herald yelled from the far side of the field.

'Cowards!' the men behind him chorused. 'Treasonous dogs and cowards!'

'Sir,' Adam's squire Eustace said anxiously, his habitual truculence gone now. Adam followed his gesture, and saw Richard de Malmaines, his charger covered by a bloody red caparison, cantering out from the enemy lines and approaching him.

'De Norton!' the man shouted. 'I see you're riding the horse you stole from me!'

'Fairly won, de Malmaines,' Adam called back at him.

'Ha, you think?' de Malmaines replied in a scornful shout. He raised his lance. 'Then win him now!'

Adam could feel the horse stirring beneath him, pawing at the turf and snorting at the sound of his former master's voice. Anger flared in his blood, all the frustrations and humiliations of the recent weeks finding sudden focus. Tightening the reins, he seized the lance from Eustace and shot his left forearm through the straps of his shield. Already he was spurring Rous forward across the stubble of the meadow. He heard Humphrey de Bohun's shout from behind him, ordering him back, but de Malmaines had turned his own horse and was kicking it into a gallop.

Now, Adam thought – now, before the eyes of everyone, he would settle his quarrel with this man.

Cheers from both armies as he rode out from the line and turned to meet de Malmaines's charge. Rous broke into a canter at once, gathering speed. The distance closed, the hooves of the horses kicking up the chaff, and Adam kept his gaze fixed on his opponent's shield. He realised he had not fastened his mail coif, and his head was covered only with a linen arming cap. This was no tournament joust; his lance was tipped with sharp steel, just like the one de Malmaines carried. The sunlight blazed around him as he brought his weapon down in a smooth plunging dive.

Moments before impact, the red-caparisoned charger breathing foam from its mouth, de Malmaines lifted his lance and aimed directly for his face. Adam's muscles tensed as he hunched beneath the rim of his shield, lifting it to protect himself while he gripped his own lance steady. The impact smashed the shield back against his brow, and he felt the steel point of the lance scoring its surface and cutting the air just over his head. He barely felt his own lance strike de Malmaines's shield.

Adam was still in the saddle but reeling from the blow. Slowing, turning his charger, he realised that his lance had shattered. Pain flashed in his skull as he glanced back over his shoulder. Anguished, he saw that Richard de Malmaines was also still mounted, still holding his lance, and bringing his own horse around for a second attack. Adam sniffed, and his throat filled with blood. With fumbling hands he groped for the hilt of his sword.

'No, no,' a voice was yelling. 'Back – now!'

Turning his head, Adam saw through the wave of pain Guy de Balliol, de Montfort's standard-bearer, cantering onto the field towards him.

'Get back,' de Balliol called again. 'Lord Simon commands you!'

And there behind de Balliol was Simon de Montfort himself, his face stern with displeasure. He raised his hand and gave one curtly imperative gesture.

Cursing, Adam hauled at the reins. Richard de Malmaines was baiting his horse, lance raised and ready for the charge, but Adam forced himself to turn aside and ride back towards the safety of his own lines. As he left the field, Humphrey de Bohun and two of his household knights rode out to cover his retreat. Richard de Malmaines snarled an insult after him, but his words were lost amid the noise of cheering.

Infantrymen closed ranks after them as they fell back, and the noise was like breaking surf in Adam's ears. Eustace was beside him now, dabbing at his bleeding nose with a rag. Henry de Hastings too, his face still flushed but his anger now changed to fierce congratulation. 'Good lance!' he cried, and dealt Adam a bruising cuff on the shoulder. 'You almost had him, by God!'

'He almost had me,' Adam managed to say, then coughed and leaned to spit blood. Nobody seemed to have heard him. Agony was flashing in his skull, nausea swelling in his gut. John de Kington grabbed him before he slid from the saddle.

*

'Here, a bitter draught but a soothing one, after time,' the physician said. Adam winced as he tipped back his head and drank from the steaming wooden bowl that the man held to his lips. Pungent vapour flooded his senses, then the vile taste almost made him gag. He swallowed heavily, and then sighed in relief as he sank back against the cushioned couch once more.

On the far side of the large tent another man lay on a table, his mail and surcoat piled on the floor beside it. He was gargling obscenities through the wadded stick clenched between his teeth as two servants pressed down on the wound in his shoulder and tried to staunch the bleeding. He had taken the injury from a crossbow bolt less than an hour previously, after wagering that he could seize the castle in a ladder attack. Three of the soldiers he was leading had died in the failed assault, while four more were wounded. But none were of sufficient rank to warrant the attentions of the bishop of Worcester's own physician.

Adam's own injury was minor by comparison. He had been well enough to ride back to the camp with the other knights as they surrendered the field to their outnumbered enemy, and had only lost consciousness when he tried to dismount and another rush of blood had burst from his nose. Now the dark red welt across his forehead was plastered with a herbal poultice, but at least the pain and the hot whirling sensation were beginning to ease.

He had first seen the wryly smiling Master Philip Porpeis, physician to Bishop Walter de Cantilupe, attending his master at the Pentecost banquet in Hereford. In his black robe the man resembled a friar, but his clothes were of the finest wool and his manners those of a courtier. He covered his clerical tonsure with a crimson skullcap topped with a stalk. At least he knew his trade; Adam had overheard somebody saying that Master Philip had been trained at the great university of Montpellier. Although, from the little Adam had seen of him, he was as adept at surgery as he was at diagnosing illnesses, and held no scruples about drawing blood. Already Porpeis had palpated his skull, moved a lighted candle in front of his eyes – both disagreeably painful but apparently necessary – and then had Adam piss into a glass jar and examined the urine, even dipping his finger in the fluid and dabbing it to his tongue. 'Well, young man,' he had said after long deliberation. 'I believe you will not die.'

Evening light fell through the opened flaps of the tent, with the smells of woodsmoke and horses, and the sounds of laughter and gruff conversation. Adam wished he could return to his own small encampment, but he had been forbidden to stir until Porpeis had made a full examination and ensured that no lasting damage had been done. He had sent Matthew to attend to the horses, and Eustace to find his broken lance, fit a new shaft and repair his damaged shield.

At least his very public injury had excused Adam from participating in the failed attack on the castle. Whether he would be so easily absolved from de Montfort's anger he did not know; he remembered all too well Lord Simon's expression of almost contemptuous disappointment as he left the field. John de Kington had suggested that Adam's reckless display against de Malmaines might have diffused some of the discord among Simon's supporters, for now at least. But all knew that plenty in the camp chafed for battle. Inglorious assaults on the castle walls could do little to dilute the hunger for confrontation.

Adam swallowed again, trying to rid his mouth of the taste of medicinal draught. He still could not understand why de Montfort had been so unwilling to attack Giffard's army. 'It was easy victory for the taking,' he said to the physician, closing his eyes. 'Why did Lord Simon hold back?'

'I'm no military man,' Porpeis said, his voice shifting as he moved around the couch where Adam lay, 'but I suspect the appearance of ease was deceptive. A ruse, in other words. Lord John Giffard wishes to goad us, like a gadfly annoying a horse. For Lord Simon, there is too much to risk for too little gain.'

Adam had to admit the wisdom of the physician's argument. At least he was beginning to feel restored now, his hours lying in the darkened recess of the tent, and the foul-tasting drinks that Porpeis had poured down his neck, finally taking effect. Adam raised his head, wincing but feeling no pain. The knight on the table was writhing and groaning as Master Philip directed the cleaning of his wound with boiling elder oil and its suturing with silken thread.

A shadow fell across him, and Adam dropped back onto the couch. He felt a tight knot of ache as his brow creased.

'Don't move too abruptly, I pray,' Joane said, placing a hand flat on his shoulder with a subtle pressure. She was dressed in a plain gown, a linen neckcloth and fillet, and she carried a jug. 'More wine, for medical purposes,' she said with a quick smile.

'Ah, Lady Joane, I thank you,' Master Philip said, returning to take the jug from her. He sniffed at it, his long nose pinching, then smiled broadly.

'From my husband's own supply,' Joane said. Humphrey de Bohun had always enjoyed fine living and good wine, and kept himself well provisioned even on campaign.

'In that case,' the physician said, fetching three cups and setting them on the low side table, 'we might put this to better use than washing wounds, I think.'

Joane sat beside the couch and smoothed Adam's face with a wetted cloth, gently wiping the remains of the poultice from his brow. Adam lay still, eyes closed, hardly daring to breathe. When he opened his eyes once more the physician handed a cup to him.

'Keep this down, young man,' he said, 'and we shall pronounce you fully restored to health!'

Adam sat upright, taking the cup. He sipped – the wine was good, especially after the vile broth, and subtly spiced.

'Lady Joane has been a great help to me,' Master Philip told Adam, inclining his head in her direction. 'I may yet employ her as a surgical assistant.'

'Since my husband insists I accompany him on campaign,' Joane said, more to the physician than to Adam, 'I need to find some occupation to fill my idle hours, whatever men may think of me. If a woman does nothing she is called indolent,' she said to Adam as she sipped her wine, 'but if she makes herself useful she is thought undignified. So be it.'

She paused to speak to one of the servants as he left the tent – in Welsh, Adam noticed. Joane's maidservant Petronilla lingered just outside the flap, peering curiously into the shadowed interior, flinching at the hint of anything bloody or gore-spattered, then peering once more.

Joane herself appeared happier and more alive now than Adam had seen her since the days before her marriage. Perhaps the life of the army camp suited her better than the stifling world of the court? He remembered well her pleasure in exercise, riding and the open air. They sat for a few moments in silence, sipping their wine and avoiding each other's gaze while Master Porpeis watched them both with studied indifference.

'I feel much better now, thank you,' Adam said, draining his cup and setting it down. He was still trying not to meet Joane's eye.

'Yes, I think so,' Porpeis said, peering at him in the dim light. 'A little concussion, a bruised head, but no lasting damage, I think. Avoid exertion, and rest well tonight, but yes – you may go.'

'Perhaps I should accompany Sir Adam, just to be sure he's quite recovered?' Joane asked, standing up.

Master Philip glanced at her, his wry smile flickering. 'Oh yes,' he said. 'An excellent idea.' Clearly little escaped him. With a light wave he dismissed them both.

The evening light outside the tent felt almost blinding, but Adam felt no pain as he narrowed his eyes. Joane lightly took his arm, as if he were escorting her and not the other way around, and Petronilla fell into step behind them as they made their way through the encampment.

'People keep telling me to avoid exertion,' Adam said with a smile. 'Do they live in a different world to this one?'

'I would welcome some exertion myself,' Joane said, lifting her skirts with one hand as she stepped through the mud. 'Several times I've petitioned Humphrey to allow me to ride out and exercise my horses.' She turned her eyes towards the wooded hills that rose around Monmouth in the last glow of the sun. 'Even with any number of men to protect me, he won't allow it. He fears that somebody would capture me in a heartbeat.'

'He may be right.'

She looked at him from the corner of her eye and a brief unspoken communication passed between them. Something that Adam could not put into words. Instinctively they had slowed their steps. The light was soft, hazed with smoke, and from the direction of the king's pavilions came the sound of the monastic choir singing the evening psalms. They were surrounded by a military encampment, baggage carts and stands of weaponry, squires cleaning and polishing armour, grooms taking horses out for exercise, tussling dogs and soldiers drinking among the tent lines. But war felt far away. The big trebuchets had long ceased their thumping, and no arrows arced from the castle walls. The blockading camp of John Giffard and his men was too distant to exert a hostile presence. A sense of peace suffused everything, here at the long day's end.

It seemed to grant a sense of permission too, a loosening of boundaries. Dangerous, Adam knew, but irresistible. Joane felt it too; he could tell by the closeness of her body as she walked beside him.

Then abruptly her manner changed. 'Holy Mary preserve us,' she said quietly, raising her eyebrows.

A pair of well-dressed young women were bearing down on them, trailed by their maids and servants. One of them was William Marshall's wife, the sister of the Earl of Derby. Adam remembered her from the Pentecost banquet, where she had been sitting with Joane.

'Cousin Elizabeth,' Joane said curtly. 'And Lady Maud, may God bless you and keep you.'

'And you, cousin,' Elizabeth replied, smiling. The other woman was the wife of Nicholas de Segrave; Adam had seen her a few times attending the court back at Hereford. Her brother Geoffrey de Lucy, he remembered, was one of the barons currently holding Gloucester Castle against Edward.

'Oh, but surely this is Adam de Norton!' Elizabeth said. 'We all heard of your deed of arms today – so chivalrous! Why so many men speak ill of it I don't know . . .'

'You were injured?' the other lady asked, leaning closer and frowning at the bruised welt on Adam's brow.

'Almost entirely recovered, thank you my lady,' he replied, dipping his head in a bow.

'Oh, but the recent news from Winchester has surely injured you too?' Elizabeth went on, her face twisted with concern. 'To hear of William de St John's betrayal of our cause . . . your betrothal to his daughter in ruins . . . And she's such a lovely girl, so I hear!'

Adam could only dip his head once more, conscious of the colour rising to his face. He felt foolish, and there was nothing he could say.

'Sir Adam needs to rest,' Joane said abruptly. 'You must excuse us.'

The two ladies made their farewells and departed, their followers trailing after them. Adam clearly heard Elizabeth's childish giggle as they moved away.

'Please forgive my cousin,' Joane said quietly. 'She has little to occupy her mind but marriages and family alliances. Her viciousness is quite accidental.'

'Is Lord Simon still holding her brother prisoner?'

'In the Tower of London, yes. Hugh Despenser's wife is his jailor. He'll probably have seduced her by Michaelmas and made his escape . . .'

Adam gave her a quizzical glance, unsure whether she was teasing him. But they were nearing his tent now, and Joane led him into the lee of a large cart piled with barrels. It was the closest place to privacy they might find in the midst of the camp. At a gesture from Joane, Petronilla drifted a few steps onward, although she appeared very unhappy about it.

'You'll recall what I said, back in Hereford,' Joane told Adam, dropping her voice. 'I wanted to thank you, for deciding as you did. It's a reassurance, having you near me. With Robert gone, and my husband so resentful of everything I do . . . I know he suspects us – God knows, *everyone* knows, but . . .'

Adam drew a quick breath. *He* had not known. Was that why Humphrey had been acting so warmly towards him recently? Was his apparent generosity and support merely a way of placing Adam in his debt, and in his power? He suppressed a shudder, then a momentary swell of anger towards Joane. She was a married woman, wife of a powerful and vengeful magnate. De Bohun had threatened Adam once; he had no protection from the man's reprisals now. But the thought was ignoble. It was unchivalrous. More importantly, he realised, he did not care.

'If all I can do is reassure you, my lady,' he said, his voice thickening, 'then you have my promise . . .'

'No,' she said, and moved closer to him. She raised her finger and placed it against his lips. 'Promise nothing. I ask nothing. I just . . .' Her words faltered, and for three long heartbeats they looked at each other. Then Joane leaned closer still, her body against his, and lightly kissed the corner of his mouth. Then she stepped away.

Adam stepped back too, and bumped against the side of the cart. A movement caught his eye and he turned quickly, with an expression of confrontation.

'I was looking for you, master!' Eustace said.

The squire had appeared around the cart's far side. How long had he been standing there? What had he seen?

'Sir Humphrey de Bohun wants to speak with you,' Eustace went on. His tongue flicked over his lips, either nervously or in relish, and there was a cold look of assessment in his eyes.

Of course, Adam thought with a plunging sense of despair. Eustace de Brumlegh was the son of Humphrey's tenant. Eustace was Humphrey's eye and his ear. And Eustace had seen and heard everything.

Chapter 17

Darkness had fallen by the time Adam arrived at Humphrey de Bohun's pavilion. Finding it had been easy enough; the blue and white striped tent was almost as large as the ones occupied by Simon de Montfort and King Henry. A brazier burned outside, and the interior was lit by candle sconces. One of Sir Humphrey's squires conducted Adam to the heart of the candles' glow, where his master sat before a chess board, idly studying the arrangement of the pieces with a cup of wine dangling from his fingers. Humphrey set the cup aside as Adam approached and bowed, then gestured for him to sit on a facing stool.

'Your behaviour today lacked restraint, and you showed no forbearance,' he declared, not bothering with any polite greeting. 'You allowed yourself to be provoked by empty taunts, and you endangered the whole army by ignoring Lord Simon's explicit command.'

Adam said nothing. Restraint and forbearance were required here too.

'Then again,' de Bohun said with a shrug, 'I might have done the same once, when I was a younger man eager to make a good name for myself.'

Adam struggled to hide his irritation. As the son of the Earl of Hereford, Sir Humphrey's good name had been granted to him at birth. Never had he had to fight for reputation or renown. This time Adam could not remain silent.

'De Malmaines challenged me directly,' he said. 'It was a personal matter. It would have been dishonourable to refuse.'

'Your *duty* was to refuse!' de Bohun snarled, raising his voice. 'And duty is the higher honour, remember that.' He took a moment to compose himself once more, and then continued. 'I have spoken with Lord Simon, and urged him to forgive your lapse. He too understands the passions of youth.'

'Thank you, my lord,' Adam said. The words felt jagged in his throat. Once again, he thought, he had been placed in de Bohun's debt.

Sir Humphrey studied Adam for a while, then snorted a laugh. 'How like Robert de Dunstanville you are becoming,' he said, smiling with cold eyes. 'He's trained you well. An independent spirit, a taciturn nature, a fondness for brooding . . . I only hope you have not adopted his changeable loyalties too, or his habitual insubordination.'

This time Adam could only shrug and incline his head. De Bohun left a long pause, staring off into the darkened recesses of the pavilion, where his campaign bed stood beside his trunks and cases. He seemed to be composing himself. Adam spoke again, just to fill the silence.

'Surely Lord Simon must confront Giffard's men sooner or later,' he said. 'They block the road back to Hereford.'

'We won't be returning to Hereford,' de Bohun said promptly, his attention snapping back to the conversation.

Adam frowned, perplexed.

'With Edward and Gilbert de Clare holding the Severn crossings,' Humphrey explained, 'we'd only be cut off there. Lord Simon's sent messengers to Bristol, ordering the shipmen to bring every craft of burden north over the estuary to Newport. We'll meet them there, board the ships and cross to the far shore.'

Adam widened his eyes. He tried not to imagine the difficulties of crossing the Severn by ship, men and horses packed together onto frail and creaking vessels. They would have to abandon their artillery, and much of their baggage.

'Simon's son is bringing a great army from London,' Humphrey went on. 'Over twenty banners – thousands of men. After we get across the Severn we'll combine forces with him, march north against Edward, and crush the rebels wherever we find them.'

'It's certainly a bold strategy,' Adam said.

'It's . . . a strategy, at least,' Humphrey replied. He exhaled loudly and touched his brow. 'Often I wonder,' he said, 'whether Lord Simon is a saint or an idiot, a military genius or a fool leading us all to disaster . . . He wears a hair shirt, did you know that?'

Adam shook his head.

'Under his tunic at all times, next to his skin,' Humphrey said. His fingers itched at the embroidered silk neckline of his own garment. 'Penance,' he said, 'and due humility, for the glory that the Lord has bestowed upon him. God knows, he may well scourge himself as well.'

He snatched up his cup and took a long swallow of wine, as if to wash down his discomfort. 'Your forty days of knight service are nearly over, I think,' he said, changing the subject with obvious relief. 'You'll stay with the army, and serve for pay?'

'I will,' Adam said. In truth, he had no choice. His lands would already have been taken by William de St John, or de Brayboef; he would find no welcome there.

'My offer of the tenancy of Crofton and its estates still stands,' Humphrey said. 'And I've decided that I shall take over your debt to the Jew Aaron. It's only right that I should do so, as my father's full ransom remains unpaid.'

'Thank you, my lord,' Adam said again, feeling the sense of obligation weighing heavier upon him. Taking on Adam's debt cost de Bohun nothing anyway, for the time being. Adam had long suspected that Sir Humphrey was running short of money, just as he was running short of influence, and of friends.

'And I thank you,' Humphrey said, his voice taking on a rougher note, 'for watching over my wife as well.'

Adam's attention sharpened. *Now it comes.*

'She is young,' de Bohun went on, 'and has a lively mind, and a disdain for constraint. I am glad that a man I can trust is close to her.'

Adam drew a long breath, waiting for what must surely follow. De Bohun's face writhed. How old was he now? Between thirty-five and forty, Adam guessed. Not as old as Simon de Montfort, or the king, or the doting husband of Joane's cousin Elizabeth. But he was surely twice Joane's age. Adam knew the stories in the romances, the tales of the young knight's unrequited love for the wife of his lord. Devotion until death. The point was the lack of requital: a form of honourable self-denial. But Adam had been denying himself for two years now, and felt no more virtuous because of that.

'I am aware,' Humphrey said, lowering his voice to a heavy growl as he leaned towards Adam, 'that my wife was not a virgin on her wedding night. I have decided to ask her nothing about this. And I ask you nothing about it either. But you must know that I cannot accept any further intimacy between you. You understand?'

His lips bulged as he ran his tongue over his teeth. Adam nodded, just once. It occurred to him for the first time that Sir Humphrey was afraid. Not of him, not personally, although that could come in time. Afraid instead of disgrace, of humiliation and ridicule, and perhaps of losing Joane.

'She is my wife,' de Bohun said thickly, not looking at him. 'You may think me a fool, and perhaps I have been one, but from now on I am determined not to be made a greater fool still. *You will remember this.*'

Then he sat back abruptly, letting the implied threat linger. The muscles of his neck were drawn tight. It had cost him an effort to say those words, and now he had no more to offer; he dismissed Adam with a motion of his hand.

*

For three days more, Lord Simon's troops remained camped before the walls of Monmouth Castle. For three days, John Giffard's gadfly army issued their challenges, and for three days de Montfort refused them. On the evening of the second day the castle garrison surrendered, declaring that they had held out long enough for honour to be satisfied, and Simon ordered the gatehouse and outer walls demolished so it could not be held by his foes. It made no odds; the following morning, news arrived of the surrender of Gloucester Castle to Lord Edward. With the fall of that bastion, de Montfort's enemies were free to advance against him.

Lord Simon broke camp the next day, dismantled his siege engines and loaded his wagons, then formed his army and led them off down the muddy roads south-westwards, with Giffard's troops trailing their march and threatening any who lagged behind. On Friday, the Morrow of the Visitation, Simon's men at arms took Usk Castle in a single assault. The day after that, the army crawled another ten miles to the town of Newport, where the river flowed into the Severn Estuary.

And at Newport, disaster unfurled before them.

Standing on the shore one evening, three days after their arrival, Simon de Montfort and his followers stared out towards the grey horizon and saw the fires burning over the water. They heard the distant screams of men and the clash of arms, the thunder of wooden hulls rammed together, the crackle of shattered oars and flaming sails and the desperate cries of men burned or drowning in the brackish waters. By the following morning the charred debris of the ships was washing up among the tidal wrack on the Severn's muddy shore. The bodies of men too, some of them blackened by fire or hacked by steel.

A handful of survivors managed to reach dry land, clinging to floating spars and wreckage. Gilbert de Clare's fighting galleys had caught them in mid-channel, the sailors said. Eleven of the ships from Bristol had been sunk, burned or destroyed. The rest had turned back. And Simon de Montfort's army was trapped on the estuary's northern shore. The commissary clerks reported that the food supplies were almost exhausted. Dark clouds rolled overhead, and the rain spattered down as warm as spit.

And where, men asked, was Lord Edward? Where was Gilbert de Clare, and the army of the Marcher Lords?

Newport was not much of a town. A few score buildings of wood and thatch surrounded on three sides by a ditch and palisade and on the fourth by the ale-brown waters of the Usk. The bank was lined with wooden wharfs and jetties, and a bridge spanned the river on tall timbers black with age and crusted with green weed.

At noon on the day after the destruction of the ships, Adam was standing near the riverbank staring out across the water. A figure was approaching along the far shore, a man running with desperate intent. Others were watching; dozens of men waiting for any news, any word that might bring hope or clarity. Simon de Montfort strode from the town church and came down to the bridgehead. Men moved towards him as if by instinct, drawn by his air of command.

The runner crossed the bridge, almost slipping on the wet timbers. He ran directly for the group gathered around Lord Simon, and everyone pressed closer to hear what the man had to say. The words carried clearly in the silence.

'Lord Edward is coming, lord! With Gilbert de Clare and John Giffard, and the Marcher Lords and all their men. Thousands of men, lord . . . The Leopard is coming!'

'Then he shall not pass!' a loud voice cried. Henry de Hastings stood forth from the crowd, his hand on his sword hilt. Other men began to shout in his support, pushing forward once more.

'We hold the bridge, yes,' Simon announced, pitching his words so all could hear. 'And if it cannot be held, we destroy it.'

'Who's with me?' Henry de Hastings yelled, drawing his sword and brandishing it above his head. His face was alight with ferocious pleasure; after being denied a fight back at Monmouth, here was the opportunity to clash with the enemy. Not a mounted combat either, fast and swirling, but a hard-slogging foot battle, face to face and toe to toe, close to the steel.

'You, de Norton!' de Hastings cried, seeing Adam in the crowd around the bridgehead. 'You're not one to shrink from a challenge!' He crowed with laughter. 'Will you stand with me now?'

Adam gritted his teeth. He knew he could not refuse without his courage and loyalties being once more questioned; besides, in his heart he desired this too. Others were already moving aside for him to pass.

'I'm with you,' he said, and de Hastings grinned and thumped his fist onto Adam's shoulder.

But in Adam's mind rose the vision of the burned and drowned men he had seen that morning, the blackened wreckage on the shore. The memory of the fight at Rochester the year before, the broken timbers of the Medway crossing and the flames in the darkness, came to him like a premonition.

*

'Shields to the fore, spears at the ready!' the serjeants bellowed, urging their men forward. 'Hold at the centre, and give not a step!'

Timbers thundered beneath the stamping of boots as the troops advanced onto the bridge. They were Welsh and English foot soldiers, spearmen and archers, with serjeants in mail and iron helmets driving them on. The men in front carried big infantry shields to screen them from arrows; the river was a bowshot wide between its spreading mudbanks, but as the troops moved out onto the central spans of the bridge the enemy archers and crossbowmen along the far bank were already lofting their shafts at them. Arrows struck the timber of the roadway and the railings to either side, and thudded into the protecting shields.

The enemy had appeared on the far bank of the river just after evensong, but they had rested for several hours after their long march. Now the sun was nearing the horizon to the west, the last rays slanting down beneath the rim of low cloud and beaming across the muddy waters of the Usk to light the eastern side, and the army of Lord Edward waiting in battle array. Banners lined the road and the riverbank. Beneath them the troops mustered, foot and horse in their thousands, all of them waiting for the command to pour forward onto the narrow wooden span of the bridge and break through de Montfort's defensive line.

As he moved up through the throng of foot soldiers, Adam felt a hand on his arm and turned to find Hugh of Oystermouth behind him carrying a leather bag.

'If you're determined to fight,' Hugh said, 'best take this. A gift from the Lady Joane.'

Adam craned his head up, staring over his shoulder at the crowd gathered between the riverbank and the main street of the town, just out of archery range. He picked out Joane among them.

'Here,' Hugh said, drawing an iron object from the bag. It was a barrel-shaped great helm, the vents and sights edged in brass. 'You might just avoid any more clouts to the skull.'

'Where did she get it?' Adam asked. But Hugh just shrugged; and when Adam looked back towards the town once more, Joane had vanished into the crowd. He pulled the helm on over his mail coif and padded cap; at once the greasy-smelling iron enclosed him, trapping his breath, narrowing his vision to two bright slashes. Adam had trained in great helms before but had never worn one in real combat. He tied the laces under his jaw, then raised a mailed hand in acknowledgement, not knowing if Joane could still see him.

'Make way!' de Hastings was snarling, shoving his way towards the front ranks of the defenders. Adam followed behind him, and John de Kington joined them.

'Make way there for Lord Henry de Hastings!' one of the armoured men cried. Adam knew him: John Spadeberd was a retainer of de Montfort, and a veteran serjeant. He had led the night attack at Rochester; Adam only hoped he proved as redoubtable here.

The pack of men at the front, directly behind the line of shield-bearers, was uncomfortably dense. Adam felt shoulders and bodies pressing on him from all sides, the smell of oiled steel and sweat-stained gambesons, the breath of men half-sick with fear, was raw and potent. The arrows were falling thicker now, smacking into the big shields and hissing past the bridge railings on both sides, some dropping to strike the men behind him. Adam knew that their own archers and crossbowmen were returning the shots, but he could see nothing of them. A sudden shout went up around him, the Welsh troops and many of the English joining in the strange screeching battle cry he had heard at Bridgnorth. From the far bank, the Welshmen among the enemy gave an answering shriek. The noise echoed inside the bell of Adam's helmet. Sweat was already pouring into his eyes, and he was struggling to draw breath.

Then the enemy came, rushing across the narrow bridge as fast and sudden as a mill-race. Packed in among the defenders, his helmet closing off all peripheral vision, Adam heard the shouts ahead of him and only had time to brace his forearm behind his shield before the enemy charge crashed against the line.

Spears stabbed and darted, shafts clattering together, steel heads ramming into shields and bodies. A man fell directly ahead of Adam, and an enemy spearman let out a shout of triumph as he pushed forward into the broken line. His shout rose to a scream as John Spadeberd's axe sheared through his knee, and he fell beside his victim. 'Hold them! Hold them!' a voice behind Adam was bellowing. 'Don't give a step!'

Pushing forward, Adam swung blows across the stooped back of the man in front of him. His blade sliced through the fore-arm of an enemy spearman, then shaved the rim off a raised shield. He could barely see anything around him now, and fought blindly, his head ringing with the muffled thunder of battle. A man behind him was driving his spear forward across his shoulder with both hands, screaming with each thrust. A choked gasp, the spearshaft fell slack, and the dead man slipped down into the mesh of bodies, to be trampled underfoot.

Adam was into the front line now, almost invulnerable in his full mail and great helm. Henry de Hastings was to his right, and John de Kington beyond them, and together they pinned the defensive line, with Spadeberd and his serjeants holding the gaps between them. The momentum of the first enemy charge had broken but more men were pouring up to reinforce them until they packed the narrow space of the bridge. A yell, and the front lines of enemy spearmen and serjeants surged forward again. Adam cut a man down with a single hacking blow, his blade shearing flesh and bone. Then the numbers were too great in front of him. One staggering step back, his feet sliding on the blood-soaked planks. No room to use his shield; he slipped his arm from the straps and let it hang from his shoulder. Reversing his sword, he gripped the midpoint of the blade in his mailed left fist and stabbed with it, driving it like a spear at the exposed bodies of the men in front of him.

Something clashed off his helmet, jolting his neck. Another blow came from the other side, an axe clashing against the steel and then deflecting hard against his shoulder. *Stay upright*, Adam told himself. *Stay on your feet and they can't harm you.*

To his right, Henry de Hastings was working like a reaper cut-ting hay. Even through his helmet Adam could hear the man's bellowing shouts. John Spadeberd hewed with his axe, bringing down another foe, and then a two-handed spear blow punched into his belly and he fell.

Adam shuffled left, panic beating at his chest, then felt the crush of men pushing him further. The bridge railing was beside him now, the timber looking flimsy and notched with cuts, bristling with arrows. Beyond it was the drop to the water below. Already men had fallen, or leaped for safety from the furious mesh of combat. Shoving back, slamming his steel-clad elbows against the men beside him, Adam fought his way towards the centre. He jabbed with his sword, point downwards, and drove it into the open mouth of a screaming spearman.

Enemies directly in front of him now, their faces filling his vision through the helm's narrow slits. Screaming mouths, broken teeth, bloodied knuckles clutching spears and axes. Blood spattered and sprayed as each man went down, and the bodies of the dead and the writhing injured were tangled underfoot.

Hard breaths, his body a pump of heat and fury. Adam stabbed forward, took a step to close with the enemy and then another. Something caught at his legs and he almost fell. Stabbed downwards, took another step. A clanging blow against his helm, then another. Somebody was beating on it like a smith beating an anvil. His throat was ragged with hot breath, and he was choking. Whirling his sword, he cut blindly to his right. A strangled cry, and the wild clanging blows on his helmet stopped. Through the pack of enemy fighters ahead of him Adam saw the face of Fulk Ticeburn. He saw the man's expression sharpen as he recognised the blazon on the shield still hanging from Adam's shoulder, saw his beard open into a full-throated scream of rage.

Then the mob around him surged, and just for a moment Adam felt himself carried by them. Was he still on his feet? He could not see the sky, nor the timber below him. The wooden railing collided with his chest, and for one moment of stark terror he felt the timber creak under his weight, and through the slits of his helm he saw the dark waters waiting for him. Not a chance down there: he would drown under the weight of his armour.

A yell and a shove, and he pushed himself back into the fight. He was too far forward now, enemies all around him. Where was Ticeburn? The shield swung on its shoulder strap, battering against his side as he jabbed and hacked with the point of his sword. His feet slipped on blood, and he fell briefly to one knee. Up again. Men crushing in all around him, wrestling him and trying to drag him down. From the corner of his eye, the angle of his helmet slit, Adam saw a weaselly man with a grey-stubbled chin crushed tight against his shoulder. The man had a dagger, a wickedly pointed misericord, and he was angling the blade upward and pushing it beneath the rim of Adam's helmet. Eyes rolling, caught too tight in the crush to move or to raise his arms, Adam watched the man as he probed with his blade, his face creased in desperate concentration. He could almost feel the bright point of the steel edging around the hem of his mail coif to touch the flesh of his cheek. At any moment the steel would be driving into his mouth, into his brain . . . Horror transfixed him. He could not move.

Then the pack gave another sudden surge. For a moment the weaselly man still clung on, desperately jabbing with his dagger. Then with a roar the axeman behind Adam's shoulder swung his blade down and cleaved the attacker's face from his skull. Blood and viscera spattered the side of Adam's helmet, spraying through the vents and eye slits, then he was staggering free once more.

*

Hands dragged him backwards, gripping him by the hem of his surcoat and the dangling straps of his shield. Adam's feet were skidding and he almost fell, but then he was bundled through the press of men and into open space, striding like a drunkard back along the bridge towards dry land.

Matthew unlaced his helmet and pulled it off, and Hugh sluiced his face with water. Behind him Adam could hear the battle still raging, but for a few long moments all he could do was suck down lungfuls of air.

'What madness was that?' Hugh was saying, clasping him by the shoulder. 'You were so far forward the enemy almost took you – did you plan to push through them all and challenge Lord Edward himself?'

Adam grinned, still dazed. But he remembered seeing Ticeburn among the enemy soldiers. The thought that he might have been dragged down, overwhelmed, at the mercy of that man chilled his blood at once.

'We held them at least,' he said, his mouth dry. He took a flask of wine from Hugh and drank greedily.

'For now, yes,' Hugh said, and gestured to his right. In the glow of the summer twilight men were dragging kegs of pitch and bundles of tow from the warehouses that fronted the riverside wharfs. Several had already scrambled down beneath the bridge timbers where they stood above the muddy bank. They were intending to burn the bridge, Adam realised. But the attackers must be held long enough for the flames to take hold.

'I need to go back there,' he said. Behind him he saw Henry de Hastings lurching back from the bridge supported by two of his men. The front of his yellow surcoat was spattered with red, and he bared his teeth in a savage grin as he passed. Other men were moving up to take his place – Guy de Montfort, Lord Simon's younger son, bearing the fork-tailed white lion on his shield; William de Boyton, his blue shield emblazoned with gold scallop shells.

'I need to go back,' Adam said again.

'You should not,' Hugh said, in a scolding tone. But from the look in his eye he knew that his words were useless. Staring towards the bridge, Adam made out horses at the far end. Armoured knights in the saddle, and the enemy foot soldiers scrambling to form a lane for them. They were intending to scatter the defenders by the shock of their charge.

'Take this then,' Matthew said, holding out the great helm. He had managed to wipe most of the blood and gore from the polished steel.

'No, I can't wear that again.'

The boy winced, pointing to the dents and scars in the metal, the marks of blades and bolts and spear points. Any one of them, Adam realised, could have split his skull or opened his face.

'*Wear it!*' Hugh insisted. This time he was not to be denied.

Adam took a long breath and then plunged his head back into the reeking barrel of the helm. At once his vision narrowed, his throat tightened. But he was already striding back towards the fight on the bridge as he tied the laces under his chin.

'Close up! Close tight and hold!' one of the serjeants was shouting. Guy de Montfort had taken his place in the front line, William de Boyton beside him. Adam pushed his way through to join them.

'They're firing the bridge?' de Boyton bellowed, the slits of his helm rotating to face Adam. Adam could only nod. 'So be it,' the other knight said.

From the far riverbank the mounted men were advancing, three of them riding abreast at a heavy trot, lances already couched. Their horses were clad in heavy mail trappers, swinging as they moved. The spearmen and serjeants in their path were crushed back against the railings, some of them hanging over the side of the bridge to escape the thundering hooves. Ahead of him Adam could see the planking of the roadway pooled with blood, wiped and smeared by feet, a couple of bodies still lying where they had fallen. The river below was ruddy in the dying light.

'Spears!' the leading serjeant yelled. 'Spears to the front – they won't charge against them!' Immediately a bristling hedge of shafts and points jutted from the defensive line. But Adam could sense that the press behind him was thinning, men dropping back in retreat towards the safety of the riverbank. The riders increased their pace, closing fast. At some point, either their horses would falter or the line would collapse as terror took hold.

Only a dozen strides remained when the leading horse went down, its hooves skating out from beneath it on the slick of blood. The animal fell sideways, spilling the rider from the saddle, and at once the horse of the knight to the left collided with it. The third rider hauled back on his reins, trying to vault the fallen animal in his path, but his armoured mount baulked and reared, turning on its rear legs. Crossbows snapped, and one of the bolts struck his horse in the fore-quarter beneath the mail barding. The downed animal was rolling and kicking, legs smashing at the timber bridge railings as the rider tried to scramble free.

'Fall back!' a voice behind Adam yelled. 'Slow and steady!'

He drew air through the vents of his helm, and realised that he could smell smoke. Behind him the bridge was beginning to burn, the pitch and tow kindled between the dry timbers of the supporting framework. The scene in front of him was lit with a livid fiery glare, the spilled blood either unnaturally bright or black as ink, the plunging horses etched with hard shadow. The fallen animal had broken a leg but managed to reach the smashed railing and fling itself into the river below. The other two knights were retreating, both struggling to regain control of their mounts.

By the time the defenders had re-formed their line the heat of the flames was falling on their backs in waves, and the glow stretched their shadows out over the bridge. The enemy foot soldiers were moving up again now, the blades of their spears and falchions flashing in the fiery light, their spear points flame-red. The defenders levelled their bristling hedge of spears once more. Sparks blew in the dense summer air. Adam felt the heat burning on his armour, the sweat turning his body to liquid. At some point he would have to retreat – would somebody send word? Would there be an order, a trumpet blast?

Then all thought was eclipsed as the rush of enemy foot soldiers crossed the bloody slick. They had archers with them

— this time, somebody was thinking clearly. While the spearmen held de Montfort's men at bay, the archers bent their bows and shot directly into them, the range so tight they could not miss. An arrow struck Adam's helm, another punched against his armoured shoulder. A third, almost at once, pinged off the side of his eye slit. His head ringing, he kept his shield up, and the arrows snicked at his armoured shins and knees.

But behind him, men were dying. A man in a gambeson fell, shot through the neck. Another serjeant dropped to his knees, an arrow jutting from his face. And now the lines were opening, the enemy were beginning to press forward again. To Adam's left, a man threw aside his falchion and vaulted the bridge railing. With a shock he realised that he was almost alone, only de Boyton and one of the remaining serjeants still held the bridge beside him.

And the enemy were still coming on. They were sliding along the railings to either side now, threatening to get behind Adam and the other defenders and encircle them. Backing, one step at a time, shield up against the arrows and sword lashing at any-one who got close, Adam and de Boyton retreated in step. Adam could feel the fire behind him, but he dared not look back. Every breath sucked in smoke. Through the slits of his helmet he could see only whirling shadows, demonic faces lit by flame, spears that jabbed and arrows that flashed from the darkness. He was in a furnace, his armour aflame, the arrows stuck all over his shield and body catching fire. He grabbed another breath, and felt he was swallowing down smoke.

Somebody was screaming his name. In the mad fire-glow he saw Fulk Ticeburn advancing on him, sword raised. Then he could no longer see, he could no longer feel. He was face down on the timbers, his face crushed against his helmet vents, and somebody was gripping his ankles and dragging him.

The world spun, wreathed in smoke. Then water crashed over his face, and he could breathe again.

Chapter 18

It was approaching midnight when Simon de Montfort led his army out of Newport, and by then half the town was in flames. Sparks from the burning bridge had carried on the warm summer breeze and lodged in the thatch of the riverside sheds. The fires had jumped swiftly to the neighbouring houses. A few men had joined with the townspeople in trying to douse the conflagration, but most had simply stood back and watched the town burn. It belonged to Gilbert de Clare anyway.

An hour after nightfall a sudden heavy rainstorm had quelled the worst of the fires, but the smouldering thatch burst into flame once more when it slackened. The bridge continued burning too, until nothing remained of the supports and the timber roadway but a charred skeleton. Lord Edward's army, trapped on the far riverbank, could only stand in the rain and the drifting smoke and watch as their foes made their escape into the night.

Adam turned in the saddle as he followed the column up the road away from the town, staring back at the fiery glow through the veils of drizzle. Hugh of Oystermouth rode to one side of him and John de Kington to the other; it had been they who dragged him from the fight on the bridge after he fell, and they and Matthew who had pulled him upright, and then removed his helmet and poured water over his face. Even then, so Hugh said,

Adam did not appear to recognise them or understand what was happening.

'We thought you'd been struck dumb,' Hugh told him. 'And maybe deafened too – it was a while before you could speak, or focus your gaze properly.'

Adam could remember nothing of that, and still felt dazed in the aftermath of the fight. Astonishingly, he was otherwise unharmed. His body felt battered, his head was ringing and his legs and shoulders were covered in bruises from the impact of arrows and spears, but nowhere had the blows broken the links of his mail. It had been a courageous defence, he supposed, and a reckless one too, but it had amounted to nothing: the bridge they had fought so savagely to hold was lost to the flames, and the army was retreating north once more in the ignominy of a night march, the intermittent rain turning the road to mud and soaking through the stooped backs of the men and the caparisons of the horses. They had left most of their carts and wheeled transport to block the streets of Newport.

On through the night they marched, few of them knowing what their destination might be but all knowing that they needed to put many miles between them and Lord Edward's army. The sky cleared, and they marched under the blaze of the stars. Swinging wide to the west of Usk, they hugged the flanks of the hills, pausing now and again to close up the gaps in their column. But soon enough they were moving once more, both horses and men walking with heads hanging, scarcely a sound except the thud of feet and hooves, the clink of bridles and armour and the occasional groan from the wounded.

Before dawn the Dog Star rose above the horizon, and by first light the column was approaching the town of Abergavenny. Sunrise lit the looming hill to the west in bright purple and gold, and ahead of them lay the shadowed country of the Black Mountains. Their enemy was far behind them now, their scouts reported no outriders of John Giffard's force on their flank, and the men in

the marching column were too footsore and weary to do anything but throw themselves down and sleep.

*

'Do you know what day it is?' King Henry asked.

Kneeling, Adam thought for a moment. In the turmoil of the
previous week he had almost lost track of time and date altogether. 'Friday, majesty,' he said.

The king made a light tutting sound. 'It is the Feast of the
Seven Holy Brothers,' he declared, his eyes fluttering closed for
a moment. 'Which is why I have asked my brother-in-law the
Earl of Leicester that we delay our departure today, so that the
proper religious observances can proceed unhindered.'

Adam could only bow his head in acknowledgement. Current intelligence suggested that Lord Edward had not pressed his
pursuit much beyond Newport, and had probably turned back
for Gloucester already, but he suspected that the king's desire to
linger here was inspired by more than just piety. Simon de Montfort had already stayed a full day and a night at Abergavenny, and
there was a long hard road ahead of them.

They were in the king's pavilion, pitched with the rest of
the camp on the meadows between the castle and the river.
The castle itself was one of Humphrey de Bohun's fortresses,
but it had not been properly prepared for the arrival of the
royal party, and the king had preferred to remain with his
household in his own familiar tents. Although much of the
baggage had been abandoned during the chaotic retreat from
the burning town of Newport, the interior of his pavilion was
still sumptuous. Carpets covered the matting underfoot, and
the painted and upholstered furniture could have graced a palace. The sunlight was diffused through layers of white linen
and silk, with gold embroidered foliage picked out with green
and red flowers.

'At least it's stopped raining, eh?' the king said, with the twitch of a smile. 'I suspect the crops will have suffered. No doubt the people will blame me for that too – unless they think that my brother-in-law Simon can intercede with God and change the weather, hmm?'

The king was coping quite admirably with the stresses of life on campaign, Adam had to admit. Henry had adopted a mildly whimsical air of detachment, as if nothing around him was really any of his concern. As if it might perhaps be amusing, seen in a certain light. He sat upon a raised chair, stroking his short greying beard, or playing with the heavy rings on his fingers as he gazed into the spangled glow through the linen walls.

There were plenty of others in the pavilion too – the king was never alone. His secretaries, chamber servants and serjeants-at-arms stood by, his chaplain waited attendance, and four members of his monastic choir knelt in silent prayer. Hugh Despenser, the square-faced justiciar, had conducted Adam into the royal presence and now stood a few steps behind him with respectfully lowered head.

'And are the soldiers still going hungry?' the king asked nobody in particular. 'I hear they refuse to eat the meat and milk-curds the Welshmen bring? They want bread, I expect, eh! But there's not a scrap of grain left, and harvest is weeks away.'

'They curse this land, and long for their homes, majesty,' Despenser said. He at least had the social standing to speak freely to the king.

'As do we all, Sir Hugh,' the king said ruefully. '*As do we all!*'

'Majesty,' Despenser said, with emphasis. 'This is Sir Adam de Norton, a knight of Hampshire.'

'Ah,' Henry replied vaguely, his gaze passing fleetingly over Adam's kneeling figure. He looked back again, his eyes gaining focus. 'Were you not one of those who fought upon the bridge at Newport?' he asked.

'I was, majesty,' Adam said, daring to look up.

'Bold deeds, bold deeds,' Henry said, fretting at his beard. 'I saw some of it, from afar. Bold deeds on *both* sides, of course . . . We can only regret the destruction of property. Still at least they can't blame me for that, ha ha!'

'Sir Adam's term of service expired some days past, majesty,' Despenser said, and cleared his throat.

'Oh, indeed? And does he wish to return to his estates? Lucky man, to do so.' His expression clouded. 'Oh, but we hear that the Lord of Basing has occupied much of Hampshire, I think? He and some others. Enterprising men . . .!'

'*Rebels*, majesty,' said Despenser. 'Rebels and disturbers of the peace, as your own proclamations have made clear.'

'Have they? Oh, I suppose so,' the king said, with a diffident wave. 'Well then, I assume Sir Adam de Norton desires to perform further service, for a royal wage?'

'I do, majesty,' Adam said.

'Very well. Who am I to say otherwise? Although we might wish all these wars were at an end, and peace restored once more . . .'

He gave the order, and one of his clerks duly wrote out a document of contract, stating that Adam de Norton would perform continued military service at the knight's wage of two shillings per day, with one shilling for his squire and six pennies each for his groom and his herald. The contract was in the name of the king, but it would be Simon de Montfort paying out the silver; for all the baggage abandoned back at Newport, the wagons carrying the royal treasury had not been forsaken.

While the royal seal was affixed, Adam advanced to the king's chair and knelt once more. Henry stooped to kiss him and seal the arrangement. The king had done this several times in recent days, Adam knew, but mostly for the greater magnates and bannerets in Lord Simon's army. Very few of the minor vassal knights remained.

But as he raised his head once more and briefly met the king's eyes, with the one drooping lid that Edward had inherited, Adam saw a cold grey fury burning there. For all his performance of mildness, Henry still longed for a very different victory to the one that his loyal subject Simon de Montfort desired. And Adam did not doubt that, given the chance, the king would see them all swinging from hempen ropes. Chilled, he backed away upon his knees.

'Now then,' Henry declared, 'I believe it is almost time to hear mass.' He stood up, visibly cheered. 'And perhaps we should pray that the Seven Holy Brothers take pity upon us, and help to bring an end to this unchristian conflict!'

Outside the pavilion, Adam paused to stretch the aches from his muscles. Clouds were rolling in once again, darkening the sky above the Black Mountains, and the air felt warm and damp. He looked up at the castle on its hillock above the meadows, the chamber block rising above the curtain wall and the tall tower capped by wooden hoardings. Humphrey de Bohun had taken up his quarters in the castle, as the king would not, and Joane was with him. For a moment a pained frown tightened Adam's brow, then he walked on.

This was what his glorious military campaign had come to, he told himself grimly. His lands were gone, and he served for coin. He was a mercenary, no different to the bare-legged Welsh archers who were paid three pennies a day. Darkness clouded his mind. But he reminded himself that he could be doing much worse.

Many of the common soldiers and several of the knights and serjeants had fallen sick; dysentery, so the physician Philip Porpeis had declared. With the sickness and the lack of food, the muggy heat and the intermittent downpours, the camp was riven with misery and gloom. Nobody even knew where Lord Simon was intending to go next, after his retreat from Newport; he was in conference with his greater magnates hourly, but none could say what his strategy might be, or whether he even had one at all.

Stamping through the mud of the camp towards his own tent, Adam passed a line of men, grooms and archers, squatting miserably over the latrine trench. *Two shillings a day*, he thought. He snorted a laugh, and the squatting men glared after him as he stalked away.

*

By afternoon the army was moving once more, west and north from Abergavenny along the narrowing valley of the Usk. The slopes of the mountains loomed over them, and they passed castles and isolated houses, several ruined or burned, others occupied by the Welsh. There were plenty more Welshmen with the army too now, short sinewy figures in hoods who carried spears, bows or bundles of javelins with them everywhere they went. The English soldiers tramped stolidly through the showers, keeping their eyes averted from both the mountains and their new allies alike.

'Apparently,' said Hugh of Oystermouth as he rode his scrawny plodding mare, 'some of the militiamen are muttering that the Welsh have been murdering English settlers and raping their wives and daughters. And that they feast on the raw flesh of beasts and men alike, washing the bloody gobbets down with curdled milk!' He shook his head disapprovingly. 'You English have been telling each other such ghoulish tales for generations, I believe.'

'Perhaps they're true?' Adam said. 'Some of the greatest men in the army believe them. Henry de Hastings is convinced the Welsh are a nation of devils.'

'Henry de Hastings is a devil himself, or the son of one,' Hugh said quietly, after checking that none of Sir Henry's retainers could overhear him. 'A man of inordinate fury and violence,' he went on, shaking his head. 'His mother was Scottish, I believe, which might explain it – now *they* are a truly savage race.'

'He seems not to hate me as much nowadays, at least.'

'Perhaps,' Hugh said, angling a glance beneath the rim of his dripping straw hat, 'he thinks you are not dissimilar to himself?'

Adam shrugged off the comment. He was gazing towards the riders further up the column, who followed the blue and white pennons of Humphrey de Bohun's retinue. Joane was among them, but she wore a hood and Adam could see nothing of her. He had only glimpsed her as they left Abergavenny, and he doubted they would have an opportunity to speak together any time soon. Unless, he thought, he made such an opportunity himself.

He was jolted from his thoughts as a band of horsemen came past, cantering on up the road. The red and white banner flew before them: Simon de Montfort's personal emblem, and Lord Simon himself rode behind it. Adam watched him as he passed on up the road: the troops fell back from his path, some of them calling out his name, some of them even dropping to kneel in the roadside mud. Amazingly, Adam realised, the awe that he inspired seemed only to have grown with adversity. Tired and hungry, retreating into a strange and fearsome land, the soldiers still trusted in the power of Lord Simon, after everything.

They rode on, and after ten miles the scouts led them north up a broad valley that climbed into the hill country. The Black Valley, it was called: *Cwm Du* in the Welsh tongue, as Hugh explained. The clouds roiled overhead, flashing bursts of hot sun over the marching men and horses and the few remaining carts and wagons. Then the rain sprayed down once more.

'We are headed for Hay I suppose?' Hugh said.

Adam shrugged. He had no idea of the country, nor the destination. Behind him Matthew rode silently, locked in his own turbulent thoughts, and his squire Eustace swayed in the saddle and appeared half asleep.

'Humphrey de Bohun has another castle at Hay,' Hugh went on, 'so we might at least find some secure lodgings there. But I believe that Llywelyn ap Gruffudd holds most of that territory at present . . .' He perked up visibly as a thought struck him, his eyes brightening. 'Perhaps,' he said, 'we are going to meet the Prince of Wales himself!'

But they did not reach Hay that night. Before the light faded, the army pitched their camp in the open valley, with a stream on one flank and the rocky mountainside on the other. The ground was dry at least, not boggy, and there was clean water for the horses. The men lit fires to dry their shoes and hose, warily eyeing the Welsh at their own fires, and their empty bellies grumbled.

The last light was almost gone when Adam stirred himself and walked through the camp. There were sentries posted all around the perimeter, and both up and down the valley, but he kept his sword with him and walked with his hand on the hilt. The new moon was not yet the merest sliver, but the stars appeared all the brighter above the black shoulders of the mountains.

Turning his back on the campfires, Adam gazed up into the sky, letting his eye pick out one cluster of stars after the next. Just for a moment he imagined that the constellations, the planets between them, were people. Simon de Montfort and Lord Edward, Humphrey de Bohun and Robert de Dunstanville, Joane, and Isabel de St John. All those who might determine his fate, who pushed him and pulled him towards contrary desires. If fate was already written in the stars, as Hugh claimed that some heretical men believed, then nothing Adam might do could avert it. But if he could gain some control over the outcomes of chance, if he could choose one over another, then fate was his to decide. His eye grew bleary, and the stars above him misted. He blinked, and they blazed once more, as cold and clear and remote as ever.

Strolling further, feigning a casual air, he picked out de Bohun's striped pavilion and the smaller tents surrounding it. He sidled closer, with more open purpose now, making sure to keep to the deepening shadows around the horse lines. *Skulking,* he thought — *I am skulking, like a thief.* From a nearby fire came the mournful singing of the Welsh, the sound rising and falling.

Luckily, he did not have to skulk for long. The flap of one of the larger tents opened, spilling a glow of rushlight from within. Joane's maid Petronilla appeared in the opening, then Adam heard a few soft words before Joane herself stepped forth and walked towards the horse lines. He followed, stepping carefully over the guy ropes and the tethers of the horses, and found Joane brushing down her jennet. She gave a start as Adam appeared on the horse's other side.

'Forgive me,' Adam said in a hushed voice. 'I was not expecting to see you out here. You have no groom?'

'A fool of a boy,' Joane said, going back to working with the brush, 'who knows nothing of the care of beasts. Better I do this myself. Besides, I wanted some fresh air. The tent becomes stifling with the smeech of the rushlights.'

'I wanted to thank you,' Adam said, keeping his voice low. 'For the helmet. It probably saved my life.'

He caught Joane's smile in the twilight gloom. Standing like this with the horse between them, few observers would notice that they were talking. 'Humphrey won't miss it,' she said. 'He has quite a few. He spoke to you back at Monmouth, I hear?'

'He told me to avoid you.'

Joane breathed a rueful laugh. For a moment she stooped down, attending to the jennet's fore-hooves and fetlocks. Then she stood again, moving around to the animal's head. The pony stirred and blew, shifting between them.

'My husband,' Joane said, in a near whisper, 'has only lain with me three times since we were married.'

Adam said nothing. The wedding had been almost a year ago.

'I don't regret that,' Joane went on, in an airy tone that failed to mask her feelings. 'He is . . . a large man, and has not learned gentleness. But nowadays he seems unmanned by bitter jealousy and suspicion.'

'Jealousy of whom?' Adam asked.

Joane directed a level gaze at him. 'Of everyone,' she said. 'Of Lord Simon and the other barons. Of his father. Of Robert . . . and of you.'

Adam exhaled. He had feared that answer, for all he had expected it.

'Humphrey prefers to tell me all about his children, by his first wife Eleanor,' Joane went on, giving the horse a final few brisk strokes of the brush. 'His eldest son is only three years my junior. All of them hate me, no doubt. I think Humphrey regrets our marriage too, now – Lord Simon's made his pact with Llywelyn, and my Welsh ancestry is not as valuable to him as it might once have been. He regrets making himself so vulnerable.'

Robert had spoken once of Humphrey de Bohun's love for Joane, years ago. Had that love endured, Adam wondered, or had marriage and the passage of time twisted it into nothing more than a perverse sense of possession?

'And you?' he asked. 'You regret it too?'

Joane ceased work and tossed the brush aside. Straightening, she looked at Adam across the horse's mane. 'At the time I had no choice, you know that,' she said. 'But I would have wished . . . yes, I might have wished that things were different.'

She smoothed her palm down the pony's neck, her hand coming to rest on its withers. Adam placed his own hand over it, and for a moment, two heartbeats, they did not move. Then she drew her hand away.

'We cannot do this,' she said quickly. 'We must not meet like this again.'

Anger flared in Adam's chest. Was it not she who had sought him out back in Hereford, and again at Monmouth? Again he had the sense that he was being used, manipulated by this woman to ease her own bitterness.

'Why?' he demanded. 'Why must we deny ourselves?'

'Because he would kill you, you know that,' she said. 'He would not want to do it – he likes you, I think, in a strange way – but he would feel it his duty.'

Duty, Adam thought; the word sickened him now. But he recalled what de Bohun had said of it back at Monmouth. *And that is the higher honour.*

*

They met the Welsh lords the following morning, to the north of the mountains at a place called Bronllys. A sturdy little castle rose on the far side of a stream, and the Welsh were assembled in front of it, hard-faced bearded men in mail mounted on tough horses, with archers and spearmen at their back. Llywelyn ap Gruffudd was not with them; instead, his white-haired old seneschal Grononwy ab Ednyfed led the Welsh host. Adam sat at a distance and watched Simon de Montfort and his chief supporters ride across the stream to confer with them. The king did not; Henry remained well apart, screened by his household clerks and chaplains. The English crown may have agreed a treaty with the Prince of Wales, but the king himself did not recognise the title or its holder.

Humphrey de Bohun kept his distance, too, and Adam noticed his expression of distaste and discomfort as the Welsh infantry cheered de Montfort. These men were occupying his lands, after all. But Adam saw Joane approach the mounted lords, and from a distance he overheard her exchanging words with the old seneschal. She spoke in Welsh, and he could not understand what they were saying. But Adam saw de Bohun's features darken with anger.

They rode on, the Welsh accompanying them for a few miles more, and reached the walled town of Hay by afternoon. The king went directly to the little chapel of St John to hear evensong and give oblations, while the rest of the army tramped wearily to their allotted billets in the houses or the castle, or to the meadows beside the Wye to bathe in the cool water before pitching their tents. Hay had been captured and recaptured countless times; in the past month alone a raiding band of Gilbert de Clare's men had sacked the place and burned the castle outbuildings, before Llywelyn ap Gruffudd's Welsh troops had retaken it. The inhabitants wore a closed and sullen look, not cheered by the appearance in their streets of yet another tired and hungry army, even one led by their own overlord and his king.

As the evening darkened, the leading men of the army gathered once more in the castle bailey. Nearly a hundred knights, and as many squires and serjeants, filled the oval within the curtain wall. A few of the Welsh that had accompanied them from Bronllys had joined them too. They stood before the steps of the timber hall, light from within falling upon their upraised faces. Simon de Montfort came from the hall and stood upon the steps, flanked by his sons Henry and Guy and accompanied by Hugh Despenser. Men with flaming torches stood at the foot of the steps, lighting them with a fiery glow.

'It's been a rough road we've walked these recent days,' Lord Simon declared, raising his voice just enough that it carried to the castle gate. 'A rough and hungry road! Some of you, I'm sure, must have thought that fortune has turned against us, and God deserted us . . .'

'No, no!' a few among the gathering called back. But Adam noticed that many more remained silent. He looked towards the gate tower, where Humphrey de Bohun stood with Joane at his side. De Bohun had said nothing.

'I ask you now,' Simon went on, a little louder, 'to remember our glorious victory at Lewes, only a year gone, when so few triumphed over so many. Remember, too, how we were defeated at Northampton before that, and forced to retreat from Rochester.'

Adam was standing near the back of the assembly, near the stables, and he heard a stir of muttered agreement pass through the crowd.

'God does not grant easy victories to the faithful!' Lord Simon cried. 'If he did,' he said with a smile, 'the foolish would think they had gained the victory themselves, instead of by the power and glory of heaven!'

A ragged burst of laughter rose from the crowd.

'No,' Simon went on, more forcefully. 'God sends adversity to try us, and to make us strong. Would he bestow ultimate victory on faithless liars, perjurers and oathbreakers?'

'No, no!' the men nearer the steps called out once more.

'For those are our enemies!' Simon told them, raising a clenched fist. 'Defeated men, who creep like dogs and spit lies like serpents! And Lord Edward, the son of our king, has been misled by these deceitful flatterers into disregarding the solemn oath he swore upon the gospels . . . Into once more violating the peace of the realm! But the king himself,' Simon said, turning and gesturing towards the doorway at the head of the steps, 'is with us!'

All raised their heads as King Henry appeared in the doorway, stepping into the light of the torches. A cheer of acclaim went up, and the king raised a palm in mild acknowledgement. Liveried serjeants stood at his elbows, and they guided him back into the hall.

'Our enemies blame me for the strife, I know that,' Lord Simon continued, summoning the attention of the crowd once more. 'They hate me, those proud and mighty men . . . Because I have always stood for truth and for justice, for the liberties of common men and the freedom of the church, they want to cast me down!'

He paused a moment, his jaw firm as he gazed out over the torchlit faces below him. 'But whose enemies are they really?' he asked. 'The enemies of all Englishmen! The enemies of the church. The enemies of God! Would the Almighty grant victory to his own enemies? To faithless men who fight with the weapons of Satan?'

'NO!' the crowd responded as one, many of them stamping their feet. Even Adam replied with a shout.

'Already,' de Montfort went on, 'my son Simon is marching from London with a great army to support us. Our enemies have retreated to the Severn, and the road to Hereford is open . . . I know many of you are discomforted by our Welsh allies, but we have a shared purpose now – Llywelyn, Prince of Wales, is strong for our cause, and we should trust him. He supplies us, guards our flank and harries the lands of our enemies.'

Cries of agreement from the crowd, although Adam could tell that many remained troubled by the alliance; the lands that the Welsh were harrying belonged to Englishmen, after all, even if they were arrayed on the other side in this war. But Lord Simon spoke again.

'What pitiful men,' he growled, shaking his head, 'what dishonourable wretches would we be to abandon hope of God's victory now? As we fight for the laws and liberties of all men, so the Lord of Battles – the God of Vengeance – stands with us. And He shall deliver us *justice!*'

He raised his fist to the darkening sky, and the cheering burst once more from the crowd before him. The flames of the torches wavered, throwing twisted shadows over the surrounding walls of the castle. Adam looked towards the gateway, but de Bohun and Joane had already departed. Lord Simon and his sons were following Hugh Despenser back up the steps to the hall. After his bold address, Simon appeared to have shrunken once more, and almost looked to be trembling. His son took his arm as he stepped back inside the building. Adam remembered what de Bohun had told him; was Lord Simon really wearing a hair shirt beneath his tunic, the coarse cloth a penitential abrasion against his skin?

The assembly broke up; most of the knights were billeted in the town, and Adam followed them as they filed through the castle gateway towards the wooden trestle bridge that spanned the ditch. Eustace for once had managed his duties adequately, and had found them rooms in a cottage behind the chapel. It would be a relief at least to be under thatch once more, instead of leaking canvas.

As he dropped down the wide stone steps and passed through the arches of the gate, Adam saw a hooded figure ahead of him caught for a moment in the flare of light from a brazier. Adam blinked; when he looked again the man had dropped his head and hurried on. Following close behind him, Adam crossed the timbers of the bridge and walked out into the open expanse of the marketplace before the castle walls.

The hooded man had been joined by two others now. The newcomers must have been waiting for him in the marketplace during de Montfort's speech; both of them wore cowls like the first, one of them in a distinctive red. Adam hung back, idling his steps to avoid drawing too close to them. Matthew fell into step beside him.

'That man in the middle there,' he said quietly. 'See if you can get a look at him. Don't let him see you.'

The boy nodded and was gone. Adam slowed to a stroll, following the outer edge of the castle ditch. It was not long before Matthew returned.

'You recognised him?'

Matthew nodded again. 'But the last time I saw him, master,' the boy said, 'he had writing all over his face.'

Chapter 19

'So we are returning to Hereford, it seems,' Hugh of Oyster-mouth reported two mornings later, when he returned to their lodgings. 'Once the army is fully rested, that is, and once Prince Llywelyn has resupplied us with victuals.'

Adam gave a mirthless laugh. Victuals would be a blessing at least – the previous evening they had dined on nettle stew and stale barley bread, all that Matthew and Hugh could find in the town's depleted market. The bread was considered a luxury, and Hugh had been lucky to get his hands on it. But the news that they would be returning once more to Hereford was less welcome.

'Meanwhile,' Hugh went on, scraping up the last of yester-day's cold stew, 'I still cannot discover anything of your hooded friend, or his accomplices.'

Adam was not surprised. He had seen nothing more of Le Brock himself, and had not found a way to pass on information of the man's presence in the town either. But de Clare's men would certainly discover Lord Simon's intentions soon enough. Hugh of Oystermouth, after all, had gained all that he knew in a morning's gossiping in the marketplace.

'So Hereford is safe then, we are to believe?' Adam asked.

'Oh surely,' Hugh said. 'Lord Edward and de Clare are back at Worcester, so I hear, guarding the crossings of the Severn.

Humphrey de Bohun believes Hereford is secure, at least. He is sending his wife there today with an escort, in advance of the army.'

'He . . . *what*?' Adam demanded, leaping up from his stool. 'Why?'

Hugh widened his eyes, his mouth full. He chewed a moment, swallowed thickly, then raised his palms. 'The talk in the market,' he said, 'is that Sir Humphrey fears his wife's intimacy with the Welsh lords. He suspects they may snatch her away, and hold her as a hostage against his claim to the de Bohun lands around Brecon.'

'Is that likely?'

'Who knows?' Hugh said with a shrug. 'It seems an extreme precaution. One might think, you know, that it suggests a distrust of his wife, rather than of the Welsh . . .'

Adam strode to the low window and leaned out into the street. A bell was ringing from St John's chapel, answered by another more distant chiming from St Mary's outside the walls. 'When is she supposed to be leaving?' he asked.

'If that bell is ringing sext,' Hugh replied, squinting towards the window, 'then I expect she will be leaving . . . now?'

Already Adam had snatched up his sword belt; he dashed down the stairs, along the narrow corridor and out into the alleyway that ran beside the house. Why he felt the need to speak with Joane again before she left, he did not know – but a strange intuition drove him. He slowed to a walk as he emerged into the sunlight of the open marketplace, conscious that he should not draw attention to himself. Between the fences and wattle pens of the cattle market the last few beasts still stood with swishing tails, while elsewhere the morning traders were packing their meagre wares onto sumpter horses and handcarts. On the far side of the market, beyond the ditch, rose the castle wall and gate with its single tower. As Adam strode across the marketplace he saw the gates swing open and a file of mounted figures emerge from within, and knew that he was too late.

John de Kington was in charge of the escort, with his squire riding behind him. After them came Joane herself – Adam knew her at once, although she was plainly dressed in a yellow woollen gown and her face almost concealed by a white linen veil and barbette. Accompanying her were her Flemish maid Petronilla and a tonsured man in clerical garb, and behind them came four packhorses heavily loaded with bundles and cases, and four mounted crossbowmen. Two other figures ran alongside the mounted group: guides, Adam guessed, who would lead them down the Wye valley to Hereford.

They crossed the bridge over the castle ditch and turned to the left, skirting the marketplace and entering Bear Street, which led to the town's eastern gate. Across the fences of the cattle market Adam watched them pass. Joane turned as she rode and peered anxiously back towards the castle, and then scanned the market and the surrounding houses. Adam tensed, catching his breath to stop himself from calling out to her. Then, as the riders vanished into the mouth of the street, he broke into a jog and followed them.

By the time he reached the corner he could only make out the backs of the mounted crossbowmen and the laden packhorses halfway up the street, with John de Kington's blue pennon fluttering some distance ahead of them. He ran a few more yards and then paused again, knowing there was no chance of catching up with them.

At the far end of the narrow street John de Kington was already turning the corner towards the Lion Gate and the road beyond it. Joane did not glance back again. Adam halted, then dragged his steps a short way further. It was only then that he noticed the second mounted group following the first.

They came from a narrow side alleyway; there were stables there, Adam remembered, and an inn. He would have ignored them, but as the three horsemen turned into Bear Street he saw that one wore a distinctive red hood thrown back upon his shoulders. Adam could not make out the identity of the other two, but he was sure that one of them was Le Brock. He was sure as well that their appearance was no coincidence. After staring a

moment more, Adam saw the trio turn the corner towards the
Lion Gate. They were following Joane's party, he was certain.

Running now, his sword clasped in one hand, Adam retraced
his steps to the lane and the house where he was lodged. Along
the corridor he crashed out through the rear door into the yard.
His horses were stabled there, beneath a thatched shelter, and in
the sunlight beside the house wall Eustace was glumly engaged
in rubbing the rust spots from Adam's mail and helmet.

'Where's Matthew?' Adam demanded.

Eustace just shrugged, and plucked at his feathery moustache.
'He went out?' he said.

Adam cursed; Matthew would be his first choice as a com-
panion, but leaving his squire here in Hay would be a mistake;
Eustace would report his actions at once to his real master,
Humphrey de Bohun.

'Saddle the two palfreys,' he ordered. 'And get ready to leave,
as quickly as you can.'

Eustace's doughy face creased into a perplexed frown, but at
Adam's repeated command he scrambled to his feet and jogged
across the yard to the tack room. No time for armour; Adam belted
his sword around his waist, then called up the stairs to Hugh.

'I'm leaving with Eustace,' he said, when the Welshman stuck his
head from the upper window. Across the yard, the squire had led the
first of the palfreys from the stable and was fastening the headstall
and bit, and Hugh hurried down the stairs and went to assist him.

'I don't suppose,' he said as he fetched the saddle, 'there's any
need to ask your purpose?'

Adam shook his head. He reached into his belt pouch and
emptied silver pennies into his palm, stacking them on the
wooden windowsill. 'Provide for yourself as best you can, and
for Matthew too,' he said. 'If we're not back here by evening,
look for me in Hereford.'

*

They were not yet three miles from Hay when Adam caught sight of Le Brock and his two accomplices on the road ahead. The man in the red cowl turned at the sound of their hooves, and then Adam saw the three of them slow to confront him.

He slowed his palfrey to a walk, Eustace closing up behind him. Half a mile or so further on, where the road passed over a low hill, Adam could make out the larger mounted group led by John de Kington. None of them appeared to have noticed the trackers that followed in their wake.

For a while as Adam rode slowly closer the three hooded men remained motionless, and appeared to be speaking together. They carried swords, Adam noticed as they drew nearer, and one had a pair of hunting javelins. Then, at a gesture from the central rider, they tugged at their reins and moved off the road. By the time Adam reached the place where they had been standing, all three were a bowshot distant and riding across open country.

'Who were they?' Eustace asked. 'Welsh robbers?'

'I expect that's what we're supposed to think, yes.' Adam replied. He continued watching the three riders as they passed across the open fields and pasture and into the scrub beyond. Their dun-coloured clothing blended into the surrounding landscape, and soon only the red cowl and the pale dappling of one of their horses marked their progress. They were making for the high ground to the east, Adam estimated. But the road ahead was now clear.

Across a stream and up the slope, he rode fast towards the larger group ahead. John de Kington's men saw him when he had covered half the distance between them. The mounted soldiers spanned their crossbows and spread out across the road as Adam approached, but it was Joane who recognised him first.

'Adam!' she called, and gestured for the men beside her to lower their weapons.

'What's happened?' John de Kington cried, turning his horse and riding back from the crest of the hill. 'Is there word from Sir Humphrey, or Lord Simon?'

For a moment as he reined in his sweating palfrey Adam considered going along with the pretence. It would be quicker, perhaps safer too. But it would be discovered soon enough.

'There are men behind you,' he said. 'They followed you from Hay. I strongly suspect there are others on the road ahead, and they mean to ambush you.'

'Us?' Joane asked. 'But why?' She appeared only perplexed, although her maid and the chaplain who accompanied them both gasped in fright.

'I cannot say, my lady,' Adam told her, 'but one of the men is a serjeant of Gilbert de Clare. It would be best if you returned with me to Hay.'

But John de Kington shook his head curtly. 'I have armed men with me, as you see,' he said. 'And with you and your squire our numbers are still greater. Sir Humphrey ordered me to escort Lady Joane to Hereford, and as his household knight I must do so. I intend to be there by evensong, and no gang of Welsh ribalds will prevent that.'

Adam circled his horse, glaring at the other knight. He knew there was nothing more to say – in de Kington's position he may have thought just the same. But John de Kington was only commanding the escort; he could not give orders to Joane de Bohun.

'My lady,' Adam said to her. 'I ask you to believe me. You are riding into danger.'

'I do not doubt it,' Joane said. She turned her gaze to the left, towards the slopes of the hills darkening under cloud shadow. 'I have been riding into danger these last two weeks, have I not? But my husband has ordered me to Hereford and there I must go.' She spoke with a clipped tone, her jaw tight, and Adam heard in her voice the echo of recent strife. Clearly she had no desire to return to Hay.

John de Kington smiled at Adam and raised an eyebrow. 'You have your answer,' he said.

'Very well,' Adam replied, glancing uneasily at Joane and then at de Kington. 'But I'll come with you.'

Ahead of them the road descended into the green valley of the
Wye, which curled eastward towards Hereford. It was an hour
past noon and the sun was hot, the air still and heavy. Clouds
covered the eastern horizon like dark smoke rolling off the hills.
They were halfway down the slope to the river when one of the
mounted crossbowmen spotted the men ahead of them.

'Six at least,' he said, standing in the stirrups and shading his
eyes. Adam rode up to join him at the head of their little column.
'There, sir, in the trees above the road,' the crossbowman reported.

'You have sharp eyes,' Adam told him. He could not see a thing
himself. 'What's your name?'

'Owein, sir,' the man replied. His accent marked him as Welsh;
he was clearly a local tenant of de Bohun.

'Stay close to Lady Joane,' Adam told him quietly. 'And keep a
close watch on her.'

'We ride onward,' John de Kington said, with a hard glare at
Adam, as if to remind him who commanded these men. But he
slung his shield from his back and slipped his forearm through
the strap. Adam wished he had taken the time to dress himself in
armour and take his own shield and lance. He felt almost naked
now, dressed in a tunic and with only a sword at his side.

They continued down the slope to the bank of a brook, crossed
by a shallow ford. The men waiting for them on the far side were
clear to see now, among the trees on the wooded slope. Six horsemen at least, as Owein had said, with others on foot. They were
rough-looking men, bearded and bare-legged; *ribalds*, de Kington had called them, but they resembled the men that Le Brock
had been leading when he waylaid Adam on the road to Hereford
months before. Adam turned and looked back, half expecting to
see the figures against the skyline, but the road was clear.

'It was Gilbert de Clare's man behind us, you say?' de Kington
asked with an exasperated frown, leaning onto the bow of his
saddle.

Adam nodded. 'And those are surely his men ahead too.'

'Perhaps,' de Kington said, although he still appeared unconvinced.

'Is it true,' Adam asked Joane, 'that Sir Humphrey believes the Welsh lords are plotting to seize you as a hostage?'

'So he claims,' Joane said, with a dismissive air. 'He'd heard a rumour, he said . . . But his mind is prone to jealous fantasies—'

'It was reported by one of his own men,' de Kington broke in. 'It was no fantasy, my lady! And those are most likely Llywelyn's men lying in wait for us.'

The two guides had been conferring in hushed voices beside the ford. Now one of them came back to speak to de Kington. 'Master,' he said, 'there's a track that follows the brook up the vale there. If we go that way we can take the road through the hills by Peterchurch. It's a rougher path, master, and a longer one, but we can avoid these robbers up ahead.'

'Then we'll take it,' de Kington decided, and gave the order at once for a change of route. Adam was peering off up the vale, aware that Le Brock and his men had been riding in that direction when he saw them last. He looked once more at the mounted figures waiting in the trees. Tempting, he considered, to set spurs to his horse, draw his sword and challenge them directly. Two knights, two squires and four crossbowmen might be able to cut their way through an ambush; but with women, packhorses and a priest accompanying them they could hardly hope to do so without taking casualties. Feeling his misgivings grow, he turned his horse and followed Joane and the other riders up the track beside the brook.

*

They skirted a boggy area choked with willow and alder scrub, where several streams and rivulets flowed together. Further onward the path rose, following the twisting brook through thickets of blackthorn until it died, and then climbing further. Dark hills closed the horizon now, and the clouds had dropped almost to their summits. A deep stir of thunder came from the south, over the Black Mountains.

'It seems we shall have rain to add to our woes,' the chaplain said, peering into the sky with a sniff. 'A wet journey, besides a perilous one!' He tugged the hem of his mantle over his head.

'You may wish to shift your seat, my lady,' Adam told Joane. 'The way ahead gets rougher.'

'Gladly,' Joane replied. She had been sitting across the saddle, her legs demurely together on one side. Now she pulled up the skirts of her gown and threw her leg astride the horse, slipping her feet into the stirrups. Her maid Petronilla, keeping her side-seat, rode up beside her and fussily arranged her gown to cover her legs.

When Adam looked to his right, he saw three horsemen against the sky, moving along the higher ground. One of them wore a distinctive pointed cowl. Turning in the saddle, Adam made out the figures behind them as well, men on sturdy Welsh cobs trotting up through the blackthorn and willow.

'I have a feeling,' Joane said quietly, following his gaze, 'that we are being herded like sheep.'

Adam nodded. He glanced towards the crossbowman who rode at Joane's other side; Owein had spanned his bow, and carried three quarrels in his belt.

They were in a broad upland valley now, the ground rising steeply to a long ridge to their left. Up ahead, fields surrounded a village, no more than a clutch of thatched huts and sheds edged with fences and byres. As they reached the margin of the fields the two guides began to run.

'Behind us!' one of the men bringing up the rear cried. Adam turned again, and saw the mounted band that had followed them up from the valley kicking their ponies into a gallop, spears raised, shouting as they came.

'Bastard guides have led us into a trap!' John de Kington snarled. He drew his sword, spurring his horse forward. 'Cut them down!' he yelled.

But there were other figures appearing from between the huts of the village now, and from the thorny coverts and hedges bordering the fields. Barefoot men in dun-coloured smocks and cowls, with short powerful bows of thick elmwood in their hands. Even as Adam spotted the first of them, they drew and shot; one of the mounted crossbowmen just ahead of Adam let out a yelp and toppled backwards over his horse's rump, a ragged-fletched arrow jutting from his neck.

'Eustace, to me,' Adam called to his squire, circling his horse. Joane saw his movement and followed, as the crossbowman Owein rode up to guard her flank. Up on the hilltop to the right, just out of bowshot, three cowled riders sat motionless in the saddle, observing the ambush.

John de Kington was halfway to the village when he caught up with the first of the fleeing guides. His sword flashed in the watery sunlight, and the running figure dropped with a spatter of blood. A heartbeat more, and de Kington's horse crashed to the ground, shot by an arrow. De Kington himself was hurled from the saddle; two more arrows struck him as he tried to stand, and a third hit his squire as he rode to his master's assistance.

Pulling at the reins, Adam turned his horse's head towards the high ridge to the left. 'Joane, stay ahead of me,' he yelled. 'And ride like the Devil's after us!'

Joane needed no encouragement; already she was leaning forward over the mane as her horse stretched into a gallop. Adam rode close behind her, with Eustace and Owein. The crossbowman loosed a shot from the saddle, then kicked one foot from the stirrup to reload, a bolt clasped between his teeth.

In the distance to the right, Adam could see Joane's maid Petronilla and the little chaplain clinging to their plunging horses as they galloped wildly in the opposite direction. The remaining two crossbowmen were struggling with the pack animals; one of them slumped over in the saddle, struck by an arrow. Then Adam saw no more.

Crossing a stream, the hooves of their horses beating the water to spray, they pushed on up the slope towards the ridge. Another glance back, and Adam saw five or six mounted men in pursuit, with the swift-footed archers running behind them. If the ground ahead grew too steep or rough for horses, he knew, the footmen would have the advantage. They had to gain as much distance as possible before then. If they could reach the far side of the ridge they might find woodland in which they could shelter, or a smooth slope down which they could ride to safety. Adam was praying through clenched teeth as he rode.

Eustace came careering past him, almost standing in the stirrups and yelling at his horse. Cries from behind them, and Adam saw the shaft of an arrow strike the young man between the shoulder blades. Eustace jerked upright, the reins falling from his grip, then slid from the saddle. His horse was still running, and for a few long yards the squire was dragged over the rough ground, one foot in the stirrup.

'Keep going!' Adam shouted to Joane and Owein, then circled back. Eustace de Brumlegh lay with his right leg twisted at a grotesque angle. His neck was twisted too, his eyes screwed shut and his upper lip curled open to show bloodied teeth. Shame blossomed in Adam's chest; he had only brought the squire with him that day because he did not trust him. But the lad had followed him anyway, and done his duty, and now his duty had killed him out here on a nameless hillside far from his home and hearth.

Another arrow zipped past, and a second buried itself in the turf beside Eustace's body. The galloping riders were barely a spear-throw distant now, the archers close behind them, shooting as they ran. With a stifled curse Adam shook off the weight of guilt, then pulled his horse back uphill and dug in once more with the spurs. On a powerful warhorse, Fauviel or even Rous, he might have stood a chance of escape. But his light riding palfrey was tiring fast, and the tough little horses of his pursuers were better at hill climbing. Anger ignited within him. How

easily they had been guided into the ambush, and how brutally
effective it had been . . . Now Eustace was dead, John de Kington and his squire probably dead too, and Joane would fall into
the hands of their killers soon enough. Adam had failed, and the
barbed arrows and the spears would end his life as well. *Senseless*,
he thought. *Senseless and stupid* . . . But he refused to die so easily.

Dragging at the reins he checked his horse's uphill canter and
turned it once more to face his pursuers. Reins loose, sword
in hand, he kicked the animal into a careering downhill charge.
They were not expecting that; the closest of the mounted ribalds
only had time to raise his head, his stubbled face opening in a
yell of surprise, before Adam's galloping palfrey crashed against
his horse. The man tried to draw back his spear, but before he
could take aim Adam's sword sheared into the side of his neck.
One down, and already the second was pressing the attack.
Adam crouched low over his mount's neck and the jabbing spear
thrust skated off his shoulder. A slash at the man's face, and he
leaned back in the saddle. Then a backhand strike with the flat of
the blade against the pony's head and the animal screamed and
backed, pitching the rider to the ground.

Two more pursuers were crowding against him now, so close
their own archers could not shoot for fear of hitting them.
Adam weaved his horse, knees pressing to left and right. This
was mounted melee fighting: he was trained in it and they were
not. His horse reared again, and then kicked out with its front
hooves. As the animal surged forward Adam leaned and struck,
the tip of his blade scoring a deep cut in the arm of one of the
ribalds. Howling, the man pulled his reins and turned to flee.

Adam's palfrey was staggering now, an arrow jutting from its
neck, blood flowing in steaming rivulets over its hide. Three more
cantering strides across the slope of the hill and the animal's front
legs gave beneath it. Adam slipped his feet from the stirrups and
threw himself clear as the saddle dropped beneath him. He hit the
ground and rolled, getting his feet beneath him and staggering

upright with the sword still in his hand. The wounded rider had pressed back into the attack, thinking that Adam was prey for the taking. Still clasping his bleeding arm, the man jabbed with his spear. Adam seized the shaft just behind the head and dragged it towards him, then slashed with his sword and cut the man from the saddle.

An arrow struck his leg, cutting through his hose, but only grazed him. Snatching the reins of the fallen ribald's pony, Adam got his foot in the stirrup and boosted himself into the saddle. To his left, four more riders were coursing up the slope, one of them the man in the red cowl. Another, closer, was keeping his distance. A dozen archers on foot too, although most were hunting the tussock grass and scrub for spent arrows.

Fighting to control his unfamiliar mount, Adam turned and turned again with his sword raised. The pursuers were moving more cautiously now, waiting for their archers to ready themselves before risking another direct attack. Taking the opportunity, Adam pulled the pony around and urged it back up the slope. Exaltation burst through him, and he shouted in triumph as he rode. But he was not out of danger yet.

Ahead of him now he could see the summit of the ridge, crowned by thorn bushes and high coarse grass. For a moment he thought that Joane and Owein the crossbowman had managed to ride clear. Then he noticed one of their horses standing a short distance away, head dipped. The sky above the ridge was bruised and lowering.

'Adam, here!' Joane's voice cried. As he reached the top of the slope Adam stood in the stirrups and gazed to his left. At first he thought there was a building there, some tumbled ruin half overgrown with bracken and high grass. Then, as he rode closer, he saw it was an oval of grey boulders jutting like giant's teeth from the rippled turf, supporting a massive stone slab laid over the top to make a chest-high table or plinth. Joane was crouched against the far side of the rocks, while Owein perched on the slab with his crossbow spanned and loaded.

'My horse went lame,' Joane called to Adam as he approached.

'I wouldn't leave her,' Owein said, 'and she wouldn't take my horse either.'

'Then we must hold them here,' Adam said.

Thunder boomed and rattled across the sky, but still the rain would not come. Instead, their enemies closed in, advancing up the slope more slowly now that they saw the chase was brought to bay. The bowmen had collected their shafts and spread out in a loose cordon around the stones, crouching in the long tussock grass. The mounted men rode up to join them. Le Brock was in the lead, his hood thrown back to reveal his leering face and the white streak in his black hair. The man in the red cowl was with him.

'Give us the lady, de Bohun's wife, she's all we want,' Le Brock called. 'Neither of you need die to protect her.'

Joane was still crouched in the lee of the stone slab. 'Let me go to them,' she said. 'If I'm really all they want . . .'

'He's lying, my lady,' Owein growled. 'They wouldn't let us live.'

Adam nodded. 'Get beneath the stones if you can,' he said to Joane. He looked at the cordon of archers, then at the mounted men as they walked their horses forward. There was no way he could fight them all off and avoid the showers of arrows too. But surrender would bring only a rapid execution.

'If you want her,' he called to Le Brock, 'you'll have to come and get her.'

Le Brock's face split into a terrible grin as he recognised Adam for the first time. 'Shame,' he replied. 'I quite liked you, young sir. But now you'll have to make your peace with God.'

His hand darted a signal, and the archers stood up from the long grass and bent their bows.

'Loose!' Le Brock cried.

Chapter 20

Owein died first.

The crossbowman only had time to snap off a single shot before two arrows punched through his gambeson. He fell back onto the stone slab, braced on his elbows as he struggled to reload. Then a third arrow pierced his throat, and with a jerk he dropped his weapon and rolled from the slab.

Adam was still in the saddle. Circling his cob around the stones, he waited for the first of their enemies to approach. But they seemed content to let the archers do the work. An arrow zipped between his horse's ears, another snagged in a fold of Adam's tunic. A moment later and he felt the shock through the animal's body as a shaft struck it directly in the haunch. The cob let out a high whinny, bucking and dragging at the reins, and Adam barely had time to kick his feet from the stirrups and throw himself free before the wounded animal dropped and rolled. Snatching up his fallen sword, he dashed to the shelter of the stone table as the cob staggered upright once more and bolted for the nearest bank of scrub bushes.

Arrows cracked and pinged off the stones, striking sparks. Squatting down with his back to one of the larger upright boulders, Adam gripped his sword with both hands. Beneath the great slab there was a hollow area, tangled with grass and dry bracken, where Joane had taken shelter. She had snatched Owein's fallen crossbow with his belt hook and bag of quarrels, dragging them into the hollow after her.

Le Brock called to the archers, and they ceased shooting. Now Adam heard the slow hoofbeats of the horses as they moved closer. He edged back into the shelter of the stone slab, and Joane joined him.

'I'm sorry about John de Kington,' she said hurriedly. 'And your squire, and the serjeant too. All of them. I'm sick of men dying for me.'

Adam shook his head. 'They didn't die for you. This is part of a bigger game.'

'I know,' she said. 'I understand it now. Gilbert de Clare's man spread the rumour that the Welsh wanted to abduct me, then paid this gang to do it. If he can sunder my husband from Prince Llywelyn, he'll weaken Lord Simon.'

Joane was pale and wide eyed with shock, fear coursing through her, but her voice was steady as she spoke. Her hands were steady too as she fixed the hook to her girdle and looped the crossbow cord over it. One foot in the stirrup, she heaved herself backwards. Owein's bow was much heavier and more powerful than the light hunting weapons to which she was accustomed, but with a gasp of effort she managed to span it.

'They're coming,' Adam said. He crawled forward again, readying his sword. Joane took his arm.

'You weren't supposed to be here, Adam de Norton,' she said quickly. 'Listen to me – take the serjeant's horse and ride clear of this place. There's no dishonour in flight.'

'I'm staying,' Adam said. He was sure of himself now, every pulse in his body strengthening his purpose. 'If God wills that I die beside you, then so be it.'

Joane took his face and turned it towards her, then kissed him on the lips.

A battering of hooves, a jingle of harness, and then they heard boots grating on the slab just above them. Adam scrambled out of the hollow as the first of the dismounted ribalds jumped down on the far side of the stones. It was the man in the red hood, a spear drawn back with both hands to stab. Adam lunged at him, driving a sweeping two-handed slash that knocked the man's spear aside and sliced into his arm.

'Adam, behind you!' Joane cried.

Another dismounted rider was coming around the far end of the stones, spear raised; the snap of a crossbow, and he yelped as a quarrel pierced his buttock. From the corner of his eye Adam could see the archers holding their distance but keeping the cordon. The man that Joane had shot had fallen to his hands and knees and was trying to crawl away, the quarrel still jutting from his rump, while the man in the red hood was stumbling into the long grass clutching his injured arm.

'Other side!' Joane shouted, as she spanned the heavy crossbow again.

Sword in hand, Adam vaulted up onto the massive slab. Le Brock had ridden up to the far side of the stones; he looked as if he was about to dismount, but seeing Adam he snarled and circled his horse.

'Hand the woman to me!' he said, stretching out his hand. 'Hand her over and you can live, I swear upon my soul.'

Adam stood upon the stone, his sword raised. This man had saved his life once, when the Ticeburns wanted him dead. Now things were different.

'Come near me and I'll kill you,' he cried. 'I don't want to, but I will . . .'

'Kill me?' Le Brock scoffed. 'You can't *kill* me, boy! I'm protected by the shadow of the cross and the saving love of Christ! I wear the holy string, remember – the holy string of St Thomas, proof against death! By steel, fire or water!' He slapped his midriff as he laughed.

Joane had scrambled up out of the hollow beneath the slab and stood braced against the stones, the crossbow spanned and loaded and aimed at Le Brock. Adam jumped down and stood beside her.

'He's a madman!' Joane breathed.

Le Brock raised his hand, giving the command for his archers to ready their bows. Adam seized Joane around the waist and dragged her downwards, towards the protection of the stones.

With a deafening crack the sky split directly overhead, and Adam flinched and covered his eyes as a shock of blue-white light blazed before him. In the afterimage he had a vague impression of a horse and rider limned in white fire. The noise of the thunder rolled and passed, and Adam opened his eyes. Joane had loosed her crossbow, shooting the quarrel into the turf, and the weapon was slack in her hands. 'Blessed Virgin protect us!' she gasped, crossing herself quickly.

At first there was no sign of Le Brock or his horse, just a lingering stink of burning hair on the charged breeze. Then Adam saw the animal and rider lying where they had fallen, Le Brock still in the saddle. A wisp of smoke rose from where the lightning had struck them. Adam crossed himself too, then did it again.

All around the hilltop the surviving ribalds and the archers stood and stared, awestruck and horrified. Then another blast of thunder came from overhead, and with wild screams all of them turned and fled away down the slopes, the wounded hobbling after them.

A moment later, and the rain fell like a heavy grey curtain, eclipsing the land all around.

Shuddering, Joane and Adam dropped and crawled back into the hollow beneath the slab. The rain was hissing off the stone above them and gushing in streams on all sides, but for now the hollow remained dry. They knelt, heads down, staring out into the grey flood as their enemies vanished before them.

'We did it, God be praised!' Joane said, then threw her arms around Adam and kissed him again. She was laughing. They were both laughing, reckless in the aftermath of shock and fear. For a

few long heartbeats they clung together. Then Adam eased himself from her embrace and stared out through the sheets of water
streaming off the slab above them.

'It's not slackening,' Joane said after a while, gazing from their
shelter. She stretched out her hand and the rain sizzled on her
open palm.

'We have to go,' Adam told her. 'Once the storm eases they'll
be back.' Superstitious dread might hold their foes off a little
longer, but they would be eager to avenge their slain, once the
fear of another lightning strike had passed.

'Let's do it then,' Joane said, turning to Adam with light in her
eyes. 'I want to be away from this place. It feels . . . cursed.'

Quickly, before they could think any further, Adam flung
himself out into the storm. He took Joane by the hand and drew
her after him, and together they ran with lowered heads to the
nearest clump of thorn bushes. There was no sign of Owein's
horse, but one of their attackers – the red-hooded man, Adam
guessed – had secured his palfrey to the bush and there it
remained, trembling and rolling its eyes in terror.

Joane swung herself up into the saddle while Adam dragged
the tether free of the thorns and tried to calm the animal as best
he could. Then he mounted behind her, got his feet in the stirrups and spurred the horse forward into the driving rain.

They were riding along the line of the ridge, and although it
was impossible to make out any landmarks in the rushing grey
murk Adam thought they were travelling south-east. The rain
seemed to come from all directions, and almost instantly both
he and Joane were soaked to the skin, their tunics blackly wet
and hanging off them. Joane's headscarf was loose and she pulled
it down to her shoulders, her copper-coloured hair streaming
loose under the drenching torrent.

For a mile or so they trotted along the ridge, over pastures of
tussock grass and around outcrops of scrub. To their left the land
fell away steeply into woodland, the trees just a dark smudge in

the storm. To the right there was nothing but a gulf of rain-filled air. Adam felt water pouring down his back and pooling around his waist, and his eyes were filled with it. He held Joane clasped to his chest as he rode, and for a long time they just rode blindly and in silence.

'There!' Joane said, as they crested another rise. She was pointing to her left, into the margin of the misty trees. 'We need shelter,' she said, wiping the rain from her face.

Adam squinted, then he saw it too. A thatched roof among the trees, tucked below the line of the ridge. He slowed the horse at once and tugged the reins, the palfrey turning eagerly towards the shelter of the wooded slope.

It was a shepherd's hut or shelter of wood and wattle, but the thatch looked thick enough to keep out the rain. Adam lifted the rope latch and pulled the door open: a single room, the ashes of a dead fire and a plank bed with a roll of blankets. But dry at least; even leaning inside for a moment was an instant relief. Squinting in the rain once more, Adam left Joane to take shelter in the hut while he attended to the horse.

There was an arching blackthorn hedge a short distance away, and Adam led the horse to the shelter beneath it, tethering the animal securely. He removed the saddle, blanket and bridle, then rubbed down the soaked hide with a fistful of dry bracken. There was no good fodder, but the horse seemed content enough to be out of the rain. Lifting the saddle and the folded blanket onto his shoulder Adam stamped back out of the cover of the hedge and through the pouring torrent to the hut once more.

Inside, he dumped the saddle on the floor and secured the latch behind him. Only then did he turn around. Joane had shucked off her wet woollen gown and hung it over a rope stretched across the room. She had removed her shoes and stockings, and in the slatted grey light through the wooden walls she stood in only her soaked linen chemise, her hair hanging loose around her shoulders.

'You should undress too,' she said.

Suddenly abashed, Adam turned his back on her as he unfastened his belts, and removed his sodden shoes and his hose. He dragged the soaked tunic over his head and slung it over the rope. Joane took the hem of his shirt and drew it off, then he turned to face her once more. She pressed her palm flat against his chest, holding the distance between them for a heartbeat. She touched the medallion of St Christopher he wore on a thong around his neck; the same medallion she had given him many years ago to protect him on his travels. Then he raised his hands and unlaced her chemise at the neck, pushing the wet linen down over her shoulders until it fell around her feet. Nothing could hold them apart now; Joane's hand slipped to the back of his neck, her fingers in his hair as she drew him towards her.

A moment later they were locked together, staggering back across the room to fall onto the narrow plank bed as Adam fumbled with the ties of his braies. They were laughing, breathing hard, the energy of peril, fear and flight still coursing through them. At first they were taut and clumsy with nervous desire, their hearts beating fast. But then their motions slowed, as Adam pressed her body beneath him. The rain pelted on the roof above them, the water hissing through the thatch and dripping from the eaves, and he felt he was drowning in her.

*

Adam did not notice when the rain stopped. But he saw the sunlight falling in bright shards across their bodies as they lay on the bed. He moved to sit up, and Joane stopped him with a hand upon his chest.

'Let's not leave,' she said. 'Not yet.'

He shook his head. 'I need to find the other horses,' he told her. 'Wait here for me, I'll be back soon.'

He kept his back to her as he dressed, pulling on the damp tunic over his bare skin and fastening his belts. By the time he had forced his feet into his wet shoes Joane was sitting up on the bed, clasping her knees and watching him from the corner of her eye.

'You'll be safe here,' he told her, evading her gaze. His words sounded unconvincing, even to him. She did not reply, and he left her and went outside.

It was still wet, the trees and bushes dripping and the ground streaming with rainwater, but as Adam climbed up onto the ridge into the sun's glow he felt his senses restored. Only now did he awaken to the full realisation of what he had done. The shame of it, and the glory too. Waves of terror and exaltation flowed through him, and he tried to drive from his mind all thoughts of what might happen next.

Less than an hour had passed before he returned to the hut, scratched and muddied and leading behind him the single pack-horse he had found caught in a thorn thicket at the base of the ridge.

'Did you see any sign of the others?' Joane called from the hut doorway. Adam could hear the trepidation in her voice.

'Nothing,' he told her as he unfastened the larger of the packs from the horse's back. 'But I saw Petronilla making her escape when we were attacked, and your chaplain too. I'm sure they're safely back in Hay by now. The bodies were gone though – the ribalds must have taken them. The other horses too.'

He carried the pack into the hut and saw Joane still sitting where he had left her, the blanket pulled around her bare shoulders. 'I think we've broken this poor shepherd's bed,' she said with a pale smile, then scratched at her shin. 'Although he's paid us back in fleabites, I think – this blanket must be jumping with them.'

'There's dry clothing for you here,' Adam said, lowering the pack to the floor. 'And some other things too – a flask of wine,

I think, and this.' He passed her the leather satchel he had found among the other baggage.

'Thank you!' Joane cried as she took it. 'May the heavens bless you, Adam de Norton, this alone I couldn't bear to lose.'

Inside was a jewellery box, some jars of cosmetics and other personal items, and a book bound in tooled leather with gold clasps. Adam recognised it at once: the old Psalter her father had given her. Joane kissed the book and then opened it in her lap, running her fingers over the faded parchment, the black rows of inked letters picked out with blue and red and traceries of gold.

'You remember we read this together, when first we met?' she asked, smiling.

Adam nodded as he sat down on the end of the broken bed. 'The psalms, and the traveller's prayer,' he said.

She leaned forward, pushing aside her unbound hair as the sun fell over the pages of the open book. Tracing the words with a finger, she began to read one of the psalms. '*Domine probasti me et cognovisti me . . .*'

'Lord, you have proved me and known me,' Adam translated.

'*Si ascendero in caelum tu illic es . . .* If I ascend into heaven, you are there,' Joane said quietly, translating the Latin as she followed the words. 'If I descend into hell, you are with me . . . Even there shall your hand lead me, and your right hand shall hold me . . .'

She drew a quick shuddering breath. Adam felt himself blushing, moved by the words but pained by the sense of sacrilege.

'We should not think of this as sin,' Joane told him abruptly, returning the book to her satchel and setting it carefully aside.

'You are married, I am betrothed,' Adam said, hating the sound of his own voice. He had been trying to keep his mind from thoughts of Isabel, and how he had betrayed her.

'My husband does nothing to deserve me,' Joane said with quick bitterness, 'and . . . I do not think God would grudge us what we've shared . . . We should not think of it in that way at all . . .'

Adam saw now that she had been thrashing through these same questions while he was gone. He heard the edge of anxiety in her voice.

'Best we do not think of it at all,' he said.

'No,' she agreed, and let the blanket fall from her shoulders. She looked at him once more, angling her gaze. 'But we have many more hours of daylight yet.'

'We can still be in Hereford for evensong, if you like,' Adam said.

He saw her smile, and the slight shake of her head. Standing up, he unfastened his belt and pulled off his tunic once more.

*

The sun was already low as they made their way along the ridge. The clouds had rolled away towards the Black Mountains and to the north and east the sky was a brilliant, rain-washed blue. In the clear air the views were massive, the broad valley of the Wye spreading beneath them all the way to the dark hills on the far horizon.

'Look there,' Joane called, pointing towards the sinuous curl of the river. She was riding the palfrey, while Adam walked beside her leading the packhorse 'I can see the tower of Hereford Cathedral!'

Adam followed her gesture and nodded. It appeared so close now. A few more hours and they would be there. 'When I've escorted you to the castle I'll need to ride back to Hay again and find Sir Humphrey,' he said, without looking back at her. 'I need to tell him that you're safe.'

'No,' she said at once. 'You must send a messenger instead!' she commanded. Then in a less assertive tone she continued. 'I'm afraid you lack the skill to hide the truth from my husband. Besides, it'll be too late for anyone to ride anywhere before tomorrow morning. Humphrey can live a while longer in uncertainty.'

Adam shrugged, knowing that she was correct. The less he saw of de Bohun the better, and he could only pray that somehow he found a path through the maze of disgrace and peril that lay before him.

'Of course,' she said, 'we could always simply ride away and tell nobody what happened. Humphrey would believe the ribalds took me, and none would know any different.'

'Where would we go?' Adam asked her. She was playing, he knew, but the fantasy was attractive.

'Oh, somewhere far away,' Joane said, smiling. She breathed in the fresh bright air. 'Somewhere across the seas . . . We could be troubadours, in the lands of Occitan, or the Empire, or . . . Or you could be a knight errant, and I your faithful groom . . .' Her voice faded. The reality of their situation was too grave for easy fantasies, however attractive – just for a moment the thought of that life, of enjoying what they had just enjoyed together every day, every night, was almost unbearably sweet. But it could never happen, and they both knew it. The word *faithful* hung in the air.

'Come on,' Adam said, swinging up into the saddle behind her. 'It's downhill from here, and the horse can carry us both for a few miles.'

They rode together down off the ridge and across rolling wooded country towards the valley of the Wye. Soon the cathedral tower was lost from view, and they followed rough tracks that led in what appeared to be the right direction. After five miles they passed through a village, and a man returning from the fields with a hoe over his shoulder directed them to the Hereford road.

Five miles more, and the light was still in the sky as they saw the river before them and the town on the far side, the cathedral and castle towers rising against the blue evening sky. They crossed the bridge riding together on the horse, Adam in the saddle with Joane seated before him, and made their way through the streets oblivious to the stares of the passing people. When they reached the cathedral Adam tightened the reins to turn the horse towards the castle, but Joane seized his hand. 'No,' she told him, 'don't take me there. Not yet.'

He knew what she meant. Once they were within the circuit of the castle walls, with the castellan and his servants all around them, she would be the wife of Humphrey de Bohun once more. He would be only a bachelor knight, the sole survivor of her escort, his clothes soaked and stained with mud and blood. The equality between them would be gone for ever.

Adam loosed the reins once more, then turned the horse to the left, towards the marketplace and the web of streets beyond. As he reached the lane that led to the Makepays sisters' yard he slipped down from the saddle and took the leading rein. With Joane riding behind him, he reached the entrance to the yard. One of the watchmen employed by the sisters was lounging at the gatepost, and as he caught sight of Adam he raised a grizzled eyebrow and jerked his thumb back over his shoulder. Perplexed, Adam led the horses after him as he passed through the passage-way into the yard.

He saw Benedict Mackerell first. Then Dulcia Makepays and a couple of her girls, sitting on a bench. All of them turned as Adam entered the yard, leading Joane on the palfrey behind him.

Then he saw Robert de Dunstanville sitting opposite them, running a whetstone over the blade of his axe. Robert straightened, then stood up, his gaze shifting from Adam to Joane, and back to Adam again. He placed his foot on a wooden block, and propped his axe beside him.

'Kneel and stretch your neck, boy,' Robert said grimly. 'And let me take a swing at you.'

Chapter 21

'What was my advice? *Get married, avoid war, and forget all about Joane de Quincy.* And yet here I find you still unmarried, in the middle of a war, and clearly making love to Joane de Quincy.'

Adam blushed, opening his mouth to speak, but no words came.

'Don't try to deny it,' Robert said. 'Your face betrays you. Apparently you value my good counsel as nothing, and I was mistaken in thinking you a person of some intelligence.'

They were sitting in the upper room above the Makepays' yard, facing each other across a rough table with cups of wine between them. Benedict Mackerell sat by the ladder that descended to the stable, where Robert had stabled his own horses and Adam's old charger Fauviel, which he had brought with him.

'Of course, if I believed you'd forced her to lechery, or compelled her in any way,' Robert said, 'I'd have used that axe on you without hesitation.'

'I would have deserved no less,' Adam replied. He remembered Robert once threatening that if any man harmed Joane or her sister he would hunt him to the deepest of the seven hells, and rend the flesh from his bones.

'But,' Robert said with a sigh, 'I could see that you were both sunk together in your depravity already, and far beyond my

judgement. I suggest, though, that you avoid my cousin hence-
forth. And keep a sword's length from Humphrey de Bohun as
well – he will hear of this before long.'

'I intend to.' Adam knew that would be difficult; keeping away
from Joane would be harder still.

'What of you?' he said, fighting down his embarrassment.
'When I saw you last you were about to surrender to Lord
Edward – you gave him your oath—'

'Ah, oaths,' Robert said, with a loose gesture of contempt.
'Haven't we all broken them? Hasn't Edward himself broken his
oath to Lord Simon? Hasn't everyone following him done the
same? When such great men betray their word so lightly, is it any
surprise that humble men like us do so too?'

He had a sly look, a half-smile. Clearly he had learned that
Adam had broken a couple of oaths of his own. But Adam could
not let him slip his responsibilities so easily. 'You seized me and
held me as your prisoner!' he said, anger tightening his voice.

'Ah yes,' Robert said, not quite meeting his eye. 'Sorry about
that. But, between friends, I'm sure you understand.'

'Oh, I *understand*,' Adam replied, his lip curling. 'Expediency
has always been one of your virtues. I just don't understand why
you've turned again, and how you came to show your face here.'

'Well, it was your squire who led me to this place,' Robert
said, nodding towards Benedict. 'I'm sure I would never have
imagined you living in such surroundings, but we must make the
best of things.'

Robert had arrived at Hereford two days before, he explained.
After leaving his chief manor at Adderley he had ridden first to
Idsall and then to Shrewsbury, avoiding Hamo L'Estrange's garrison at Bridgnorth. Near Shrewsbury he had joined forces with
Ralph Basset of Drayton, de Montfort's Keeper of the Peace,
who had just surrendered the town and castle. Together, and
with twenty men at arms at their back, they had ridden down
to Hereford, only to find the rest of de Montfort's army gone.

'I heard that you'd followed Lord Simon to Newport, but that he'd been turned back and was expected here once more,' Robert had said. 'So I decided to wait and see what God's providence directed. I admit I had not expected to see you so soon, and looking like a drowned dog too, with my cousin Joane riding behind you.'

'And what have you done with Belia?' Adam went on, still in his tone of accusation.

'She's gone to Nottingham, to live with her people there,' Robert told him. 'It was . . . safer, we decided. Until her child is born at least. Sadly, my manorial household and tenants proved to have very narrow minds. There was some doubt as to our being properly wed, and the usual questions about Belia's faith . . .' His voice choked with anger, and he thumped his fist down on the table. 'How dare they ask these things?' he demanded. 'And, by the death of God, what business is it of theirs? May each and every one of the baseborn dogs burn in the everlasting fires!'

'She went gladly, then?' Adam asked, as his own anger cooled.

'She did not! She would have preferred that I accompanied her – can you imagine that? No . . . she was not happy at my decision to come here. Words passed between us that I will not relate. Words I am blackly ashamed to recall.'

Adam nodded. Knowing them both, he could well imagine the scene.

'But she was right, you know,' Robert said, and when he glanced up Adam saw him blinking a tear from his eye. 'She was right to free you, back at Bridgnorth. I heard about it from Benedict, once we'd hoisted him back inside the walls. And I was . . . I was glad. It did not feel right to seize you, and I was not thinking clearly. I see now that I should have let you do whatever you thought best.'

Adam was silent for a moment, startled. Seldom had he heard Robert make so open an admission of error, or so simple an apology.

'And now you've chosen to follow me, is that it?' he asked.

Robert snorted a laugh. 'See it that way if you choose. Perhaps I just decided, once I'd swallowed down the disgrace of surrender, bent my knee and made my oath to Edward, and trailed back home with my head hanging low . . . Perhaps I just decided that this is who I am. A knight, a warrior. I could have lived the rest of my life in peaceful occupations, and never again known the thrill of combat. The chance of victory. And there is a chance, even now – you agree? Because if Simon de Montfort wins this war and I were not fighting at his side then I would sicken and die from grief and dishonour.'

'And if he does not?'

'Well then,' Robert said, and grinned. 'We gave it a throw of the dice, eh?' He thought for a moment, rubbing his thumb over his moustaches. 'Perhaps that's all there is to it,' he said, lifting his wine cup. 'Perhaps what we call honour is nothing but pride, at the end of the day. Pride – and the fear of what other men would say of us if we failed.'

*

Simon de Montfort's army returned to Hereford three days later, on the Morrow of St Swithun. They made a sorry spectacle as they filed across the bridge and into the town. Most were still short of food, hunger gnawing at them, and many were grey-faced and stumbling with sickness too. Morale leaked from them at every step.

Earl Simon himself took up his old quarters in the Bishop's Palace, with Humphrey de Bohun lodging in the adjoining buildings. Joane went to join her husband at once; she had returned to the castle shortly after arriving back in town, unwilling to endure Sir Robert's scornful glares. The rest of the army invaded the houses and pitched their tents in the open spaces, just as they had done before. The markets were empty, the townsfolk resentful, and through the dog days of July few sang the bold songs of English liberty and freedom any more.

But Matthew and Hugh of Oystermouth returned with the army, and they brought Adam's baggage and armour with them, and his horses too. In the upper room Hugh sat with Adam and Benedict and Robert's squire Giles, drinking thin ale and listening to Robert once more repeating the story of his change of heart and allegiance – a story, Adam noticed, that grew more polished and less honest with every telling. The bad feeling that had once existed between Hugh and Robert seemed forgotten now. But the same was not true for everyone.

'And so we left Adderley,' Robert was saying, 'and went south to my manor at Idsall, where Belia departed, not without misgivings on both our parts, I should say, not knowing what lay ahead of us . . .' He broke off as Matthew came stumping up the ladder from the stables, where he had been attending to the horses. The boy halted at the head of the stairs, gazing blankly back at Robert.

'And no thanks to this one here,' Robert said, his voice suddenly icy. He stood up from the table suddenly, his stool clattering, and with one long stride across the floor grabbed Matthew by the neck and shoved his head down. '*You*,' he told the boy, 'were supposed to go with Belia! You were supposed to stay with her – she trusted you! She even believed she could reform you!'

He snarled, and slapped the boy hard across the side of the skull. Adam had stood up as well, but before he could move, Robert shoved Matthew away from him in disgust. 'I had to send Wilecok and his wife to escort her to Nottingham instead,' he explained. 'God alone knows what will happen to them now . . .'

'You can't blame him,' Adam said, his mood darkening. 'It was your own—'

He broke off abruptly as he saw from the corner of his eye Matthew rising from the floor. A blade glinted in the light from the open window. 'No!' he cried, dashing towards the boy.

But Robert had moved quicker still. Before Matthew could strike at him he seized the boy's forearm and twisted it, knocking the knife from his hand with his fist. The blade clattered onto the floor, and Robert held his grip, pushing Matthew back against the side of the table. 'Come at me like that once more,' he snarled, 'and I'll split you end to end!'

Then he released the boy. Adam placed himself between them. 'Go!' he commanded Matthew, and with one parting glance of pure outrage the boy clattered away down the ladder again.

'Told you, did I not?' Robert said, seating himself at the table and reaching for the ale jug. 'That young person is a killer. He's dangerous.'

We are all dangerous, Adam thought. Robert's hand did not even tremble as he refilled his cup.

*

Nine days later, the Feast of St James the Apostle, and Adam stood amid the assembled congregation in the Lady Chapel of Hereford Cathedral. Morning sunlight shone through the high lancet windows to the east, falling on the golden altar-cloth and the five gleaming swords that lay upon it. As the resonant sounds of the antiphon swelled from the choir, the priest blessed the swords with holy water. Then he turned to the five young men kneeling upon the tiled floor before the altar.

All five had spent the night in silent vigil and prayer, after bathing in rosewater and dressing in tunics of spotless white. One of them, John de Beauchamp, had just passed his twenty-first birthday and was now ready to claim the barony of Bedford as his inheritance. The other four were lesser squires, chosen to be his bachelor companions in knighthood.

As the priest recited the prayers and crossed the air before him, Adam remembered his own knighting ceremony, on the field of the Battle of Lewes. For him there had been no rosewater bath, no white tunic or prayer vigil. No altar either, and no priest to lecture him on the duties of faith, justice and charity. For Adam there had been only the sweat and the blood of battle, the stench of death in the air, the aching fatigue in his body. But his knighting was no less honourable for that. More so, perhaps; while de Beauchamp and his comrades had the sanctified glory of the ritual, they had yet to earn the honour that their gilded spurs would bestow. Only combat could do that, and prowess on the field of war.

Across the crowded chapel, Adam noticed Robert de Dunstanville standing in the congregation, his head lowered and his hands clasped before him. Robert caught his eye with a quick smile, and Adam knew that the other man had guessed his thoughts exactly. The same man that had performed Adam's knighting now presided over this ceremony: Simon de Montfort, grave and firm-jawed, dressed in a tunic and mantle of plain midnight blue, stepped from the side of the altar and approached the five kneeling aspirants.

'Lift your hands to heaven,' Lord Simon commanded. 'Your eyes to the light, and your hearts to God.' One by one he gave each kneeling man the slap that would awaken them from evil and remind them always of their oath. 'Now arise,' he told the first of them, 'and be a knight.'

At his gesture, John de Beauchamp rose to his feet, hands still clasped in prayer above his head. Two attendants took the first sword from the altar, scabbarded it and girded the sword belt around his hips. Two more fastened at his ankles the gilded spurs of knighthood. 'Keep watch faithfully in Christ,' Lord Simon told the young man, in a quiet voice that nevertheless carried to the rear of the chapel, 'and be always praiseworthy in fame and prowess.' And he gave him the kiss of peace.

Sir John de Beauchamp turned to the congregation who had gathered to witness and approve his knighting. His face shining with emotion, he drew the sword from its scabbard, kissed the hilt, and then flourished it before him. Two squires brought his new banner, blessed by the priest, and presented it to him: red quartered with yellow, crossed by a black diagonal, the arms of the Beauchamps of Bedford. Then Lord Simon knighted the four other young men, and the ceremony was complete.

'Well, that is how it's supposed to be done,' Robert said quietly, sliding up beside Adam as they filed through the dimness of the cathedral. 'But it was not like that for me either, needless to say.' He gave a quick smirk, and Adam smiled ruefully back. Passing the chancel screen, they knelt in unison before the great crucifix, each thumping their chest and muttering the Paternoster, before walking once more towards the cathedral porch.

Robert's return to de Montfort's allegiance had gone unchallenged. By now, it seemed, such shifts and twists of loyalty were accepted as commonplace. Besides, the twenty veteran men at arms that Robert and Ralph Basset had brought with them had secured their quick forgiveness for the surrender of Bridgnorth and Shrewsbury. With so many of Lord Simon's knights now untried young men like John de Beauchamp and his companions, he needed all the experienced warriors he could attract to his banners. And Robert de Dunstanville still retained a formidable reputation as a fighter, no matter how tainted his name.

Adam walked beside him now into the morning sun outside the cathedral, both of them with the same nonchalant swagger, their hands propped on their sword hilts. Around them were others who had come from the chapel: household men, bachelor knights and great barons mingling together. Adam saw Humphrey de Bohun, and looked away sharply. The two of them had already made their peace, at least in public: Sir Humphrey had thanked Adam for identifying the threat to his wife, and for saving her from the attackers and escorting her unharmed to Hereford. In de Bohun's eyes, in the heavy politeness of his manner and the grit in his voice Adam could sense the roil of bitter suspicion, of great anguish and great rage. But to accuse Adam directly would be to accuse his own wife too, and Sir Humphrey would not risk that. Not in public, where others might hear and know of his humiliation.

His life was in the balance though, Adam knew that for sure. He had been scrupulous in avoiding Joane, just as Robert had urged. Several times he had seen her passing through the town, and their gaze had once or twice flickered together for a heart-beat. She looked tired, Adam noticed, and worn down, with dark smudges beneath her eyes and a tightness to her lips.

But now, as he strolled through the crowd outside the cathedral, Adam felt a different unease weighing upon his spirits. Robert was not slow to notice his gloomy distraction, and slapped a hand down onto Adam's shoulder.

'Speak,' he commanded. 'Be open with me. Frankness of speech, so I hear, is one of the chivalric virtues!'

Adam forced a smile. They had heard much of chivalry from the priest, and from Lord Simon too. 'It's really nothing, I . . .' He let his words trail off, shrugging.

'You're not still smarting at my treatment of your groom, surely?'

'No, it's not that,' Adam said quickly. Matthew had apolo-gised, to Adam and Adam alone, for his attempted attack on de Dunstanville. Adam in turn had advised the boy to keep well away from Robert. It seemed the best course, for now.

'So it's your soul that troubles you?' Robert said, with a tight grin. 'Your lewdness with my cousin? Find a priest and confess your sins – no need to wait till Lent, you know.'

But Adam had done that already. The confessor had been frus-trated in his breathless desire to know the name of the woman with whom Adam had sinned so grievously, and to have Adam describe both her person and what they had done together in great detail, but had granted him absolution nonetheless. His penance was to give alms for four successive Sundays, and to abstain from eating meat until Michaelmas. That at least would not be difficult; there was scarcely an edible beast remaining in Hereford.

But Robert had an insistent air that Adam knew well. He would not be satisfied with evasions.

'Perhaps it was the ceremony that discomforted me,' Adam said. He dropped his voice as he spoke. 'The knighting. Hearing so much about the virtues of chivalry, the honour of our order . . . And then looking around me and seeing nothing but conflict and betrayal, knights forgetting about Christ and justice and throwing the land into turmoil.'

Robert grunted. 'Such has it been since ancient days,' he said with a shrug. 'Often the loudest yelps of virtue come from the foulest of men.'

But we should be better than them, surely, Adam thought. Nearby stood Guy de Montfort and John FitzJohn, with a gang of rowdy young men that had formed around them, eager to praise and be noticed by them. In truth, the morning's ritual had only deepened a disquiet that had been growing in him ever since his return to Hereford. And Robert clearly knew that he was concealing his true feelings.

'When you came back here,' Adam began, tentatively. Robert raised an eyebrow, waiting for him to continue. He looked suddenly very alert.

'It was not solely to fight for de Montfort, was it?' Adam went on. 'Nor was it for your own honour, your own pride.'

'No?' Robert said, his eyebrow still cocked.

'You came back,' Adam went on, before caution could halt his words, 'because you felt guilty about the way you had treated me at Bridgnorth. You came back here because you believed that by fighting at my side you could restore the bond of trust between us.'

'I did?' Robert mused. He stared into the sky, plucking at his moustache. 'Strangely, Belia believed the same,' he said after a while. He drew a long breath, and when he looked back at

Adam his eyes had grown cold and hard. 'So I must tell you
what I told her – I fight for no man but myself, and no man's
honour but my own. My fate is not your responsibility, Adam
de Norton.'

Then abruptly he turned his back and stalked away. Adam
stared after him, remorse battled with the heat of his affront.
Then a burst of noise drew his attention, and he turned to see Sir
John de Beauchamp riding from the yard of the Bishop's Palace,
his warhorse caparisoned in red, yellow and black, as the cheers
of the surrounding men sent the pigeons fluttering madly from
the pinnacles of the cathedral.

*

'I have an offer to make you,' Lord Simon said later that day,
opening an oyster shell with his clasp knife. 'And some news,
that you must keep to yourself, for now.'

Adam said nothing as the earl lifted the shell to his mouth and
tipped it back. He had been surprised to be summoned to the
high table, and given a seat at de Montfort's side. The feast was
laid in the hall of the Bishop's Palace – the king dined separately
at the castle, attended by Hugh Despenser – and reflected the
wider food shortages, with no trencher bread or white wast-
rel loaves. But there were plentiful fresh oysters in honour of
St James the Apostle, washed down with golden Rhenish wine
from Lord Simon's own supply.

'The news arrived today by messenger,' Lord Simon said, casting the empty oyster shell onto the clattering heap beside him.
'Would you like to hear it?'

'If it pleases you, my lord,' Adam said, with feigned nonchalance. He picked up an oyster and dug his knife into the crack of
the shell. The hall was filled with the noise of men, their raised
voices and laughter, and the skirl of pipes and vielles. None but
Adam could hear what Lord Simon was saying.

'It comes from my son. He marched a fortnight past, with six-teen bannerets and the London levies, into Hampshire to crush the rebellion of William de St John and his confederates.'

Adam paused as he prised open the oyster, his hand tightening on the knife handle. 'He was . . . successful?' he asked, without looking up.

'Indeed he was,' Lord Simon said, apparently oblivious to Adam's anguish. 'He retook Odiham and then marched on Win-chester, where the citizens closed the gates against him. He was obliged to break into the town, and to give his troops licence to plunder it. Thankfully, and by God's grace, they mainly restricted their violence to the Jews.'

Adam lifted the open shell, sucked down the oyster and swallowed it, though he feared it might choke him. All too well he recalled how the men of London had treated the Jew-ish community of their own city the year before. He thought of Belia, and of Matthew. 'And William de St John?' he asked. Already he was imagining the army rampaging across the familiar fields of his homeland, the burning buildings, the bodies flung in ditches. *What of Lord William's daughter? What of Isabel?*

De Montfort angled a quick glance in Adam's direction. 'I believe he managed to flee with his sons,' he said, shrugging. 'In the meantime, my own son Simon is marching his army north-wards, and should be at Oxford by now. Soon enough we'll go out and meet him, and end this uprising by Lord Edward and his accomplices. And then, you see,' he said, taking another oyster and opening it with a vigorous twist of his knife, 'I shall need somebody to exert control over Hampshire once more.'

'Exert control?' Adam asked, frowning.

De Montfort turned to him, holding his gaze as he tipped the oyster into his mouth, then smiled as he chewed and swallowed. 'I intend to seize lands from those who have rebelled – de St John, de Brayboef, de Cormayles and the rest. I would prefer to give those lands to men I can trust. I have a manor there myself – Chalton, perhaps you know it? That too needs a new tenant.'

Adam knew of Chalton, on the downs to the south of Petersfield. It was one of the largest manors in the district, and worth more than sixty pounds a year.

'And then there is the matter of appointing a new Keeper of the Peace,' de Montfort said. 'Perhaps you might be worthy of such a position yourself?' He paused a moment, but before Adam could summon an answer he went on.

'Some men, I know,' he said, 'use such gifts to stuff the beaks of those who squawk for favours. But I prefer to bestow them on men who do not ask, but merely deserve them. I believe you are a deserving man, Adam de Norton, and I intend to reward you as you deserve.'

Breaking de Montfort's gaze, Adam looked across at the lower tables flanking the dais. He saw Humphrey de Bohun peering back at him, a frown shading his features. What Lord Simon was offering Adam now was several times as valuable as Humphrey's own offer of lands and lordship. And Simon de Montfort, Earl of Leicester and Steward of England, would make a far more powerful and exalted lord than Sir Humphrey could ever hope to be.

Was this, he wondered, how these things happened now? Had de Montfort grown so mighty that he could simply break some men and lift others to fortune and high position? Perhaps, Adam thought to himself, England had always been governed in that way. Did de Montfort still wear a penitential hair shirt, scratching and scouring the skin under his tunic, or was such humble piety beneath him these days?

'Does the exercise of power offend you?' Simon asked, with a slight smile. He took a sip of wine, then picked up another oyster. 'Some say that I am turning into a worse tyrant than the king and his ministers ever were, I know that,' he said, still in a wry tone. 'Such men will always kick at the yoke when others govern them, no matter if that government is used for good or evil.'

Swallowing the oyster, he washed it down with another mouthful of wine. Then his brow creased and his voice hardened. 'But when we are blessed by God with great power and fortune,' he said, 'we must use what we have to bring justice and peace to the land, to defend the poor and the holy Church, and to reform the kingdom as best we can. Otherwise,' he said, turning to Adam with an expression of furious contempt, 'all that we touch will turn to filth!'

Adam held his gaze, letting the silence stretch between them. At the back of his mind he heard the echo of what Richard de Malmaines had once said. *'Lord Simon is old, and believes too many of his own lies . . .'* But he nodded.

'Quite so, my lord,' he said. 'And I would be honoured to accept what you offer. Except . . . I must speak for William de St John. He's been a friend to me, and I do not wish to profit from his ruin.'

De Montfort remained unmoved a moment, then grunted. 'Very well,' he said. 'Your loyalty does you credit. But be sure you do not confuse personal attachment for virtue. *He who does not give what he loves does not receive what he desires . . .'*

He turned away then, speaking to the newly made Baron of Bedford, who sat at his other hand. Adam drank wine to cover his discomfort. From the lower table he saw Robert de Dunstanville's questioning glance. He mimed a shrug and looked away.

'Friends,' de Montfort declared suddenly as he stood up, his voice booming across the hall. At once the noise of voices died into a hush, the musicians falling silent. 'Friends, I'd thought to keep this to myself for now,' Lord Simon went on, in an affable tone, 'but why should I not share it with you?'

A few men called encouragement to him, and he grinned.

'My son, the younger Simon, is at Oxford,' de Montfort cried, 'and marching north with a powerful army to Kenilworth Castle, which lies only a few days' east of here. Soon we shall join our forces with his, and finally crush this rebellion!'

Enthusiastic roars from the men lining the lower tables. Henry de Hastings began banging his fist on the tabletop, and others joined in. But Adam was sure he was not the only one wondering how they would cross the Severn, how they would evade Lord Edward's scouts and ambushes and slip past his powerful army at Worcester. That seemed not to matter any more.

'The very day we hear that my son has reached Kenilworth,' Lord Simon declared, raising his hands to command a momentary silence, 'we will raise our banners once more – yours, Sir Humphrey de Bohun, and yours de Hastings, and yours, Fitz-John. And our new Baron of Bedford's too – and together we will march forth to join him, and to seek the victory that God has ordained!'

'Victory, victory!' Henry de Hastings yelled, standing up. Guy de Montfort was on his feet as well, and John FitzJohn. Adam saw Humphrey de Bohun joining them, and two score other knights and barons. Robert stood and joined their shouts, although he wore a sardonic smile.

And Adam was on his feet too, as the shouts of furious acclaim echoed back from the high beamed ceiling. He was shouting along with them, borne by that clamorous torrent, even though his heart quailed in his chest.

Battle was coming once more. And this reckoning would decide the fate of England, and of them all.

Chapter 22

In the soft evening light the river appeared placid, the willows along the bank hazy with the coming dusk. The boatman poled his raft with steady strokes, the timbers roped and nailed together from wreckage and driftwood but holding up well. On the raft King Henry sat on horseback, his old grey head high and proud, looking neither to one side nor the other as he glided across the stream towards the far riverbank.

Adam remembered the boatman well. He had seen him at Ribbesford many weeks before, ragged and desperate as he begged Lord Edward's soldiers for compensation after they destroyed his boat. Now the same man was here, miles downstream below Worcester, ferrying the king across the Severn. Doubtless he would be paid handsomely for his services.

'We should try and get across too, before darkness falls,' said Benedict Mackerell.

Adam agreed. They had arrived at the river late in the day, and so far the crossing had already taken two hours. Getting to the far bank, either by one of the various makeshift punts and rafts or by the two rough fords the scouts had located, would be a hazardous business in the dark.

'We'll swim the horses across,' he said, 'and find a camping ground on the other side. Matthew can follow us with the baggage in the first raft he can find.' Matthew, he remembered, could not swim.

A little upstream from the ferry crossing a line of men were forging through the water, following a rope strung from one bank to the other. Tired, still desperately hungry, many of them weak with sickness, they crossed chest-deep with their weapons held over their heads. The two thousand Welsh spearmen and archers who had followed Humphrey de Bohun from Hay were even less happy; like Matthew, most of them were unable to swim.

It was a Sunday, the Morrow of St Peter's Chains, and they had marched from Hereford that morning directly after mass. Word had reached them the day before that Simon de Montfort's son and his great army from London had arrived at Kenilworth; word, too, that Lord Edward's men had ridden north from Worcester unexpectedly, towards Bridgnorth or Shrewsbury. With the Severn unguarded and the troops at Kenilworth await-ing them, there was not an hour to lose. For more than twenty miles, de Montfort's army had slogged along lanes and over hills, all through the Lord's day. There was no bread, but the fields they passed were heavy with harvest wheat and barley ready for the sickle. Lord Simon promised that there would be grain at Kenilworth, with good English food and ale enough for every-one.

Now, as the long summer evening neared its end, the footsore army spilled across the river, horses and men and wagons either splashing through the water or borne across on rafts and punts. On the far side of the river lay Kempsey, one of Bishop Walter de Cantilupe's manors. They would camp there for the night, and press on for Kenilworth Castle the next day.

'Have you ever been there, master?' Benedict asked, as they led the horses up from the water. 'To Kenilworth, I mean?'

'I have not,' Adam told him. He had stripped to his braies for the crossing; now he took a rough towel from the saddlebag and scrubbed himself dry. 'But I'm told it's one of the mightiest fortresses in the kingdom,' he said. 'Two circuits of walls, and a great lake all around it. We'll be safe enough there, at least.'

He reminded himself that Benedict's father was a vassal knight of William de Saint John, now Edward's ally. The squire had followed Adam from Hereford without comment or apparent misgivings, but Adam could not help wondering about his allegiances all the same. Would Kenilworth truly represent safety for the young man, or was it now the stronghold of his father's enemies? Whose side would Benedict choose, if matters came to battle? Doubtless he would find out soon enough.

They found a camping ground between the yew trees at the edge of a churchyard a short distance from the river. Adam rubbed down the horses while Benedict helped Hugh of Oystermouth pitch the tents. Robert de Dunstanville joined them while it was still light; he had come across on one of the rafts an hour beforehand.

'Word from Worcester,' Robert said quietly, kneeling at Adam's side while Benedict and Hugh tried to light a fire to dry their clothes and heat their thin soup. Adam could tell from Robert's grim expression that the word was nothing good.

'Our scouts lost track of Lord Edward and his men,' the knight said, 'only a few miles upriver from the town. We have no idea where they are now.'

'Christ's mercy,' Adam said under his breath. Instinctively he raised his head and stared into the lowering light, as if he might see Edward's armoured horsemen crashing out of the evening shadows all around them. Robert gave him a reassuring touch on the arm.

'They won't be upon us any time soon,' he said. 'But we can't very well move from here until we have firm intelligence of where they've got to. An ambush while we're in a marching column would be disastrous.'

Adam nodded, trying not to envisage the scene. 'Then we should get what rest we can while we have the chance,' he said.

Hugh and Benedict were crouched over the fire, nursing their little blaze. The day had been long, and even the prospect of a bowl of thin vegetable stew before sleep felt like a blessing. Riders were still coming up from the river, the last of the men straggling across dragging the carts and baggage wagons with them. Standing beside the fire Adam watched as a mounted party rode up from the riverside. They were in silhouette against the last glow of the sky, and he did not recognise them at first. Then he made out the blue and white banner, and saw Humphrey de Bohun riding at their head. Behind him came Joane, riding with her maid and her chaplain. She looked in his direction for a moment as she passed the churchyard, and he thought she saw him, but he could not be sure.

*

The morning sun had not yet burned the dew from between the trees when the first cries of dismay and alarm sounded through the camp. Thinking they were being attacked, his imagined scenes of the previous evening made flesh, Adam grabbed for his sword and called for Benedict. But quickly he realised that there were no sounds of combat, no screams of pain or fury. Instead, there was only shock, and then a rapidly spreading sense of panic.

Hugh came running back from the riverside, where he had gone to gather firewood and water. 'Lord Edward's attacked Kenilworth!' he blurted as he reached the tents.

Robert had already come striding over, with his squire behind him.

'What's this?' he demanded, 'what have you heard?'

'Yesterday before dawn, even before we'd left Hereford!' Hugh explained in a breathless rush. 'His soldiers must have ridden through the night, and they attacked Young Simon's men as they were sleeping in the town and priory . . .'

'In the *town and priory*?' Robert repeated, with a glance of incredulous fury.

'Why were they not in the castle?' Adam demanded.

'From what I've heard,' Hugh went on, holding up his palms as he steadied his breathing, 'Young Simon's men had spent the night carousing in the stews of Kenilworth, the baths in particular . . . Edward's soldiers caught them in their beds, killed some and captured most of the rest . . .'

'And their leader?' Adam asked. 'Did they capture Young Simon himself?'

'It seems they did not,' Hugh said. 'One story has it that Young Simon escaped and paddled across the lake to the castle, after leaping naked from his bed . . .'

'And leaping from the arms of some strumpet, no doubt!' Robert cried. He pressed his fists to his forehead, teeth clenched. 'My God the stupidity of that boy!'

'He had others with him, older men and more experienced,' Adam said. 'They should have counselled him better.' Young Simon was three years his senior; surely Adam himself would not have been so complacent?

'It's all true, messires,' said a servant, pausing as he ran between the tent groups. 'Lord Edward's captured the Earl of Oxford and Gilbert de Gaunt, Baldwin Wake and William de Monchensey, many others too! He's dragged them back to Worcester with him as prisoners.'

'But the castle still holds out?' Adam asked him. 'Young Simon still holds Kenilworth, with at least some of the garrison?'

'So they say, sir!' the servant replied, then made a hurried gesture and ran onward.

'And Edward's back at Worcester,' Robert said, more gravely now, fretting at his beard. 'He's less than five miles from us . . . We should move as soon as we can muster.'

Adam could only agree. But move they could not, and as the morning went on and the day grew hotter and the church bell rang terce and then sext the sense of panicked alarm filling the camp slowed to a paralysing dread. Adam sat by the wall of the churchyard with Robert, in the dappled shade of the yews. Bees buzzed heavily around them, and the torpid heat seemed to forbid speech, just as it forbade decision.

Lord Simon remained in the manor house with the king and his leading nobles, with Humphrey de Bohun and Hugh Despenser, Henry de Hastings and Nicholas de Segrave. Now and then servants and soldiers came slinking back from the doorways and windows to report what they had overheard, but there was no firm news, and no clever strategy that might extricate them from the jaws of their enemies. In the sullen heat of the afternoon, men began to doubt the genius of Simon de Montfort, and to wonder whether God had deserted him and his cause.

Evening was coming on by the time the order came to muster; they would march through the night, swinging wide to the south of Worcester and avoiding Edward's scouts. The vintenars of the infantry barked and growled, the wagon-masters yoked their beasts and the knights formed up their retinues and watered their horses at the riverbank.

'Where are we bound?' Benedict Mackerell asked. Some men had said that the eventual destination was London, others believed they would be making for Kenilworth. But by the time the army formed up in the last shades of twilight, kicking the pale dust from the baked road, word of the destination of their night march was already passing along the column.

'Evesham,' Adam told his squire. 'We're going to Evesham.'

*

'Does anyone know where we are?' he asked, several hours later.

Turning in the saddle he looked back at Benedict, following him on horseback, and Matthew bringing up the pack animals.

'We're just following you, master,' Matthew said.

Adam turned again and gazed around him into the darkness. It was a warm night, the air still and clammy, the waning half-moon covered by cloud. No sign of the other riders, or the rest of the army. Were they still on the road? Or was this just a dry patch of field?

A shape formed ahead of him, a horse, hooves beating dull on the parched earth. Hugh appeared, raising his hand as he drew closer, and Adam repeated his question.

'We must have missed the path in the dark,' Hugh said. 'But if we listen carefully we might be able to hear something. It wasn't too long ago there were riders and carts ahead of us.'

They gathered closer, as if for protection in the great gulf of the surrounding night. All fell silent, stilling their horses, listening into the darkness. Adam had known the difficulties of long night journeys before, the ease with which travellers could become sundered one from the next, and wander off on diverging courses. All the worse when the travellers were a mile-long military column trying to move quietly. He remembered the night march they had made before Lewes the year before, up onto the hills above the town. That had been hard enough, and they had been climbing on foot for most of the way.

Just for a moment, as he sat listening to the subtle noises of the land around him, he considered that it might be easier like this. Nobody could blame them if they lost their way in the night and dropped out of the column. Dawn could find them far away, riding freely towards a different future. But that would not work, he told himself. Robert was with the army, and Joane. Lord Simon too – and Adam's fate and future depended solely on him now. With his lands taken and ravaged, his betrothed in the camp of the enemy, Adam had nowhere and nothing to which he could flee. Unless he cared to spend the rest of his days as a homeless wanderer, he would have to rejoin the others.

'Not such a good view of the heavens tonight,' Hugh said quietly, his saddle creaking as he leaned back and tipped his head up. 'Too much cloud up there. But the great conjunction still bears upon us, I'm afraid.'

'The great conjunction?'

'Yes!' Hugh said, and Adam saw his eyes widening in the darkness. 'Ten nights ago. Saturn and Jupiter in conjunction, just before dawn. I saw it myself – a great and terrible sign. I would not like to expand on what it foretells.'

Adam trapped a shudder between his shoulder blades. Here in the depths of the night on a lost road with battle looming it was hard to suppress a sense of dread.

Benedict made a shushing noise, then an apologetic mumble. 'Over there!' he whispered. All of them turned, staring into the black country to their left. A moment more and they heard it: the quiet squeak of an axle, and the thudding of hooves. A stir of voices too. Riders, carts and packhorses were moving along a road not a hundred paces away.

'You have good ears,' Adam told Benedict, then nudged his horse to the left.

As he approached them, the figures on the road slowed and halted, several turning to confront him. Adam heard the clicks of crossbows being spanned, the clink of steel. '*Lux Aeterna*,' he said, speaking the password quietly. 'We are for de Montfort.'

'Adam is that you?' a voice replied. As the carts started off again and the horsemen spurred wearily to follow them, Adam saw that he had joined the tail of Humphrey de Bohun's household, and Joane was with them. Waiting until she had moved up to join him, he turned his horse and rode beside her. In the darkness there was no sign of de Bohun or his knights. Joane's maids and servants dropped back behind them, and the men of Adam's retinue lingered with them, and after a short while they rode side by side with empty darkness around them and only the suggestion of moving figures on the road ahead.

'Bishop Walter will meet us at Evesham,' Joane said as she rode, her voice sounding much closer in the darkness. 'My husband wishes me to go with him when he leaves once more.'

Adam was not surprised. Since her cousin Elizabeth had been sent home by her husband William Marshall, and Geoffrey de Lucy's wife had gone to join her own husband after his surrender at Gloucester, Joane was the only noblewoman remaining with the army. Only Humphrey de Bohun's suspicious and possessive nature had prevented him sending her away sooner.

'And will you go?' Adam asked. He could just make out her white fillet and neckcloth in the gloom.

'Would you come with me if I did?' she asked, dropping her voice.

'Lady, I cannot,' he told her.

He heard her sigh, and perhaps her quiet laugh. 'Ah yes,' she said. 'Honour compels us all.'

Adam wanted to argue – but then he realised that she could be in much the same position, if de Montfort were defeated. For a time they rode on in muffled silence.

'Do you regret what happened between us?' she asked, her voice softening to a whisper on the night air.

'No, how could I?' Adam said at once.

'Neither do I,' Joane said.

'Does Sir Humphrey suspect us?' They were riding very close now, their knees almost touching.

'Of course – *everyone* suspects us! But he will get no confirmation from me,' Joane said. 'And I'm not with child, you should know.'

Adam was glad that she could not see his sudden blush. The thought had not even occurred to him, and he was ashamed of that.

Voices came from behind them, and the shapes of riders up ahead as the advance slowed and bunched. Joane drew her horse away from Adam's, and moments later her servants surrounded them and they were separated.

The marching column pressed on through the night, and an hour later the darkness began to thin and the land appeared around them, grey shapes of trees and fields, hedgerows and isolated buildings. A river too, looping and curling away to their left.

They had closed up again, and Adam rode at the tail of a baggage cart with trudging foot soldiers to either side of him. The sky was still heavy with cloud, but along the eastern horizon a stripe of clear sky glowed pale greenish blue with the coming dawn.

Flowing in a tight loop, the river enclosed within it the little huddled settlement of Evesham and the great walled precinct of the abbey. As he followed the road along the waterside Adam saw the tower of the abbey church standing tall and black against the sky. The riders ahead of him were urging their weary horses over a wooden bridge into the town, pennons trailing and heads lowered. Then he was crossing over himself, into the web of streets still dim and cool with night's shadow.

In the open area before the abbey's western façade the principal men had drawn to a halt, surrounded by a swelling crowd of townsfolk shocked at the apparitions appearing among them from shades of morning.

'It's the king himself!' Adam heard one man calling to his wife, in a tone of awe. 'King Henry and Earl Simon de Montfort!' another cried.

They were shocked, too, at the three hundred mailed horsemen that accompanied the new arrivals, the hundreds more servants and camp followers and the thousands of ragged, footsore infantry, many of them Welsh, who were pouring across the bridge and into the streets of their town, filling the dawn with uproar. Adam rode on through the crowd to the gates of the abbey precinct, and saw in the greyness the king dismounting from his horse, helped down from the saddle by one of his serjeants-at-arms. The abbot rushed to greet King Henry, kneeling before him and kissing his hand. Walter de Cantilupe, the elderly Bishop of Worcester, followed him.

Hugh Despenser was saying something, while Lord Simon remained on horseback, his expression grave and guarded.

'No, no, Sir Hugh,' the king replied, in a brittle tone of command, and raised a finger. 'We cannot continue until I have broken my fast. And how could I deign to pass through Evesham without hearing mass sung in this magnificent church?'

Peering up at the darkened bulk of the abbey, he spread his palms in unfeigned admiration. Despenser said something in a lower voice.

'We could go straight to mass as soon as Matins is complete, your majesty,' the abbot said hurriedly, still on his knees. 'A very early mass, to be sure – but sung, yes, in honour of your royal presence . . . Bishop Walter, perhaps, would preside?'

And only moments later the matins bell started to ring, the clear brightness of the sound opening the morning and summoning the dawn. Adam heard the ringing as he led his retinue around the southern side of the abbey precinct to a small meadow beside the wall of the abbot's orchard and the infirmary, where several other groups had already settled themselves to rest while they had the opportunity. The grass was wet with dew, but the coolness was refreshing. Cockerels were crowing in the town behind them.

'See what food you can find,' Adam told Hugh, passing him a few pennies. 'Bread if they have it. If the king is breaking his fast then so shall we.'

Matthew was already taking the saddles and packs from the horses as Benedict set about lighting a fire. Adam took Rous and Fauviel and led them down the sloping meadow of long grass, still misty in the dawn, to the riverside to drink. He stood among the sedge grasses while the horses dipped their heads to the water. Across the river and the hazy flatlands the sun was just coming up, a hot red orb in the strip of clear sky at the horizon. Just for a moment as Adam stood and looked at the sun, breathing in the scents of the river and the horses, the fresh grass underfoot, he felt suffused with a sense of extraordinary contentment. For the first time since leaving his manor months before, since Lord Edward's escape from Hereford, since his own escape from Bridgnorth, he felt he was in exactly the right place at the right moment. The horizon glowed with clear golden light, as if heaven itself was opening, and Adam felt washed by its brilliance.

What day was it? He thought for a moment, then realised. *The Eve of St Oswald's.* Tomorrow was the day they had set for his marriage to Isabel de St John. A day, he saw now, that would surely never come. The sadness of that thought welled through him, mingling with his previous contentment. Then it was gone.

Adam became aware of a figure at his side, and turned to see Robert staring into the sunrise too.

'We'll have fighting this day,' Robert said. 'Today perhaps, or tomorrow for sure. I feel it in my blood and bones.' He seemed to smile as he spoke, and to another he might have appeared to relish the prospect, but Adam could see the tension that lined his features in the sun's glare.

'We'll not get to Kenilworth then, you think?' Adam asked.

Robert shook his head. 'Nor do we intend to. Young Simon will sally forth this morning with his remaining troops and meet us midway. Unless Edward meets us first. No doubt he'll be up and out with his hounds already, questing for his prey. Not a man to lie abed when there's hunting to be done.'

Hunting, or killing, Adam thought. A breath of cool breeze came from the river and sent a feverish tremor through his body. Fear fluttered inside him. 'May God grant that Young Simon meets us before Edward does,' he said, mastering himself, 'and brings us the strength to oppose him.'

From the corner of his eye he watched Robert, gauging his mood and intent. Robert noticed his scrutiny. 'I see what you are thinking,' he said, and smiled. 'Believe me, if I had any notion of slipping away into the dawn I would have done so already. As would you, I'm sure.'

'I would have no reason for it,' Adam said, although he knew that he had considered doing just that, back in the darkness of night. 'You, though . . .'

He heard Robert's rueful laugh. 'Great God, are you still carrying me upon your conscience?'

'Not exactly, no,' Adam said quickly, unable to hold back the clip of annoyance. 'But you have lands to which you could return. You have Belia, and soon you'll have a child . . . If you left now, Lord Edward would know nothing of it . . .' He fell silent. Even to suggest such a thing felt shameful now, in the clarity of this sunrise.

For a moment Robert seemed to digest what Adam had said. Then he threw back his head and laughed again. One of the horses raised its head from the water and nuzzled Adam's side.

'Believe this,' Robert said, and turned to him. He reached out and clasped Adam's shoulder. 'Whatever happens this day, there is nowhere I would rather be but here.'

*

Hugh of Oystermouth had a dozen eggs in the bowl of his hat, with a large bunch of fresh-cut parsley and a nugget of dry bread he had found somewhere. Matthew already had a fire going, and the Welshman was heating butter in a skillet as the boy beat the eggs with the chopped herbs and crumbled breadcrumbs. From the abbey the bells were ringing once more, and by the time breakfast was almost ready they could hear the choral voices drifting from the church where the king and Lord Simon were hearing mass. The sun was bright and low, beaming from beneath the lid of dark cloud to illuminate the meadow and turn the smoke from the cooking fires into a glowing blue haze.

They listened for the sound of the sacring bell, signalling the moment of the Elevation of the Host, and as it chimed they knelt and bowed their heads towards the sunrise for a few reverent moments. Then they ate, sitting on the dew-damp grass.

'I wish we had ale,' Hugh said, scraping his spoon around the inside of his wooden bowl.

'I wish we had wine,' Benedict replied, rubbing at his face. 'Will there be wine at Kenilworth, do you think?'

'More than enough to drown us all, I'm sure,' Adam told him. He had not repeated what Robert had told him by the river; better that such things were revealed when the time came. Matthew remained silent, eating slowly and casting quick glances around him.

'They say in the town it's another thirty miles to Kenilworth though,' Hugh said, setting aside his bowl and stretching himself on the grass. He yawned at the heavy sky. 'Better we stay here, I'd say. Ale or no ale.'

Adam was tempted to agree. After spending the whole night in the saddle he did not relish the idea of pressing on once more, especially as Simon the Younger was supposedly marching towards them anyway. But it would be all too easy to slip into fatigued lassitude, to surrender to sleep and lose a day . . . Shaking himself, he climbed to his feet and strode across the meadow towards the abbey precinct.

He saw the approaching horseman as he turned the corner of the infirmary wall. A solitary rider coming down the main street at the gallop, drawing his horse to a staggering halt before the abbey gateway and leaping from the saddle. As Adam broke into a jog he recognised the man: Lord Simon's personal barber, Nicholas, who doubled as his herald. Other men ran to seize the reins of the man's sweating horse, calling out questions, and the barber threw a quick answer over his shoulder then ran through the gate into the abbey precinct.

Mass was finished, and those who had attended were emerging from the great church. Adam followed Nicholas and those who had questioned him into the abbey yard; he saw the man running into the crowd of worshippers, picking out Lord Simon at once and going to him.

'What's happened?' somebody cried out.

'Did anyone hear what he said?' another man demanded.

'An army,' said one of the serjeants at the gate. 'He said there's an army coming over the hill from the north – and they're carrying Young Simon de Montfort's banners!'

Already there were glad cries and cheers as the news spread between the men gathered outside the church. 'God has delivered us!' one man yelled.

Adam too felt the sudden lift of his spirits; they would be reinforced that very day. Now, surely, they would have the strength to face Lord Edward . . . But he felt a shadow at the back of his mind, a cloud of uncertainty that drifted, threatening to cover his joy. This was too soon to exult. This was too easy a salvation.

He could hear Lord Simon calling out orders now, striding through the crowd with Nicholas running before him. Behind them lingered King Henry, pale and wan in the morning light and apparently forgotten by all. Men were dashing into the abbey buildings, following Nicholas into the passageway that led to the cloister and the dormitories. Adam followed the throng, and from the upper windows the monks peered down at them, some in eager anticipation and others with resentful disdain.

Nicholas had disappeared inside the building once more by the time Adam reached the cloister. Together with the other men he stood in the open space of the cloister garth and stared upwards; the barber was scaling the narrow internal stairway to the high tower of the abbey church, the highest point in all the town.

The tower rose against the bruised sky, lit starkly by the morning sun. Men squinted, shading their eyes from the glare as they gazed upwards. A few heartbeats later and they picked out the figure of the man at the tower's top.

'Can he see anything from up there?' Adam asked.

'Nicholas has the sharpest eyes of any man I know,' a voice beside him said. Adam turned to find Lord Simon at his shoulder, with his son Henry de Montfort and Hugh Despenser. All of them craned their necks, staring up at the tower.

Then the man on the tower top shouted, waving his arm. He disappeared, and they heard his hurried steps as he dropped back down the spiral stairway. A moment more, and his head appeared again from an arched window above the cloister.

'My lord,' Nicholas cried, 'they're up on the hilltop, thousands strong. But it's not your son's banners they're carrying now . . . May God have mercy upon us, my lord, for we're all dead men!'

Chapter 23

Chaos engulfed Evesham. 'Make ready! Make ready!' the ser-jeants yelled, as the noise of men struggling into armour, squires and grooms bringing up mounts and weapons, harnessed horses blowing and dragging at their reins filled the abbey yard and the cemetery of St Lawrence. Chaos, and panic too, the taste of it in the air like the reek of blood. The people of the town and the monks of the abbey stared from windows and doorways, wondering what strange hell had been summoned with the dawn.

In the stone-flagged passageways of the cloister men barged and swore, fumbling at their belts and bellowing for their ser-vants. The cloister garth was filling, knights and clergymen drawn in their scores to the still centre of the whirling turmoil: the figures of Simon de Montfort and his sons, Hugh Despenser, Bishop Walter, and the king.

Off to one side, leaning on a stone pillar of the cloister walkway and idly chewing a stalk of grass, Robert de Dunstanville appeared unmoved by the frenzy. He watched, with studied indifference, as other men swirled around him and the crowd in the garth grew. And Adam watched him, and wondered what he was thinking.

'My lord,' cried Ralph Basset, the baron who had ridden down with Robert from Shrewsbury. He was addressing Lord Simon. 'My lord, we haven't slept or eaten properly since leaving

Hereford, and our men and our horses are exhausted. There's a thousand men up on that hill who want our flesh – why make it easy for them? The abbey precinct and church have strong walls, we can defend ourselves here until your son and his army come to our aid, and our strength is restored.' A few other men raised their voices in agreement.

'No,' de Montfort replied at once. 'No, my friend, churches are the place for chaplains. Knights should be found instead on the field of battle!'

He stood at the centre of the square cloister garth, his back straight and his head tipped back slightly, as if he were gazing into the heavens. In the morning light his face appeared grave and solemn, the web of wrinkles around his eyes tightened as if in pain. Lord Simon looked like a martyr, Adam thought. Like a man preparing to die.

'But our enemies outnumber us by three to one, lord,' another man called. 'We should retreat from here – cross the bridge and burn it behind us, as we did at Newport . . .'

'*No,*' de Montfort said again, louder and more firmly still. 'No, the soldiers of Christ do not flee! Anyone who wishes to depart may do so – they may go with Bishop Walter, and save themselves – as for me, I'm prepared to die for justice and the law, if that is required. Prepared, and thankful.'

'Father, don't talk of death,' his son Henry said. 'Don't despair of victory—'

'I don't despair,' Lord Simon said abruptly, cutting him off. 'Although I know it's *your* proud arrogance, and the arrogance and foolishness of your brothers, that's brought us to this end!' The sudden bitterness in his voice was shocking. 'But so be it,' he said, flinging up an open palm.

Silence for a few moments, then Henry de Montfort turned abruptly on his heel and stalked away towards the abbot's lodgings, his brother Guy trailing after him. The sound of released breath filled the cloister garth.

'Friends, fellow Christians, let us be thankful,' Bishop Walter declared into the muttering hush. He spread his arms, raising his crosier high. 'This is a holy battle you fight this day, for God and the law. You are holy warriors! All shall be marked with the cross, and all shall be shriven and receive absolution!'

But as Lord Simon too left the garth, pacing wearily after his sons, the hush broke up into angry speech, accusation and recrimination. Panic was stalking through them all, throwing them into confusion.

'No surprise your resolve slackens, Basset!' John FitzJohn was ranting, his voice clipped, edged with terror. 'You were the last to join us! You and your friend de Dunstanville over there as well!'

Henry de Hastings called to Robert, a snarl in his voice. 'Is that your real master up there on the hill, de Dunstanville?' he said, flinging an arm towards the north. 'Where's your loyalty now? Will you flee to join him?'

Robert shrugged himself away from the pillar he had been leaning on and stepped forward, one hand hefting his axe and the other on his sword hilt.

'I've heard a lot of bold talk of chivalry and honour,' Robert said. He swung the axe up onto his shoulder. He still appeared entirely at ease. 'But now all I hear is the gnashing of teeth and the chattering of fools. Well, I pity the man who calls himself a knight and then shrinks from battle when it comes.'

'Yes!' a few men cried. 'Hear him!'

'What could be greater chivalry,' he declared, raising his voice and flourishing his axe, 'than going out to fight as one against three? Where could greater honour be found? And if we die, what of it? We die well. We die as knights!'

Cheering from the throng; several men drew their blades and lifted them to the sky. Even Henry de Hastings looked grudgingly impressed.

Robert looked quickly at Adam, and winked. 'Whatever happens today, stay close to me,' he said quietly.

Then he turned and walked with an easy step back into the shadow of the cloister.

Outside in the abbey yard, Adam found Hugh and Matthew waiting with the horses, and Benedict with his armour and helmet. As they helped him into his mail chausses and padded aketon he gave them his instructions. 'Hugh, you and Matthew must go with Bishop Walter and his retinue,' he told them. 'They'll be leaving before the hour is passed, over the bridge and away to safety.'

Hugh looked back at Adam with anguish in his eyes. But he nodded.

'Benedict,' Adam said to the squire. 'I give you the choice. Go with Hugh and Matthew, or come with me. I will not take you into battle unprepared.'

'Please,' Benedict said, and his words caught as his throat tightened. 'I want to come with you. Don't send me away . . .'

'Very well,' Adam told him. But he could not meet the young man's eye. He was grateful when Hugh held up his hauberk and he could immerse his head in the heavy web of mail links. He had fought in battle as a squire himself, the year before at Lewes. But Benedict was only eighteen years old, and had not gained years of combat experience on the tournament circuit. *God protect him*, Adam muttered quickly, raising his head to the sky. *God protect him, if I cannot*.

'You'll ride Rous, and carry my spare lance,' Adam told Benedict, as Matthew helped the youth into a spare hauberk. The squire was grinning as his head emerged from the steel hood of the mail coif, his face shining with joy. 'Keep close behind me,' Adam said, before his misgivings could overwhelm him, 'and try to stay clear of the melee if you can.'

Matthew saddled and bridled the warhorses, both Rous and Fauviel stamping and restive in anticipation of battle. Hugh was sitting cross-legged on the ground, his tongue between his teeth as he sewed two strips of white linen into a cross upon the breast of Adam's green surcoat. All around them men were preparing, knights and their retinues forming up, the Welsh spearmen and archers and the English militiamen shuffling together in bands, everyone bristling and hard-faced, steeling themselves for battle. From above them came the clanging of the abbey bell, ringing the hour of terce.

A palm thudded into Adam's mailed shoulder, pinning him in place. Adam's hand darted at once to the hilt of his sword. For a moment the man who had accosted him was unrecognisable; it had been a long time since Adam had seen Sir Humphrey de Bohun clad in his fine steel mail, his blue silk surcoat and jewelled belts.

'Listen to me,' de Bohun said, stepping in close, and Adam heard the word hissing between clenched teeth. 'You must speak to my wife. Speak to Joane. She refuses to go, and I have told her she must . . .'

'Where is she?' Adam said, eyes wide.

'In the church. She refuses to go with Bishop Walter, and says she'll remain here . . .' His voice choked off, and he mastered his emotions. 'I know you have . . . a certain *influence* with her,' he said. 'Use it now. Use it, for her sake. Convince her to take herself away from here to a place of safety. I . . . I ask you. If you care for her . . .'

The passion in the man's words amazed Adam. For the first time, he realised that Humphrey de Bohun truly did love his wife. Even if that love was polluted by bitter jealousy, suspicion and spite. Truly he felt the anguish of having led her into danger.

'I'll speak to her,' Adam said, and Humphrey released him at once. Passing his scabbarded sword and belt to Benedict, Adam crossed the yard to the porch and entered the church.

In the deep gloom, the air was still rich and thick with the incense of the mass. Adam walked quickly along the northern aisle, blinking as his eyes adjusted to the shadow. Night still lingered here, the whole vast space of the church plunged into dimness.

But very soon he became aware of the figures all around him, the throng of people huddling in the nave and the aisles to either side. They pressed away from him as he approached, repelled by the crunch of his armoured feet, the gleam of his mail, as if he were a harbinger of the battle to come. Most of the people in the church were army servants, clerks and clergymen of the knightly retinues; the few women appeared to be camp followers, laundresses and soldiers' wives. Peering among the clustered heads and bodies, Adam could see nothing of Joane, and despaired at finding her.

'Where is Sir Humphrey de Bohun's wife?' he demanded of one tonsured clerk, who crouched beside the chancel screen. 'Where is Lady Joane?' The man gibbered something and shook his head.

'She's in the north transept,' another voice said. Adam turned to see Master Philip Porpeis, the bishop's physician, emerging from the shadows. 'You should find her easily enough.'

'Thank you,' Adam said, grasping the man by the hand. 'Are you remaining here as well?' he asked.

Master Philip shook his head. 'I wanted to, as certainly my skills will be needed. But the lord bishop wishes that I not be separated from him once more, and sadly I must comply.' He inclined his head, then laid a palm on Adam's mailed shoulder. 'I wish you God's strength and mercy,' he said. 'And I shall pray that we meet again.'

Adam could not miss the despairing note in his voice, and for a moment he watched the man pace quickly away towards the daylight of the porch. A painting on the wall caught his eye, as his vision grew sharper: the enthroned Christ, sitting in judgement on the Day of Doom. To one side, the figures of the blessed soared up towards paradise. To the other, the naked figures of the damned tumbled into hell.

Tightening his jaw, Adam fought down a shudder of dread. Then he turned and plunged into the crowd once more, shoving his way through the throng until he reached the north transept.

'Adam!' Joane said. She was kneeling before one of the side altars, her chaplain and her maid Petronilla and several of her other servants accompanying her; all were in attitudes of prayer, but all appeared too distracted to pray.

Taking her hand, Adam helped her to her feet. 'Your husband came to me,' he told her, speaking quickly and quietly. 'He wanted me to ask you to leave this place. I think he's right – you must not stay here.'

'I cannot leave, not now,' Joane told him. They were standing as close as they dared, their hands clasped. Adam saw her maid directing baleful glances in his direction, as if all of this were his fault.

'Joane, if this battle goes badly . . . if we are defeated, then you'll be in great danger here.'

'But this is a holy place!' Joane said, with a quick half-smile that did little to hide her nerves. 'Surely God will protect us from any harm?' She held his gaze for a moment. 'Listen to me,' she said, more urgently. 'All that I care about is here. If my husband should fall . . . if *you* should fall . . . then I will have nothing. Do you understand?'

'Yes,' Adam said, feeling the shock of her words running through him. The truth of them. He knew at once that his pleas would be in vain. 'I would beg you to leave, but—'

'But it would do you no good.' She smiled again, sadly and with more genuine feeling, and tightened her grip on his hands. Then she embraced him, pressing herself against the hard links of his mail. He kissed her hand as they separated.

'Fight well,' she said. 'May God protect you. Find me when this is done. Wherever we might be.'

*

Adam was still swallowing back his anguish as he strode down the north aisle once more towards the door. The incense in the air, the scent of close-packed humanity, was suddenly choking, and he gasped with relief as he emerged into the fresh morning daylight.

Near the porch a group of men were gathered around a horse in a red and white caparison. They were helping another man into his armour, and with a jolt of surprise Adam realised that it was King Henry. Those assisting him were serjeants-at-arms – all of them de Montfort's men now – and they were dressing him in a plain mail hauberk and helmet, and the red and white surcoat of Lord Simon's own household. As he stood and watched, Adam heard the king's voice rising, thin and querulous: 'But why must I wear it? This is unheard-of . . . Will I be protected? Will I be recognised at all?'

'Don't worry, your majesty,' one of the serjeants said, with only the vaguest note of deference, 'we'll be all around you, keeping you safe. But we wouldn't want anyone to mistake you for the enemy . . .'

Adam watched a moment longer, then walked on towards the gates of the abbey precinct, where Hugh and Benedict were waiting with the horses. 'Matthew's disappeared,' Hugh said at once, his expression tight with concern. 'I can't find him any-where, and the bishop will be leaving directly!'

'Don't worry, he'll find you soon enough,' Adam said. He raised his arms as Benedict pulled the surcoat over his head, marked with white crosses on the chest and the back. Then the squire buckled his waist belt, fastened the sword belt across his hips and the gilded spurs to his ankles.

Across the yard, near the great west doors of the abbey church, Bishop Walter and a line of priests and friars were attending to the confessions of the fighting men, and granting absolution to them. Just as they had done before Lewes, Adam remembered. And their position now was similar to that at Lewes, but in reverse: their enemies had occupied the heights overlooking the town, after a night march, while de Montfort's army were in the town and priory. Only now, of course, the enemy had the advantage of overwhelming numbers as well. *Do not think of such things*, Adam told himself, and crossed the yard to join the men waiting to be shriven.

Kneeling on the worn flagstones, his mail crunching, Adam pressed his palms together and closed his eyes. '*Benedicite pater*,' he said.

'*Dominus exaudiat nos*,' came the reply. Adam saw that it was the bishop himself who stooped over him.

'*Confiteor deo omnipotenti* . . .' he said, reciting the words and then the Creed quickly and steadily. 'I acknowledge to God and to all the holy company of heaven that I am a sinner . . . I have sinned in thought, word and deed . . .'

He could confess anything now. Any sin, any crime or enormity, and the stain of it would be washed from his soul. Was he not a holy warrior, signed with the cross? Only moments before, Bishop Walter had given the sacrament of the Eucharist to Lord Simon and his principal nobles in one of the side chapels; the aura of sanctity still lingered about him, a golden light of divine blessing.

The bishop laid his fingers lightly on Adam's shoulder, stilling his words. There was no need to say more.

'*Ego te absolvo*,' he said, sketching the cross in the air above Adam's head. Righteous battle in the name of God, justice and Simon de Montfort would be his penance. For that, all his sins would be forgiven. He would be among those soaring up to heaven at Christ's command, not tumbling down into the gaping maw of damnation.

As he stood, light-headed, Adam felt a sudden rush of pure pleasure and fulfilment. A sense of rightness, like he had felt earlier at the riverbank. The first sun was gleaming from behind the abbey church now, filling the yard with radiance, although the sky above was darker and heavier still and the air had grown warm and clammy and charged with a strange bristling energy. The bells had started ringing once more, a steady insistent clanging, although Adam did not know why.

Slipping his foot through the stirrup, he swung himself up into the saddle. Benedict passed him his lance, then mounted the second charger. There was still no sign of Matthew, but in the chaos of the muster, and with Bishop Walter and his retinue preparing to depart, it would be impossible to track him down.

'I'll be riding with Ralph Basset,' Robert said, walking his horse over to join Adam. His squire Giles and a pair of serjeants rode at his back. 'Will you join me?'

'I will,' Adam told him. 'Gladly.' The Baron of Drayton had long experience fighting on the Welsh frontier, and the men of his retinue knew their business too. If anyone might stand a chance of surviving this battle, it would be them.

On the far side of the yard, Humphrey de Bohun and his knights and squires were in the saddle too, powerful in their livery of blue and white, with the golden lions and fleurs-de-lis on their banners. De Bohun saw Adam gazing at him and his brow creased in a silent question. Adam shook his head.

A trumpet sounded, the blast echoing back off the façade of the great church, and Simon de Montfort and his great retinue came riding across the yard towards the gateway. Lord Simon himself was at the fore, with the king behind him in his plain armour and livery, no crown upon his plain iron helmet. The Scots knight Guy de Balliol followed, carrying de Montfort's personal banner, the rampant fork-tailed lion displayed on blood red. Men cheered and cried out his name as their leader rode by, but Lord Simon stern and tall in the saddle, not turning his head.

As they rode out beneath the arched abbey gateway, de Balliol failed to lower the banner, and the spearhead clashed against the arch. With a crack the banner toppled, the shaft broken near the tip. Groans of dismay came from the onlookers.

'God help us now,' Robert said. 'If that is not a sign—'

'Think no more of it,' Adam said quickly, although he too was shaken by the sight. He could see that many of the foot soldiers who had witnessed the accident were even more gravely disturbed.

But they went on out of the gate, filing through into the broad street outside the abbey precinct and forming up in a single great column beneath their banners. Bishop Walter and his people had gathered beside the road, the bishop weeping openly as he embraced Lord Simon from the saddle and prepared for his departure. Where the road branched off towards the bridge the bishop and his entourage left them, a ragged throng of townsfolk and camp followers going after him, many with handcarts piled with belongings.

'I still can't find Matthew,' Hugh of Oystermouth said, running up beside Adam's horse. 'I can't leave without him . . .'

'You must,' Adam said. He leaned from the saddle and clasped Hugh by the arm. Then he reached into his belt pouch and took out the ebony and silver paternoster beads that Isabel had given him so many months ago. 'There's a pouch of coin in my baggage,' he said. 'Take it, and take this too.'

He pooled the beads into Hugh's open palm. 'Find your way back to Basing,' he said, quickly, firmly, 'to the court of William de St John. Give these to his daughter Isabel. Tell her . . . tell her I'm sorry. And ask her to pray for me if she can.'

Hugh closed the beads in his fist, nodding as he blinked back tears. He opened his mouth to speak, but no words came.

'Now go,' Adam said, brusquely to hide his own feelings. He waited until the Welshman had hurried after Bishop Walter before snatching a parting glance back at him. Then he straightened in the saddle once more and rode onward.

The air had grown heavy and still, the clouds pressing down, and Adam beneath the weight of his armour felt the sweat breaking on his body. At the town wash house, de Montfort reined in his horse and circled back to address those that followed him. Men crowded closer, trying to catch his words. Standing in the stirrups, Lord Simon called back over the heads of his retinue.

'If any more wish to leave us,' he cried, 'this is the moment. Many among you are young and untried, many have wives and children . . . Cross the bridge and you can save yourself, for we ride into great peril.'

Adam heard many around him replying that they would not flee. John de Beauchamp, the young Baron of Bedford, shook his head vigorously and shouted that he would stand with Lord Simon.

'Sir Hugh,' Simon called to Hugh Despenser. 'Considering your great age, you may wish to depart . . .' He grinned; Despenser was a decade his junior. 'Think how much wisdom you have yet to offer to this kingdom!'

Laughter from those who overheard him. But Hugh Despenser looked grave. 'No, my lord,' he said, in a low voice that carried to them all. 'Let it be. Today we shall all drink from one cup, just as we have in the past.'

De Montfort nodded, still smiling. There was nothing more to say. He tugged at his reins, turned his horse and gave the signal to advance once more. As they passed the last houses of Evesham, the Welsh infantry bringing up the rear under Humphrey de Bohun's command let out a massed bellowing shout, raising their spears and bow staves. The noise echoed back from the river and the lowering sky. Birds wheeled overhead in startled profusion.

Robert was laughing, his eyes wild; Adam caught his mood and laughed too. He looked around him, and felt the strength in their numbers. Surely, Adam thought, they could break through anything. A sudden wild exhilaration lifted his spirits.

The hillside rose before them, a steady climb of a mile or two to the crest. Fields of wheat and barley fringed the lower slopes, broken by orchards and clumps of trees, all within the enclosing loop of the river. Higher up, the ground was open meadow and sheep pasture. And there on the ridge stood the enemy. Still distant, their banners were a shimmer of colour against the sky.

'May God save our souls,' somebody said, 'for our bodies are theirs!'

Then from overhead came a deep rolling percussion, a boom of thunder that travelled across the sky. The warm breeze gained force, turning to a black wind that roared low across the earth and tugged at the banners and pennons. Up on the hill crest the lines of the enemy rippled like grass before the scythe. Thunder cracked and rolled again, the black clouds pulsed with lightning, and suddenly it felt as dark as midnight.

Horses kicked and pulled at their reins, twisting their necks as the riders fought to keep control. The wind coursed over them, and then out of the blackness came the flurrying rain. Water-drops exploded off the dry ground, seething in the dust and hissing off the armour and shields of the riders. Another crack of lightning, the sky splitting in a livid white flash. Then the rain slackened, the wind eased.

A moment more, and the sun broke through the clouds. Trumpets blared, drums began to rattle. From the hill crest came the distant bleating of the enemy's horns. The tight mass of horsemen closed up, dressing their ranks, and as the sun glittered all around them they began to advance once more. Messengers were riding back down the slope, carrying orders from Lord Simon to his captains.

'What are they saying?' Ralph Basset demanded, twisting in his saddle to track the riders. He was a weathered man, nearing fifty, with a creased and leathery face. One of his squires rode out and back.

'The earl wants Sir Humphrey to move the infantry forward, sir,' the squire reported. 'But Sir Humphrey refuses to change his position.'

Basset grunted, his lips twisting. 'Daresay de Montfort would prefer to use them to screen our advance,' he said. 'Not surprised de Bohun won't let him – they'd be cut down like chaff.'

Only a few scattered companies of foot soldiers had followed closely behind the advancing horsemen, most of them English militia. As Adam looked across their ranks a figure caught his eye, a slight young man in a brown cowl, carrying a spear and with a knife stuck through his belt. A shock of startled recognition as the figure raised his head: it was Matthew. But now the trumpets began to sound once more, the shrill discordant braying rousing the horses to quicken their pace without the need for the spur. The leading riders had begun moving up the slope of the hill onto the pastures and meadow, the remaining infantry were running to keep up. Another shower of rain passed over them, then the ground steamed in sudden hot sunlight.

Again the pace doubled, the leading horses breaking into a heavy trot up the slope and the rest powering after them. At the crest of the hill the line of enemy banners widened, new divisions moving forward on the flanks. Now Adam could see why Lord Simon had wanted the infantry: Edward's forces threatened to envelop their advance on both sides. Their only hope lay in a frontal attack on the enemy centre, and a desperate attempt to break their line.

'Lace up!' Ralph Basset cried as he rode, and the squires of his retinue passed helmets forward to the knights. Benedict rode up alongside Adam and gave him the heavy iron barrel helm; Adam was unwilling to put it on at once, knowing that as soon as he did he would be half-blind and half-suffocated in its metal casing. Instead, he breathed deeply, smelling horse sweat and leather, and wet grass on the breeze.

'Ready?' Robert called. Adam looked to his right; Robert stretched out his arm, and Adam grasped his hand. 'Yes!' he called back.

'To victory, then,' Robert said with a grin. 'Or a glorious death!'

He laughed, and Adam laughed with him. He remembered this wild thrilling energy. They had felt it before at the tournaments, and at Lewes. He relished it now, while he still could. Before the first shock of combat, the first sickening pulse of terror.

Adam stretched his legs out, feet wedged tight into the stirrups. One long breath, the blood rushing in his head, and he pulled on the helmet and tied the laces under his jaw. He shot his left arm into his shield straps, reached with his right hand and felt the shaft of the lance in his palm as Benedict passed it to him. Through his mind ran the words of the Lord's Prayer.

Pater noster, qui es in caelis, sanctificetur nomen tuum . . .

His horse began to trot, and his vision narrowed to two jolting slits of light. Ahead were the backs of Basset's retinue knights, his red and yellow banners whipping in the breeze, the enemy line growing closer, then rapidly closer still as Lord Edward's men sounded their horns and began to charge.

Adveniat regnum tuum. Fiat voluntas tua . . .

Head down, shield rim bashing against his helmet, Adam braced himself in the saddle and held his lance angled upward, ready to bring the steel tip arcing smoothly down to the point of impact — *like a plunging hawk*, he thought. But there was nothing smooth, nothing controlled about this charge.

Sed libera nos a malo . . .

Sed libera nos a malo . . .

All he could hear was the battering of hooves, the screech of trumpets and the noise of his own blood in his ears. And, above it all, a voice away to his right.

'*Death!*' Robert was screaming, brandishing his axe. '*Death!*'

Chapter 24

The charging armies met at the brow of the hill, all formation disintegrating as horses and armoured men rammed
together. Lances clashed and buckled, and the air was filled with
a blizzard of flying splinters. Horses screamed, several going
down at the first impact. Adam saw one of Ralph Basset's knights
struck by a lance, the point slamming in under his helmet rim
and piercing his neck. He saw the man's head jolted back, heard
the snap of his neck, then the body toppling from the saddle. A
touch of the spurs and Fauviel surged on forward, shoving aside
the riderless horse.

Adam dropped his lance and couched it – too soon, too sudden – but with the men ahead of him packed so close he could
barely miss. He felt the thud of impact, the grate of steel as the
lance point scored across the face of a blue and yellow shield.
Then the blow went wide, Fauviel plunging onward. The stallion had never been in the melee before and was half-mad with
terror. All around them was the mesh of combat, the brutal col-
lision of beasts and men, and the flicker and stab of sharp steel.

The enemy were wearing red crosses on shoulder and surcoat, Adam noticed – were they too holy warriors now? Did
they too fight in the name of Christ? Drawing back his lance
again, he angled it at a red-crossed knight and lunged. The point

caught and grated on the man's mail, then a savage downward blow from a mace shattered the shaft. Adam threw the weapon aside, stretching out his empty right hand for his second lance. But Benedict was lost somewhere behind him. Instead, Adam snatched for his sword.

To his right, Robert was slashing with his axe from the saddle, but Adam could barely see him. Through the eye-slits of his helmet he saw only flickers, darting steel bright in the sunlight, jostling shapes of horses, the flash of heraldry, the sun off a shield. His horse was plunging beneath him, caught in the mad dance of the melee. Down between the kicking trampling hooves, the wounded and the dead cried out for mercy.

Trumpets from both sides. *Rally*. Adam tightened his reins and slowed the wild careering of his horse. Backing, he felt Robert close up on his right, one of Ralph Basset's knights on his left. A space was opening as the enemy too dressed their ranks. Fallen horses and downed riders lay between them, some of the animals hamstrung or crippled, kicking their legs as they tried to stand.

The horns screamed a second time. 'Again!' Ralph Basset yelled, his voice muffled by iron. 'Again, and we break them!'

They moved in a wedge, driving their sweating chargers forward into the crush of battle. Adam wanted desperately to tear off his helmet, but with every ringing blow against the steel he knew it was keeping him alive. Terror seized him, clasping him by the throat. He could not live through this; nobody could. Then a moment later his horse gave a sudden lunge and all he felt was the coursing exhilaration of motion, of wild destructive fury claiming him entirely. Robert barged against him from the right, then reeled away again, swinging powerful blows with his axe.

Open ground ahead, and Adam pushed on into it. An enemy rider turned, presenting an open target, and he struck, feeling his blade hacking at the mail links with all the strength of his arm. A blow to break bone and sever muscle. But he did not even hear his victim cry out. A lance rammed against his side, driving hard spikes of pain through his torso. A breath, and the pain doubled. Ribs bruised, maybe broken. Sweat pouring all over his body, greasing his limbs. He could bleed to death and not know it.

Fauviel staggered beneath him, and he feared the horse would fall. The terrible pit beneath the fighting opened, the crush of fallen bodies kicked and trampled by the horses. He saw the blood streaking the muddied grass. Then his charger staggered back upright, lifting him, and he was back in the fight once more.

'We're breaking them!' somebody cried. 'On! Keep on!'

Sure enough, the mass of opposing horsemen ahead was thinning. Some were already retreating, backing their horses in skittish sidestep as de Montfort's attack ripped a breach in Lord Edward's formation.

'Turn, cowards!' a knight was bellowing at them, tipping back his helmet. He wore a red cross on his blue surcoat. 'Turn, damn you! Remember your shame at Lewes!'

De Montfort's men were over the crest of the ridge now and far across the flat ground of the hilltop. But slowly, with the strength of their overwhelming numbers, the enemy were rallying. Adam saw the red chevron banners of de Clare's men down the slope; Earl Gilbert had pivoted his whole line against de Montfort's left. Now his riders were galloping across the open ground beyond the battle's swirl, eating at the flank of Lord Simon's army as they rode down the riverbank towards the town of Evesham.

Steam rose from the soaked ground and the bodies of the horses. Adam's eyes were flooding with sweat, and he could not wipe them or blink it away. The noise of his own breath in the helmet vents was near deafening, and the wound in his side flared and pulsed. There were a lot of men on foot around him too now, knights either unhorsed or with their chargers killed beneath them. Several fought back-to-back in small groups, fending off the assaults of the mounted enemy.

Then, directly ahead of him, Adam saw the fork-tailed white lion dancing above the melee. Beneath it rode a young knight on a white horse, the de Montfort arms on his shield crossed by a blue bar. It was Simon the Younger, Adam thought with sudden elation – de Montfort's son had arrived with his army from Kenilworth and plunged into the fight. *Surely the battle was won . . .*

He spurred his horse forward, into the turmoil around the standard. '*A Montfort! A Montfort!*' he yelled, his voice booming inside his helmet.

But he soon realised his mistake. The knight on the white horse was not Simon the Younger, but his brother Henry. And now Adam saw the other horsemen, closing in from the opposite direction. Hundreds of them, all wearing the sign of the red cross, with Roger Mortimer's banner at the fore. The powerful retinues of the Marcher Barons had swung their line from the right and ploughed into Lord Simon's flank. Like a wave they engulfed Henry de Montfort, driving his household knights away from him with the force of their charge.

Shards of brilliant sunlight sliced between the combatants, and Adam rode blindly. He felt the shock as Fauviel rammed his chest into the flank of an opposing horse. The rider tried to swing his lance back; Adam smacked it aside with his shield, hacked his sword down into the haunch of the enemy mount. The rider dug in with his spurs, and he was gone.

By the time Adam caught sight of him again, Henry de Montfort was disarmed, attackers on all sides of him. Too far away to ride to his aid, Adam could only watch as one of them pulled the young man's helmet off, another seized the rim of his coif and dragged his head back, and a third aimed a savage blow with his axe, chopping down into his exposed throat. The attackers separated, but Henry de Montfort was already dead, his blood spattering down the white flanks of his horse.

Roger Mortimer's knights were crashing through the fraying mob of men around de Montfort's standard. Adam pitched in

his saddle as his horse leaped, dodging another animal that collapsed to the ground ahead. As he regained his seat Adam glanced
downward and saw the fallen rider: Hugh Despenser, his face a
bloodied mask.

Mortimer's flank attack had driven de Montfort's men off the
top of the ridge and a short way down the western flank, but
already they were rallying, the horns shrilling over the clash of
metal and the battering of shields and bodies. Adam kept Fauviel
on a tight rein, turning the charger in a short-stepping circle
until he picked out Lord Simon's banner once more. Even as
he glimpsed it, he saw the rider who carried it, Guy de Balliol,
struck with a savage blow between the shoulder blades, the banner slipping from his grasp to fall between the fighting men.

Screwing his helmet desperately from side to side, for several
punishing heartbeats Adam could see nobody but the enemy all
around him. Then an avenue opened, the briefest gap between
the struggling forms, and Adam saw Lord Simon standing in the
stirrups as he struck at his attackers. Another rider came galloping towards him, Roger Mortimer himself with his gilded great
helm flashing in the sun, his lance couched at the charge.

Adam cried out a warning, spurring his horse forward. Too
late: Mortimer drove his lance into the chest of de Montfort's
horse, and Lord Simon went plunging forward over the mane,
into the bloody chaos below.

'No!' Adam yelled. 'No!' But the words rang only in his own
ears. Before he could kick again with his spurs a blade struck him
on the shoulder, bursting pain down his spine. Adam backed, fighting his horse around. A second strike, the sword clipping the top
of his shield. His helmet blocked his peripheral vision, and Adam
could see nothing. He aimed short hacking blows in the direction
of his attacker, trying to keep his shielded side towards him.

The two horses turned beneath them, and then the man was
right in front of him, the red shield raised to display three severed hands. *De Malmaines.*

They were too close to strike effectively. Adam let his sword drop and swing on its wrist strap, leaning from the saddle to slam his mailed fist against de Malmaines's helmet. The other man was fending him off with crabbed blows. His blade grated and clashed against Adam's mailed arms and shoulder. Getting a grip on the helmet rim Adam dragged at it, hauling de Malmaines to one side as he pressed at Fauviel's flanks with his knee. The horse caught his movement and backstepped, haunches low, and Adam clung to the other man with his grip burning.

De Malmaines roared, wrenched his sword arm clear, and aimed a savage underarm stab. The blade pierced Fauviel's throat and drove in deep. Adam felt the shudder beneath him, then the convulsion of the pained animal. He released de Malmaines and clung to the saddle, his sword dangling and clashing. A sudden blow against his helmet, denting the metal into the side of his face, and Adam dug in his spurs, agony in his skull and blood in his eyes.

Fauviel bolted, galloping wildly with blood pumping from his wounded neck. Clear of the whirling fury at the heart of the melee, clear of de Malmaines, and then the gallop turned to a crashing fall. Adam kicked his feet from the stirrups at the last moment, then felt the rush as he was hurled from the saddle.

He struck the ground hard, and knew nothing.

*

Up. *Get up.* He could not see, and the metal reek of blood swamped his senses. But he could feel the fighting above him and around him, the air pulsing with savage movement. The ground beneath him, the mud in which he crawled, trembled. He was lying on his side, he realised. Something was pattering against the side of his helmet. Rain, perhaps. With clumsy hands he clouted at his chin, scrabbling for the helmet laces. Then he remembered to pull his hands from the mail mittens, and tried again. Fingers clawing, he got the laces undone but still the helmet would not come off. He could not breathe. He could not see. Frantic, both hands clasping the dented steel barrel of the helm, he wrenched at it until at last it came free. With a sobbing gasp of breath he flung the helmet away from him. Pain bathed his face.

Scrubbing a filthy palm across his blood-welted eyes, he opened them and saw the rutted turf, the gore sprayed and spattered over the grass. One of Fauviel's legs was still jerking. Another horse leaped over him as he lay, hooves kicking up dirt that showered onto him.

Adam blinked, sucked air between his teeth and tried to raise himself on his elbows. At any moment he expected the lighting flash of a blow that would open his skull and end his life. He crawled, dragging himself until he could lie against Fauviel's steaming belly, propping himself up.

'No mercy for traitors!' somebody was yelling. 'No mercy!'

Between the legs of the jostling horses he could see the ground scattered with fallen men. Other men too, fighting on foot, hewing at each other. Only a score of paces from where Adam lay a knot of figures struggled in the mud of a hollow, grappling and punching. One of them tried to break free, and through the glaze of pain Adam recognised Simon de Montfort. Another figure was striding closer, a knight in a gilded helm. The knight raised a misericord dagger in both hands and then stabbed it downwards, punching it into the back of Lord Simon's neck through a rent in his mail.

Adam drew breath to shout, but his throat locked and he could only stare.

The other men closed around the body as it fell. They lifted swords and daggers and began to hack, a mob of them now all jostling together. For a few long heartbeats Adam saw nothing. Then, as the men parted, he saw the exposed and bloodied flesh, the mauling of the body. He heard the crowing cheers, the wild exultation of the slaughterers. Horror was pumping through him, but in that moment he was too stunned to move.

Up, he told himself again. *Get up.*

Shoving against the hot carcass of the fallen horse he managed to get his knees beneath him and lever himself upwards. Nausea filled his chest, and he fought it down. He was hurt, he knew, perhaps badly, but amid the overall pain he could not distinguish where the wound might be. Getting to his feet he began to run, heavy and stumbling in his mail hauberk and chausses. He had dropped his sword, the wrist strap broken, and for a moment the loss of that excellent Solingen blade, the same weapon Lord Simon had given him on the field at Lewes, grieved him more than anything. Then he remembered that Simon was dead, and all was lost. He snatched up another sword from the ground, a notched and bloodied weapon, and ran onward.

The fighting was behind him now, the knot of surviving men and horses drawn tight as the enemy swarmed around them. But mounted men and foot soldiers were ranging in a wide circuit, some trying to flee while others hunted down the fugitives. Here and there little swirling melees broke out as small groups tangled in combat. The clash of weapons and the cries of the fallen sounded muffled and deadened by the muddy ground and the soaked sky overhead.

Veering between the fallen bodies, Adam made his way along the slope of the hillside. Horses galloped past, and he heard the cracked laugh as one passing knight lunged at him with a spear. As he dodged away, Adam grabbed the neck of his surcoat and pulled at it until the linen tore, then cast aside the white cross that identified his allegiance.

Ahead of him three dead horses lay in a pile, as if swept there by the waters of a flood. One had the stub of a lance jutting from its chest. A fortune in prime horseflesh, butchered in moments. A tide of blood flowed down the slope from the carcasses of the horses, broad as a stream and splitting into rivulets. He slipped as he made his way through it, falling heavily on his side with a gasp of pain.

Beyond the dead horses a gang of men surrounded a captive knight. The prisoner was on his knees, pleading for his life – Adam could not hear the words, but as he raised his head from the churned gore he could interpret the gestures well enough. One of the captors dragged off the man's mail coif and arming cap, and Adam saw that it was John de Beauchamp, the handsome young baron knighted only a few days beforehand. De Beauchamp was weeping, hands clasped in prayer as he threw back his head and begged for quarter.

'No mercy for traitors!' one of his captors cried, and with a cruel laugh plunged his sword into the young man's open mouth, driving the blade deep into his throat.

On his feet again, stunned but still moving, Adam headed towards the higher ground – better that way, he thought, remembering the sight of the riverbank flowing with Gilbert de Clare's men. A short distance away, just over the crest of the ridge, the red and white de Montfort banner was aloft once more, men on foot gathered around it in a last stand.

Closer, an iron-grey destrier lay dead on the slope. The red and white caparison drew his eye at once, and Adam took a few steps closer. He recognised the horse, but only when he saw the discarded shield lying beside it did his heart punch in his chest. White with a red lattice: Robert de Dunstanville's arms.

Hefting his sword, he broke into a staggering run.

Robert lay at the edge of a narrow field of trampled wheat. The stalks all around him were stippled with blood. Adam called out as he drew closer, and then yelled with relief as the fallen man raised his head.

'Adam!' Robert said, his voice a rasping croak. His helmet was gone, his ventail hung loose and his beard was matted with sweat. Adam came to a halt beside him and dropped to one knee, Robert stretching up to embrace him with one arm. Their mailed bodies grated together.

'Merciful Christ, I thought they'd killed you,' Robert gasped. His face was grey-white and waxy.

'They killed Lord Simon,' Adam told him, easing him back down. 'Mortimer and his men – I saw them. His son Henry too, and Hugh Despenser . . .'

'And Ralph Basset, and my squire Giles, and half a hundred more,' Robert said, and then grimaced as the pain racked him. 'And now there's only us.'

'Where are you wounded?' Adam asked. He could see no injuries on Robert's body at first. But as the fallen man dragged aside his surcoat, Adam's brow chilled and he caught his breath. Blood was leaking through the punctured mail of his friend's abdomen, just below the coat of plates he wore buckled over his hauberk.

'It was Hamo L'Estrange,' Robert said, with a cough of grim mirth. 'Got me with a lance at the charge. Never go into battle against your dead wife's brother, I would suggest.'

'Let me help you,' Adam said. He could see that the coat of plates was paining Robert, and he ripped the surcoat open at the sides and fumbled with the straps and buckles that secured the armour.

'There's water . . . over there,' Robert managed to say through his teeth.

Adam nodded. He wrenched the straps free and then peeled the armour away from his friend's torso. Robert gasped in relief, his body shuddering. But when Adam glanced down, his throat tightened and he looked away quickly. Robert's entire lower body was streaming with gore.

'I'll get you a drink,' he said. 'Don't move.'

The water flask was lying a little further along the field's edge, the strap clasped in the hand of a dead groom or servant. Adam snatched it free and then ran back to join Robert. Pulling out the bung he poured water over his friend's face, washing away the streaks of blood and the mask of sweat and dirt. Robert sucked the water through his teeth and grinned. 'Take some yourself,' he said in a breath, then inhaled sharply. 'You look ghastly.'

Adam tipped the flask back, drenching his face with the last of the water and then letting it spill into his mouth. It was blood-warm, and blood-tasting as he gulped it down. As he wiped his face, he realised that his eyes were streaming tears.

'It's bad, isn't it,' Robert said.

Adam could only nod. They both knew that few survived a wound to the gut, especially from a lance. L'Estrange would have driven the steel deep and hard. It was only surprising that Robert had not died instantly. If he could find a horse and get his friend into the saddle, Adam thought, there was a chance of escaping the battlefield and saving his life. Otherwise, his death was only a matter of time.

Somewhere on the slope above them a band of de Montfort's dismounted knights were making their last stand, gathered around their banner while Lord Edward's men rode at them with lances and axes. The noise of the fighting was a wild high percussion on the blood-scented breeze. Closer, men on foot were already stripping the corpses of the slain.

As he raised his head, Adam caught sight of a mounted figure on the far side of the wheatfield, riding at a trot and leaning from the saddle to stare at the fallen bodies. He recognised the horse first, the red hide glowing with sweat. It took him only a moment longer to recognise the rider.

'Benedict!' he called. He raised his arm, and saw the squire's quick grin. Shaping a prayer of thanks to God, Adam got to his feet.

'I'll be back,' he told Robert. 'Try to lie still.'

Benedict had already turned his horse as Adam pushed his way through the trampled wheat. Adam paused and blinked, his vision sharpening, then let out a warning. Another rider was gal-loping fast down the slope behind the squire, his lance couched, the red caparison of his warhorse billowing. Benedict heard Adam's shout and twisted in the saddle, but Richard de Mal-maines was already upon him. The lance struck the squire in the

side, punching through his mail and piercing his chest. Benedict
threw up his arms and toppled backwards, dead before his body
hit the ground.

With the notched sword in both hands Adam advanced the last
distance to the open ground. He felt very calm now, the horror
and anguish falling away from him, his mind focused entirely on
what he had to do. He carried no shield, but de Malmaines had
still not noticed him; the knight slowed his destrier to a trot,
dragging at the reins to turn and seize the fallen man's horse.
It had been his own once, Adam realised. Perhaps he had recognised it, and that was why he had attacked Benedict?

Sword raised, Adam charged from the edge of the wheatfield.
One flashing strike opened the chest of de Malmaines's horse,
and the animal stumbled as blood sprayed from the wound. De
Malmaines fought with the reins, but the destrier's legs folded
and it fell. Adam took three long strides backwards, lifting his
sword again. He had saved this man's life on the field of Lewes,
but now he intended to take it. De Malmaines had thrown himself from the saddle skilfully, and his armour had protected him
in the fall. Already he was clambering to his feet again, clumsy
for a moment in his armour and still dazed. Adam rushed at him.
No chivalry now.

De Malmaines had dropped his shield, but he blocked Adam's
first strike with his mailed forearm as he drew his own sword. At
once he slashed back, a low horizontal cut that rang off Adam's
armoured chest. He was still wearing his enclosed helmet, while
Adam's mail coif was thrown back on his shoulders and he was
bare-headed. Faster though, and breathing easily. He could hear
de Malmaines panting like a cracked bellows.

They circled, feinting. Then de Malmaines stamped forward,
aiming a fast lethal chop that would have opened Adam's skull
had he not dodged it. Adam grabbed the blade of his sword in
his mailed hand and used the weapon like a spear, driving the tip
beneath the other man's helmet rim. De Malmaines staggered

back three steps, but the links of his neck armour remained unbroken. Then he roared, the sound inhuman from inside his helm, and attacked once more.

Their blades clashed, steel whining, and they shoved against each other. De Malmaines ground his sword upwards until the edge caught in a notch in Adam's weapon, then he began to twist it. Jaw set hard, Adam bunched his muscles and pushed again with both hands, trying to drive de Malmaines back until he could free his sword. De Malmaines let out another choked gasp of effort, blowing froth through the vents of his helmet. Then, with another steely roar, he twisted his grip.

And Adam's blade broke.

He staggered forward, de Malmaines's sword whipping against his head and cutting his scalp. But he managed to throw his weight against his adversary, driving him a few steps back again. Adam glanced at the stub of shattered steel in his fist. He looked downwards at the ground, searching desperately for a better weapon, but saw nothing. He took a long stride backwards.

The rutted ground caught at Adam's spur and tripped him. He fell, arms flung out, to sprawl on his back at the edge of the trampled wheat. Richard de Malmaines laughed, half in surprise, took a moment to steady himself, then lifted his sword for the killing blow.

As he did so, a figure rose from the grass behind him. Adam saw him, and caught a shout in the back of his throat. Matthew was still wearing his brown hooded cowl. He had lost his spear, but the knife was in his hand as he rushed at his enemy.

Only at the last moment, as he drew back the weapon above his head, did Matthew let out a cry of murderous triumph. Richard de Malmaines twisted, grunting in surprise, and the boy rammed the point of the knife with both hands into the eye slit of his helmet.

The knight's mailed body arched in shock, and the blade grated against the steel of his helmet as Matthew pulled it free to stab again. Yelling in pain, de Malmaines flung up his sword arm and blindly aimed a hacking blow at his assailant.

The blade cleaved through the boy's collarbone and cut deep into his chest. De Malmaines released his grip on his sword and let the body fall, then he crumpled to his knees. He raised his mailed hands towards his helmet, but the blood was pouring from the eye slit. A convulsion ran through him.

Then Richard de Malmaines toppled forward and fell beside the corpse of his killer.

*

'You put your man down?' Robert asked, as Adam dropped down beside him once more. His face was white as old bone and sheened with sweat, and there was blood on his lips and on his teeth as he bared them in a smile. He must have heard the sounds of combat, even if he could not have seen it.

'Matthew did.'

'See. Told you the boy was dangerous.'

His fate shall be upon your conscience, Adam thought, hearing the voice of the moneylender Aaron in his mind. But he felt no guilt. Matthew had taken upon himself the terrible vengeance that he had so long desired, and Adam could not have stopped him. God had willed it so.

Crows were filling the air above them, a multitude of them fluttering and hacking around the bodies of the fallen, calling across the dark sunshot sky.

'Always there at the death, our sable friends,' Robert said with a grim chuckle, and Adam wondered where he had heard that before.

Robert's laugh choked off. 'You know why I really came back?' he asked.

'I think I do,' Adam told him. 'It wasn't for me, was it. Or for Lord Simon's victory, or for honour—'

'Whatever that word means,' Robert said with a grimace. But he nodded. 'You understand now, then,' he went on, each word shaped against the pain. 'I came back because I am a coward.'

Adam started to deny his words, but Robert spoke over him. 'I knew that the woman I love would never be accepted as my wife,' he said. 'The child she bears would never be called my child, either by her people or mine. I came back here because the battlefield is the only place I understand. Because I am a knight, and I cannot live in this world any longer.'

Adam tried to speak, but his throat was too tight. Tears flooded his face, and he made no move to wipe them away.

'Don't remain here to die,' Robert said, as the last of his strength ebbed. 'They're killing the prisoners. You must flee . . . Find Belia and tell her . . . that I was thinking only of her as I died. Tell her . . . that her name was the last word I uttered.'

'I will, upon my oath,' Adam said. He held Robert's hand clasped in his own. 'But you won't die yet. I forbid it!'

He forced himself to laugh, and Robert thanked him with a grin.

'When did I ever take orders from you, boy?'

Then a wave of pain jolted him rigid, and his lips drew back from his teeth. Adam seized him by the shoulder, feeling the dying man's grip tighten fiercely. The wave passed, and Robert opened his eyes once more. He frowned.

'*Belia*,' he whispered.

Then his eyes clouded, and he was gone.

Adam raised his head and knelt upright. He eased his hand from his friend's grip and looked around him. There were men forging through the wheatfield, de Clare's and Mortimer's foot soldiers armed with spears, a few dismounted knights and ser-jeants with them. He heard their cries and roars, the noise of their cruel triumph. He did not care. Death felt meaningless to him now. With his palm he closed Robert's eyes, then laid his crossed hands upon his breast.

Don't remain here. That had been Robert's dying command, and he had to honour it. But what choice did he have, alone and on foot with the hunters closing in around him?

Then he looked the other way, and saw the stallion Rous standing at the edge of the wheatfield, head down and cropping the long grass, the reins dangling.

And Adam knew that he was not fated to die in this place after all.

Chapter 25

He was halfway down the hill towards the town when he saw the man on the road ahead of him. The slope was covered with fugitives from the battle, but this one was different. Dressed in full mail, a white cross on his blue surcoat, he was limping and calling out to anyone who approached him. 'For the love of Christ! For the love of Christ, help me!'

He was wounded, his sword was gone, his helmet and shield too. His jewelled belts and gilded spurs marked him as a fine prize for anyone who cared to capture him. But the victorious troops of Lord Edward and Gilbert de Clare did not appear to be in the mood to take prisoners. Alone, unarmed and on foot, even the son of the Earl of Hereford was nothing but prey now.

'De Norton!' he shouted as Adam rode closer. 'De Norton, in God's name, you must help me!'

Adam tightened the reins, slowing Rous to a brisk trot. The Welsh and English foot soldiers under de Bohun's command must have broken and fled the moment they saw the knights outpacing them up the hill. Whether Sir Humphrey had been struck by one of his own men while he was trying to rally them, or by the advancing enemy outriders was immaterial now. With his retinue knights and squires either dead or scattered, Adam was his only hope.

The temptation to swing the horse in a wide pass and leave Humphrey de Bohun to the enemy was strong. Just for a moment Adam considered it. To have left Robert de Dunstanville dead on the battlefield only to rescue his half-brother seemed a bitter irony. But for all the anguish de Bohun had caused him, he was not callous enough simply to leave him to die.

'To the abbey!' de Bohun was saying, limping towards Adam with a hand raised to grab at his bridle. 'We have to get to the abbey – find Joane – you must help me!'

Biting back a curse, Adam brought Rous to a champing halt. He slipped one foot from the stirrup, then stretched out his arm. De Bohun seized his hand, got his foot in the empty stirrup and with a gasp of effort heaved himself onto the horse behind him. There was no good seat behind the high war saddle, and the injured man had to perch uncomfortably across the animal's haunches; but as soon as he was up, Adam spurred Rous forward once more. The horse was skittish, labouring under the weight of two armoured men.

'Robert's dead,' Adam called back over his shoulder as he rode. De Bohun was clasping his waist, slumped forward against him. 'De Montfort's dead too – I saw them cutting him down—'

'I know,' de Bohun said, his voice grown thick and slurred. 'I foresaw it . . . I tried to warn him, persuade him to flee, but he would not . . . almost as if he wanted to die . . .' Adam had no idea whether he was talking about Lord Simon or Robert. Sir Humphrey appeared lost to the pain of his wound, and to the urgent desire to evade the doom that was consuming everyone behind them.

Riding between the open fields towards the first houses of the town, Adam felt the shock and anguish which had numbed him shift to a fierce despairing rage. They had been so close to victory, or so it had seemed . . . But the death, the totality of the slaughter seemed overwhelming, unthinkable. Could God really have decreed it?

Jaw set, burning with the pain of wounds he was only now beginning to feel, Adam drove the reeling thoughts away from him. His only desire now was to find Joane and flee this place together if it was still possible. Already, as he rode down the main street into Evesham, he could see that his chances were narrowing fast.

There were enemy soldiers in the town, infantry skirmishers and cavalry outriders who had dashed on ahead of the advance. A few of them casting appraising glances, but none cared to chance an attack on a pair of knights on horseback, even wounded and obviously fleeing, when there were so many softer targets around them. Already they were plundering the houses, driving the inhabitants into the streets.

As they passed the wash house and the turning that led to the bridge, Adam saw a great mob of people filled the neck of the street: townsfolk, servants and fugitive soldiers, many of de Bohun's Welshmen among them, bellowing and screaming as they pushed towards the river crossing. But sounds of fighting came from that direction too. Adam stretched his head up and saw spears and banners in the distance, the flicker of arrows against the sky. The enemy had moved down the far bank of the river and blocked the bridge. Now the only escape from Evesham was by swimming across the loop of the river itself.

Adam could see the abbey ahead of him now, the wall and gateway and the great church rising behind it. Fugitives scattered before them, both men and women running in confused panic and terror. A horse lay on its side, legs kicking as it tried to stand. Nearby a broken cart spilled its load across the street. The smell of smoke laced the morning air.

The gates to the abbey precinct were still half open, and Adam turned the horse and rode on through the archway. On the far side the yard was still deep in cool damp shadow, the façade of the church rising black against the sky. The yard and the adjoining cemetery swarmed with people, many of them crowding around the porch and the church doors and trying to get inside. Most had fled from the battle; squires and serjeants, Welsh and English foot soldiers were together throwing off their gambesons and mail and casting aside their weapons, crying out for sanctuary within the sacred bounds of the church. Dragging on the reins Adam brought Rous to a halt, hooves clattering loud on the cobbles.

'Go inside and find Joane,' Humphrey de Bohun ordered as Adam dismounted. 'I'll wait for you here.'

'No,' Adam told him. 'You're coming with me.' He was already seizing de Bohun and dragging him from the horse. The man was heavy, and wounded more seriously than Adam had realised; a blade or arrow had struck him in the small of his back, close to his spine, breaking the links of his mail and punching in deep. The man's left hip and leg were soaked in blood.

And Adam was wounded too. The cut he had taken on his head was flaming, and his ribs ached fiercely with every breath. No time to consider that now. The clash of hooves sounded in the street outside the abbey gateway, and the yells and whoops of the enemy. Adam wrestled de Bohun from the horse and pulled one of the man's arms across his shoulders, holding him upright.

'There's no safety out here for any of us,' he said, gritting his teeth as he fought down the aches of his injuries. 'We need to seek sanctuary in the church.'

De Bohun nodded, his head hanging, and stumbled along beside Adam as they made their way into the press of bodies around the great porch. Adam had no weapon, but with his free hand he began to shove at the men ahead of them.

'Make way there!' he shouted. 'Sanctuary! Make way!'

He was dragging de Bohun along beside him, the older man a deadweight on his shoulder. After a moment somebody in the crowd, a wiry man with a creased face who wore a grimy leather coif, took Sir Humphrey's other arm and they supported him between them. 'Make way there, you swine!' the man bawled, thumping at the people in front of them. 'Make way for these sirs!'

'Thank you, friend,' Adam said across de Bohun's bent neck.

'If he dies, I take his belts and spurs, and you don't try to stop me,' the man replied.

The mob drew them in, bodies pressing close on each side, funnelling them towards the church doorway. One moment they were outside in the shouting elbowing turmoil, the next they were suddenly inside the deep scented gloom with everyone spilling away from them.

'Sanctuary!' Adam cried out to anyone who might hear him. 'We claim sanctuary!'

'Get him to the presbytery, or the transept,' the man in the leather coif said. Adam was just concentrating on dragging de Bohun as far from the doors and into the depths of the church as possible. As his eyes adjusted to the dimness, he saw that the space of the nave was still crowded with huddled figures, the aisles and the choir beyond the great carved and painted screen packed as well. There were families in here, camp followers and army servants, along with the men of the noble households. Monks and priests from the abbey were working their way between the groups of people, trying to persuade some of them to leave, giving medical help to others where they could. The stink of blood was rising through the smell of the incense and the packed bodies. Wounded men lay on the worn paving, groaning and calling out in English, French or Welsh, their voices echoing in a vast roar from the soaring arches overhead.

'Adam!' a voice called from the tumult, and Joane dashed from the shadows of the side aisle. Just for a moment Adam's heart leaped, and then it plummeted: he had hoped she might already have fled to safety.

'Is that Robert with you?' Joane asked as she drew closer. 'Is he badly hurt?'

Adam saw the disappointment in her eyes as she realised her mistake. But now she was beside him, clasping him briefly in an embrace. Her maid and chaplain were still with her, Adam noticed. Between them they guided Sir Humphrey's staggering steps along the aisle. The man in the leather coif kept his hold on de Bohun's other arm.

'Are things as bad out there as they look?' Joane asked Adam, taking his arm as they passed the rood screen and through into the north transept.

'Bad, yes,' Adam replied. He turned to her and tried to meet her eye but could not. 'De Montfort's dead. And . . . Robert too.'

She hid her face quickly, but Adam heard her stifled cry. In the choir beneath the central tower, men lay along the stalls and slumped across the tiled floor. Few had any compunctions about violating the sacred spaces of the church now. At the far end, smoothly polished stone steps rose to the presbytery where the high altar stood. There were people there as well, huddled around the holiest place in the abbey.

Easing Humphrey down onto the presbytery steps, Adam groaned as he dropped to sit beside him. Joane passed him a flask of wine and he drank, then poured some of it into de Bohun's mouth.

'You're bleeding,' Joane said. 'Your head . . .' She turned to her maid. 'Fetch a surgeon,' she told her, 'or some dressings if there are any to be had.'

Adam held up a hand. 'Your husband needs help more than I do.'

He looked at her now, and in the light that fell from the great east window above the altar he saw the anguish on her face, the pallor and the deep graven lines of distress. Joane's eyes were shadowed, dark with fatigue and gleaming with tears. Sitting on the step beside him she took both of his hands. 'You saw Robert?' she asked.

'I saw him,' Adam told her. 'I saw him, fighting like a champion.' He laughed through clenched teeth, and tasted blood. 'It was L'Estrange that brought him down,' he told her. 'I found him lying on the field . . . I was with him when he died.'

Joane buckled, catching a sob in her throat as her hands tightened. 'I'm glad,' she said as she looked up again, tears flowing down her cheeks. 'I'm glad you were with him. Glad he did not die alone.'

And now none of us will die alone. Adam looked away from her, down the length of the church. Through the carved lattice between the nave and the choir, and the ornate fretwork of the rood screen with its painted figures and great crucifix, he could just make out the doorway to the porch. The chaotic scramble had eased now, but there were still figures struggling around the arched opening. Trying to close the doors and bar them, Adam realised, against the flow of stragglers still trying to get in.

Sunlight shone through coloured glass, lighting the church interior and the haze of scented smoke. Adam's eye was drawn to the painting of the Doom high on the wall, and the figures of the damned and the saved, some ascending while some were cast down into torment. Which group, he wondered, would he be joining, when the moment of death and judgement came? To his left he saw a boy of eleven or twelve sitting with his back to the base of a pillar, staring back at him. For a moment he thought of Matthew.

Then the thunder of voices and battering steel sounded from the far end of the church.

Adam had hoped, when he first got here, that he might be able to find Joane and flee with her, leaving de Bohun safe in the sanctuary. He knew now that his hope had been in vain. The enemy were here; they were outside, hammering at the doors and yelling for entry. The men who had shown no mercy to their prisoners on the battlefield were showing none now.

'In the name of God!' one of the priests begged, standing before the rood screen with his hand raised. 'In the name of God, respect this sanctuary!'

But his words were drowned out by the wave of wailing and screaming from the western end of the church. The enemy had forced the doors, ramming or hacking them open, and now the victorious soldiers were pouring into the church itself. The cries of panic changed quickly to shrieks of pain as the murdering began.

'You have to leave us,' Adam told Joane. 'We won't be able to protect you, if they find you with us.'

'No,' Joane said. 'Never – I won't leave you again.'

'Listen to him,' Sir Humphrey said, heaving himself up onto his elbows. He had been slumped motionless for so long, it was a shock to hear him speak. 'Listen to him, wife, and do what he says.' He spoke grimly, forcing the words. 'If you ever had any care for me, do it for my sake. If not, at least do it for his.'

'He's right, my lady,' Joane's chaplain was saying. 'We must take shelter in the crypt, with the womenfolk and clergy . . .'

'Go!' Adam told her, seizing her arm.

Joane stared back at him. Waves of violent noise and motion seethed around them. Panicked figures dashed past, rushing towards the high altar.

She tried to speak but could not. Then her maid and the chaplain took her arms and pulled her upright. She mouthed a last word to Adam, but he did not hear what she said.

'De Norton,' de Bohun said, stern through his pain. 'Get me up to the altar. They might respect that sanctuary at least.'

Adam nodded. Joane and her maid were descending the steps into the crypt with the other women and the children, her chaplain following and the remaining monks and the abbey priests piling hurriedly after them. But most of those sheltering in the church were making for the altar as well; a tide of them came boiling through the openings in the chancel screen, flooding between the stalls of the choir and up the steps to the presbytery, to fling themselves onto the tiled floor before the altar. On their knees they prayed for deliverance.

'Bugger this, I'm off,' the man in the leather coif said. He released his grip on de Bohun and like a snake he was gone.

Taking the older man beneath the arms, Adam heaved him up off the steps and dragged him across the presbytery floor. Fleeing men buffeted him on both sides, but he managed to drag Sir Humphrey to the altar and sit him there with his back to it. Others crowded tight around them, crying for God's mercy and stretching out their hands to touch the altar cloth or even the gold candlesticks that stood upon it, as if they might grant some added protection.

Until now, Adam had only heard the torrent of violence flowing from the other end of the church. Now he saw it too. The intruders were spearmen, axemen and archers, serjeants and crossbowmen in mail among them too. Few if any knights that Adam could see. But as they stormed through the church from the porch and the open doors, half-blind in the sudden gloom and seething in their fury, they resembled nothing more than devils. As if the great slaughter up on the hill had opened a rent in the fabric of the world, and hell had come pouring in.

The devils were striking out at anyone they could see, killing without thought or mercy. Already they had cut down those remaining in the nave and the side aisles, driving the rest before them through the chancel screen and into the choir and presbytery. And at the head of them was Fulk Ticeburn.

Adam knew him at once. Fulk had an axe and was swinging it with both hands, roaring as he slew. His brother Warin was with him, armed with a falchion and cackling madly as he aimed wild chops at anyone within his reach. A few tried to beg for mercy. Adam saw men falling to their knees, palms clasped in entreaty. He saw Fulk Ticeburn's savage grin as he swung his axe down, severing his victim's hands at the wrist and cleaving his skull.

Some of the priests had remained, and they were trying to calm the fury of the invaders. Some of the monks too, kneeling in attitudes of prayer amid the carnage. Wide eyed, barely able to breathe, Adam watched as a priest was stabbed in the neck, a monk battered to the floor. The attackers were sparing nobody. *Nobody*.

'No mercy for traitors!' they were yelling, heaving out the words as they laboured at their reaping. 'No mercy!'

Blood sprayed and spattered over stone pillars and tiled floors. Fulk Ticeburn's axe split another man's head, flinging gore over the painted carvings of saints and martyrs upon the chancel screen. Around the high altar the bodies were pressed in a struggling mass, those towards the outside trying to fight their way closer to the altar itself. Nobody seemed to be putting up any kind of fight against the killers. Terror had consumed them all, and disbelief at the violation of their sanctuary. Adam was crushed in on all sides, pinned against de Bohun's chest as he fended off fists and elbows.

'Can you hear me?' Sir Humphrey said in a gasp. He paused a moment. 'I want to tell you . . .' he said. 'You and Joane. I know it all. I thought I could not forgive you, but now . . . If we are to die then let us die as friends, agreed?'

Adam twisted his head and stared back at the man, incredulous. 'Very well,' he managed to say. 'But let's try not to die yet.'

Struggling to sit upright, he raised his head above the throng.

'A sword, in the name of Christ!' he shouted. 'Who has a sword?' He stared about him, shoving at the men closest to him to see if any were armed. One of them swore back at him in Welsh.

'Here,' a weak voice said. Looking down, Adam saw another knight lying nearby, his mail crusted with mud and dried blood. It took him a moment to recognise William de Boyton, the man he had fought beside on the bridge at Newport. De Boyton held his sword in his left hand; his right was clasped to his chest, almost severed at the wrist. 'I can't use it,' he said. 'Take it, with my blessing.'

Adam's hand closed around the worn hilt, and immediately he felt his assurance return. At the same moment, Warin Ticeburn reached the steps of the presbytery and looked towards the altar. Adam saw his expression shift from bafflement to wonder, then to savage joy. 'It's him!' he cried to his brother, pointing with his blade. 'It's the bastard de Norton!'

The wave of attackers had so far held back from invading the inner sanctuary of the presbytery, but as Warin Ticeburn leaped towards the steps the rest surged past him. Deafening screams burst from the cowering throng around the altar, roars of fury and outrage, and the demented laughter of the killers. Warin was struggling towards Adam now, his falchion raised, as other men shoved past him to spear and stab at the mass of defenceless fugitives. Grasping hands pulled at the golden altar cloth, and the candlesticks and sacred vessels swayed and toppled among the heaving bodies.

The killers could not miss; their every blow and lunge found its mark. Blades hacked flesh, maces and clubs broke bones and burst heads. The noise of steel cutting and mauling meat was overwhelming. Everywhere was blood, flowing in streams across the smooth tiles, spattering over the exposed stone of the altar. Men were slipping in it, smearing it in great lurid swathes beneath them as they struggled and fought. Some had begun to resist now, throwing off their crippling fear to grapple the attackers with open hands, dragging them down into the roiling scrum. But the resistance did not last long, and ended in a flurry of blades.

Adam stood with his back to the altar, de Boyton's sword held in a low grip. Warin Ticeburn was battling his way towards him, shoving other men aside. Adam waited for him to come. He felt a great stillness inside him, a calm focus as the bloody chaos roared around him. This, he knew, would be the place he died. But he would fall with sword in hand.

'Ha!' Warin cried as he broke through the last knot of bodies and flung himself at Adam. Braced against the altar, Adam remained motionless until his attacker was almost upon him.

Then he took one stamping stride forward, bringing up the sword in a sweeping arc just as Warin's falchion flashed at his head. The blade slashed Ticeburn's wrists as it drove the blow aside. Then Adam wheeled the sword and brought it down again, with all his strength behind it.

He struck Warin Ticeburn between the eyes, the honed steel biting into his skull. The man staggered as Adam ripped the blade free, blood streaming from his wound. His weapon fell from his hand as he flung his arms wide and toppled backwards into the churning mob behind him.

A club smashed at the back of Adam's leg, and he dropped to one knee in the lake of gore. He managed to raise his sword again to parry another strike, then flick the blade and wound his attacker. He needed to get up, to die on his feet. But pain was shrieking through his body, threatening to overwhelm him. A spear stabbed his shoulder, not breaking his mail but shoving him backward, and he toppled to lie across de Bohun's body.

Sir Humphrey was still alive, his arms raised to shield himself as other bodies crashed around him. On his far side, Adam saw two serjeants dragging William de Boyton's mail hauberk up to his shoulders and stabbing him repeatedly in the back, their daggers leaving red gashes in his linen aketon.

Fulk Ticeburn had seen his brother's body among the dead, and he was bellowing with fury. His teeth gleamed through his beard as he gripped his axe and hunted among the scrum of fighting men for his prey.

Adam felt the chill in his blood as their eyes met. Ticeburn fell silent and smiled. A terrible sight, even in the heat of battle. Fulk did not charge. He did not rush his attack. Instead, he merely walked, pacing slow and deliberate as death itself through the chaos. Planting his feet carefully in the pools of blood, stepping over the bodies of the slain, he raised his axe and held it above his head as he advanced on Adam. In his eyes was nothing but murder.

Humphrey de Bohun struggled out from beneath Adam's body. Pushing himself up to sit, he raised both hands. 'Spare us!' he yelled in a cracked voice. 'Spare us – I am the son of the Earl of Hereford . . . My father will pay a great ransom!'

Fulk Ticeburn appeared not to hear him. Several other men merely laughed. Amid such slaughter, any idea of mercy felt like insanity. But there was another voice calling out now, a stern and steady voice that rang like a bell. Adam could not make out the words, but he could discern the stillness that followed them. He lay slumped against de Bohun, still gripping the sword but barely with the strength to raise it and defend himself. Fulk Ticeburn stood over him, raising his axe for the killing blow as the strange hush fell all around them. Only the groans of the injured and dying and the chanted prayers echoing from the crypt below filled the sudden quiet.

'This is your death, de Norton!' Ticeburn said, with furious spite. 'This is for my brother Warin, and my brother Eudo, and for the lands you stole from us!'

A thud, and Ticeburn's knees gave beneath him. He dropped to the bloody tiles, the axe spilling from his hand. Behind him was a serjeant armed with a short club.

'Less chatting, churl,' the serjeant said. 'Listen when your master commands!'

Breath burst from Adam's chest as he heaved himself up on braced arms. The killing had ceased. The enemy soldiers, blood-ied weapons in their hands, moved aside now with bowed heads as a man climbed the steps from the choir to the presbytery. The newcomer wore armour, and was flanked by men in full mail, knights and serjeants. He came to a halt in a shaft of sunlight, staring around him at the gore splashed and spattered up the pillars, the blood in lakes across the tiled floor, the mounds of mauled corpses and wounded men surrounding the high altar.

Propping his fists on his hips, his yellow surcoat and jewelled belts gleaming, his ruddy hair dyed golden by the sun, Gilbert de Clare twisted his face into an expression of sour distaste.

'What a foul mess,' he said, and nudged one of the bodies with his toe. 'Let no man say that I ordered it!'

'My lord, some of them still live,' said the serjeant who had clubbed Fulk Ticeburn insensible.

'Indeed,' de Clare replied, stepping rather daintily around the spreading lake of blood to view the bodies. Adam felt de Bohun shift beneath him. Sir Humphrey was dragging himself clear of the carnage, raising his hand.

'I see Humphrey de Bohun there,' Lord Gilbert said, with the twitch of a smile. 'I suppose his father would be most upset if we killed *him*.'

'And the others, lord?' one of the other serjeants asked.

Gilbert de Clare idly scanned the bloodied mass of people sprawled around the altar, picking out the living from the dead. His pale eyes rested briefly on Adam, then flicked away. 'Their fate's not mine to decide,' he said. 'But if they are to die, they can do it in the daylight and not defile this holy place any further. Bring them!'

Chapter 26

Across the yard of the abbey precinct and out through the gateway, the captors stripped their prisoners of their belts and spurs and made them kneel in the mud of the street. Adam kept his head up, ignoring the flare of pain in his ribs, the burning wound on his scalp. Humphrey de Bohun was kneeling beside him, slumped on his calves and rasping every breath as he fought down the agony of his own injuries.

There were others who had been taken alive from the church, but few lived long. Adam watched dispassionately as the few surviving Welsh archers and other foot soldiers and army servants were slain with knives, their hands tied behind them. He expected nothing but death himself, and wished only that his captors would get on with it. De Clare's men were herding the people who had sheltered in the crypt out of the gates now, the monks and clergymen either in stunned silence or loudly praising God for their deliverance. Adam stared at them as they emerged, anxious for a glimpse of Joane. But he heard the women before he saw them, their screams and violent weeping as the killers of their menfolk drove them out of the church. The slain had been dragged out by their ankles only moments before, knocking their heads over the stone thresholds, and their bodies lay flung in heaps in the yard.

'Have mercy, I beg you sirs!' one woman cried, two others holding her upright as she wept. The captors ignored her as they went about their work. Joane followed the group out of the gateway and into the street, but she did not scream or cry out. Her face was stark white, her eyes staring. Adam could not tell whether she was in deep shock, or transfixed by anger.

'Get those screeching women away from here!' Gilbert de Clare snapped, waving his hand. It was the only time that Adam saw him at all disturbed.

A procession was coming down the wide main street of Evesham. Formed up under their banners came the victorious companies, the retinues of Mortimer and the Marcher Lords, de Warenne and the Earl of Pembroke. Some of the towns-people cheered them, hoping for their clemency, but most of those who remained just stood in the streets and watched the cavalcade pass.

Adam was surprised to see that they had other prisoners with them too. Not everyone had fallen victim to the killing lust of the victors. Henry de Hastings rode by himself, arms tied behind his back and his horse led by a grinning serjeant. Guy de Mont-fort was with them too, walking with shuffling steps between two guards. Lord Simon's youngest son was red-eyed and sniff-ing back tears, his black wing of hair falling to obscure his face.

After them came the king. Henry, third of his name, restored now to full power and freedom. He was still dressed in the plain armour, the red and white surcoat that de Montfort's men had forced him to wear, and he carried his left arm in a makeshift sling. Apparently, he had been injured in the fighting, before his son's knights had identified him and dragged him to safety. He looked merely bewildered now as he rode with the victorious army, his thin grey hair plastered to his head with sweat and a pale, pained smile upon his face.

And after the king came the conqueror. Lord Edward rode on a champing black warhorse caparisoned with the royal arms of

England. One fist propped on his hip, he gazed to left and right with an expression of masterful scorn. Unlike his father, and so many of his followers, he appeared to have come through the battle entirely untouched. But he wore the glow of achievement and of prowess, and the mantle of fame. The Leopard, in his hour of triumph.

Men ran to take his bridle as he drew to a halt before the abbey gates, others to hold his stirrup as he dismounted. For a moment it looked as if Edward was about to make a speech or pronouncement. But he merely scanned the throng of men before him with his lazy eye. Then he turned to Gilbert de Clare, who waited beside the gateway. His voice carried clearly.

'I understand your men have violated the sanctity of the holy church, Lord Gilbert.'

De Clare merely shrugged. He might even have smiled. 'Some of them found it difficult to restrain their zeal for slaying your enemies, my lord. But it was not my men alone. John de Warenne's reavers joined in as well.'

Edward made a sound in his throat. Hard to tell, Adam thought, if he was amused or displeased. From the gateway behind them came the cries of the wounded and the dying, and the wails of the women.

'Anyway, they're not all dead,' de Clare went on. 'These are alive, for example.' He gestured towards Adam and Sir Humphrey, still kneeling beside the abbey wall. 'I make you a gift of them, lord,' he said.

Edward inclined his head in acknowledgement, then stalked closer. His men at arms and household knights followed behind him, ready for anything.

'Sir Humphrey de Bohun, is it?' Edward said as he approached. 'A shame you did not fall on the field of battle, Sir Humphrey, for all the disgrace you have brought your family.'

De Bohun raised his head. His lip curled, and he tried to spit. Just for a moment, Adam felt a tremendous bond with the man.

'Well, we cannot rightly kill you now, however you might deserve it,' Edward said, ignoring the gesture. 'You shall be my lawful prisoner.'

'And the other, my lord?' one of the serjeants asked, his hand on the hilt of his dagger.

Lord Edward took a pace closer and stooped over Adam. For a moment it appeared that he genuinely did not recognise him. Unsurprising, Adam thought; his hair was matted, his face streaked with blood and dirt, his surcoat torn away and his mail blackened with filth. He lifted his head, hardly daring to meet the Leopard's gaze. Then he did, and for a few long heartbeats Lord Edward studied him. Malice flickered in his eyes, and a frown formed between his brows. Then his lips twitched into a smile.

'Yes,' he said, 'I remember this one. De Norton. A traitor, and a breaker of oaths. But I recall he aided me once, on a tournament field in France.'

Adam stared back at him, unblinking, motionless.

'Well then, I repay the debt,' Edward said. He straightened, clicked his fingers. 'Both shall live,' he said.

Already he was walking away.

Adam drew a long breath and held it, trying to slow the heavy drumming of his heart. Two guards pulled him to his feet. Two more were dragging Sir Humphrey onto a makeshift wooden stretcher. On the far side of the street, across the trampled mire of wet mud and horse dung, Joane stood with her maid and the other members of her household, fenced around with armed men. She was staring back at Adam, unflinching and silent.

Then abruptly the crowd of men surged forward, pressing into the street. Another procession was moving down into the town now, from the hill where the battle had been fought. This one came marching on foot, to the battering of drums and the clamorous honking of bagpipes. Men with hunting horns blew the mort as they carried their trophy on a pole between them. At first Adam could not make out what it was, but he heard the reactions of the spectators gathered in the street. Some laughed, others cheered and applauded, while a scattered few let out deep groans of dismay and cries of horror. Guy de Montfort dropped to his knees and covered his face.

Stuck on top of the pole, Adam realised as it came jolting closer above the throng, was the severed head of Simon de Montfort. His hands were nailed below it, and what looked like his legs and feet dangled beneath, swinging grotesquely. Something was draped across the nose and open mouth as well, a hank of bloody flesh that Adam recognised too soon to look away.

'My God, my God what have they done?' de Bohun groaned, raising himself from the stretcher to sit upright.

'They've unmade him,' Adam replied.

De Montfort's head was adorned with his own severed genitals. Adam's stomach clenched, and he turned his gaze to the muddy ground until the gruesome trophy had been carried onward. The noise of the horns and the honk of the pipes drifted in its wake, and cheering came from the meadows below the abbey, where Lord Edward's troops were assembling.

Adam looked across the street, but he could see no sign of Joane. He hoped that she had already departed, or that the crowd around her had shielded her from sight of the horror. Two of the guards were lifting de Bohun on his stretcher, bearing his weight between them as they moved off after Edward and his retinue. Another prodded Adam in the small of the back.

As he started forward, Adam felt more alone than he had ever done before. He was alive, but he could almost envy the fallen. With pain in his heart, he turned and looked up the street towards the green rise of the hill beyond the town. Robert was still lying up there, his body abandoned where he had breathed his last word, in the company of the noble dead. The summit appeared placid, with no sign of the bodies of the slain or the fury of battle that had raged across it only an hour before, but the sky above was thronging with carrion birds.

'Wait!' a voice cried. 'Wait, I must see my husband!' From across the street, Joane was hurrying to join them, lifting the skirts of her gown as she crossed the churned mud and filth. 'I must see him,' she demanded, 'it's my right!'

The guards carrying Sir Humphrey looked to the serjeant who commanded them; he gave a curt nod, and they set down their load once more. Joane dropped to her knees beside the stretcher, but Humphrey turned away from her with a groan, hiding his face in the crook of his arm. Adam could not watch.

'Treat him well,' Joane said to the guards as she got to her feet. 'He is the son of the Earl of Hereford,' she told the serjeant. 'Treat him with the respect he deserves.' She was reaching into the purse at her belt, drawing forth coins and passing them to the serjeant and the attending soldiers.

Then, as she stepped away, she seemed to stumble slightly in the mud and swayed towards Adam. Without looking in his direction she stretched out her arm; he took her hand, and quickly she pressed something into his palm. Distracted, the guards saw nothing, and a heartbeat later she was striding away across the street once more.

Adam waited as long as he could endure, then opened his palm slightly and glanced down. A creased slip of parchment, crudely sliced with a blade from the pages of a book, then scored and folded tight. Inked words were visible on the upper side: *Si ascendero in caelum tu illic es . . .*

The words of the psalm they had read together from her precious Psalter, that afternoon in an abandoned shepherd's hut on a distant hillside. He heard her voice in his mind, speaking the verses: *If I ascend into heaven, you are there. If I descend into hell, you are with me . . . Even there shall your hand lead me, and your right hand shall hold me . . .*

Then the guard prodded him once more, and Adam gave an angry shrug. He lowered his head, and began to walk.

Historical Note

The slaughter at Evesham on the 4th of August 1265 was considered shocking even at the time: 'the murder of Evesham', the chronicler Robert of Gloucester calls it, 'for battle it was none.' By the chivalric conventions of 13th-century warfare, knights and great nobles were not supposed to die in combat, but rather be taken prisoner when defeated, to be held for honourable ransom. At Evesham, however, more than fifty knights were slain, together with countless others. One of the abbey monks later described the massacre of fugitives who had sought sanctuary in the church after the battle, mentioning in particular the corpses heaped around the high altar, and the blood running down into the crypt below.

But if Edward and his allies hoped that their vengeful savagery would erase the memory of de Montfort for good, they were mistaken. In the decades after the battle, Lord Simon continued to be regarded as a hero and champion, particularly by the common people, and was the subject of popular songs and verses. Many of his former supporters, and even some of his foes, came to venerate him as a secular saint and miracle-worker. The dismembering of the earl's body contributed to a cult of relics: his severed head had been sent as a gift to Roger Mortimer's wife, but one of his feet ended up encased in gold at Alnwick Abbey, while one of his hands was kept at Evesham. His supposed place of death on the battlefield, meanwhile, became a site of pilgrimage. A spring appeared there, and its waters were reputed to heal eye ailments. You can still visit the site today, although the spring is just a grassy cleft in the side of the hill these days.

Simon's last moments are described in a number of sources, but there are discrepancies between some of them. One of the most vivid of these accounts was discovered as recently as 2000, written on the back of a manuscript kept at the College of Arms in London. I've chosen to follow Dr David Cox's amended translation of this narrative: de Montfort was stabbed in the back of the neck with a 'sharp weapon', Dr Cox believes, rather than struck with a lance as previously suggested. This accords with the description in the *Lanercost Chronicle*, which specifies that the killing blow was dealt with a dagger. A number of sources also describe the sudden darkness and thunderstorm that preceded the first clash of arms – a couple have it happening at the moment of de Montfort's death, for added drama and religious significance.

While we have descriptions of the battle itself, and of Edward's dramatic escape from Hereford at the beginning of the war, the events that lay between them remain rather hazy. Only one chronicle relates in passing that Bridgnorth was captured after a 'short siege' (*brevi obsidione capti*), while another describes John Giffard's challenge to de Montfort outside Monmouth. The same account mentions the fight on the bridge at Newport, while others say merely that the town was burned. I have attempted to stitch together from these fragments the most plausible narrative, although determining the reasons for these events has sometimes required more imagination.

Edward is compared to a leopard in the *Song of Lewes*, the contemporary verse that I mentioned in my previous book, *Battle Song*: 'A lion by pride and fierceness, he is by inconstancy and changeableness a pard, changing his word and promise, cloaking himself in pleasant speech.' Leopards at this time were both a heraldic form of lion, and a hybrid beast born of an unnatural union between a lion and a 'pard', or mythological devil-cat. Edward's grandfather King John was also nicknamed 'the Leopard', in the 13th-century story of *Fouke Fitz Waryn*. So, while it's possible that nobody aside from the anonymous author of the *Song of Lewes* actually referred to Edward himself by that name, the chance that they might have done so is too tempting to ignore, and I am not the first writer to bestow the dramatic title upon him.

The comet that Adam notices in the opening chapters was one of the most prominent in medieval history and was recorded as far away as China. Various writers mention its first appearance in July of 1264; the date that it disappeared is less certain, although one chronicler mentions that it coincided with the death of Pope Urban IV in early October. Adam's explicit-sounding address in Hereford, meanwhile, was quite common in the Middle Ages; towns all over England, from London and Oxford to Norwich and Newcastle, had similarly named thoroughfares. All were renamed in a later and more prudish age; Hereford's is now called Gaol Street, although it was still known as Grope Lane as late as the 1750s.

Many today will associate medieval hunting with the grand chase of the stag, but the most common form of the hunt throughout England was the so-called 'bow and stable' method. This was conducted at all times of year and by all classes in society; there is a description of a hunt of this sort in the late 14th-century poem *Gawain and the Green Knight*. It could also be quite dangerous; in an earlier century, both King William II and his nephew were accidentally shot dead or mortally wounded by arrows while engaging in it.

The ritualised dismembering – 'unmaking' or 'undoing' – of the dead animal was also a popular scene in medieval stories and poems. I am unaware of anyone making a connection between this hunting rite and the mutilation and display of Simon de Montfort's body after Evesham, but I suspect that onlookers might have noticed a similarity, if only a mocking one.

Acknowledgements

Once again, I must thank my editor, Morgan Springett, for his care and attention to detail in bringing this novel to completion. My sincere gratitude, as always, goes to Narmi for her constant support and encouragement in both the brighter and the darker moments. I am also very grateful to the Society of Authors and the Authors' Foundation for their assistance during the writing of this book.